GREY 4:

THE RECONNECTION

Spectrum Series
PART FOUR

By Allison White

Grey: The Reconnection

Copyright © 2018 by Allison White.
All rights reserved.
First Print Edition: September 2018

Limitless Publishing, LLC
Kailua, HI 96734
www.limitlesspublishing.com

Formatting: Limitless Publishing

ISBN-13: 978-1-64034-441-9
ISBN-10: 1-64034-441-1

Dedication

To my family for
promoting the hell out of my books.

Chapter One

Liv

"Do I look fine?" I ask Charlotte, pivoting on the sleek black heels. I run my hands down the short sleeveless black dress Jaimie lent me. I'd never ever buy something as chic as this. But I have to admit, where the dress lacks in appropriate length, it makes up for in elegance. Or maybe that's because I *look* elegant wearing it. More…like a woman. "Say something, Char. I need to know if I look like a hideous clown or I *will* pummel you with my wacky hammer."

She chuckles and waves a dismissive hand at me. "You look stunning. Doesn't she, guys?" She looks to the other two girls, and they nod, checking me out. "Hey, now! Stop checking out my sister's goods, which you cannot have…" Her brown eyes bounce to me as she drawls, "They're reserved for Nick."

"Oooh," Jaimie and Julia both encourage her ridiculous comment.

"Screw you, guys," I spit and turn back around. I clamp down on my bottom lip and do my best to bite back the blush in my cheeks. "It's just a date, nothing big."

"Just a date? Yeah, right," Julia scoffs, and I look in the mirror, giving her a pointed look. She holds up her hands and laughs defensively. "I'm just saying, I never thought I'd see you date anyone that's not crazy-ass Grey."

"He is not crazy," I snap without meaning to. Why am I still defending him? Protecting his "honor?" They look at each other warily, and I let out a breath to calm myself. "Are you saying that I should just keep pining after someone who loathes me? Who, even after all I've done to make up for the one terrible thing I wish I could take back, would rather see me in pain than give me another chance?"

"No, of course not, Liv," Jaimie pipes up, walking over to me and flinging an arm around my shoulder. She bares an optimistic smile as she tips my chin up. "We all want the best for you. Jules is just saying…what you and Grey had was so, I don't know, epic…I guess? And she never expected you'd be going out with someone else."

"I thought you two would always be together," Julia clarifies, her dark brown eyes softening, almost as if she's guilty. But I get what she means.

"I thought so too…" I mutter.

The room grows silent for too long.

Before anyone could get totally bummed out, Charlotte jumps off the bed, clapping her hands together. "Okay, let's not get all reminiscent right now. Our girl is going out on her first date since forever." She slides up behind me and slings an arm around my other shoulder, smooshing her cheek with mine; I can barely hold back a laugh. "And we are going to support and love her. Am I right, gals?"

"Yes!" Jaimie squeals, pinching my cheek.

"Eh." Julia shrugs her shoulders.

"Jules…" Jaimie says in a warning tone.

"It's okay, Julia." I laugh at her ever-loving hostility toward me, even though she has definitely grown on me as time went on. I turn with the girls still clung onto me like soaked clothes to my skin and smile a Jaimie smile, hopeful and determined. "You'll come around to Noah. It'll take a while, but you will."

"I don't know," she sighs as she stands and walks over to us, a small smile coating her lips. "The kid looks like he's had a seven-twenty credit score since he was *two*."

"Jules," Jaimie whines, but her girlfriend just rolls her eyes.

"Not gonna lie, I thought the exact same thing," Charlotte admits.

"Guys," I groan, and they collectively laugh.

The doorbell rings, and we all freeze.

"Guys still do that? You know, come up to the door?" Jaimie says.

"I guess so," I mumble, my heart in my stomach from nerves. "Well, I've gotta go. But I will text you guys when I'm coming back," I say, but mostly to Jaimie and Julia. Apparently, anything romantic makes them really horny. One time, we were all just casually watching *Just Like Heaven,* my favorite

3

romance movie, and next thing I knew they were making out on the bed. I had to lie and say I wanted to get something to eat from the cafeteria, but really, I had to leave before I saw what I couldn't un-see.

They follow me downstairs, even though I tried to shoo them away multiple times. I love that they want to protect me and everything, but I am an adult. A stupid adult who has mental issues because of a failed relationship, but an adult nonetheless. Meaning I can handle anything that comes my way. And if I can't and I get hurt, I will learn to accept it and move on. Just as I am doing right now. I'm learning that I shouldn't live like this, so pained and unable to breathe, and moving on to something healthier. Although it feels as though I am ripping off a Band-Aid that's made me feel safe and secure, it's become sour and isn't keeping my wound healed and protected. I have to get rid of it before my whole body shuts down.

I throw the front door open and gasp.

"Mason?"

He's wearing the same clothes he wore last night, but his shoes are in his hands, his neck is covered in hickies, and his hair is a complete mess.

"H-hey, guys." He nervously smiles and waves using his free hand.

The girls and I gasp simultaneously.

"He did it..." Jaimie trails, eyes wide.

"The cherry's been popped!" Julia snickers wildly, clapping her hands and ignoring her girlfriend's attempt at shutting her up.

"Shut up, no way!" Charlotte chuckles.

"Stop it, guys." I flash them an evil eye and gently pull Mason inside, who is as red as a tomato, maybe even redder. I shut the door after him just in case Noah pops up and sees I have an entire entourage, which would be very weird...but he knows who my friends are, so maybe he wouldn't be *too* surprised. "He just lost something very important—"

"Want some help finding it?" Julia mutters, and I hit her with my shoulder. "You set yourself up with that one."

"Hush!" I shush her, and he shyly averts his eyes. "Come in. Noah's on his way now, but you can tell me everything that happened. You're always here for me, and I want to do the very same—"

"Noah's pulling up!" Jaimie announces shrilly.

"What?" I whip around and watch as Noah's Porsche slowly pulls up in the large driveway. My blood runs cold, the nerves starting up once again. I bite my lip and turn back to Mason. "Later, okay? As soon as I get back, I want to know everything."

"Maybe not *everything*," Charlotte assures sheepishly.

I open my mouth to reassure him, yes, everything, because I kind of gave him details about my first time. At the time, he was the closest thing to me, and I couldn't *not* tell him. I'm pretty sure that's what all best friends do.

"Later, I get it. But I want to know how your date goes—" he begins.

"We all do!" the girls jump in.

Mason and I laugh, and he rolls his eyes. "Have

fun, okay?"

I take a deep breath I didn't know I needed and nod. "I will."

He pulls me into a surprise hug, and I melt into it, wrapping my arms around him. "And remember to use protection," he jokes in a whisper.

"I could only hope you did too," I snip right back.

He pulls back and laughs as I do too. "Touché."

The doorbell rings again, and we all snap our heads to it, because we know exactly who it is.

"Scatter. Go!" I shoo them away, and they stick their tongues out before going up the stairs, but I can see a peek of their bare feet on one of the stairs. They're such—ugh! I can't help but laugh, though, because they're the best things to happen to me. I can't thank God enough for them. Without them, I'd most likely be in that group home in Nebraska.

I take several breaths and plaster on what I hope is a convincing smile while opening the door.

Instantly, my eyes connect with Noah's, and we both are at a loss for words. We each take in the other with either shock or adoration. I am mostly leaning toward shock. He is dressed in black slacks, a crisp white dress shirt, shiny black loafers, and an Armani suit jacket. He looks absolutely...ravishing. I can smell his expensive woodsy cologne from here, and my mouth waters slightly. He really does clean up nicely, huh?

"Say something, fools!" I hear Julia scream from the stairs.

Noah chuckles, and I do too, but I am blushing from the inside out, mortified.

"Sorry about that. We should…" I point behind him.

"Yeah." He steps out, and I admire how great he looks with gelled hair. I step out too and close the door behind me, admiring his dimples. They seem to be even deeper with him dressed like this.

It's silent again, but this time I can't even hold back my smile.

"You look—" we both begin, stop, then laugh.

I nervously curve my hair behind my ear, and I swear he sucks in a deep breath.

"You go," he says, but I shake my head. He nods, quickly bites his lip, then rasps, "You look…fucking amazing. Sorry, sorry—that sounded—I sound like a caveman." Aw, he is so cute when he's unsure of what to say.

"That's quite all right, Noah," I assure him, and he shakes his head, almost like he's in a daze. "You look amazing yourself. Very…sharp."

Can I be any more of an idiot? Sharp? Is that all you have to say, Olivia?

"Thank you, m'lady." He bows his head slightly, and I erupt into giggles. His eyes glimmer as he straightens up to his towering height. "I wanted to look good, um, for you. Does that sound stupid? Is *this* stupid?" He gestures between us, and I know he's referring to the fact that we've been friends for our whole childhood, and now we're going on a date.

"No, it isn't. I'm glad we're doing this," I admit shyly, rocking back and forth on my heels.

"So, we should probably get going," he says, putting an arm on my lower back. I flush bright pink, but he is too busy nervously checking his watch to notice. *So cute.* "I have a reservation for…" He stops and looks at me with a half-smile. "I should probably keep that a secret, huh?"

"It'd be more suspenseful." I shrug, mirroring his half-smile.

He rolls his eyes playfully and escorts me into the passenger seat. "Then you'll find out what I have planned much later."

"Can't wait." I wink at him, and he laughs. "Stupid," I groan, holding my head. Hopefully, I won't make myself out as an idiot for the rest of the night.

***

"Did you have a good time?" Noah asks, but I know he can tell I did by my shameless grin. I know he enjoyed himself by *his* ear-to-ear grin, like he just won the big jackpot: that jackpot being me.

He took me to a super fancy restaurant named Luigi's, then took me to see a rom-com right after. It reminded me so much of…I have to take another breath to keep myself from comparing this incredibly normal, healthy night to *that* night.

"I had the best time, Noa—" I begin.

His lips cut me off. I quickly shut my eyes and try to melt into his chest and let myself ignite by his lips. Nothing happens, but I still kiss him back and allow myself to get used to his minty breath.

When he pulls back, he beams at me. "I did, too," he says softly, then takes a step away, shoving his hands in his pockets, cheeks pink. "I'll call you tomorrow."

I nod, unable to conjure words. I watch as he jogs back to his Porsche and drives away. I stand in front of the front door for what seems like hours before Mason pulls me inside. He has me tell him every detail of the night, and I tell it as if I am relaying a magical date beyond this world. Although his eyes tell me he doesn't believe me, he takes it all in silently, then tells me he's happy for me. He tells me how his night with Mateo went, and I listen half-heartedly. I am just too in my head with a million thoughts to pay attention, and I have to stop him, feigning I am too tired to keep my eyes open.

As I slide under my bed covers with memories of that truly wonderful night that still has me blushing from head to toe, I close my eyes and will my brain to scratch it out and replace it with tonight. I am moving on, and with that…I have to get rid of the past.

I unlatch his charm from my wrist, my heart in my toes, and slide it under my pillow. It has been helping me get some sleep, but I will not wear it any longer. Not when it reminds me of what I can never have. Never again…

Chapter Two

Grey

I can feel my heart tip-tapping away on the tip of my tongue as I run. My calves tighten and strain as I twist around corners and push myself faster and faster until everything besides me blurs. I dive through people on the sidewalk without missing a beat. Some give me nasty looks and curse at me, but the rock music booming in my ears blocks them all out. Before I train in the gym, I like to get a few miles in. The weather is perfect for it, and I want to get in my cardio to get my heart under control. There's nothing worse than getting tired after a few minutes in the ring. And if your opponent sees your heavy panting or slow foot movements, you're done for.

As I pass by a local diner, I am tempted to enter, but I can't. I want to be light and quick on my feet. And that's not possible if I'm like a boulder gunning for the next shot. So, instead, I run to a market and slow down. I take out my headphones, barely out of breath, and get a fruit salad and a water. I swear, after this tournament, I am pigging the fuck out. I eat and drink on a park bench and rest for a few minutes, ignoring Dean's calls. I know what he wants me to do—we all have for a very long time—but I'm just not ready to come face to face with it just yet.

I finish my salad with a sigh, then get back on my feet. I run for another half an hour, then end up back at the gym. I head straight to the back, throw my shit in my locker, and walk over to the workout machines. I curl my growing biceps, using hundred-pound dumbbells for about twenty minutes. After that, I rotate through each heavy-lifting machine that pushes me to my limit, and I exceed beyond them greatly. David says I shouldn't push myself like this, but I won't get that top title or champion belt without pushing myself.

"Grey!"

"What's up?" I turn around after setting down a weight and standing from the bench.

David walks up to me, sweating himself. "I got a fight for you at Fort Lauderdale around eight," he informs me.

I sigh as I walk over to a punching dummy, him on my tail. "Can't. I'm a little busy tonight," I say vaguely, starting to throw my hands strategically.

"Then get un-busy," he says sternly.

"I can't, David," I huff out, throwing my fists left and right.

"Why not?" he questions.

I throw my fist a little harder, and the dummy swivels around. "Because I can't, David."

11

"Because of *The Knights*?" he questions, lifting a dark blond eyebrow.

I don't answer.

He steps in front of the dummy, lips twisted and eyes narrowed into sharp daggers. "You know nothing good will come from being in that fucking gang, Grey. Get out now, or you'll leave another way we both know *won't* promise you *breathing*."

I appreciate him looking out for me, I really do. He's been like my brother for so many years, always looking out for me when no one else would or wanted to. He actually pulled me out of Indiana, not just because of my mother kicking me out, but also because I was involved with the gang. Even then, he was concerned for my safety and preached that I had to get a better life.

But there is no better life for me. I was just a shit kid that grew into an even shittier man who still thirsts for violence and breaking young girls' hearts. I'm a fucking serial heart-breaker. What *better life* does he see for me? I fight for a living, and I am madly in love with one girl but am with another. I deserve shit. And if being in the gang is shit, then I am where I belong. And David can't help me. He should have given up on me all those years ago, because it didn't help anything.

"It's honestly none of your fucking business what I do beyond the ring, David," I spit, feeling like shit as soon as the words leave my mouth.

His jaw tightens, and he jabs a finger at my bare chest. "Everything that deals with you and your safety *is* my business. I have been looking out for you since you were *sixteen* years old. After your mother kicked you out, who took you in and drove you to and from school when you threatened to drop out? Huh? Who turned you to MMA to take your anger out? Who got you into therapy sessions to deal with whatever was kicking in your brain? Hmm?"

I'm silent, because he's right. He's been there for me since day one. Maybe even before I told him my mother put me out. Maybe when he saw me doing all kinds of drugs and alcohol at those parties. Maybe when he first saw past my bloody fists and foul mouth.

"That's what I thought," he grits out.

"I can't just drop out of it. You know that," I remind him.

He shrugs. "Find a way."

"It's not that easy," I breathe softly.

I close my eyes and fall back on the bench, pinching my nose bridge. I can feel him fall next to me, but he doesn't say anything. Neither of us speaks for what feels like hours.

"What does he have you do nowadays?" he asks, but it sounds like he's accusing me of something.

"Nothing you should worry about," I reply quickly and stand. I should get to the gang spot now, or he'll send one of his goons. Lord knows David won't be able to hold back his anger for the gang with one of their imbecile members strolling through like they own shit.

"Like that gas station robbery?" he says, and I freeze but don't turn around. "Really weird how you weren't here that night for a sparring match I set up for you and Rodriguez..." He lets the words

13

hang heavily in the air, and so do I.

***

"Why the hell didn't you answer when I called?" Dean barks as I enter the venue, but he doesn't seem as angry, as he is winning a pool game. He lands two pocket shots at the same time, then straightens up, taking a long drag of his blunt. He smirks devilishly when I pick up a cue stick to join, some members stepping back with a wave of his hand.

"I was training," I tell him, then land a blue shot in a pocket.

His lips turn up. "Why do you even busy yourself busting your knuckles for them when you can do that full-time for me…" He pauses, sinking another ball, his eyes lighting up. "…for double the price?"

I shrug and coolly lean against the table. "Passion calls."

He lets out a roar of a laugh that sends the others on edge, but I don't even flinch. "Passion," he scoffs, sliding his tongue across his lips. "Passion got you into trouble with that little redhead beaut you're running around with. *And* got you heartbroken the second time around with Blue."

I stiffen and let a beat go by before asking, "Blue?"

His eyebrows shoot up, and his lips round into an *O* as he playfully looks around at the laughing members. "Whoops." His eyes meet mine, and they're rimmed with mischief. "You didn't know your little honey bunny and I are acquainted, huh?"

Blue…big blue eyes…he fucking means Liv! God damn it, that fucker Nate got her involved with this! What the absolute fuck does she see in him? All he's doing is setting her in sight of a monster hungry for sweet blood. Her blood.

"No, I didn't," I mutter and line up for another shot.

"She is quite the girl, though," he says, almost dreamily. "Quite a fire in her. A *spark*."

"Does she?" I land three pocket shots. I stand up and play this around in my head. "Don't you have more important things to do than toy with her?"

"Eh." He shrugs and glances at me while he bends down over the table. "I've only seen her once or twice. I'm just hoping you haven't seen her at all." He sinks a shot and shoots me a hard, cool glare. "Have you?"

Do my dreams count?

"No," I lie without hesitation.

His lips quip into a knowing smirk. "So she's available."

Over my dead fucking body…but he can easily have that arranged.

"Don't think she's your type."

Silence fills the rather buzzing area.

He laughs and wags a finger at me as he stands. "You know me so well. I'm more of a redhead kind of guy."

"Don't think about my girl," I joke with smile. But seriously, he can't. Even though she and I aren't anything, I feel like I should do her a favor and protect her from this ass.

He laughs with me, and the members fall in like the followers they are.

We play a few more rounds where he wins because I let him, then chill out in the back, smoking weed. He offers E, but it's a little too early and I'm not in the mood.

"Who's ready to party tonight?" Sam makes a loud-ass entrance.

I roll my eyes. "Not up for it," I grumble.

"You and Liv, man. Boring-ass people," he says, falling into one of the chairs opposite the couch.

I perk up, but not too much because Dean is still next to me. "Why'd you invite her? You know she'd never be up for it."

"I invited her a few days ago, such a bummer." He snickers, nodding at me. "She's got a cute ass, I'll give her that. Too bad she's got a stick up it—"

I tackle him to the ground and punch him in the mouth. Members gather around and cheer me on, and all hell breaks loose inside me as I punch him over and over. All I see is red, blue, and white-knuckled fists turning crimson, almost black.

I am finally pulled back by Dean, who looks at me with an unreadable expression. Before he can make any assumptions, I shrug out of his hold and say, "He shouldn't have opened his mouth."

"Ready to use your fists for good?" He looks fishy, like he's planning something. And when he gets to planning things…let's just say they don't end with unicorns and rainbows.

I glance at Sam, who is cursing every word he knows at me, then at Dean. I turn to the front door and begin walking. "Always."

16

Chapter Three

Liv

Miami is one of the most beautiful cities I've ever seen. Despite the heat, it is a pool of generated excitement, bright colors, cheerful laughter, and all-around amusement. I let the realization sink in as I lay on the sand of South Beach. The day is too perfectly warm to stay inside the house, so we all decided to pack a bag of sunscreen and beach towels and hit the road. We ended up here and are now relaxing as the sun does its work.

The girls are playing volleyball with a few guys they met, Mateo's getting Mason and me flavored slushies, and Noah is somewhere in the water trying—and failing—to surf. Mason is next to me under the huge umbrella, while I am a bit out in the sun, trying to get a little tan. Nothing too serious, though. I don't want to go to David's party looking like an orange popsicle. I made sure to apply a bit of sunscreen on my body and make sure to turn on each side so one side doesn't get too much or too little.

"Perk up. It's a *Baywatch* moment," Mason says excitedly, shoving my shoulder with his toes.

"Great, record it for me," I mumble into the towel beneath my body.

"I don't think my boyfriend would appreciate that, and neither would yours," he jests.

I pick up my head and glare at his annoying grin. "Gross." I finally turn around, leaning on my elbows. But when I spot what he's talking about, my jaw drops into the sand.

Noah is running out of the water, his fit body, muscled and lean, soaking wet. His V-line is very prominent and disappears into his light blue shorts. He's flashing a deep-dimpled smile at me as he shakes out his golden-blond hair. I never realized how blatantly attractive he is. Well, I am very aware of it now.

"You know, this beach allows girls to be topless," Noah says as he sits on the end of my towel.

I flush red and gently push him with my foot. "Why would I take off my top, perv?"

"I am not a perv. I'm just letting you know," he defends, raising his hands with a cheeky smile. "You'd get better *coverage…*"

"Fuck off." I laugh with a squeal when he grabs my foot and drags me onto his lap. I feel incredibly feverish with this skin-on-skin contact. But he doesn't even seem to notice. Part of me is stung; maybe he's been with so many girls he doesn't even realize…

He whistles and fans his face. "Is it me, or did it

just get hot in here?" His eyes flicker down to my bottom pressed on his knee, and I flush red with a little bit of relief he hasn't man-whored himself out *too* much.

"Oh, shut up!" I sit on the ground beside him, but he brings my legs in his lap and lets them stay there. I hide my smile as he begins to rub them. I lay down and poke Mason's outstretched foot. "Where's your boyfriend with the slushies?"

"There was a magician," he replies.

Noah stops rubbing, and he and I stare at Mason.

"A magician was performing by the stores, and he likes them," he explains, and Noah and I share a look. "What? That's not weird. He likes magicians. Geez." He flushes bright, bright red as he lays back down, defending his boyfriend.

"I find it cute," I say honestly, and Mason smiles at me.

"I can do magic," Noah claims.

"Yeah, right," I scoff.

"I'm being serious," he deadpans.

I squint my eyes at him in disbelief. "What kind of trick can you do?"

His serious expression is muddled by his boyish smile. "I can make your panties disappear."

"Noah!" I whine, but I can't even hide my laugh.

"Nice one," Mason cackles, and I grow even hotter.

"Shut up." I stick my tongue out at him, and he does it right back.

"Slushy incoming!" Mateo announces as he jogs up to us. He falls beside Mason, gives him a chaste kiss, and hands us our slushies.

19

"Thanks, babe," Mason gushes.

Noah leans over and takes a large sip, then beams at me. "Thanks, babe," he mocks.

"Don't steal my slushy," I groan, pushing his head away, but he bounces right back and does it again with a proud smirk. I roll my eyes and let him take a few sips before I lean against his shoulder and drink the rest. The cold drink does wonders as it slides down my chest, but Noah's hand twirling my bikini bottom's string and his previous joke sparks the heat again, tenfold.

"You guys should join us." Jaimie sinks to the ground, breathless.

"And be all sweaty and out of breath like you? I don't think so." I scrunch up my nose, and Noah squeezes it lightly. I swat him away and sling an arm around his neck. I somehow feel closer to him than ever, and he doesn't seem to mind one bit.

Julia eyes me as she collapses next to her panting girlfriend. "I didn't know you guys were so buddy-buddy," she accuses.

I gulp and anxiously twirl the end of his hair. "Didn't know we had to broadcast it to the world."

She still isn't on board with Noah and me being a thing, but I don't even know if that's what we are. We've only been on one date, and he hasn't brought up what we are officially. Just friends trying something new? Or much, much more…? I want us to be one of the two that would crush *him*, but I have to remind myself that I must move on or I won't get better and I'll have to bulk up winter clothing for Nebraska. I hate myself for thinking like this, like Noah's a means to an end I don't want to come to, like I'm selfish. And I am…but it doesn't mean I can't develop feelings for him, right?

"So, I think we should leave now before it's time for you to go," Jaimie pipes up, cutting the unknown, thick tension between Julia and me. She looks between us and smacks my leg with an assuring smile. "I think she'd like the vases I found while browsing the shops the other day. Or we can search for a gift that'll knock the others out of the water."

Noah arches an eyebrow. "Vases? Gifts? What's happening?"

I look at him and frown. I forgot to ask him to come with me to the party. "I'm going to a friend's party, and I have to bring a gift."

"You don't *have* to." Julia shakes her head.

"It's the right thing to do, plus I really do want to." I pause and flush for some reason. "They're getting married. They could use a few things…if not, one nice item for their house." I turn to Noah and add, "And I'd love if you could come with me." Mason was supposed to come with me but has plans with Mateo that day.

"Of course I will," he says, then grins from ear to ear. "You are too sweet," Noah sighs and tenderly kisses my cheek.

I laugh while Jaimie awws, and my smile digs even deeper in my cheeks. That is until I open my eyes and look over his shoulder. Grey is walking by with two guys flanking his sides. My heart skips as his eyes lock with mine…then shifts to Noah, all around, then back to me. I hold my breath in anticipation, but he looks away and keeps walking. That stings for some reason, but I pull back and quickly stand.

"We should go," I tell Jaimie, glance at Grey, who is already staring at me...then turn away and begin walking.

***

"You look very pretty, Livvy," Noah compliments me as we pull up in front of the house. The house is large, blue with white trim and colorful beds of flowers. There is a chalkboard announcing the party with his and Holly's names in fancy handwriting in the driveway.

"Thank you," I mumble around my thumb as I gently suck the skin nervously. That little exchange of eyes with Grey before I abruptly left the beach pushed me off the sky-high cloud I resided in with Noah. Now, I've landed on my butt in the cold, hard reality of black eyes and rude remarks I will no doubt encounter the minute I step out of this car.

He squeezes my thigh. "You okay?"

I nod with a forced smile. "It's just...Grey's gonna be here and—"

His lips cut me off.

The kiss is short, and he rests his forehead on mine and says, "He doesn't matter. You're here for your friends, right?"

He doesn't know David is like Grey's brother, and I'm more so here because I promised I'd be here after blurting it out without thinking about the *G* problem.

"Yes."

He pulls back, hand on the door handle. "Then let's go and support them."

I nod, sucking on my bottom lip.

His brows furrow. "Or shall we skip the party, buy a tub of ice cream, and watch some chick flicks?"

"There is no need." I crack a smile just because he'd actually do that for me. *See? We can work in a relationship; he's...nice.* "I think I'm fine now. I just needed a little time to prepare."

He reaches over the center console and takes my hand in his. "I'll be by your side the entire time." His words are more than reassuring, so I get out and take his hand. He pulls me into his side, and I laugh. I grab the wrapped box in the trunk and pull him along the driveway and into the backyard, where music is playing and general chatter can be heard clear as day.

Blue and silver balloons are hung in a gorgeous willow tree in the far-right corner of the massive backyard. There are white-clothed tables, a built-in dance floor just next to the medium-sized pool, and a bar and grill. A DJ is on the back porch, blasting summer songs; I think this one is by the group *DNCE.*

I find David and Holly by the grill, talking within a small group of people dressed in pastel colors.

"You made it!" Holly launches her arms around my neck.

I laugh. "Of course I did. And I got you something." I hand her the box, and she squeals.

23

"I'll put this with the others." She rubs my shoulder with a grin. "Thank you so much." She hugs me one more time before skipping away like an energetic bunny that's been given a carrot.

David faces me, cold beer in hand. "Glad to see you've made it," he says, cooler than his soon-to-be wife.

"I'm glad too." I glance around. "The place looks amazing."

"Thanks." He nods, mirroring my polite smile.

"Yeah…" I trail, unsure of what to say. I still feel iffy around him since, you know, the *G* thing.

Silence fills the warm air, and I nervously rub my hands on my bare thighs. "So, who's this?" he asks, staring at Noah with an unreadable expression.

"Oh." My cheeks warm. "This is Noah, my…" I shift my eyes to him, and he shrugs.

"Her very good friend," Noah finishes for me, pulling out his charming smile as he leans forward to shake David's hand.

Oh, thank God. That would have been embarrassing if I introduced him as my boyfriend, since we have yet to talk about it.

Holly comes back over, and I introduce Noah to her as well, smoother this time. I make small talk with them, nervous there'd be an uncomfortable gap, given the situation. Thankfully, Holly fills every inch with details of the wedding, like reservation card designs, the venue, the cake, and much, much more. I was very grateful for her chatty side.

Noah and I join the dance floor when a couple began talking to them. His hands are on my hips, and we're bopping around to some pop song that has a very catchy tune. So far, I haven't seen Grey, so a genuine smile has found a home on my face as I dance with him, my hands snaked around his neck.

"Having fun so far?"

I am about to reply when my luck runs dry and my eyes lock with a pair of cool black ones.

I ignore the flutter in my stomach and look into Noah's brilliant green eyes. "Yes, the best!" I get closer to his chest and turn us around, so he is all I see, and not…*him.*

Chapter Four

Grey

"Why the hell did she bring him?" I mutter under my breath. I narrow my eyes at the happy couple across the pool. The minute she saw me, she turned around faster than you could say, "What the fuck is she doing here?" They're now drinking bubbly champagne and talking with some people. Her hand is on his shoulder, and his is around her waist. And she is laughing so loud, you could probably hear it from Nebraska.

"Why do you care?" Rose asks from beside me.

I glance at her and scoff. "I don't," I lie and take a long sip of my ice cold beer. I end up finishing it and groan. "She just shouldn't have brought someone no one knows or cares about. It's an important event."

She just hums like the pretentious thing she is. "Sure, that's it."

"Yep, it is." I bend down to the cooler and grab another beer.

"So it has nothing to do with the fact that you're not over her?" she questions with attitude, her hand on her hip.

"I couldn't be more over her." I pop open the beer and take a long drink. I wipe my mouth with the back of my hand, the same time Liv is looking around. If you didn't know any better, you'd think she's looking for me. She finds me and stares at me, then at Rose, then turns back around and continues talking animatedly.

Rose hums again, and I roll my eyes. She's always been so annoying. But now she's annoying with a purpose, which is ten times worse.

"Don't you have anything else you can do?" I snap at her. "I'm sure Holly would like to yap about the lip gloss she's wearing on the *big* day."

"I'd rather talk about lip gloss than your bitching over someone who deserves better than you," she grits through her clenched teeth.

I turn to her, Liv and her boy-toy be damned. "Great, because being around someone who's just pissed I don't want her can get *really* fucking irksome."

"Screw you," she scoffs and stomps away.

"In your dreams!" I snap. It'd be too bad if she accidentally fell in the pool…

I down the rest of the beer, then drink another and another, but they do nothing. I am still very aware of *her* and that fucking Ken doll across the pool. It wouldn't be bad at all if that fucker fell in the pool…with chains linked around his feet… Wow, I am getting quite buzzed, aren't I? But still, it's not doing that much. I hit up the bar and take three shots. That's when the liquor finally hits me, hard.

I take a random blonde's hand and take her onto the dance floor. I dance with her along to the fast rap song, sipping a new cracked-open beer. As she shakes her ass on me, I stare across the pool. Liv's dancing with that pansy. Her back is turned to him, and he has his long-ass ape arms slung around her small waist. Fuck, she looks so beautiful. Her natural curly hair blows in the wind, and some sticks to her perfectly puffy pink lips as she laughs.

Fuck! Stop thinking about her. And stop looking, for God's sake, you pussy.

But my subconscious is right: I should focus on this five dancing on me. Liv gave me another chance, and I shot her down for her sake. It just hurts and annoys the fuck out of me to see her dancing on him like he's what she *really* wants. I know she doesn't like him like that. I can tell by how stiff she looks each time she really thinks about what's she doing. I can tell by the tiny little dimple on her cheeks she gets when she makes a forced smile. I can practically smell her want for someone across the way…me, fuckers. I mean me. But she isn't meant for me; she's for him, as much as I despise it.

There is no world where me and her would actually work. We tried it once, and it ended in a disaster. Even if she didn't do what she did, I think she would have found my dark past and not-so-bright future too much and left me for the douchebag in khaki shorts and polo who's too scared to dance frisky-like with her. He's holding onto her like he's trying to rein in an aunt who drank too many wine coolers. Speaking of which, I can see her lips from here. So pouty and reddish and wet, I think she drank one or two cherry coolers...

Stop fantasizing about her, Jesus H. Christ.

"Where's my gift?" David jokes with a jackass of a smile as he walks up to me.

I crack a smile before downing the rest of my beer and tossing it in a trash. "I'm right here, you ungrateful bastard." Disregarding the girl stumbling away from me, I spread my arms open, and he rolls his eyes but gives me a bro-hug.

"Did you keep the receipt?" he says like the smart-ass he is.

"Fuck you." I laugh.

"Enjoying the view?" He nudges me, and I quickly shake my head.

I drag my eyes away and scoff at the ground. "What are you talking about?"

"You know what I'm talking about," he assures with a knowing smile.

I roll my eyes. "Why'd you even invite her? You know what she did to me."

He sighs and rubs the back of his neck. "I ran into her, and I couldn't *not* invite her. Plus, I genuinely wanted her here, and I know Holly definitely did too. She's a nice girl."

"What a sweetheart, going behind my back and shit," I gripe through my teeth.

"Don't do that," he breathes.

"Don't do what?" I scoff. I think he's had one too many champagne glasses.

"That. Hate her so much it pushes others

29

away…like Rose," he explains, "when we all know you don't remotely hate her. You just think you have to because of your twisted-ass, hard-headed-ass mind."

"You don't know what goes on in my head," I say, not knowing what to say really because he's right. I just…now it's too late to try to be anything with her again. She's already got someone new who actually deserves her.

"Sure…" He squints at me, and I roll my eyes because he's acting like he knows everything that goes on in my head. Trust me, the best therapist in the universe wouldn't be able to understand what's going on up there.

"David! Where are you?" Holly hollers, and I cover my ears, grimacing. *Fuck, I'm wishing him all the luck with this parrot.* "Oh, hey there, Grey!" She waves at me, freckled cheeks bright as a tomato and auburn hair swept up in a stylish hair-do.

"Hello, Holly." I hesitantly wrap my arms around her when she launches into me. I pull back after her heavy scent of cinnamon spice and grape wine coolers becomes too much.

"Where's Rose?" she asks, linking her fingers with David's.

I shrug and look around aimlessly; I don't really want to find her. She's being a fucking pest at the moment. "Somewhere around, she'll show up," I tell her noncommittally.

"You should look for her. She's your date," she whines.

"Like I said, she'll turn up." She is really testing my patience.

She squeezes my bicep with a frown. "We're gonna start opening presents in a while. *Find her.*"

I give her a tight-lipped smile but let it drop when they finally walk away. There is no way I'm getting stuck with one girl I can barely tolerate while watching the girl I actually want. I'd rather drink and watch the fakeness drip around me as everyone talks and laughs and has the time of their lives.

I go to the bar and grab another shot and am walking back to the pool-side when I make the mistake of looking across. Liv and lover-boy are dancing, but they've left the aunt-stage and are dancing more risqué than before. My blood boils, and I glare at his hands that are traveling around her lower back, close to her ass. And she isn't putting up that much of a fight against it.

That just pisses me off.

"Hey, Holly kept bugging me to find—what are you doing?" Rose stops talking when I swing her back into my chest. I grab her hips and shush her when she tries to talk again.

"I'm sorry about what I said earlier. You're right," I whisper in her ear and glance across the pool, locking eyes with a pair of eyes that rival the crystalline water between us. "I should get over her."

"By making her jealous?" She whips around and jabs a sharp finger at my chest. "I am not some toy you can just—oh…" She shuts up when I kiss her under her chin, then down her neck and right under her neck. I gently spin her back around and wrap my arms around her, swaying her hips side-to-side.

I move us closer to the pool, push some people away, and broadcast our little tango.

What I am doing is petty as hell, but if she can dance with another guy and have him be all up on her, why can't I do the same with Rose? At least we've been in an actual relationship, whereas she and Mr. Barbie are like two different species trying to live under one roof—it won't end pretty nor would it ever work.

Liv looks me up and down and stumbles on her boy-toy's feet until they stop dancing altogether. He tries to ask why she stopped, but she can't stop looking at me. And when he looks over, I smirk as widely as possible and send him a little smirk while lightly nipping under Rose's chin. She moans slightly, her eyes closed in bliss.

"Gift opening time!" Holly announces loudly, and the music cuts off abruptly.

I swing my eyes from her standing on a table back to the happy couple. Liv is staring at me with an unreadable expression...or is that anger? But what the hell should she be angry about? She's the one who started this in the first place. At least she looks as miserable as I feel inside. Good. Now we're sort of even.

"Let's go, babe," I whisper in Rose's ear.

She nods, and I give the couple a wink before leading her to the back patio. There are a bunch of wrapped gifts surrounding the sitting couple. What? Is this a fucking baby shower? Is there something David's not telling me?

They get through two dozen gifts, and I have the strongest urge to plunge a knife through myself on repeat with each squeal and "Oh my God!" that escapes Holly every few seconds. Mine was a big-ass pack of condoms, to which everyone laughed like it was meant to be a joke. It wasn't, though. He's already doing one of two things I've vowed to never ever do: get married, the other have children. One forces me in a relationship with one person for the rest of my life when divorce rates are sky high, and the other just ruins life, plain and simple.

Liv's present was an immaculate white and blue vase. Of course it must have cost like three hundred bucks or something.

I am half tempted to bounce and find something more exciting, anything really, when they land on a particular gift: a "Welcome Home" rug. What really sets off bells in my head was Holly's response.

"We should set this down now before you forget. You know how bad your memory is."

"Why would you do that? It's just a rented beach house," I pipe up, and many people glance at me like I've lost my mind. I lift my eyebrows expectantly when the celebrated couple share a meaningful glance. "Well? Don't all speak at once."

David exhales heavily and rubs his neck vigorously; he's definitely hiding something big. "Can I talk to you in private...?"

I scoff and look around at the rest of the people, who look afraid to say something, in fear I might lose my shit. Too fucking bad it's going to happen if no one says nothing at all. "No, just tell me here. Why the fuck is that mat necessary on a *rented* beach home?"

He opens his mouth, then lets it drop. "I think

33

you know why…"

He's fucking living here now? Without *telling* me?

My eyes widen for a brief second, but then I grit my teeth together and ball my hands in fists. "No fucking way. You wouldn't…you'd tell me."

"Grey, can we step to the side—" He sounds jittery, nervous.

"Fuck you, David!" I storm through the crowd, pissed off beyond belief. I thought we were fucking brothers who told each other everything. I guess not.

Chapter Five

Liv

In times like this, I wish I could put the world on pause. Just so I can think carefully without looking like a fish out of water. The minute Holly showed off the rug, I knew this would happen. Grey is a very hot-headed person, one that doesn't deal with change well. David is Grey's savior, a brother, really. And now he's uprooting from his position as Grey's rock through hard times and leaving him behind. Grey will wash back into the turbulent storm he previously escaped from.

And although he just tried to make me jealous—which he totally did, that bastard—I want to make sure he's okay, that he's not completely breaking right now. No matter how much he makes sure that I pay for what I did…he'll never be able to stop me from caring about him. I don't think I will ever be truly able to stop the instinct to nurse his wounds or make sure he's just okay. It sucks because I know we can never ever be a *thing* again, and I'll have this massive part of me that almost consumes me, to be at his aid.

But he isn't mine anymore. Not my responsibility. Not my concern, at least, he isn't supposed to be. I lost my obligation to look after him the minute he walked away, taking my heart with him like the thief he is, no matter how right it was. He has a new person there for him now—Rose—and maybe she can do a better job. They were in love first. She probably knows him and what to do to help him more than I do.

I glance around the dimmed crowd for her. No one's really speaking as David runs after his friend. It's awkward as someone clears their throat, highlighting how crazy uncomfortable the air has become. And it becomes even more unbearable as shouting and curses are thrown in the direction the two men disappeared into. Holly attempts to diffuse the tense atmosphere by showing off a collection of kitchen pots, but it does nothing to draw the attention of her nosy guests.

David finally storms back and heads past his struggling fiancée. He's coming my way, but I find Rose walking up next to me. Oh…of course he'd want his best friend's girlfriend to calm him down. I take a step back, not knowing if my face looks as fallen as I feel on the inside.

"I need your help," he says, and I turn away. I don't want to invade where I don't belong.

I head to Noah, who looks lost and concerned, when David grabs my hand. I turn around, and he's looking at me expectantly. I look between him and Rose, who looks unreadable as she catches my gaze.

I look away, flushed, and finally manage to find words.

"With what?" I ask, but we both know what he means.

"With Grey," he sighs and looks around before lowering his voice. "You're like a Grey whisperer, and I need your help in getting him to calm down."

"Why should he? You're abandoning him, like—" I begin, quite annoyed and automatically on Grey's side. Well? What did he expect? That I'd be fine with him leaving his best friend who relies on him so heavily, though he likes to act strong?

"It's not like that," he says quickly, then sighs again. "Can you just please help…?"

Cheeks warm as a million suns, I shift my gaze to Rose. "Why me?"

He reads my lost expression and says, "I think he needs you right now."

If Rose is stung by his words, she doesn't let it show. "He's right." She takes a step back and shakes her head, cheeks stunned blossom-pink. "Grey won't listen to me," she admits. "He never has."

"But…" I cast a look over my shoulder at Noah. His eyebrows are scrunched together, and he nods his head as if he can hear this absurd conversation. As if going after my emotional, sometimes cruel, ex is okay. Like he trusts me alone with him. I look back at David, who looks anxious now, as if Grey will actually explode in anger if I don't go out there to him in this second.

"Wait one second," I tell him, then rush over to Noah. "I don't have to go if you don't want me to,"

I pant out, holding onto his forearms. He is the one I'm supposed to look after, though he seems perfectly stable and isn't the one who "needs me" at the moment.

"It's okay, go ahead," he says without a hint of jealousy or any other emotion.

I string my eyebrows together, and he cracks a smile. "Really?"

"Yes." He leans down and kisses my forehead. "I'll be right here."

Why is he so amazing? I pray I don't hurt him.

I lean up and peck his lips—nothing. But I smile because he's great, sparks or not. And who the hell needs sparks when he is literally the best human?

"I won't take long." I kiss him again, then jog in the direction David came from. I make the mistake of peeking over my shoulder. David looks restless, hands covering his face. Rose is chewing on her lip, rubbing her arms in worry or sadness, I don't know. And Noah, his hands are tucked in his khakis, and he looks the same way he looked the night of my birthday, when that door flung open, revealing his hurt expression. Common sense is screaming at me to run into his arms and tell him to drive me far from this Grey-infested party and move on. But my heart, my heart is connected with my feet, and it's pulling me in the direction of my first love.

The music starts back up the minute the latch on the side gate shuts. I can faintly hear murmurs about the drama going down, and Holly is resuming her gift showcase. Everyone can finally breathe now that the foolish, hung-up ex is finally going to calm down her upset ex-boyfriend who ruined the party's mood. If only I could breathe too. I'm actually doing the opposite; I'm having my damn lungs stolen away from me in the rudest way possible.

I immediately find him sitting on the curb, head in his knees.

"Grey?" I say softly, and he goes rigid.

"Fuck off, Olivia," he replies, clearly agitated. And he clearly doesn't want to be bothered, by me especially. Too bad I'm apparently the *Grey whisperer*. I wonder if I can resign now…or if I have to wait until I'm, like, seventy and haven't been able to settle down with a nice guy.

"Such a nice quote," I joke as I sit a few inches away from him. "Should be stitched on a throw pillow. It'd be a hell of a decoration, don't you think?"

He side-eyes me hard, then glowers at the street. "I am not in the mood."

"Seriously?" I scoff. "I couldn't tell from your sulking posture and your looming gray cloud over your head." I snicker to myself, but he just glares at me silently. "Get it? Because of your name? Grey and *gray*…?"

I am met with silence.

He looks at me sideways. "Why are you here?"

"David invited me—" I start, but he slices through my words.

"No, I mean *here*. Next to me. Trying to…do whatever *this* is." He gestures to me with his hands.

I take a deep sigh and think about what I will tell him next. Something tells me I shouldn't say I'm mostly here because David asked me to calm him down. He'd just lose his shit again. And he looks like he's calmed down some. I don't know whether it's because he's had a tiny bit of time to let the news process or because I'm here. I do know that I'll never find out because he'd never admit to the latter. Ever. He is the most stubborn person I know.

"Because I want to," I finally say.

He scoffs and rolls his eyes. "Yeah fucking right. David sent you, didn't he?" He quickly stands, and I scramble up after him. He's turning away from me, and it stings when he pulls his hands away as I reach for them. *Now I know how he feels, frustrated and like I'm not being listened to. I suddenly am very apologetic for not hearing him out all those times.* "You shouldn't even be here."

"I'm here because you just found out some pretty big news—" I defend myself.

"You shouldn't be *here* at all!" he snaps, veins pounding under his neck. I snap my mouth closed and watch as he rolls his eyes and pivots on his heels, furiously rubbing his face. "At this party, with *him*—"

"Why do you care why I'm here or why I'm with him?" I cut him off, and he looks at me incredulously. "Because last I knew, we were through. Done. *Over.*" My voice grows softer and softer with each word. "I gave you that note…and you never replied. I took that as the last possibility of there being an *us* and was okay with it. Dying on the inside a little, yes, but okay nonetheless." I take a breath and look away from his hurt expression. "This isn't about us, though. I am here right now because I genuinely care about you. And not just as a significant other, but as a *person* who cares about your well-being."

"Then leave," he whispers.

"Stop being so damn stubborn and let me help you, Grey," I say, fed up with his BS.

"If you care about my well-being so god damn much, then fucking leave!" he screams in my face.

"Fine!" I scream and push him back. I turn on my heels, stomping up to the backyard gate. I can't believe I ever thought I could still help him. He's always been so freaking hard-headed, but he's even worse now that he won't accept my help. He still thinks I have some god damn agenda against him, and I'm growing too tired to keep explaining to him that what I did was a mistake I am paying for every single day.

I am almost at the gate when I am whirled back around.

"Don't leave," he says, his face softened.

"What the hell, Grey?" I grab my hands from him and rub my eyes. He can be so confusing. It was stressful then, and it still is to this day. "Do you want me here or gone?" I put my hands on my hips and pull my best stern expression. He has to choose whether he wants my presence or not. I will not keep getting jerked around by him. I refuse it.

He chews on his lower lip, and his dimples poke into his cheeks as he twists up his face. Like a baby stuck between two toys, he narrows his eyes at me and thinks so hard, I can practically see his thoughts fly through his head.

Finally, he rolls his eyes and kicks his foot at the grass. "Here, I guess…"

I think I hide my smile as I nod and say, "Good,

now stop being an ass and come with me."

His dimples grow deeper when he smirks.

I gasp, knowing what he's thinking.

"Get your mind out of the gutter, Wyler." My cheeks warm immensely.

"I didn't say anything," he defends, raising his hands. But that cheeky little grin is still sloping his mouth.

"Yeah, but I can read your mind." I walk over to the curb, and he follows. We sit down, just a few inches apart.

"Oh, can you now?" he jests.

"Yep, clear as day." I smile and feel a certain tugging in my chest when he grins from ear to ear. For once, he isn't scowling at me like he wants to see me at my lowest. He actually looks sort of relieved. I know, it's weird, but I feel a big sense of relief too. "So, David…" I clear my throat. It felt too good between us, and I still haven't done what I was sent out here for. Even though he looks well under control now.

He groans and looks super pissed, like he totally forgot why he's out here in the first place. "Can you believe it? After all the years of us being like brothers, he's leaving me for a girl. She's okay and everything, a little fucking chatty, but she's his and he loves her. I have no problem with her, but he just wants to get up and move so far fucking away?"

"Did he tell you *why* they're moving here?" I know David would tell him the whole situation.

"Something about her family being out here or some shit like that," he hisses and throws his hands up. "But what the fuck am I? Am I not his family?

His brother is locked up, and they're on the worst fucking terms ever. His parents are dead, and none of the rest of his family really reach out to him unless they want something. But me? I've been there since day fucking one." He looks away.

"I was there when his aunts tried to squeeze money out of him. I was there when his grandmother died, who was closest with him. I was there when he thought he was shit and that Holly wouldn't want him; I listened to him babble about planned dates and everything. Yet he's just fucking getting up and leaving me? How is that fucking fair?" he rants until he is out of breath at the end. He finally looks at me for a reaction and shakes his head. "Let me guess, you think what he's doing is right and I'm just a big fucking baby?"

"No," I frown, placing a hand on his knee.

"Really?" He sounds shocked.

I nod. "I mean, I get her family being here and everything, but I do get it. He was everything to you, he *still* is, and he's just leaving you. When he asked me to come out here, I was instantly on your side. What did he expect? For you to be totally okay with it? I mean, eventually you will have to be, because he's still your best friend, but for right now, you get to be a little mad."

"So he did send you out here," he says, completely missing everything else I said.

"Yes, but that's not the point—"

I become mute when he suddenly pulls me into his chest, arms around my neck. I'm stiff and don't know what to do. I am surprised. He's supposed to be hating me, not *hugging* me. Do I hug back or...?

"Sorry," he mutters, cheeks kind of pink as he pushes me back. He turns to the street and draws his knees up to his chest. "I just...I just kind of needed..." He glances at my shocked state, then sighs at the road and shakes his head. "Nothing. Sorry. I just...he's fucking leaving me, you know. He's been my rock. He saved me when I needed him the most. And now...now I have no one." His voice shatters, and I think I see his eyes gloss over with tears.

"What about Rose?" I ask, swallowing a dry lump in my throat.

He looks at me and stares for a long time, brows knitted, lips pursed, and eyes roaming my face. I feel heated, like my lungs are being sucked dry by a vacuum.

"She isn't mine, not really," he finally says.

I nod and glance at the road, too nervous to hold his intense eyes. "Oh..."

"Yeah." His voice hasn't repaired itself. He's breaking down, and I literally can't just sit here and let it happen without trying to coax him, even a little bit.

Damning his supposed hatred toward him and damning the boy waiting for me back at the house, I scoot over to him and throw my arms around his waist. I nuzzle my face in his neck's crook, my hair covering him like a protective shield. He smells deeply of cologne and Clover cigarettes. He feels bigger beneath my small hands, more muscular. But he is still plush, and he is still huge, and he is still mine to take care of. Like a huge teddy bear that keeps ripping himself open, letting out cotton. I'll always be there to stuff them back in and sew him back up. Always.

I tense for a second when I feel his arms slink around my own waist, but then I feel myself fall into his hold, like instinctual relief. I'm twisted so my chest is pressed into his, and his growing stubble scratches my collarbone. I giggle, and he bounces a little with his own deep laughter. I close my eyes shut and bask in the silent glow of his heavy scent, and his huge but soft arms, and the electricity running throughout my limbs like live snares.

Chapter Six

There was a breakthrough yesterday. It started when he said he actually wanted my help and for me to stay by his side. It really vaulted forward as we talked and joked like old times. It felt so good being able to see his adorable dimples pop into the conversation...but I felt like I was in heaven on earth when I hugged him...and he hugged me *back*. I honestly thought he'd just push me away and storm off. But he didn't. He accepted my comfort and returned it.

And those few seconds that turned into whole minutes were beyond euphoric. He's always been so tenacious when it comes to warding me off or showing any kind of affection he used to, so when I felt those strong arms wrap around me and heard him sigh in contentment, I nearly lost my mind.

Even though it is the next day, I can still remember everything. The quick beats of his heart drumming against my own. The distinct smell of cigarettes and cologne. His thick stubble rubbing against the crook of my neck each time he took a deep breath. The way he held me like he didn't want to let go. Like if he did, the world would come crumbling down. And when we did let go, I actually felt my world crack a little.

"Heads up!" Charlotte calls out from beside me.

I quickly dodge to the side, barely missing the tennis ball. I watch as it bounces off the gate and rolls to the side. I pick it up, apologize, and hit it back over the net. I was so caught up in my thoughts that I almost had my head taken off. I wish there was a way I could get him out of my mind, even if it's just for a second.

"Sorry," I mutter, but she just shakes her head.

Today, my mother managed to drag her, me, and Noah to the country club. I'm surprised I've been able to avoid the place for so long. It could have been avoided the entire summer, but she pressed so hard for me to come. Unable to resist her stern persuasion, I agreed. It's not as bad as I thought it would be, though. Despite the few glances here and there after my reputation of being a fool for falling under the vile influences a "bad boy," I haven't been looked down at *too* badly. Too badly is them basically shunning me and my parents, which would put a first-class stamp on my trip to Nebraska.

Noah eyes me, and I feel so guilty. I must have stayed with Grey for maybe an hour, though it could have been less. When I'm with him, it's like time has no meaning. Like I am in a time loop of his laughs and his dimples and his cigarette-soaked shirts and his messy black hair and his...*everything*. Thinking about it all now has me warm, and it's definitely not because of the sun beating down on us as we play tennis.

It's Charlotte and me against Noah and his father, Robert. He's a nice man but a beast when it comes to tennis, which makes a lot of sense since he basically spends his summer in the lavish club. Charlotte didn't want to come for the same reason as me—snobby tycoons—but Louise can be pretty persuasive when it comes down to it. Once she convinced me to take three AP classes instead of four, which was pretty hard to do, considering how much I love the hard work.

When we finish, I am out of breath and cramping up. We walk over to the shaded patio table, where my mother and Noah's mother are chatting animatedly. A young girl rushes over from the sidelines and freshens their lemonades, then runs back to her post. I roll my eyes in slight disgust as they pay her no mind and drink from their sweating glasses, like their sparkling juice just came from God above and not a girl busting her butt to keep them satisfied.

"Who won?" Mother asks when she sees us walking up to the little table.

"Us, of course," Noah says with a cocky smile as he wiggles his eyebrows at me. "There was no chance for them with *me* playing. I'm a champ at le tennis," he jokes, but all I can give him is a distracted smile. His brows knit, and he smiles at me nervously. I look away and fiddle with my charms. I can't look at him. Even though I didn't do anything explicit with Grey, I still feel dirty. As though being next to Grey is enough to make me guilty of betraying him.

"I don't think that should be something you should be bragging about," Charlotte says with a playful roll of her eyes.

"My baby can't help winning. It's in his blood," Gemma, his mother, coos, pinching his cheek.

"Jesus, Mom," Noah groans cutely, scrunching up his face. "Don't do that. It's humiliating."

"Oh, am I embarrassing you in front of your girlfriend?" she jokes, waggling her eyebrows. *I see where he gets his teasing from. It's in his DNA.*

I can't help but laugh at that, especially with his shy smile and pinkish cheeks.

"There's always next time," Mother says with a warm, suspecting smile as she lays a hand on my bare knee and rubs in a supposedly comforting way, but all it does is make me stiff and questioning. "Maybe you can show her some of your moves?"

I flush bright red and sit up. Her hand falls. "Mother," I hiss in a low voice. She makes it sound like she wants him to have sex with me, like she's my pimp or something. Gosh! She can be so damn shameless, so ruthless when it comes to my life that she just has to have control, or *she'll* go insane.

"You know what I mean, sweetheart." She laughs it off and looks at me as if *I'm* the one who's lost her mind. "Get your mind out of the gutter."

"What gutter?" I scoff, and she visibly grinds her teeth.

She's probably mentally contemplating what I should wear on my way to Nebraska.

A thin layer of silence fills the sweltering air.

"But you were great at tennis once," she continues, subtly narrowing her icy blue eyes. "You must have spent maybe three weeks training and beating your father, game after game." She laughs, and I catch Charlotte glaring at her like she wants to strangle her, but I shake my head softly, and she makes a *humph* sound. "Maybe Noah here can refresh your skills."

"Mother," I warn.

"I think it's a lovely idea, Elena," his mother raves, clapping her white-laced gloves together with a shining white smile. "I always knew you two would end up together." She sighs and brushes his hair out of his eyes while he rolls them at his mother's touch. "But then she got wrapped up with that *boy* at university…"

"How is that any of your fucking business?" Charlotte finally snaps.

"I should be asking you the same thing," Gemma snips.

"Calm down now, ladies," Robert, Noah's father, says with a light laugh that's supposed to diffuse the tense atmosphere. But with the way everyone is glaring at one another, I don't think it's working quite as well as he hoped.

"You two have been growing very close. Why not throw a little more one-on-one in there?" Mother continues to publicly push Noah and me together.

This is why I haven't told her we are together, because she'd jump up and begin arranging our wedding. But I'm just nineteen years old. I haven't even finished college yet, but I see the heart eyes when I look at her, and I know I can't divulge all a daughter is supposed to gush about with her mother.

Sad, really. But it's just how it has to be if I want to succeed in the life I've planned for, and a career comes way before a family.

I push my chair back and stand. "I'm going to go take a shower." I give Mother a look to back off. "I feel really sticky and gross after that grueling game. Thank you very much, Mr. Wells." I playfully wink at him, and he clutches his heart. I giggle and send Noah a meaningful look for him to follow me and stalk off to the country club's mansion, giving Charlotte an assuring shoulder squeeze.

When I get inside, I keep my head down to avoid all the pearl-wearing women's judging eyes and the men's gossip while on their way to the golf course. I swear, it's like high school when it comes to these people. They look down at each other and put one another down as it is, but when it comes to us kids, the next generation in line for their pearls and Porsches, they act as if we can't make a single mistake or we won't be *allowed* to wield the golden country club access card. As if I'd actually want it. I'd burn it the second I got my hands on it. I wouldn't want to voluntarily be involved in this conniving world of theirs.

I find myself at the massive inside pool. The water is brilliantly crystal and is surrounded by reflective glass walls and exquisite marble sculptures. There is also a large jacuzzi. But since today is such a nice day, most of the members are either on the golf course or at the racetrack near the club to watch the horses and throw money into gambling.

"Hey, you okay?"

I turn around. "No, Noah, I am not okay," I reply, frustration sinking into my voice.

He frowns. I hate that my mother is the way she is. He'll never be able to be *with* me without feeling overwhelmed. What boy would stick around with my mother progressively shoving us a million steps forward?

"I get it, your mother's insane. Whose isn't?" He chuckles, and his dangerously dark green eyes sparkle. "Mine still treats me like I'm twelve and need to wear a fucking *bib*."

A laugh sits on my chest, but my anger burns it away.

"You don't get it." My hands go wild, swinging from side-to-side. "She just keeps pushing and pushing for us to be together. There is no *doubt* she's planning *everything* for the future. And I mean *everything*. And it just makes me so angry because she just can't do this. What if you don't even want me? What if no one does? She shouldn't be allowed to do this and drag you into it. I care so much for you, but she's being such an insane person, and I'm scared you'll want to leave me," I rant, gasping for breath at the end. I close my eyes, taking a few steps back to clear my mind.

"Liv, you should take a breath—" he says worriedly.

"I can't. I'm trying, but she's just driving me insane!" I admit, clutching my hair.

"Do you feel like you're on fire right now?" he questions, eyebrows raised.

What does that have to do with anything?

"Yes, what kind of question is—Noah!" I gasp

52

as I am pushed back and free-fall into the water. I quickly catch some breath before I submerge and pinch my nose closed. I watch as Noah dives in and grasps my waist, pulling me to the surface. When I emerge, my ears pop, and I gasp frantically for air. "What the crap, Noah!" I smack his shoulder, but he's just smiling from ear to ear.

"What? You said you felt like you were on fire!" He defends himself like the maniac he's being.

"So you push me into the pool knowing I can't swim?" I screech.

"I can be insane," he exclaims, and I'm speechless by his raspy voice, eyes glistening, jaw sharp from his open smile. "I get it from my mother. I literally just told you that. Do you not *listen* to me when I speak?" I roll my eyes, and he laughs more broadly, lifting my chin up. "I'll gladly distract you from your insane mother, if you want."

A memory of Grey saying the same thing pops into my head, and my breath becomes shallow as I remember how he accomplished that...

"I'd love that," I say breathlessly, and his dimples sink into his cheeks like plush-cushion pillows. "Thank you." I lean forward and kiss his nose. Then I pull back and look around. "Gross, we're still in our clothes...and *shoes*!" I clench my feet around his waist, looking down at my see-through chest and my tennis skirt rising up. I can't be any more on fire right now.

He laughs at my expense but swims us over to the edge anyway. I climb out, feeling like a billion pounds are on my back. I consciously undress into my underwear, so relieved I'm wearing matching pink underwear and bra. But when I look over my shoulder and look at Noah, I turn the color of his briefs that does his…um, *manhood* justice. I quickly look away from his rows of abs and sit at the edge of the pool. He jumps in and pulls me in; I am held up in his arms, and I become an even deeper shade of shameful.

"Ready to swim, buttercup?" His dimples and little smile are going to be my personal torture.

"Readier than ever." I smile back just as brightly, I hope.

Ten minutes later and I am flailing like a fish out of water, ironically, and he's laughing at me.

"It's not funny, Noah! I can't swim. It's just not possible." I pout, and he pokes my nose to piss me off. I bite his finger, and he groans and swims backward until his back hits the artsy tiles.

"Maybe you just need some motivation," he says, and I hold my breath. His eyes are glued to my lips…then they meet mine, and his lips slide to the right.

"Maybe…" I whisper and glance at his reddish lips.

He closes the inch gap I didn't even notice and kisses me. I wrap my arms around his neck and thread my fingers through his hair. He presses one hand on the wall behind me and cups the lower part of my back with the other. He tastes sickly sweet and his tongue still feels foreign, but over time it will become second nature and I will feel something. But at the moment, I am only feeling the coolness of the tiles on my back and his large hand.

A singing ringtone halts our little make out.

"I think that's me." I smile apologetically, and he nods. The smile drops, and I answer the phone, the guilt weighing on my shoulder as Jaimie talks. And no matter how much I try, I can't really understand what she is saying. All I can focus on is the hopeful, wide smile on the boy who genuinely likes me and how I felt nothing when he kissed me with *everything* he had.

Chapter Seven

Julia's birthday is Saturday, which is in three days, but Jaimie wants to throw her a surprise party before the day actually arrives. She wants it at a really popular club. She says then it'll *really* be a surprise. I think it's sweet, and I would have loved to help her plan it, but she says my sense of fashion would slow her down, which is in no way offensive in her eyes. However, I couldn't just sit back and let her make little changes, since she's already begun planning two weeks in advance. I find it amazing and frightening how well she kept the party a secret for so long, especially since she knew she was going to come to Miami.

She acts the same way Julia acted when she planned Jaimie's surprise party. I think it's adorable as heck. Well, her planning a party for her girlfriend. Not the freaking out and screaming at the workers who are helping set up the venue. I helped the workers who got the brunt of her demands. I understand why she is so high-strung, though. She

56

wants the absolute best for her girlfriend. I just wish I could have a partner as dedicated to making me happy like her. And a relationship where my heart isn't on the chopping block or where my mother has inserted herself so much, it feels like I am being suffocated.

I inhale deeply and pause in spreading the white cloth over a tall table. I have to clear my mind because I'm trying to help Jaimie. I exhale heavily and continue to cover the tables. After I finished laying down all the cloths, I placed golden sparklers on each table. When Julia wanders in, they will all be set ablaze and confetti will pop from basically every single direction. I think it's a little *too* much, but I wouldn't ever tell Jaimie that. She is allowed to go all out and do whatever to please her girlfriend. Even if it means the chance of inhaling pieces of shiny paper or having my hair set on fire is extremely high.

"Wow, you really went all out..." I muse as I look over Jaimie's shoulder. A pair of big brown eyes covered in black eyeliner stare back at me...in the form of icing. That's right, Jaimie's ordered a huge cake that resembles Julia, leather jacket, eyeliner, brooding expression, and all.

"Thank you," she says with a smile.

"Wasn't really a compliment," I mutter.

"Can you help me move it to the center?" she asks.

"Sure." I help her move the cake that no doubt weighs one hundred pounds. "Couldn't you have gone with a normal cake?" I ask, out of breath after the cake is set on the round table.

"Um, no," she scoffs incredulously. "My baby is the best, and she deserves the best." Her head tilts back, and a warm smile lightens her features as she beams up at the cake. "And nothing less."

I shrug and stand behind her, staring up at the cake. "I guess it is kind of awesome. Kind of scary too…but still awesome. She's gonna love it."

"Duh, of course she's going to love it." She flashes her hair over her shoulder while giving me a cocky wink. "If you haven't noticed, I'm pretty fucking awesome."

"Whatever you say." I playfully shrug, and she glares at me. "Kidding, kidding! Look around. You did all of this by yourself."

She looks around with a resigned sigh as she twirls a lock of her dark hair. "You're right…I am so getting some tonight." She bites her lip as she zones out into whatever creepy sexual fantasy has sparked her interest.

"And that's my cue to leave." I sneak away as she really starts diving deep into her subconscious, making weird faces. I slink off into one of the dark corners with purple velvet couches and sink into one of them. I'm going to give Jaimie a little time to snap back into reality. But in the meantime, I pull out my phone and frown at the two missed calls and one text from Noah, all asking if I'm okay, since I left him in the pool so abruptly.

Noah is honestly the best person, and he doesn't deserve this. We were in the middle of some pretty intense, intimate kissing, then I just got up and practically ran out of there. And all because I didn't *feel* anything from a kiss. A kiss! Who cares if I didn't feel a drop of desire when my lips touched his? You didn't have to feel the heavens move or explosions inside of your stomach every time you kiss a guy…right?

Even after dating Grey, I'm still horribly inexperienced when it comes to relationships and feelings that come along with it, which is insane since he and I felt so right, so perfect, like we were making up our own rules as we went along. Or maybe the all-consuming feeling of pure bliss and darkness and perfection was the standard, and I'm just not going to ever feel them with Noah. *Or* I will feel the same as I did with Grey with another guy, just not Noah…?

I don't know, but I'm getting a headache the harder I think.

Luckily, the vibrating of my phone snaps me out of my muddled thoughts.

I hesitate when reading the screen.

"Hello?" I bite my lip and nervously shake my leg, awaiting the person to reply.

"Liv…" Rose gulps, "I need your help…"

***

A few hours later, I have switched out my tennis skirt for a pair of skinny jeans, black booties, and a lavender tube top. To be safe in case it becomes chilly tonight when I leave the club, I pair the outfit with a jean jacket and wrap my hair up in a bun with bangs.

I look around the packed club. There is a surging crowd of people on the multi-colored light-up floor that grows with each new group of friends that heard about the party online. I feel as though I'm going deaf with the loud music playing. I wish I had bought some earplugs so I could drown this out. I am half-tempted to take my Coke and hide in the bathroom. And I wouldn't even care about how unsanitary sitting on a toilet of a club is, as long as I could have some peace and quiet.

Julia came in about a half hour ago, and true to my prediction, I almost had my hair set on fire and I am almost positive I swallowed confetti.

Now, I'm waiting for someone.

"Liv!" I swivel my eyes all around and barely make out Rose's raging red hair as she emerges from the crowd. She breaks into what I think is a smile of relief as she nears the bar.

"Rose." I return her warm smile and stand. She wraps her thin arms around me, and I laugh uneasily before wrapping my arms around her, returning her hug. For a few seconds, we stay like this, until she backs up and stares at me with misty eyes. "What's wrong?" I pull her down to sit at the bar.

"Nothing, I just…" She sniffles and grabs a napkin from a stack on the bar. I watch as she dabs under her eyeliner, then croaks, "Grey…he's been such an asshole lately."

"That's kind of his thing," I joke lightly, and she smiles sheepishly. "Sorry." I gulp and flicker my eyes away, but she grips my arm. I look back as she waves her other hand dismissively, sniffling some more.

"It isn't your fault…much." Her eyes drift to the floor.

"I'm sorry, but what did I do?" I try and succeed in catching her eyes.

"Isn't it obvious?" she scoffs, rolling her eyes as if I'm the most oblivious creature on the planet. "He's in love with you, Liv. And I don't think he ever really stopped." She stops talking, and while I try to swallow her words, she sniffles hard and cries, "I tried, I really did, to give him another chance. For us to be together. But I can't, not when he's still so hung up on you."

I am at a loss for words.

"I'm sorry, I didn't mean to cause you harm, Rose." My voice sounds as I feel, weak and deflated.

"Oh, it's not your fault." She wipes under her nose and tries a grin, but it lacks a solid foundation and wobbles a little. "Look at me, crying in the club. Am I a song cliché or what?" She laughs, and I join her.

"How about you forget about Grey, and drink?" I suggest, and her blue eyes light up.

"I'd love that!" She shrugs off her jean jacket, revealing a red blouse. She orders a line of shots for what I assume is also for me.

I feel the harshest gutting feeling ever of guilt. Like always, Grey has changed his mind in the flash of an eye and now wants me again, but he's hurting Rose in the process. I am not okay with it at all. I'm trying my *absolute* best to move on, and he isn't helping by doing things like this. It pisses me off, and I make a mental note to confront him and tell him to treat Rose better and give her what she deserves the next time I see him.

Which, I hope, isn't soon…because my guy is coming toward me right now.

"Are you done having girly time yet?" Noah groans into my neck, arms coiled around my waist. His lips brush against my skin, and it tingles. I thank the heavens for *some* kind of response. I take it in stride and break into a grin. But then I glance at Rose, who is smiling at me almost forcibly, like she's dying on the inside, seeing me happy with another guy while the one she wants, *wants* me. I feel horrible for flashing him in front of her.

"No, I'm not." I pull him away from me. "Noah, you remember Rose, right?"

He nods, green eyes pinched contemplatively. "From that hella awkward dinner?"

She laughs, cheeks flushed pink. "Unfortunately, yes. It's nice to see you again." She outstretches her hand, and they shake hands.

"Eight shots," the bartender with multiple face piercings and a bored look announces, pushing the drinks to us.

"I'll chip in." I begin to dig into my purse, but Rose puts a hand on my wrist and hands the man money. He walks away before I can even grab my wallet.

"There's no need," she says, pushing four of the drinks to me.

"But I could have helped with that," I say and quickly add, "I'll get the next one, whenever that shall be."

"Whenever that shall be, it is." She raises a glass and winks at me.

I laugh and try to hand Noah one of the glasses,

but he says he isn't down for drinking tonight. "But it's a party. Come on, Wells," I tease him, brushing my shoulder against his.

"I'm the designated driver, remember?" he reminds me.

"Fine." I turn to Rose and raise the glasses. "Here's to a night of fun and celebration!"

"Celebration!" we holler before we knock back the shots of tequila.

I make up my face as the sting buzzes behind my tongue. She and I divide the rest of the drinks between us, then slide onto the dance floor, finding our group that consists of Mason, Mateo, Julia, Jaimie, and Charlotte. They're all eating pieces of Julia and dancing around. I cut a piece for myself, and I have to hand it to Jaimie: the cake is pretty good.

I take Rose's hands and dance around, Noah holding onto me from the back. My head feels woozy, and the floors look like part of those dancing games, and I go for the high score. She seems to notice the game too, because her feet are going everywhere, and she bumps into me. Noah laughs and wraps his arms around the both of us. I wiggle my butt against him and giggle as his eyes grow dark. Rose laughs, her hand thrown against her lips as we stumble trying to hop around. I think I take my jacket off because I feel so hot in the midst of a hundred people all moving around.

I am so gone, but I instantly know something is wrong when Rose stops dancing and stares over my shoulder like she sees a ghost.

"What is it?" I feel like I know before I even turn

around.

Dean, Grey, and a few other intimidatingly large guys are entering the club.

What the hell is he doing here...and after what he did to Rose?

My blood feels like it's been set on fire, and I grind my teeth together.

"I'll be right back." I take a step toward them, but Noah takes my hand.

"Where are you going?" He doesn't see them, and I don't want him to. I have to confront Grey, and I won't be able to with him lingering over me, with the chance of them breaking into a fight because of testosterone and whatnot.

"I'm going to the bathroom," I lie.

"Hurry back," he says, and I return his nod.

"Don't," Rose warns, taking my other hand.

"I'll be fine," I say with a drunken smile, pulling my hands into my chest. "I'm the *Grey Whisperer*." I give her what I hope is a discreet wink, then push away from the group. I weave through the crowd, eyes zoned in on Grey, who is looking around. I bet he doesn't even know he's crashing the party. Well, I'm going to inform him right now.

As if sensing me before I can even get to him, his eyes flicker to mine. "Liv?" he questions.

"Looks like Blue's had too much to drink," Dean jests with an annoying smirk, standing in my way of the giant with no freaking emotions.

"Outta my way," I slur and push past him.

He laughs and steps back, cocking his head at me with an undecipherable expression. *Weirdo.*

"Liv, what are you doing?" he asks me, like I'm

not allowed to be near him. I don't want to be near this talking tree that is a big meanie; I just want to tell him off for hurting my friend with good-smelling hair and oceans for eyes.

"I...am telling you off, *mister*," I snarl. He doesn't look impressed, so I snarl a little more and add a little more toughness by jabbing a finger at his chest. "You keep fucking with me. Telling me you hate me one second...then you want me. Then...you don't like me." I press my palms against his hard chest, nearly melt and moan, then push away, finding my point for this, bringing myself back into his warm chest and, again, almost moan because he is sooooo soft. Jesus! "Then you want me...then no! 'Go 'way! No, Liv, you're horrible! You blah, blah, blah'—pick a fucking emotion, dude! You're hurting my *heart*..." I mumble, tears bundling in my eyes, then sniffle and add with a little finger wave, "And Rose's, too. And she is a precious flower who deserves...*much* betterrrr." I drag out the word and nod affirmatively, placing my hands on my hips.

He stares at me like I've grown another head that's named Frank...then shakes his head and says, "What the fuck are you on?"

"The ground, duh." I laugh then burst out crying. "Too much tequie," I mumble, falling into his chest.

"You mean tequila?" he questions with a hint of a smile in his voice.

I smile against his chest and wrap my arms around his waist, patting his butt. "Mmmm, tequie, tequie." I shake my hips a little, poking his amazing butt cheeks with a little giggle and hiccup.

"Come on, Liv. Let's get you home," he says and begins to pick me off his chest, but I cry out on the top of my lungs and shake my head.

"Stay on tequie, with mmm butts." I giggle and begin to fall into a puddle on the ground. "Tequie!" I scream, and he hoists me up onto my feet, and I sigh in relief. "Tequie…"

"What the fuck is going on here?" Noah barks from behind me.

I turn around and wrap my arms around Grey's neck, smiling lazily. "'Sup, BF."

"Let go of her." He ignores me and takes a step forward.

"She's too drunk. I'm taking her home," Grey explains through gritted teeth.

"You don't get to do that," Noah barks and holds out his hands. "Hand her over."

"I am not something to *hand over*." I roll my eyes at the ridiculous men.

"Fuck that, and fuck you," Grey hisses, completely ignoring what I just said.

Noah takes a step forward, and I widen my eyes. He wouldn't do anything to hurt him, would he…? Is it bad I don't know which guy I'm talking about?

"Do something," I hiss at Dean.

He steps up between the two with a smirk. "Calm your tits, everyone. There will be no fighting…" he promises, and I sigh in relief. "Until I've bet my money on Grey. Get at him, G!"

"Seriously?"

In the flash of an eye, Grey's fist swings into the air, and I prepare for all hell to break loose.

Chapter Eight

Grey

I let my fist fall before it can connect with his face. I have to think about this. If I beat up this Ken motherfucker, Liv will freak out and push me away. She did exactly that the time I tried to help at that glamorous mansion party, after she fell in that pool and I gave Golden Boy what he had coming. And there is no way in hell I trust her to be trashed around this fucker *and* Dean. I don't like the way Dean is eyeing her right now, like he has something wicked up his sleeve. I know what's usually up that tatted sleeve of his—absolute terror.

"I don't want any problems," I semi-lie through clenched teeth. "I just want to get her home. That's it. Not that I have to answer to you."

"You do, actually, because we're *together*," he hisses, then smiles like the snake he is. "If anyone's taking her home, it's me."

He takes a step forward, grubby hands outstretched for my girl...yeah, you know what? I

67

said what I fucking meant. After all this time apart and all the heartbreak and everything in between, she is mine, and she will always *be* mine. He or any other collared guy can try to get in the way of us, but he won't succeed. I mean, look how she's latching onto me like she's too afraid she'll die if she lets go. I know for sure that if she does, I might be the one who goes down.

"Listen, you irrelevant swine, you are just a plaything for the moment. I, on the other hand, know how to take care of this and her, so get your little fucking hands away from her and go back to partying with your *Barbie*, Ken."

"There is no way in hell I am letting you take her *anywhere*," he hisses.

"Noah," Liv whines, and I freeze as she turns to face him.

Is she about to reject me again?

"I want my bed, and he won't try anything. If he does, I'll shoot him in the foot, m'kay?" She beams up at him, and I let go of a breath I didn't know I was holding back.

"I'll take you home," he says softly, taking her hands.

I have to look away and clutch my own before I let my desire win over and knock the fucker out.

"You gotta take care of the others," she explains, gesturing to the crowd, referring to her group of friends.

"Make him do it," Golden Boy scoffs, shooting a "deadly" glare at me.

"Fuck no, I don't care about the others," I scoff.

"I am offended!" I hear Jaimie scream

somewhere in the crowd on the dance floor.

How the hell did she even hear me? It's so fucking loud in here!

"Noahhhhhh." Liv drags out his name while slowly falling to the floor.

Before she can hit the floor, I snag her back into my chest and flash her "BF" a grin.

"See you around, fucker." I wink at him and nearly laugh at his fists. As if he could do any damage. I could have his ass cold on the floor in point-two seconds. Make it point-one if he tries to test me even further or even attempts to touch her. There is no doubt in my mind she doesn't actually like this little boy. But if he keeps entertaining me like this, I don't mind him being around...for the time being, of course.

I hastily bypass Dean and the gang members, shooting down any fucker who looks at her in any perverted way. And I am almost out of the club when my forearm is clutched. I stop, my blood running cold, because I instantly know who it is without having to turn around.

"This doesn't look like you're *over* her...now does it?" Dean drawls from behind me in a tone that makes me shiver. I know what he is capable of, and I don't ever want to hurt the girl mewling like a little kitten in my arms. I want to protect her and show her that I still do really care for her...but what if she gets hurt in my arms more than anywhere else, more than with *Noah?*

But then it hits me...I'm selfish, and I won't let him or anyone else dictate my feelings for her.

"Guess it doesn't," I answer him, side-eyeing

him.

He lifts an eyebrow, clearly surprised by my defiance. When he says nothing in return, but stares into my eyes coolly, I know there will be repercussions tomorrow. But for right now, I have to get her home and out of harm's way. I don't know what kind of prowling fuckers would try and take advantage of her, this intoxicated. Getting her to safety is more important than Dean's wrath.

I exit the club and slide my jacket around her, noticing she's shivering like a Chihuahua. She gives a muffled thank you while rubbing her eyes. I save her from walking into a pole, barely bite back a laugh, and guide her to my parked car a block away. When we get to it, I open the door and buckle her in, then jog to my side and slide inside. I pull the car out of its parking space and head toward her ridiculous mansion.

"Where—going?" she mumbles, her face snuggled in my jacket.

"I am taking you home, like I said I would," I explain, and she scrunches up her face.

"No home." She shakes her head.

"Yes, home." I nod.

"No," she says more firmly, then sighs and peeks her giant blue eyes over the black leather. "Mother will be upset. It's late, I'm seeing leprechauns *everywhere,* and she doesn't like you."

"Leprechauns?" I laugh.

"G-uh-reyyyyy," she whines.

"She won't even notice you're drunk. Just rush up the stairs. Say you're not feeling well, and she can fuck off. I'll drop you off a block away or

70

something."

She doesn't even try to think about my plan. Just shakes her head frantically like she can get rid of it that way, face unrecognizably twisted up. "Too much tequila, she'll sniff it. Like, like a bloodhound. Great nose."

I laugh loudly, gripping the wheel. "Of course she'd have a hellhound nose."

"I said *bloodhound*."

"Does it matter?" I glance at her, and she actually stops to think, then shakes her head with a cheeky shrug.

"Not really. A big ol' mean dog either way," she says, and I laugh even louder.

"You're really funny when you're drunk," I tell her, and she grins.

But then she turns the words in her head and pouts so adorably, I am tempted to reach over and pinch her cheeks. "Wait, what about when I'm sober?"

I shrug and hold back half a smile. "Eh."

"Rude!" She reaches over the center console and jabs her finger at my cheek.

"Settle down, girlie." I swat her small hand away from my face and push her away from me without looking away from the road. I know how That Night still affects her, and I want to get her to safety. Not in another accident that will turn around and scar *me*.

After a few minutes, she pipes up, "I'm hungry."

"What do you want to eat?" I ask, playing with my bottom lip.

She doesn't respond.

I glance at her and see she's staring at me. "What?" I laugh, a little uneasy. She can be pretty unpredictable when she's drunk. Last time, she tried to eat me. And now she's admitting she's hungry again…you do the math. She might be thinking about lunging at me and eating my face like a petite zombie.

"Nothing," she finally says, then giggles and "whispers" under her breath, "Totally lying."

I roll my eyes and smile at her childish-ness. "What do you want to eat?"

"You," she says, and I look at her, kind of thrown off guard. But then she giggles again, tries to—but fails—to hide it, and declares, "I would like some of the Fro'sYo."

"One…froy'syo? Coming up," I say, and she claps her hands. I can't even hold back laughter on that one.

We arrive a few minutes later, and I lead her into the FroYo place. There isn't that long of a line, since it is around one in the morning. And whoever is in the small place are partiers who are feeling the same weird craving for sweet yogurt, sorry, *FroYo*. What a stupid fucking term. Why not just say frozen yogurt? And why even eat the crap in the first place? Isn't it the same shit as ice cream? Hipster people, I swear.

I step off to the side when my phone begins to ring. "Order what you want," I tell Liv, and she nods so frantically, I think her head is going to snap off like a bobble-head figure. I smile at how cute she is but snap back into reality. "What do you want?" I snap into the phone.

"I could do without the sass, thank you," Jaimie says.

I roll my eyes and pinch my nose bridge. "Again, what do you want?"

"I *want* to know that my friend is safe and sound," she replies.

I scoff and slap my hand to my side. "As if I'd hurt her."

She scoffs for the longest time. "Do you want to go down the ever-growing list of times you hurt her?"

I sigh and run my tongue between my lips. "No, I would not. What's up?"

"I'm gonna need you to bring her to your house. I would say bring her to Noah's, but his mother's good friends with Liv's and would rat her out. And her mother's home and she will put her under lock and key if she sees her daughter trashed and coming home with the likes of *you*," she says, straightforward.

"Um, ouch?" I refer to the last part.

"Oh, don't be a puss. You know it's true."

"I guess…" I trail and glance over my shoulder to make sure Liv is all right. I gasp, finding her taking *shots* of sprinkles in tiny paper cups. "Liv!" She stops halfway through a cup and looks at me like a puppy caught eating from a cookie jar. "Stop taking *sprinkle shots* and order your damn yogurt!"

She is silent, un-moving…then bursts into tears. Actual tears!

"Jesus Christ…" I mumble, rubbing my face.

"Is that a baby crying?" Jaimie questions, confused.

"Yeah, I'll get her to my place and make sure she's fine," I promise, then hang up before she can go off into a rant. She doesn't particularly like me at the moment, but it's very understandable. I've been a major dick, well, more than usual.

"Miss, you can't take shots of the sprinkles," a young girl behind the counter chastises, unsure if Liv's a mad woman.

I take the half-eaten sprinkle cup from Liv's hands, place it on the counter, and point a finger at her and sternly say, "No more sprinkle shots." I nod to the girl with the poofy ponytail and say, "Order what you want."

"Anything?" she squeals, biting her lip.

I think I just died and went to heaven.

I can't even hold back a little of my grin at my girl as I nod. "Anything," I confirm.

"Yay!" She starts jumping up and down. She rushes over to the glass case of yogurt and toppings and begins pointing out what she wants. "I want strawberry flavor, gummy bears, chocolate chips, like, *lots* of chocolate chips, and sprinkles, like, *looooots* of sprinkles." She grabs my hand and pulls me over, jabbing the glass. "Tell her I want sprinkles, Grey, *tell her!*"

"Sprinkles, lots of sprinkles," I emphasize, widening my eyes.

"Got it," the girl says, obviously creeped out by this beautiful nineteen-year-old girl acting like she's *nine*.

Liv bounces around, mumbling something about a *sprinkle-fort in her stomach* as her FroYo is made.

I laugh so hard I feel my muscles burn, but I

couldn't give less of a shit.

The girl makes her order, and I pay for it. We leave, and I make sure to buckle her in before slipping into the car. She eats the entire thing on the way to my house. When I pull up to the house and park in my spot, I look over and burst out in laughter, I almost cry. Her entire mouth is nearly covered in pink-colored yogurt and sprinkles.

"Aw, babe, you made a bit of a mess," I coo mockingly, reaching over and swiping some onto my finger.

She stares at me with dark eyes, her tongue swiping over her lips, catching most of the yogurt.

"You look better than the Fro'sYo," she whispers.

"What?" I let my lips slide into a smirk, because I know she is so fucking gone and will not remember any of this tomorrow.

She stares at me with a hungry gaze for a few more seconds, then bursts into a nervous kind of fake laughter. "Totes kidding..." She laughs for a long time, and I just smirk at her, amazed at how her drunk-self is coming on to me. Which means this is what she really wants, me, because her sober-self would never say or do any of this with me. Not without overthinking until her brain fries.

"Sure you are." I wink at her, and she completely gushes, hand over heart and teeth clipping onto her mouth. I laugh a little, then swing out of the car and round it. I open her door and help her out, stabilizing her as she wobbles. But when she continues to stumble and nearly bust her ass, I decide to just lift her up and walk her into the house for the rest of the way.

"Yay, I'm on a ride! Wheeee!" she cries out as I go up the stairs.

"Quiet, *princesa*," I hush her, but I don't give a fuck if she wakes anyone. She can be as loud as she wants; she deserves it the way I've been such an asshole to her. I struggle opening the door with her bouncing like an over-excited child in my arms. I finally get it open and kick it closed. I walk into my room and throw her onto the bed.

She screams and descends into a huge fit of giggles. I smile as I kick off my boots and take off my shirt.

"I'll get you some water," I tell her, and she nods, squirming out of her jeans.

I bite my lip and watch as they fly off, leaving her in a pair of white panties and showing off her short but silky legs.

"Hot," is all she says, looking like a fucking sex-goddess with her hair curly and disheveled, my jacket nearly swallowing her, and eyes dark, lips swollen from the numerous times she's bitten them.

Don't fuck her, don't fuck her—she is intoxicated. Do. Not. Fuck. Her.

"Oh, fuck me," I mutter, feeling the front of my pants get tighter each second she smiles at me with an innocent look, but damn if she knows what she is doing. *Fucking minx...*

I turn around and leave before I can do anything, and I mean *anything* to please this fucker down south. As I grab the bottled water, I close my eyes and take a deep breath with my forehead against the cold surface. "She's drunk, she's drunk, she is fucking drunk," I chant over and over, until I feel myself cool down. I wet a paper towel to clean her face. I push off the fridge and walk back into the room.

I stop at the door and grin. She is face planting on the bed, limbs bent at odd angles. She's passed out. I jump into action and try to take the jacket off of her so she'll sleep better, but she basically *growls* at me. I laugh and raise my hands defensively. I then wipe away the lingering yogurt and sprinkles around her mouth until she's clean, then toss the mess in the garbage bin by the door. I grab the sheet and cover her body. I begin to sneak out so she can have the whole bed to herself, but she grabs my wrist and yanks me to the bed, whispering in my face, still very much asleep, "Stay…" then lets out a little burp, a pause, then a very faint whisper, "Too much tequie…"

"Oh, Liv." I laugh but slide into bed next to her after taking off my jeans. I stay on the far side of the bed, but she growls again, crawls over to me, and latches onto me like a newborn koala.

"Better," she sighs, then snuggles her face in my neck, tongue pressed against my skin, and hair completely covering my face.

"Liv," I groan with a little laugh. But even with hair getting caught in my mouth and getting hot in general, I fall asleep like a baby and have the best sleep I've had in a very long time.

Chapter Nine

Liv

The next morning, I wake to the brutal sounds of banging pans and loud music. I cover my ears, but the sound drills through my palm, having no chance to keep out the wretched sounds. My head feels like it's on a wooden stick and is being twirled around on top of a campfire. I make the mistake of opening my eyes, because the burning sunlight pours through the blinds and nearly makes *me* blind.

Oh jeez...how much did I drink last night?

I sit up on my elbows and feel my head tilt to the side. I close my eyes and try my best to block out the noise. But when I realize this won't be happening, I push the heavy comforter to the side and gasp at what my eyes take in. My jeans are missing, leaving me in my underwear and a leather jacket...that's it. But when I sit up against the headboard and raise my arms, assessing the light leather, I spot a familiar "G" on the left breast of it.

"Grey...?" I breathe, feeling my stomach twist

into impossible knots. I sweep my eyes over the room I'm in—I must be in Grey's house, in his bed. I'm wearing his freaking jacket. The jacket I got him, to be precise. I smile like a giddy fool as I realize he didn't just burn it after what happened. I wonder if he still has the gloves…"Not important." I shake away the silly thought and stand up. Big mistake. I trip on my jeans and fall on my face. "Ouch! Fuck, fuck—ow!" I think I broke something. Either my nose or my spirit, either one wouldn't be much of a surprise.

I expect Grey to run in here and help me up because I am a hungover ball of pain, but with that damn music blasting through the house, I doubt he even heard me fall.

I hobble out of the room and wince in the hallway. My head is throbbing so hard, I think my body is actually vibrating. I lean against the wall and rub my temples for a good two minutes. I run my tongue through my lips and feel a tug at the back of my throat; I'm deathly thirsty. And I feel as though if I don't get a drip of water soon, I will pass out. I push off the wall and take my time inching out of the hallway.

I stop in my tracks when I see Grey in the kitchen. His back is to me, but I admire him all the more. Unlike his front, his back is mostly saved from ink, but it still has some that are just jaw-dropping. And his muscles are ripped and a tad larger than the last I saw him shirtless. His jeans from last night are low on his hips, and boy, does his butt look amazing. I tilt my head and feel my mouth become drier with every square inch of his perfectly marred skin I take in.

Sensing my shameless stare, he looks over his shoulder. He looks surprised for a split second, but then he realizes I'm basically checking him out, and his pink lips slant in a knowing smirk. He reaches over to a stereo on the counter and turns the music down to the point of toleration.

"Morning, princess," he says, his voice deep like the Pacific.

His voice isn't the only thing in the room similar to the Pacific...I think naughtily.

Fire embeds itself in my cheeks and neck, and I consciously cross my arms. "Um, w-what happened last night?" I ask.

He looks almost offended, facing me while raising a thick brow. "You don't remember what went down last night?" His eyes grow dark, and I flush even hotter when they flicker down at my bare legs. I try to cross them, but there is no use. And it's not like he hasn't seen me naked before. But still...why is he looking at me like that? "Shame." He shrugs and licks his lips before turning back to the stove. "Looks like I'll be the only keeper of last night's *events*."

My jaw drops.

Does he mean...? But we didn't...I wouldn't *do* that with him. I wouldn't...I mean...my eyes wander to his butt. Now he's just showing off. I bite my lip but then feel my subconscious slap me back to reality.

There's a possibility you betrayed Noah by having sex with Grey—focus!

"What do you mean, Grey?" I ask, narrowing my

eyes.

He whistles, flipping a kind of burned pancake.

I storm over to him and push his shoulder, making him face me with a nauseating smirk, or is it because I feel like emptying my entire body because of my hangover…? The world may never know. But *I* do know I will get this stubborn man to tell me what happened last night.

"Tell me, Grey." I poke his chest repeatedly.

He just covers his heart and winces. "Ouch, I can't live on. You've wounded me terribly. Ah! I think I see the light!"

"Don't you dare go toward that light, Grey Wyler!" I command and lunge for him.

He easily scoops me up and places me on the counter, my legs wide open around him.

I am the Pacific; the Pacific is me.

"Fine, I'll stay in the darkness…" He pauses, and I nearly melt into a puddle of bones and mush when he tugs my bottom lip, eyes blacker than ever, peering into me senselessly. "As long as you come with me."

Tsunami alert! I repeat, tsunami alert!

"Wet!" I scream and gasp, clapping my hands over my mouth.

He raises an eyebrow, lips twitching. "What?"

I open and close my mouth constantly, trying to find words. "I am…I have to pee. That's it, gotta pee, pee, pee!" *Gosh, I sound like a freaking first grader.*

He makes a sound from his chest, like he's doing everything possible to hold back a laugh, but he's not quite succeeding. "Sure." He winks at me like

81

the ass he is, and I am basically on actual fire at this point from embarrassment. The minute he steps back, I jump down and run back into this bedroom.

"Jesus, Liv. Get it together," I mumble, sitting on the bed and rubbing my face. He and I were a couple before. I've seen him naked and vice versa. We have done…*it*. Why the hell am I acting like a church girl that's just seen a man naked for the first time? I need to stop acting like he is affecting me so much. I am not *with* him anymore; I am with Noah. Sweet, sweet Noah who doesn't deserve my sexual longing for another man. I need to suck up whatever… *feelings* I have toward Grey in *that* way and transfer them to Noah.

I am so busy coaching myself, I almost don't hear the vibrations.

I grab my phone out of my jeans pocket on the floor and answer.

"Hello?" I rub the side of my face.

"Livvy, are you okay? Where are you?"

"I'm with…" I am hesitant to relay to him that I'm with my ex. "I'm with a friend," I end up telling him, and I instantly hate myself for lying to him.

"Jesus Christ, I've been calling you all fucking night," he curses, and I'm taken aback. I've never heard him curse before, well, not at me, at least.

"Sorry," I say, my voice clipped.

"Shit," he curses again and takes a deep breath that sounds ruffled over the phone. "I didn't mean to snap at you like that."

"It's okay." I clutch the thin sheet beneath me, rubbing the fabric.

"No, it's not." He pauses again. "Are you okay?

Did anything happen last night?"

"No, no—I'm okay," I reassure him with a small smile.

"That's great, now where exactly are you so I can pick you u—"

"Do you want sugar and milk with your coffee, or just plain black?" Grey bursts through the door, his voice loud and very *distinct.*

I widen my eyes, and Noah pauses.

Crap!

"Wait, you're still with Grey?"

"Still?" He knew Grey practically kidnapped me. "What do you mean still?"

"I *mean,* I thought the asshole would have actually dropped you off at a friend's or something after he took you from the club," he says, and I mentally scratch my brain.

What is he talking about? I am so confused.

"What the hell happened last night where you would be okay with Grey *taking* me—oh, right!" Images of last night pop up in my head and scroll around like a slideshow. Of him strolling in the club, me screaming in his face, the crying. Him nearly punching Noah but taking me out and that strange look Dean gave me. I shiver thinking of it now. Then I am sucked into the memory of me practically wanting to jump his bones in the car, to him buying me yogurt, me doing shots of *sprinkles,* all the way to me again, wanting to fuck him—or him to fuck *me*—when he threw me on his bed.

Oh my gosh, I was a mess…what was I thinking doing sprinkle shots?

And, you know, the wanting to have sex with

him?

Yeah, that too...

I feel like I've been thrown in a volcano.

"Liv, hello? I said what is the address?" Noah barks into the phone.

I draw my attention back to him and open my mouth, but the phone is snatched from me before I can utter a word.

"That won't be necessary." Grey stares at me while he smiles like the little devil he is and hangs up.

"What was that for?" I stand up abruptly, feeling woozy. I push past the sudden dizzy spell and lunge for my phone, but he raises it high in the air. "Give me my phone back!"

"No, you'd be wasting your breath on him," he scoffs like he's all that.

"Too late, I already am by speaking to you," I sass.

"Touché." He smirks.

"Thanks." I smile, proud of myself.

"But you're still not getting it back." He taps my nose, and I groan. A loud buzzing fills the room, and we both stare up at my phone lighting up. He snaps his eyes to me with a cocky grin. "Someone must be excited to see me," he drawls, glancing downward.

I flush like I am laying on the sun and try to cover my eyes. I almost forgot I am practically naked.

"Give me my phone, please!" I plead.

He sighs and looks at the screen. "I'll bring you home. Just don't call him back or answer him if he

84

calls again."

"Why not?" I grab the phone and see it is Charlotte calling me.

I look up and am surprised to see he is frowning, hands dug in his jeans' pockets.

"Just don't...okay?" He rubs his lower lip, pinching it, and I find myself nodding.

"Fine..." A small silence lingers between us. But then I remember Charlotte is calling, and I clear my throat. "I'm gonna step outside."

I go out on the back patio where there is a small secluded beach and a swing. I sit on the swing and finally hit accept.

"Hell—"

"*Ella no está contestando su teléfono, me da mi martillo*—" (She isn't answering her phone, hand me my hammer—)

"No need for that, Char," I speak up quickly.

"Liv?" She sounds shocked but happy. And then anger settles in, and she rants, "What the hell is wrong with you, girl? Don't you know how to pick up your god damn phone? I've—*we've*—been calling and texting you all damn night and morning."

I wince and glance at my notifications: all texts from her and my friends. "I am so sorry. Tell the guys I am extremely sorry. I didn't mean to worry any of you. I just...I kinda just woke up a few minutes ago, actually."

She sighs like she's trying not to act on her desire and pick up her favorite weapon of choice. "Where are you?"

"Grey's," I tell her hesitantly, scared of her

reaction.

"Why are you at his house?" she screams, then laughs anxiously as she tries to get her breathing under control. "Sorry, please tell me how you ended up at your ex's house."

"I got too drunk last night, so Noah had him take me here. I couldn't go home because my mother would chew my soul alive, and his mother would definitely tell my mother. I guess the safest place was…here." I shrug.

"Wait, Noah *let* Grey take you to his home for the night?" she asks incredulously, obviously not believing a word I am saying. But I can't blame her. I'm confused too.

"Yes." I nod even though she cannot see me. At least I think Noah let him bring me here, though he did sound surprised to know I'm here…I don't know, I'm too hungover to figure it out.

"Well, fuck…" she trails, then asks, "Did you guys do anything, you know…?"

I gasp and look around nervously, as if Noah will pop up and skeptically watch me answer. "No! Of course not!"

"Mm-hmmm…" She pauses, then gasps. "But you wanted something to happen, didn't you?"

Again, I'm searching for the right words, but nothing comes out.

She gasps again and bursts into laughter. "Holy fuck! You *did* want something to happen!"

"Shut up!" I rub my hot cheeks. "I did not want anything to happen, because I'm with Noah."

"Right," she says, but I can just feel her annoying, knowing smirk thing she does when she knows she's right. Not that she is at this present time…oh, Lord, please help me.

At the moment I'm going to respond to her, I hear a loud crash behind me in the house.

What the heck was that?

"Grey?" I call out, slowly standing up.

"What's happening?" Char asks.

"I don't—" I start.

Another crash, but much bigger.

"Liv—"

I drop the phone and take off into the house. My heart is pumping, and I feel my stomach tighten at the possibility that he's having an emotional breakdown for some reason. It happens a lot when a person with his disorder stay off their medication. But since he's been off of them for a long time, even before I knew him, I thought he was able to deal with them without throwing furniture around. Guess not…

"Grey!" I burst into the room.

He is a complete wreck, and so is the room. One of the dressers is thrown on the floor, splinters and chunks of wood littering the ground. His shirt and hair are ruffled like he's been yanking at both religiously. I gasp at a hole in one of the light blue walls and blood on one of his balled-up fists. And his face, oh God, his face…flushed beyond comprehension and tears streaming out of bloodshot eyes.

"Help me," he whimpers so low, I feel my heart split into a million different pieces.

Without knowing what has set him off or if there is a sharp splinter in my way, I run over to him and wrap my arms around him, nodding with tears in my own eyes.

"I'm here." I kiss his chest and nod. "I'm here."

Chapter Ten

His grandfather died of terminal lung cancer last night. His funeral is in a few days, and he is leaving to go to his family's birthplace, Venezuela. Tonight. All alone. When I heard that, I felt my insides grow weary. I hate the idea of him attending his grandfather's funeral all by himself.

Apparently, they had a deep connection, and when he found out…he lost his mind. He explained that it felt like a part of him was forcibly ripped out of him. With the way that he was crying a storm into the side of my neck and held onto me so tight, so securely like I would melt away if he dared let me go…I feel like I know the feeling.

The feeling of having something you care for so deeply be snagged right out of your caring hands. I felt it eight months ago. So I know somewhat of what he felt, but not enough where I could tell him that I "understand" or "it's going to be okay." Whoever tells him that isn't in his boots, walking around in his skin.

We stayed that way for a long time: my arms

caged around his large, lean body and his face buried in the crook of my neck. The only other time I witnessed him freak out that way was when his mother popped up in his apartment. I saw pure, raw anger, confusion, fear, and panic swell in his eyes. And at that moment, I felt it. The unsettling, black hole-sized space in the back of my heart open and form around the idea of protecting this poor, confusing tatted boy with eyes of darkness, yet having possessed so much light he didn't even know about.

And when I saw those emotions brew behind his eyes again, I felt every single boundary I had put up after he walked out on me eight months ago shatter, and I knew. I knew I wouldn't ever be able to hold back from doing anything to stop the tears from rolling down his cheeks or hugging him or just about anything it took to help the weeping boy that needed a little shedding of light in that dark vast place hidden just behind his heart. He had to see it, no matter what. Even if I got hurt in the process...my well-being has been on the back burner since the first time I saw him, I think.

The problem is, what about Noah? I'm not saying that I will do anything with Grey. The door on us is closed, locked, and the key has been thrown away. Random, meaningless sex or not. I don't want to hurt Noah. Feeling so deeply for Grey, though, it isn't so much in the sexual department as it is in the department where I feel so irrevocably attached to him in ways that could never be truly cut, is basically the same as betraying him. I am not caring for him in the same way as I should. I'm not drowning in searing waves of electricity just from one single touch. And I should be with him, but I just can't.

Is there something wrong with me? Am I just not trying hard enough?

A million and one questions run through my brain, worsening the headache from my hangover I'm still suffering through. I wrap an arm around my grumbling stomach. I don't know if I'm hungry or extremely nauseous.

Nonetheless, I step through the front door of the beach house, trying to be as quiet as possible. I am trying not to wake anyone. It's still morning, and the others, excluding Charlotte, may still be asleep. Plus, I'm afraid if I make any kind of loud noise, my brain will detonate.

Take that for your pristine porcelain walls, Mother, my subconscious spits bitterly.

My plan goes to crap when I hear flip-flops smacking on and off the marble staircase. And boy, are there a bunch of them…

Prepare yourself, prepare yourself! I chant over and over, readying myself for the pounding questions and wailing cries of relief that I'm okay, then the roaring anger I didn't return or notice anyone's calls or texts.

A lifetime of preparing wouldn't help me.

First, it was Louise, "*¿Dónde estaba en el nombre del Señor, niña? ¡Estaba intentando contactarte toda la noche!*" (Where in the name of the Lord were you, little girl? I was trying to reach you all night!)

Next was Charlotte, "*Debería aplastar el cráneo*

91

de ese idiota. ¡El martillo, por favor!" (I should really smash that idiot's skull in. The hammer, please!)

Then Mason, "Dude, where the hell did you go last night? You had me so freaking worried!" He wrapped me in a tight hug, and I hugged him back even tighter.

Mateo joins in the hug and says in a muffled voice, "Don't do that again, okay? There is something called taking your fucking phone off silent, you know?"

"Babe," Mason warns.

"Sorry," he mumbles, then adds, "Really, I'll kill Grey when I see him."

I want to tell him to lay off considering the news he got this morning, but Julia's cut in before I could get a word out.

"Thanks for ruining my party." She sounds super pissed, and I instantly feel horrible. Everyone is worrying over me when yesterday was her day, not mine.

"I feel like shit," I say, then flush and glance at Louise's shocked expression. "*Disculpa mi lenguaje.*" (Sorry, excuse my language.) I then look back to Julia and take her hands once the guys have released me. "I will make it up to you."

"How about sending us to an exotic country, like you did when Grey totally fucked up *my* party?" Jaimie suggests, sounding extra pissed too.

Jeez, he and I are always ruining someone's party...I feel like utter crap now. What is wrong with us?

I look at Julia. I wouldn't mind. "Well?"

"A vacation to another country wouldn't change the fact that you messed with my groove last night," she snaps, and I wince.

Jaimie whines.

Julia rolls her eyes and resigns, "But I guess a trip to Italy wouldn't be so bad…"

"Yay!" Jaimie jumps onto her girlfriend's side, arms encasing her small waist. "Make it Rome and you'll get something special tonight. And I'll give you a hint: it starts with a V."

Everyone collectively groans, disgusted. And I join in too, because, um, gross. But when do they ever hold back on what goes down in their bedroom? They're a very shameless couple…but you can't *not* love them.

"Don't be nasty," Charlotte mewls, face scrunched up.

"Oh, get your heads out of the gutter, people," Jaimie scoffs, then a mischievous grin forms. "I just meant: *very* amazing head from moi." She pokes her cheeks and bats her eyelashes, and everyone begins to disperse, each muttering how they're "nasty" and shouldn't reveal too much information. "What? I don't believe for a second that you all haven't gotten banged by another human being," she argues as she drags Julia along with her to catch up with them as they huddle into the living room.

I stand here for a moment, wondering how I became friends with such weirdos.

"Cool weirdos," I correct myself.

I struggle up the stairs with the massive headache growing larger and larger with every nerve-wracking beat.

When I finally make it to my bedroom, I trudge directly to my ensuite. I twist on the bathtub faucet. A shower would not be enough to soothe my aching muscles and the nefarious scream ringing in my head. I strip away my clothes and add bath bombs and soap into the quickly rising tub. The end product is a soft orange and dark pink color that looks really pretty.

I sink into the water and press the button on the expensive tub that starts up the jets. I thought my mother was splurging way too much by buying this tub, but man, am I extremely grateful for her inability to make smart shopping decisions.

About twenty minutes into the bath, I nearly doze off, feeling relaxed and the headache slowly disintegrating, when I hear a knock at the door.

"It's me," Noah says before I can even open my mouth.

"Oh, come in." I sink lower into the thick bubbles to cover myself.

The door pushes open, and he steps in, closing it after him.

He turns and our eyes lock. But then his eyes shift to the bubbles, one of my legs peeking through my makeshift bubble-shield, and his pinks turn the color of the soap used in the bath. I believe I am the same color as I look away and self-consciously arrange the bubbles a bit in case something else wants to make itself known.

"I'm sorry, I can come back later?" he suggests, smoothing his fingers through his hair.

"No, it's all right—you can stay," I assure him with a smile.

He just nods, face glued to the ground.

An uncomfortable silence fills the room.

"So, you came here for something?" I say, trying to fill in the silence.

He turns to me, looks shocked for a second like he forgot I am completely naked, save for my terrible wall of protection made of bubbles, then clears his throat and tries on a crooked smile. "Yeah, I did." He looks hesitant for a moment, but then he finds his natural confidence and walks over to the tub. He grabs the wooden chair that holds my clothes, places them on a rack, and swivels the chair in front of me and sits, facing the back of the chair.

I raise my brows expectantly, and he blushes even more, if possible.

"Sorry I'm being a spazz," he says. "Not very often I am in the presence of a pretty naked girl."

"I doubt that," I mumble, looking into the bubbles. But looking in his eyes when I bring my attention back to him lets me know instantly that I am wrong.

"I'm serious, buttercup," he relays. "Despite my past, none of them compare to you. You're like this kind of wildflower, exquisite and rare."

I gulp at his sweet words and avert my eyes from his, unable to look into those green eyes. "Thank you…" I raise my hand to my lips and nervously play with my lower one. But then I realize I've stolen Grey's tick and let my hand drop. I feel hotter than ever at the image of him and give my full attention to Noah, who has been rubbing his neck nervously.

"No problem," he mumbles.

"Yeah…" I grumble.

"Hey," he says, and I look up.

"Yeah?"

He pauses.

"How come you only got home twenty minutes ago? I called you way before that…" he questions, and I gulp.

"Oh, yeah…I, uh…I had to help comfort Grey," I say, though it sounds more like a question.

"Oh?" He frowns.

"Not like that," I say, then sigh, having to reveal something that's left him a complete wreck and is a personal thing. "It's just…he got this call that his grandfather passed, and they were really close. I couldn't just leave without knowing he was okay, especially after his hospitality to me last night."

"Oh…makes sense." He nods to himself, then quickly adds, "But sorry about his loss. That sucks."

"Yeah, it does." I bite my lower lip and feel another silent pause coming. "I'm sorry, you were saying something earlier…?"

"Oh, right." His eyes light up. "I just wanted to make sure you're okay."

"It's not like Grey would hurt me," I immediately defend him, and he raises his brows. I sink lower into the tub and shrug, my voice turning lower, "not physically, at least."

"Still…" I face his serious expression, cheeks sucked and lips taut. "Are you okay?"

"Despite the raging hangover?" I laugh lightly and roll my eyes. "I'm rainbows and leprechauns."

"Good." He smiles from ear to ear, but there's something he isn't saying. I can see it in his eyes.

"What is it?" I question him.

His dark eyebrows curve. "What do you—"

"What aren't you saying, Noah?" I cut him off, kind of impatient. I have my fair share of partners withholding things on their mind and making me lose mine because of it. I won't go through it again. I just won't.

"It's just…" He sighs and closes his eyes. "Did anything happen between the two of you?"

"Seriously?" I feel my cheeks rise in critical temperature from both shock and anger. I wish my emotions weren't so easy to decipher based on my cheeks.

"I'm sorry, I'm sorry," he groans and slaps his hands over his face and leans down, then pops back up, lips between teeth. "It's just, I know the *epic* past you two have and—and I was just worried you or he would…Fuck, I'm the worst, aren't I? It sounds like I have no fucking faith in you, but I do, trust me! It's him I don't trust—" he rants.

"We didn't do anything," I tell him, but he doesn't even hear me over his blinding fear of me betraying him, which has been my own lately.

"I should have taken you and rented a room at the motel or something. How could I have let you leave with that guy? I could have watched over you at the club, but Dean and the gang fucking walked in and I knew he would just try to start something and—"

I clutch the tub's edge and lean up to kiss him, tasting his words on my tongue.

It lasts for a few sweet seconds, but then my skin bubbles with goose bumps and I feel ultra-uncomfortable. So I sink back into the tub and let the bubbles almost swallow me with coverage.

He has some on his chin, and I giggle at the dazed look on his face. "Whoa," is all he says, and I laugh some more.

"Does that satisfy your worry?" I ask teasingly.

"It satisfies something, all right," he says with a little laugh. I can't stop myself from joining him.

"Nasty." I stick my tongue out at him.

"You're nasty," he coos, lightly pinching my tongue.

"Ouch!" I laugh and pull back. He and I laugh so hard the sound bounces off the tiled walls. I like this, the easiness that ignites between us when we're just joking around. I swear it becomes so much harder when we kiss or do anything romantic, but that isn't detrimental to being in a relationship.

Our laughter is cut short when my phone begins to ring.

"I got it," he says, walking over to my clothes.

"Thank you," I mouth to him as he digs my phone out of my jeans' pocket.

"No problem," he mouths back as he hands me the phone.

I smile as I answer the phone and press it to my ear. "Hello?"

"Hello, is this Olivia Westerfield?" a woman answers.

"Yes…" I say unsurely. I should have looked at the caller I.D. Whoever this lady is, she sounds stern, professional even.

She continues speaking, and as she does, I swear it isn't real. Tears fill my eyes as she goes on and on, answering my questions, completely oblivious to the fact that I'm having a major dance party on the inside.

"Yes…yes…thank you so much for the opportunity. Yes, thank you, again." I hang up the phone and stare long and hard at the bubbles.

Noah carefully takes my phone from my palm. "Okay…what was that about?"

"I've been accepted into the Psych Program…again," I say breathlessly, still shocked.

"What?" I look at him and feel relieved, and ecstatic tears leave my eyes. "Oh my God! That is amazing!" I can tell he wants to hug me, but he holds back, considering. "How are you not freaking out right now? You told me how big this opportunity was."

"Oh, I am freaking out." I laugh and shake my head in disbelief. "It's just taking me a while to process it." I can't believe this!

"Don't process, just react!" He grabs my hand.

"Okay, I'm so fucking freaking out!" I launch out of the tub and wrap my arms around him. I don't even care if I'm naked and freaking out even more because of the fact. I'm doing as he says, reacting! "I got into the program, Noah! Again! Fuck! The most elite and hardest program in the field, and I got in twice! Can you believe it? How am I special?"

"Don't even get me started," he says and hugs me tighter.

I squeal and melt back into the water. But I am too excited to stay still. I splash around excitedly, and he laughs and throws his arms up.

"I can't believe this!" I scream at the top of my lungs.

"Quiet the sex down, please! Thank you!" I hear one of those cool weirdos yell from downstairs.

I clasp a hand over my mouth and giggle, meeting Noah's wide, mortified eyes.

"Crap! What do we do? What do we do?" I repeat, and he grabs my hands and leans forward.

"We celebrate, of course!" he exclaims. "First, we go out clubbing tonight. We tear up the fucking town because you *did* it. Then, we stretch out the celebration all through the week, because, guess why…you fucking did it!" He grabs me out of the tub, and I laugh and squeal as he spins around, my naked body flushed and dripping against him.

"Getting dizzy!" I yell.

He stops, and I stumble a bit, my stomach clenching.

"Sorry." He is the definition of red as he sets me down and looks away.

I quickly grab a towel and laugh at his excitement. And although I should be shouting my accomplishment from every roof in town and think of myself—because I fucking did it!—I can't get rid of the image of Grey sitting on the plane, alone, trying to hide his tears as he heads to his grandfather's funeral…alone. The crystal-clear snapshot brings actual tears to my eyes and tugs on my heartstrings, the strings that are connected with his.

"Livvy? Did you not hear me?" Noah cries, shaking me by my shoulders a little.

"Hmmm?" I lift my eyes and meet Noah's wide

green ones that are absolutely shining.

"I said: are you ready for a week of victory?" he reiterates, but a little less enthusiastically, having realized I'm not totally in the moment.

I open my mouth to say, "Hell yes!"

But that image, that fucking image, nearly sends me to my knees in tears. Him, all alone, heart-broken, all alone…

"No." I shake my head.

"No?" He laughs uneasily.

I shrug his hands away and take a step back. "No," I say firmly.

Chapter Eleven

"What?" Noah says breathlessly. He looks so confused and a little scared.

"I said…I said no," I affirm, nodding my head as if to cement the insane idea myself. But I highly doubt nods are enough to swallow what I'm thinking of doing. I have to look away and storm into my bedroom; the look he was giving me was too intense, too emotional for me to register.

I pull out my luggage and begin packing frantically. I rush around my bedroom like I'm a chicken without a head. I don't know what I'm doing. Yes, I do. But it is too insane to linger on the thought for too long. Because when I say it in my head, I get this little jolt in the back of my mind and I jump a little like I've been nipped in the butt. I am going to Venezuela with Grey. Wow! There goes that electric shock.

"What are you doing?" Noah watches me cautiously from the ensuite.

"Packing," I tell him vaguely, folding a soft pink blouse.

"For what?" he asks, then stops, and I glance at him. But as it sinks in what I mean, I look away. "You're not seriously doing what I think you're doing, are you?"

When I shift a few jeans to the filling luggage, he smooths his hands over his hair.

"You are!"

"It's only going to be for a week—" I try to explain.

"You're going to another *country* with Grey, your fucking ex-boyfriend!" he screams, and I cringe.

"He needs me right now, okay?" I say calmly, trying to get him to lower his voice. I don't need everyone to find out, not like this, not right now. They'd just tell me how stupid and irrational I'm being. And I will probably listen, and I can't afford to do that. Not when Grey needs me more than he ever has before. The thought of him alone during such a trying time with no one who understands him the way I do kills me from the inside out.

"So?" he booms, and I sigh.

"Do you desperately need me right now?" I question.

"Does *he*?" he asks accusingly.

I look away and brush past him to the closet. "You don't understand."

"Of course I don't *understand*!" he shouts, and I whirl around, walking up to him.

"Will you please lower your freaking voice?" I hiss, consciously glancing at the door.

"No, I will not lower my voice!" he screams defiantly. "You are jetting off to another fucking country with your ex-boyfriend, whom you just spent the night with."

"I already told you I didn't sleep with him," I defend.

"Another country!" he exclaims.

"I get that, Noah!" I clutch my head; the headache is coming back tenfold.

"I don't think you do!" he counters, and I roll my eyes. "Would you be okay with me going to fucking Canada with one of the girls I used to fuck?"

I gasp and push him away from me. "You can do whatever the hell you want, but unlike you, my goal wouldn't be to *fuck* my past. I'm only going because he needs someone. He's going through a lot."

"But why does that mean you have to go to his rescue?"

Because I love him!

"Because I can't handle him suffering," I go with instead. My voice stretches thin and cracks at the end. I watch as the words crash on the ground. He looks more hurt than he would if I had gone with what I cried in my head.

"Why the hell not?" he exclaims. "He sure has put you through a hell of a lot of suffering himself. So why do you feel like you have to go out of your way to make sure he isn't in too much pain? Why don't you just let him be? He deserves it after all he has done."

"No one deserves to feel like there is no hope," I croak, and he tilts his head. "No one deserves to feel dead on the inside. No one deserves to be alone...not even Grey. Especially not him." I shut my eyes to trap my tears, but a long warm strip slips past my eyelash barrier.

"Why not him especially?" he whispers.

"Because…" I chew on my lower lip as I try to think of a way this won't hurt him. But then I open my eyes and take in his face: screwed eyebrows, flushed cheeks, and messy hair—and I can't. Because he knows why and he's already hurting, and I don't want to drive the final nail through him.

"Because you're still in love with him," he finishes for me.

I don't answer. But I assume he reads my trembling lips and shedding tears and formulates his own answer.

"For fuck's sake, Liv," he breathes, taking a step backward.

"It isn't like that," I argue, taking one forward.

"Oh, it isn't?" He sounds utterly pissed, and I cower back.

"No," I say weakly.

He rolls his eyes and threads his fingers through his hair. "I know how you two were before."

"That doesn't mean I'll do anything with him. I'm only going for support—" I reason.

"That's what I am afraid of!" he yells, cutting me off.

"What?" I shrug my shoulders defeatedly. "You're so afraid I'll fuck him the minute we're out of the country? Do you have no *faith* in me?" My voice raises as my patience for his wild rage grows paper thin.

"It's not you I don't have faith in, Olivia." He sucks air through his clenched lips and shakes his

105

head, arms thrown up, done with this heart-breaking conversation. "Have fun on your trip," he says and walks out.

I jump and close my eyes when the door slams behind him. The breeze flowing in from the cracked window makes me shiver, and I am very aware that I am practically naked. Flushed, I quickly get dressed in a pair of jeans, a loose white shirt, and a brown leather jacket and run a brush through my hair. I lean against the window after locking it and let out a long breath. I stand here before my knees become too weak, so I sit on the bed and let my face fall in my palms. "Fuck!" I curse as loud as I can and pick up a pillow and throw it at the door.

I never wanted to hurt Noah like this. He's a very sweet guy, and I just caused him pain, all because I care too much. I feel as though it will be the death of me. But I can't just flip a switch and stop caring altogether. And even if there was such a way out, I wouldn't dare go near it, because my caring for him and overall being compassionate is what makes me *me*. Without it I'd probably end up like Grey, and he needs me with my switch on, or he'd be drowning in the silent darkness.

A light knock sounds on the door before it opens.

"Can I come in?" Mason asks, his head sticking through a tiny crack.

Wordlessly, I nod.

I cup my ears, watching his footfalls until the bed sinks a little with his added weight.

It is silent with the exception of my loud thoughts whirling around my head.

"You know, you don't have to go because you

feel sorry for him," he says.

I guess Noah told him, probably everyone, what's happening when he stormed out.

"I do not feel *sorry* for him." Maybe I do a tiny bit, but that's because any normal human would feel bad for someone who lost a loved one. I roll my eyes, annoyed he's getting on my case too. I just need one person on my side who can see from my perspective. I stand up and begin packing again.

"Then why are you going, Liv?" He gets up and grabs my wrist, stopping my rapid packing. "Because you know you don't *have* to continue to deal with him."

"Out of everyone, I thought you would understand." I sigh.

"Why would I understand?" he exclaims. "I have been warning you from him from the very beginning, only to protect you. But you didn't listen, and look at what happened."

"I'm sorry I couldn't stop myself from falling in love despite your oh-so-fucking-vague warnings!" I snap. He furrows his brows, and I point an accusing finger at him. "You warned me but didn't specify why. But even if you told me he hurt your sister in a really fucked-up way or was in a gang or—or he simply was too fucked up to process, I'd probably still be in love with him. I'd still have fallen for him, because I love him! Okay? Can you understand that?"

He scoffs and looks away, a vile smile hanging on his mouth corners. "You sound insane."

"Maybe I am. Maybe that's why we were so perfect for each other!" I throw my arms out and bite back a sob. "Maybe that's why I still care for him so damn much. I couldn't care less about myself unless *he* is all right."

"That's sick," he croaks and tries desperately to catch my eyes. "Do you not see how fucking sick you are? How you're putting your neck on the line for your ex, your fucked-up ex, by the way, who has done so much wrong—"

"Like I haven't done any wrong!" I slice through his words, breathless. "Like I haven't betrayed him in the worst way possible? Mason, I have gotten used to how cruel he can be, only because that was and will always be a huge part of him. That darkness in him that helped hurt your sister is still in him…but I swear, it was gone when we were together. I helped him see some light in himself…but I screwed it up. And I have to find it for him again. It…I wouldn't be able to move on if I don't."

"You don't need to *fix* him—"

"Yes, I do!"

Mason stills and slowly shakes his head. "You are so obsessed with him that you don't even see it."

"I am not obsessed with him."

"Yes, you are!" he screams, and I close my eyes, holding back a flinch.

I just shake my head, biting my tongue. This has already turned to shit; I don't want to hurt him like I've hurt Noah. He's still my best friend. He means well, but he just doesn't understand I need this to find closure. I finish packing my luggage, and he sighs, his foot tapping impatiently.

"Why are you really doing this?" he asks.

"I told you, he needs my help," I answer with a tired sigh.

"Tell me the real reason, Liv," he demands.

"I just did!" I snap, growing enraged by this entire conversation. We've never spoken so heatedly before, and it's giving me heart palpitations.

"No, you didn't!"

"Believe what you want." I finish closing the luggage and drag it off the bed. "I've tried to make you all understand that moving on is like trying to swim to the top of the ocean, but you can't swim. And trust me, I know what that feels like *exactly*." He flinches. "And I will get rid of that feeling even if it means I black out a little. As long as I am able to breathe again, I will do anything. Do you understand that?"

***

I leave the house, unable to undergo anymore arguments with the people closest to me. I left everyone else voicemails. I know how much crap I'll get for not telling them directly, but I honestly can't deal with any more pain for the day. I've taken all I can, and I'm barely standing as it is.

I chew my bottom lip as I stare at the doorbell. I haven't thought this through, and the old me is screaming in fear of the unknown. I haven't planned what to do or say if he says I can't go with him. But I will never know if I don't push that damned button.

I've been standing here for about ten minutes, thinking and then overthinking some more.

Finally, my fingers feel sticky with sweat from standing in the sun for so long. And I push the doorbell. I inhale a deep breath and wiggle my fingers that are clasped around the luggage handle. I pray this goes well, because if it doesn't, I'm not sure what to do next...

The door swings open, and I am met with Grey: ruffled black hair, sharp black eyes, and an even darker frown. He is still the same as I left him, but more ragged, shirtless and rocking a pair of low-hanging Levi jeans.

Silence fills between us like a pestilent force.

"I hope crying babies don't freak you out," I breathe, my throat constricting with each word.

He eyes me, then shrugs. "Are you pregnant?" His voice is much thicker than the last I heard from him, which was around an hour ago, maybe a little more.

I feel my skin warm up like an inferno. "No, no—I mean, on the plane. There's usually a crying baby..." I stop, feeling his eyes seep through my flushed skin.

"Where are you traveling to?" he asks, tilting his head.

My lips twitch into a small, awkward smile. "Um, Venezuela?"

His brows furrow, and he crosses his arms, leaning against the door, but stays silent.

Bastard...

I clear my throat and drop the smile, unable to hold up its weight. "Listen, I know you will never forgive me for what I've done to you. And still, I am forever apologetic toward you. I want to move onto a fresh page between us. But that doesn't mean I have forgotten about the way we used to be and the feelings involved, which were pretty damn strong." I lick my lips nervously at his lack of input. But I've come too far to stop now.

"Anyway, uh…I know how hard your grandfather's passing is on you." His fist flexes…well, there is some life in him. I return my gaze to his intense eyes and finally get out, "And I wanted to go with you…you know, for the funeral." I take another deep breath and avert my eyes to the ground. "Because I don't want you to be lonely while going through this. I know how—how hard the death of a loved one can be."

Tears sting my eyes, and I try my best to suck them back up with a sniffle, but it comes out louder than expected.

He is still silent.

I raise my eyes to wipe away my tear, but he beats me to it.

I freeze in place and feel steamy goose bumps run along my spine as one of his marred knuckles wipes the warm tear away. Then he cups my cheek and gives me a small slant of his soft pink lips.

"Help me pack?" He nods inside the house, and I feel my shoulders lighten.

I beam up at him and nod quickly. "I'd love to."

He hitches his lips up one side, then does something that he hasn't in a very long time. He lets me in.

Chapter Twelve

Grey

I am firmly convinced that Liv is insane. It has to be the only reason that she has stuck around for me even after all I've done to her. I have hurt her too many times to count. I have seen her cry, watched her soul break, and put her through every bullshit my dumb ass could think to throw at her. And she caught them all like a fucking professional and came out unscathed. Though I know for a fact that she isn't completely the same as when I first saw her, freaked the fuck out by the opposite sex breathing the same air as her in a closed-off room.

From the moment I saw her, I was intrigued. She was so god damn beautiful, and it didn't just stop on the surface of her silky, flawless skin. It soaked deeper than that, to her very core, but I wouldn't find that out until I smashed through the obnoxious wall she'd built to keep any *distractions* out for her future or what-the-fuck-ever. And boy did I have to smash through a thick boundary. But when I finally broke through, I discovered how vulnerable and passionate and *frisky* she could be. Basically, everything her mother was desperately afraid of: her daughter being human and not a freaky robot who wore buns and dressed like she went to job interviews every single day.

When she fell for me, she fell hard. Like, face-planted through the earth until she hit hell, hard. And even though I fell even farther than that until I smashed through the center of nothing, I used how hard she fell for me and did as I pleased. I pissed her off, I broke her, I twisted her soul, and I became inhumane. But only because I knew she would come back to me and I loved to test how much she really loved me. My fucked-up self took pleasure in the fact that the one thing I loved more than life itself would always come crawling back to me.

I know, how fucked up can I be? Apparently, very. I always have been. But when I met Liv and grew to love her so fucking much, it just got so much worse to the point that I sent her to the hospital. To the point that she cried more than she smiled. To the point that she possibly ruined her relationships with her best friend and boy-toy. To the point that she would come with me to a whole other country, just because she wanted to make sure that *I* was okay.

So, like I said. She is either really fucking insane…or too damn good for her own good.

I think it's a mixture of both. My insanity, that I could easily have passed on to her. I should have warned her to stay away. I'm pretty sure I did. I warned her how dark I was and how I didn't want her to drown in the darkness of despair with me, but she is the most stubborn person I know. And she's always been good. I could never rub anything like that onto her. All I ever could rub off on her is being an asshole, which comes quite naturally to me.

I'm pondering all of this as we're walking up to the airport. As normal, it's busy with people coming in, going out, and waiting for their ride. There's a lot of honking, multiple foreign languages, and a strong smell of musty coffee and cheap perfume. This is why I hate airports. They're too crowded, loud, and smell.

We enter the huge building that is built entirely of glass and steel. Checking in our bags cost a little money, but I wordlessly pay for them before she can even say anything. She has spent way too much money on me in the past, for example the five hundred dollars she paid bailing me out of jail. The one hundred and change I just spent is definitely not enough, but I'll find a way to pay her back in full. I don't like having debts hanging over my head. Although I don't think she desperately needs the money back or even wants it, I will give it back. It's a good thing my abuela paid for our tickets.

"You didn't have to do that, you know," she says softly, like she's afraid I'll snap at her.

I sigh, hating she automatically thinks that will be my reaction.

"Yes, I did," I whisper back to mock her, and she glares up at me. I just smile down at her, and her own lips pull into a little something. *I'll take it.* "Are you hungry?" I ask.

She nods. "I'm starved. I haven't eaten all day."

"Seriously?" I try my best to sound cool, but I can't help the little pique in my voice. I meant to give her breakfast when she woke up this morning, but everything turned to shit, and I just threw it away. I wasn't able to stomach anything. The realization of why we're here in this pretentious glass building hits me in waves, and I take quick breaths to keep from flipping out in public and becoming one of those stupid viral video stars on Facebook.

"Yeah, and I'm not sure if the plane will serve quality meals," she says, looking around for a place to eat.

"Too bad we didn't just take your private jet," I joke when she grabs my hand and pulls me to a café.

"Yeah, it is too bad." She looks over her shoulder with the cutest little smile.

I widen my eyes in surprise and peer down at her. She hides behind her hands to cover a giggle. "I was kidding, but you actually have a private jet?"

She shakes her head and stands on her tippy toes to look over the guy who's in front of her shoulder. "Not me, my parents. They use it for business trips, but mostly my mother." Her voice is clipped toward the end, and I shift on my feet. Her relationship with her mother is completely destroyed, and I am the sole reason behind it. I kinda can't help but feel bad, but the witch was a witch before I came into the picture. She would have likely ruined it whether I was in the picture or not, so…

We don't talk for the rest of the time she orders

food: a bacon, egg, and cheese, and a large black coffee.

"No sugar or milk, just black?" I make conversation as we exit the busy café, and she's sipping her steaming coffee.

She nods and shoots me the wicked smile she swiped from me. "Just like your soul."

"Hey!" I nudge her with my shoulder, and she bursts into my kind of laughter: eyes squeezed shut, nose scrunched up, cheeks flushed pink, and a light aura around her that draws my dark side to her instantly. "And here I thought you were the nice one."

"I am nice!" she defends as we snag two seats by the window.

"Yeah, right." I roll my eyes, and she giggles some more. I smile at her at the moment my pants buzz. I hold up a finger, and she nods and turns her attention outside the window at the large planes moving around as I dig my phone out of my pocket. I look at the screen and roll my eyes, shoving it in my jacket pocket. I stare out the window, my leg shaking.

"Everything okay?" she hesitantly asks.

"Yep," I answer, voice clipped.

She exhales and taps my shoulder. "Grey?" She sing-songs my name.

"Hmmm?" I don't feel like talking.

"Was that...was that David?" Her voice is fragile, her lips pressed together.

"Mm-hmmm." I give a brief nod. I haven't talked to him since he announced he's staying here, in Miami. I know it's incredibly childish, but I don't give a fuck. He promised to always be there and have my back. How is he supposed to do that when he's almost twenty hours away?

"There's a plane called Antonov An-225 that weighs one million, two hundred, eighty thousand pounds," she blurts out.

"What?"

She shrugs and takes a sip of her coffee. "Sorry, it just got weird, and I know an awful a lot about airplanes."

"Why?" I tilt my head in fascination with this weirdly amazing girl.

She takes a nervous chew and shrugs again. "I like to know things?"

"Kinda forgot, because of how obsessed you were with me," I joke, and she grows tense and looks out the window, taking another big bite. "What's wrong?"

She shakes her head and takes a large gulp from her cup. "Nothing," she says with a smile. I know she's lying, but I don't want to push it, like she isn't pushing to talk about David.

"So, you and David haven't talked since the party?" she asks, and I let out a little laugh.

She still pries. How could I ever forget that?

I shake my head no. "Tell me more about planes."

Her eyes light up, and I swear it is the cutest thing. And then she goes on and on about planes, about how they are lightning proof, and what they are made of, how they are made, and so much more. A human should not know so much about one topic, and so vividly and accurately, but of course she does. She's Liv.

About an hour later, it is finally time to go on.

"Ah, shit," I murmur when the buckle is attached.

I fucking *despise* airplanes. The idea of them, the concept—just everything. Who wants to be thousands of feet in the air, cooped up in a tin box, with loads of people you don't care for? Not me. That's for fucking sure.

"Everything okay?" Liv asks with a small pout. "We can switch seats…" she suggests.

I look out the window past her and quickly shake my head. "No thanks, the middle is good."

"Excuse me, is this seat—" A man with a huge stomach, a thick beard, and beady eyes asks, pointing to the end seat with my leather jacket in it.

"Taken. Move along, Dirty Santa," I snap, and he grumbles a nasty reply before waddling down the aisle with the rest of the passengers.

"Don't be so rude, Grey." Liv pinches my arm.

I turn to face her. "Excuse me if I don't want some sick guy hacking up his lungs beside me on a *six-hour* plane ride."

"How do you know he's sick?"

There is a loud-ass cough behind us, and no doubt it is the guy who was clutching a wad of tissues in his grubby hands.

She blushes. "Oh."

"Yeah." I nod.

It takes a while for everyone to settle in, but finally, it's time to take off.

I grip the empty seat handle beside me on my left and pinch my lower lip anxiously. Liv's popped earphones in her ears and has her face plunged into a book. The plane runs down the runway, and I feel my stomach clench in anticipation. Fuck, oh fuck, I hate this part. I only flew once, when I was coming here to America from Venezuela. I was eight then, but fuck did I hate it back then, and I still hate it now. I feel so nauseated.

"You okay?" Liv whispers.

I glance at her concerned expression and give a tight nod. "Oh, yeah. I'm completely—holy fuck." I close my eyes when the plane tips up and begins to fly into the air. I feel like my heart is floating in my chest, just waiting to be slammed down to my feet.

She doesn't say anything.

Her small hand clasps over my balled-up right hand, and I feel at ease immediately. I open my eyes and shift my gaze over to her. She's staring up at me with a bright smile and even brighter eyes. Cheeks popped with color, nose scrunched, and aura blinding white.

I don't feel the effects of the plane lifting off anymore, because she's touching me. All she has to do is touch me…and I'm basking in light I do not deserve.

Chapter Thirteen

Liv

"Ladies and gentlemen, we have landed in Venezuela. We hope you all have a great trip and check out the beautiful sights of the country," one of the pilots announces over the PA system. At this, the snapping sound of seats unbuckling ensues all around me. Passengers grab their things and begin trailing down the aisle, relieved to finally leave after sitting down for nearly six hours. My own feet feel like they've fallen asleep on me, and my neck is a mess. But it's nothing a little walking around can't fix.

I take mine off with one hand; my other is still gripped by Grey. I smile a reflective smile when remembering how he looked at me when I took his hand in mine. I saw how apprehensive he looked when boarding the plane. He shot so many nervous glances around, I was afraid his eyes would magically turn into actual bullets and shoot up the plane. And when we first took off, I couldn't take it anymore. The look of true terror, the sweat on his forehead—I just had to comfort him.

I had expected him to rip his hand from mine and move into the empty seat. But he didn't do that. Instead, he looked at me with this look I still can't decipher. Awe? Adoration? Relief? I think it could have been a mixture of them all and maybe bits of shock and hatred. But not toward me. Why would he hate himself? I don't know, and it doesn't matter.

After, he just sort of fell asleep on my shoulder. He must have the worst neck pain, to have been bent over so low for six hours. What really amazes me is the fact that he never once loosened his grip. I thought he loathed me so much, he wouldn't be able to stomach sitting next to me for hours, but he proved me wrong and held onto me like the world would come to a fiery demise if he let go.

"Grey?" I speak low and gently shake his shoulder. "We've landed."

"Mmmm, go away, Prince..." he trails, waving his hand in my face before turning his back on me.

I feel myself grow incredibly hot in my cheeks as passengers chuckle, watching me trying to wake a grumpy man from his slumber. Mind you, he's still holding—more like *squeezing*—my left hand. I stand up and pull him upright and rub his scruffy cheek.

"Grey, you have to wake up. The plane has landed."

His eyes slowly flutter open, and I am locked in a bubble of awe of how beautiful he is, even if he looks sort of constipated. I laugh at my thoughts, and he scowls even harder than before.

121

"What's so funny?" he grumbles.

Your face.

"Nothing." I smile and stand, but he moves, and I'm yanked back into his chest. He has the tightest grip ever. I don't say anything but raise my brows as he yawns and stretches his back, pushing me into the seat in front of us.

"Sorry." He gives me a tight-lipped smile, but he's too irritated for whatever reason to let it last long. He glances at our interlocked hands, and I quickly, nervously, avert my eyes. "What's this?"

"Don't ask me. You were the one who wouldn't let go." I smirk, watching his reaction. He narrows his eyes at me and laughs dryly. I laugh, nearly snorting at how pink his cheeks are.

"Shut up!" he cries and pushes my hand from his.

I finally stand, unable to stop laughing. "Aw, don't be embarrassed." He stands up, and I playfully poke his chest. "I knew there was a big ol' softie afraid of something under this tough jacket and these tattoos of yours."

He grabs my wrist and tips my head back. "We all have fears, so don't you go high and mighty on me." His lips slip into a crooked smile that makes my stomach churn with hellfire. "What's yours?" His voice is low and gritty.

Losing you forever…

"Clowns?" I lie, and it sounds more like a question.

His eyes shift between the both of mine while he flicks his tongue out the corner of his pink lips. I try not to stare at it or the way his thumb is gently caressing the back of my hand.

"Then how do you live through the day after seeing yourself in the mirror every day?" He breaks the silence and brings out two big guns: his deep-deep dimples and glimmering black eyes.

I gasp and feel the tension between us fade away. "Screw you!" I push past him and walk down the aisle. We are the only passengers left on the plane, but the attendants have begun cleaning up after us. I made sure to clean out our aisle from all the chips I ate and beverages they offered. How I managed to get through the flight without using the bathroom once will be a mystery. Though I think it had something to do with the two-hundred-pound fighter crushing into my side, which I surprisingly didn't really mind.

He catches up to me and throws an arm around me as I step off the plane and into the portal that bridges from the plane to the airport. "I think you already have, multiple times, if I remember correctly."

"Grey!" I try to push his arm off, but he just pulls me tighter into his side.

He hisses through his teeth and bites his lip. "Oooh, *princesa*, don't wear it out or you won't be able to scream it again."

Oh my God! He's insane.

I anxiously look around for little children or people in general. "Grey, please, stop." I am no longer able to resist the warmth taking my cheeks by storm.

"That's a first." He wiggles his eyebrows, and I slap a hand over my face. My God, he can be so embarrassing. But at least he's in a better mood than when he woke up on the plane. He descends into roaring laughter that has me shifting on my feet for some reason. He directs us to baggage claim, and we stand with other people waiting for their luggage to pop up on the rotating conveyor belt.

It's quiet between us, but it's a comforting silence. As I watch bags go around and round, I realize a lot of girls are looking at us. I think it's because of Grey—he's the most handsome—I mean, he is pretty attractive; there's no denying that. They must be wondering what I'm doing with him. But I notice they aren't just looking at him; they're looking at my shoulder. I don't understand it until I look down and freeze. Grey's arm is wrapped around my shoulder, I'm playing with his large hand, and he has his other hand slung around my waist, my behind almost close to touching his front.

I feel hotter than the sun, but I have no time to correct myself, because he perks up and announces, "I see them!" He drags us over to the belt, and we snag our luggage. We still haven't let go of each other's hands as we stroll through the airport toward the exit. It feels good, almost too good for me to comprehend. But then my pocket buzzes, and we stop so I can reach for it.

Noah.

He must see the screen, because he says in a low, gravelly voice, "I'll go see if my uncle is here."

He's gone with my luggage before I can open my mouth.

I frown at his retreating back that gets lost in the crowd. "Fuck," I curse under my breath and close my eyes briefly to gather my thoughts. I lick my lips and exhale before moving to the side and answering the phone.

"Liv?" he says.

"Hi, Noah." I smile widely, even though he can't see me.

Silence sparks.

"How was your flight?" He sounds like he's trying his best to not give up on me. I don't know if he should try not to; I have a feeling I'll only end up hurting him. But he's a good guy, and I want to try with him, really.

"It was okay," I tell him. "I watched a couple of movies and slept for a little while, but I kept waking up because of the snoring bear next to me…" I stop talking. *Why did I just bring up Grey?*

"Oh, you sat with Grey?" He spits out his name with a certain thickness of hatred, it makes even me shiver.

"Um, yes…but he was out the entire flight," I say quickly, as if it's any consolation to make him feel better.

"Mm-hmmm," he hums with a tired sigh.

I sigh too. "I'm so sorry how we left things…I didn't mean to upset you. I just made a rash decision and—"

"It's all right," he cuts me off, and I can just see him running a hand over his hair. "Listen, I need to go. I'll talk to you later."

"Okay, bye, No—"

The line dies.

I huff out a heavy breath and shove my phone in my back pocket. He hates me. I don't think I can live with this pressure in my chest. I close my eyes and thread my fingers through my hair and clutch tightly, trying to pull my thoughts together to make sense.

Suddenly, a hand is curved on my hip, and the pressure is non-existent.

I lift my eyes and find Grey searching my face.

"You okay?" he asks, his voice low and raspy.

I give him a tight smile and nod. "I'm perfect," I tell him, but I don't even believe myself.

His raised brow and little hum tells me he agrees. "Sure…" He stares into my eyes for a really long while, and I feel my palms grow sweaty. I let them fall to my side, but my right meets his, since he is still holding me. His fingers trace my skin, and I take in a deep breath and exhale shakily. His touch will forever have this strange, fiery effect that threatens to melt me into a puddle of arousal.

Arousal? Yeah, it's time he takes his hand off.

He drops his hand, catching my wandering eye. "He's here." He sounds closed off again, and I frown as he backs away and walks out of the airport, leaving me behind.

Did I make a mistake coming here? I have these two guys I really like hating me. Except one of them can't keep his freaking hands off of me.

I push my conflicted thoughts to the side and follow him out. I instantly find him shutting the back of a green pick-up truck. He catches my eye and enters the backseat of the truck. I walk over and throw open the passenger door. I am immediately met with a pair of big dark brown eyes. A dark-haired, mustached man wearing a thin button-down

126

shirt and a tank top smiles down at me with a crooked smile I instantly stamp as the family smirk.

"You must be Olivia!" he exclaims with a fruitful boom of laughter as I climb inside.

I click on the seatbelt and thrust a hand out with a smile. "And you must be…" I trail and instantly hate myself. Grey told me absolutely nothing about his family. Great, now he must think I'm terrible for not knowing his name when he's gone out of his way picking me, a stranger, up along with his nephew.

"Fernando," he finishes for me, slapping his puffy palm into mine and shaking abruptly. He takes the other and rubs the back of my hand. I can't help but giggle. Is this back-of-the-hand rubbing a family thing too? Geez, Grey can't be original, can he? "Grey was always a little asshole," he jokes, and Grey rolls his eyes, proving his uncle's point.

I laugh even harder, even snorting, which I really wish I didn't do. "I really am sorry, but I have to tell you." I lean closer and whisper just loud enough for Grey to hear me, "He hasn't changed at all, maybe even got worse."

"Oh, screw you!" Grey snaps while his uncle reels back in laughter while clapping his hands.

I shoot Grey a look and mouth, "Oh, but you already have."

He narrows his eyes but has no comeback.

Proud, I wink and turn back in my seat.

"Oh, I like you, Olivia," Fernando boldly says, pulling out of his parked spot. "You call little Grey out for being what he doesn't even try to hide, asshole."

"If you guys don't stop calling me a fucking asshole…" Grey warns, gritting his teeth.

"You'll what?" I provoke him, smirking in the rearview mirror.

His uncle is a mess, with a tanned round face like a red tomato.

My pocket buzzes, and I pull out my phone and open it up.

I wouldn't keep doing that if I were you, Grey texts.

Panicked, I shoot my eyes to the rearview mirror.

He's the one smirking, and it's the real deal.

I blush and sink in the seat. I keep quiet for a little while, but Fernando is an excited man, I've quickly learned. He talks loudly and fast about anything and everything. Like his growing garden of spices in his backyard, how he won the biggest room for him and his wife in the house we're staying in, and much more. And as amazing it all sounds, I just can't stop staring out the window.

Venezuela is much more beautiful up close than seen online. The water we pass over on a very long bridge is the most beautiful blue I've ever seen. And the coconut trees are towering. I can see a few enormous buildings in the distance across the water—the city. And on the far side I can spot a little bit of mountains—the country. I would love to visit every place and document, but I don't think it'd be appropriate, seeing why I am here in the first place.

My eyes wander, and I find Grey staring in the rearview mirror…at me. I blush a little and hold his gaze, feeling conscious with my head peeking out of the window a little, my hands clutching the door. I look away at the approaching shoreline of the ocean as we're getting over the bridge. I assume he's caught himself and gives me time to take in this beautiful country. But when I look again, he's still staring at me. And this time…I don't look away.

***

"Olivia! Oh, you look just as beautiful as Grey described." A lady wearing a floral apron, graying hair, and a warm smile greets me loudly with wide eyes as I get out of the truck.

"Abuela," Grey groans and rubs his face, leaning against the truck.

I laugh at how embarrassed his grandmother's made him and walk into her arms. Shows him he isn't as invincible as he likes to portray. I love it, and I love her. She smells like dough and lime floor cleaner.

"It's so nice to meet you…" I trail when I pull back. "I'm sorry." I smile apologetically and throw my thumb over my shoulder in Grey's direction.

"Ah, he's still an asshole." She nods knowingly with a cheeky little smile.

"What the hell is it—call out Grey day?" Grey snaps behind me, and I laugh again and stick my tongue at him over my shoulder.

He shows me the middle finger, and Fernando snorts as he walks up to us.

"He's still an asshole," he confirms, and she nods. He walks into the house behind her, and I smile.

I love his family already.

"I am Alma," she informs me, then takes my hands in hers. So wrinkly and soft, I love her. "And you are really beautiful!" she exclaims like she's making a boastful toast, and I giggle as Grey hits the truck with his foot. "Boy, you calm down before I set you in the corner or send you to bed. Now come over here and give me a hug." She sounds like his mother, and from the way he calms down but still crosses his arms and pouts like a child, I'm guessing he really took her for his. A pang in my chest makes me sad, because his mother is in an asylum. That's random, but then another pain arrives as I realize she is to him as Louise is to me, an alternative mother figure. We are a lot more alike than I thought...

Grey rolls his eyes and walks over to us. "Hello, Abuela," he mumbles as he bends all the way down to hug her. She is very short; I'm guessing he got his height from his mother's side.

"It is so good to see you," she sighs, rubbing his back.

"Same," he grumbles, and I giggle behind my hand. This is so cute. He stands up and quirks a smile at me, nudging my arm. "Shut up." He rubs his neck and his cheeks, embarrassed.

"Well, come on. I oughta show you where you're sleeping and whatnot." She smiles as she rubs her hands on her apron, turning to the rusting white gate.

We follow her up some steps, and I examine the two tricycles laying in the over-grown, brownish

130

grass. I stare up at the two-leveled house and its chipping white paint. We walk through a red door with an adorable door-knocker of a cupid and into a small foyer where she instructs us to take off our shoes.

Grey groans like he's forgotten the rules since being here but kicks off his boots aimlessly. I sigh and place our shoes and a few others neatly in a metal rack. She laughs at me, but it's in a sweet way, like I finally understand her struggle. I smile at her, and she leads us up a rickety staircase to the second floor.

I look around at family photos and find myself smiling at a lot of the ones that had a little pouting Grey. Like always. He really was a little asshole...but he's grinning and looks generally happy in a lot. I sort of can't believe I'm walking through Grey's childhood. On the ride to the airport, he explained that he lived here until he was eight. A year after he was born, his father went to America for a better job than working graveyard shifts at construction sites. His mother gladly went with him, leaving him behind while they sorted out their finances and living arrangements. This went on for seven more years, like they had forgotten him, until one day they finally had him come to America.

"Well, this is it," Alma says from down the hall.

"Where's the other—" Grey begins.

"You didn't tell me she was coming until last minute," she tries to whisper.

I frown and walk over to them. I had stopped to stare at a picture of Grey chasing one of his cousins with a baseball bat, dressed in all black. Typical.

"What's the…oh." I snap my mouth shut and stare at the *one* twin bed against the wall. "Oh…"

Chapter Fourteen

Alma believes Grey and I are in a relationship. That's why when he told her that I was coming, she thought she didn't have to worry about finding another place for me to sleep. When she assumed we were together, I have never felt more embarrassed in my life. But it is fair for her to assume so, since Grey spoke so highly of my beauty. I still can't believe he gushed about that to his grandmother. When I asked him about it, he brushed me off, claiming she's insane, that it runs in the family, but she's related to him on his father's side, and his *mother* is the one with the mental issues. Hmmm…

Anyway, he and I agreed we would take turns sleeping on the bed. I would take the floor one night while he gets the bed and vice versa. He offered taking the couch in the living room, but I quickly shot that down when I saw how small it was. He's quite tall, and he'd be uncomfortable and cramped, and this is *his* family, his childhood home. I would feel horrible and out of place if I took the more

133

comfortable option while he suffered.

Tonight, I would take the floor.

"Hell no, I'll take the floor," he says when I tell him.

We're putting away our clothes in the little brown dresser by the door. I frown as I move a few blouses to my side of the dresser.

"It's your house, Grey. Your family event, I am the guest," I point out and pass him as he puts some rumpled, smelly black shirts away. I grimace, and the urge to wash and iron them is strong, but I have no place to do such.

"This isn't my house anymore," he reminds me.

"It wouldn't be right if I took the bed," I counter.

He leans against the dresser, arms crossed, eyes pointed. "You said you didn't get any sleep on the plane because of me, right?"

I open my mouth to reply, but then it drops closed. I had let that slip as a sort of teasing thing a little earlier when he complained about his sore neck. I just didn't know it'd come back around and bite me in the butt later.

"That's what I thought," he says with a cocky smile.

I narrow my eyes at him and toss balled-up socks at his chest, which he easily catches with a short, mocking laugh. "You're very annoying, you know that, right?"

"I've been called worse." He shrugs.

"Like asshole?" I tilt my head, a smirk slowly winding on my face. *My turn to mock.*

"Like you're a ray of sunshine!" he snaps and throws the socks back to me. I, however, am not quick to catch them because of the pair of jeans in my hands. It hits me in the head, and I bite my tongue while he throws his head back in the most annoying laughter, clapping his hands like his uncle Fernando.

"That's why you got the lovely title, *asshole*!" I spit and storm over to the dresser, placing my jeans in order by color. I am standing up when I feel a light thud on the back of my head. I whirl around and find him laughing his butt off, another pair of socks a foot away from me on the ground.

"Classic!" he exclaims like the extreme goofball he is.

"Oh, it is so on!" I rush over to him, and he stops laughing and runs out of the room. "Stop running!" I scream after him, but he just continues to laugh and run faster. Curse him and his incredibly long legs. They're like skyscrapers.

"Just give up, munchkin. You will never—ah shit!"

He shuts up when I jump onto his back.

"Got you now, a-hole!" I screech and throw my hands around his neck. I squeeze his cheeks, and he tilts from side to side like those huge blow-up things that stand in front of car washes or dealerships.

"Stop *pinching* me!" he cries out, but a laugh sits behind his words, making me smile from ear to ear.

"Not until you apologize," I tell him.

"Hell no!" he declares, then proceeds to go down the stairs. Only problem is, he doesn't walk down. No, he *runs* down them. I bounce up and down haphazardly, and I clench my legs around his waist and tighten my arms around his neck.

"Grey!" I cry out and bury my face behind his ears, praying he doesn't slip and crush me to death. He laughs the entire way and actually jumps off the last step. I nearly fly off his back, but I make sure to hug tighter to his body. Finally, I jump off and smack him hard on his chest, flushed hot in the face from how much he is amused by this. "That was not funny! I could have *died*!"

"But did you, though?" He waves his face near mine, and I back up and grunt.

"I could have," I pout.

"But did you? Die?" He takes steps toward me, but I retreat from him and his nauseating smug look.

"No, but—"

He closes the gap between us, and I stumble back, pushed against one of the floral chairs in the living room. "I wouldn't have let you *die, pequeña princesa*."

"I am not little," I argue, trying my best to bite back a smile. I shouldn't like how close he is to me or how heavily he smells like spices that lingered in his uncle's truck.

"Oh, but you are. The littlest thing I've ever seen," he teases, making a show of catching my eye as I move my head around. He presses his nose against mine, tongue peeking out to slide across his lips. "So small, I could just *eat* you up…hmmm?"

He is really close. Like, too close…too…close…

I should reply. I definitely should. I think it's been a while since I've spoken, right…?

He raises an eyebrow expectantly.

Bastard.

"And you're just a big asshole," I finally manage to find words. For a second there I thought I forgot how to speak.

He just smirks but doesn't say anything to freak me out.

"Love birds, it's time to come outside," a voice says, but Grey is unmoving. His eyes stay glued to mine, and I can barely feel my heart beat in my chest; it's moving too fast for comprehension. "Your *primos* are back from the square. Come on, boy! *No hagas esperar a todos*." (Cousins. Do not make everyone wait.)

"You should listen to your grandmother," I choke out.

His eyes squeeze like a trigger for a brief second, then he huffs out and stands straight.

"Let's go meet my *primos*," he says and winks at me before turning around and strolling over to his waiting grandmother.

When they go out to the backyard through the kitchen, I finally let out a breath I didn't know I was holding back.

"Wow," is all I can say. I feel like I have to check a mirror to make sure I don't look like a very round peach and my hair is intact.

"Olivia, that includes you too," Alma says as she rushes over to me in this cute old lady walk Louise does all the time. She really reminds me of her. I bet they'd make great friends. They both know how to boss people around but still look after them with love and care.

"Sorry," I say quietly, but she waves it away as she simultaneously hustles me to the back. I am overwhelmed at first glance. There are so many…*primos*. A lot are playing soccer on the wide grass, cursing and teasing in Spanish. The adults are either watching and laughing and scolding them for cursing or eating what's cooking on the grill.

"Everyone, this is Olivia, Grey's girlfriend," Alma introduces me in a very loud voice while rubbing my arms.

Everyone pauses and turns to me. I see Grey leaning under a tall tree with a swing, smirking at me in that signature, annoying, smug look of his. He doesn't even try to interject and help me out, just watches me make a fool out of myself in front of his family.

"I…" I begin to explain the situation when Alma shakes me a bit and whispers, "Most of them don't speak English. Would you like me to translate?"

I make eye contact with Grey and, somehow, it's like he heard, because his smirk stretches into a full-on grin, enjoying my torture.

I make a note to "accidentally" step on him when I use the bathroom in the middle of the night.

"No, that's fine. Thank you," I tell her, then turn to the awaiting crowd. *"Hola a todos. Yo Afortunadamente, no soy la novia de Grey. Pero rezo por la pobre chica cuando la encuentra y la atrapa con sus garras."* (Hello, everyone. I, fortunately, am not Grey's girlfriend. But I do pray for the poor girl when he finds and traps her with his claws.)

Everyone laughs, and I feel extremely proud when I find Grey with steam practically blowing out of his ears. I laugh and bounce my eyebrows to mock him.

For the next few hours, I am introduced to just about everyone. The pack of girls I found in the corner of the party near the coolers are the more grown-up *primas* and *tías*. They are pretty cool and love to gossip about the neighborhood women and some show called *El Señor de Los Cielos*. Apparently, the last season left on a major cliffhanger that dealt with a character being shot in the back. Sounds interesting, but not my thing.

I rotate around the party, then around eleven, there is a big bonfire made in the middle of the grass. I stand back and watch as everyone gathers around the logs. A few minutes later, a huge bottle of vodka is passed around, and a man with a scar running across his right eye and dressed in a plaid shirt begins speaking. I try not to pay attention too much, because it seems like a family thing, but everyone has been nice to me and seems to accept me either way. I catch snippets of a story about a man named Nathaniel, which I am guessing was Grey's grandfather's name.

I am about to walk over to listen to more as the bottle is passed down, but someone bumps into my shoulder, and I am dragged up the stairs.

Grey.

"Where are you taking me?" I ask curiously, casting a glance over my shoulder to see if anyone saw us. I don't want to appear rude for disappearing so suddenly without excusing myself.

He doesn't answer me.

We go up the stairs and down the hall. I think he's taking me to our room, but he continues down the hall. He makes a turn and stops walking down a short dead-end. I stand back, but he doesn't let my hand go as he reaches up and tugs on a hanging string. The attic. He brings the small stairs down and goes up first. I hesitantly go up after him. The dusty space is pitch black and filled with clutter. A few streams of moonlight pour through, washing over the grungy, creaking floorboards.

I follow after him out of a window and try not to look down. It is angled enough that we can walk without much difficulty. My heart is wrapped around my tongue the entire time we walk, though. How is he acting so cool about this? Unless...he's probably done this a million times before.

He abruptly sits down and tugs me down with him. I stare at him. "Why are we here, Grey?"

He's staring off into the distance of the tree above the backyard. "Drink?"

"What?"

I look down and see he is offering me a vodka bottle.

"Um...sure." I reluctantly take the bottle from him. He lets my hand go and hangs his head, knees wide apart and fingers looping around each other.

I take a few sips then hand it back to him. "Can you tell me why we're up here?" I question, careful with my words. He looks irritable, and I don't want to upset him. There must be a reason he just dragged me up here without a word.

He's nearly drunk a good quarter of the drink before he sucks in air and nods. "They're telling stories about him."

"Your grandfather," I state, and he slowly nods.

"Oh." I pout, and he nods again, then takes a long sip. I watch and watch until I've had enough. I bring the bottle down and tip his chin toward me so he's facing me. Tears dabble in his eyes, and I feel my heart swell, waiting to break when the first tear drops. "I am very sorry for your loss, Grey."

He shrugs, tugging on his lower lip. "What can you do, right?"

I look to the bottle and shrug. "Drink?"

He moves to take it, but he holds my hand for a while.

"But not too much," I instruct, then smile softly. "I want you here with me."

He stares into my eyes for an unnerving amount of time, then nods. "I'm not going to be the best company tonight, princess," he says, almost apologetic as he takes the bottle. He holds it with both hands and tsks, shaking his head. "I shouldn't have brought you up here. I'm sorry." He brings his head back as he takes a large swig of the strong liquor.

"So why did you?" I ask, and he shrugs, wiping the back of his hand across his wet lips, black eyes soaring straight through me.

"I didn't want to be alone."

Oh.

"Oh," I voice my lackluster thought.

He eyes me for a while and adds, "And I just felt like I need you by my side."

Oh... "Oh," I repeat, but with a smile this time.

He breaks into a smile and starts laughing. "You're cute," he blurts out, and I bite my tongue and turn away, barely biting back a laugh.

"Someone's getting a little tipsy," I tease, willing myself to pale in color.

He tugs at my hand. Sparks fly the moment his calloused palm touches mine. "I don't have to be tipsy to tell you that." The emotion passing between us is too much; my heart feels like it is going to burst any second.

"My turn. Remember, I still want you here." I take the bottle from his hand and murmur, my mouth on the tip, "Plus, I'm going to need your help getting back in the house. Or for you to act as a cushion for me to land on if we fall."

I take a large gulp and listen to him laugh and snort, which is the cutest thing ever. I try my hardest to bite back a laugh, but some liquor drips down my chin. He laughs even harder and leans into my side. I finally can't take it anymore and spit it all out.

I groan, "Aw, look at what you made me do!"

He gasps and waves a finger at me. "That was not my fault."

"Yes, it was!" I argue, waving a finger back at him.

His whacks against mine, and I burst into laughter again. Our foreheads touch each other, and I find myself leaning into his chest, the liquor settling on my temples. We laugh and laugh and laugh until the stories below us turn from sober to funny memories. Up here, we bask in *ours*.

Chapter Fifteen

The next morning, I wake up to the sight of Grey's bare ass.

I quickly sit up, mouth dry and head throbbing like I smashed it through glass.

"What's...uh—" I mumble, brushing hair out of my face.

He flashes me a smug smirk as he steps through a pair of black boxers. "Good morning, sunshine."

"What happened last night?" I grumble, my throat thick. I think we had a little bit too much to drink last night. How did we even get down from the roof without falling off? Ugh. I should have thought that through. But I haven't been able to think much, not when *he* is around.

"Oh, we just had the best sex of your life," he says casually.

"What!" I scream, feeling my heart beat faster, to the point where I think I'm having a mini heart attack. I clutch my chest and watch as his serious face drips away, and a more annoying, amused one takes place. He looks like he's holding back

143

laughter, but finally, he can't hold it in anymore and hits the dresser as he laughs like a drunk hyena.

"Ugh! That is not fair! Do *not* do that ever again!" I grab the pillow from behind me and toss it at him, aiming for his enormous head. Unfortunately, he dodges and winks at me.

"You have terrible aim," he insults.

"And you have a terrible…*butt,*" I lie, and he scoffs and tsks me, waving a finger at me.

He walks over to me and leans on the bed, pushing his face close to mine. Annoyed by how wonderful he smells and how the scruff on his face is doing odd things in the pit of my stomach, I crawl back, and he quirks his lips in a knowing smile.

"Now, you and I both know you're lying." He pauses, and I hold my breath to keep from imploding when he slides his tongue through his supple lips, then eases forward and rasps out, "Am I right?"

"Y-yes," I stutter, without thinking.

Wait…what?

"I meant no—you tricked me!" I accuse and raise my foot to push him away, because I know if I got too close to him with my hands, I was a goner. But he grabs my ankle and pulls me, so I fall back onto the bed. How could I have forgotten? He has a freaking fetish with grabbing me by my ankles. I swear, no limb of mine is able to keep him away.

"I tricked no one," he drawls.

I suck in a surprised breath when he hovers over me. His elbows are on either side of my head, and I am suddenly *very* aware of his naked, inked chest. I know I should say something or try to get him off of me—he was always so horny in the mornings—but I can't. I feel paralyzed, but definitely not from the waist down, if you get what I mean. His head tilts the same as mine does as I take in his face up close.

I'm trapped, and the longer I am under his powerful eyes, the more I'm sucked into his aura of perfection. From the natural puffiness of his reddish pink lips, to his carved, high cheekbones, to his almond-shaped eyes. I reach out and, like a sailor trapped in the melodic song of a siren, I bite my lip as I trail my finger, feather-light, against his top lip.

His gaze intensifies to the point of my stomach twisting and turning. With the way he's staring down at me, his hot chest close enough to mine that I feel like I am inside a furnace, and the way his messy black hair hangs in his eyes—I feel as though he's wringing me dry. I am parched, and boy, is he a tall drink of water…

Did I just say that?

"What are you doing to me, Grey?" I whisper, pinching his full lower lip.

His eyes darken, if possible, and threaten to swallow me whole. "You tell me…" I suck in a large breath when I feel his palm slide up my bare leg. I must have shoved my jeans off before I got into bed or while I was in it. Ugh, I don't remember much of last night. I am still contemplating how we made it back in in one piece.

His hand gripping my flesh abruptly brings me out of my distracted mind. I think I am just trying to center myself on anything other than the feeling of my heart drumming in my head or the way my hands have taken to cupping his very sharp, rock-hard jaw…

"I couldn't in a million years," is my raspy reply.

Is he moving closer? Or am I? Is he holding me tighter, or does my body naturally spark on fire?

I should stop him, because…um, because…he is really warm. I think I really am engulfed in…uh, in him…

"Olivia! *Te gustaría venir a la—oh mi,*" Alma exclaims, bursting through the door.

"Alma!" I sit up quickly and knock my forehead with Grey's.

"Fuck!" He curses the same time I do and falls back off the bed. He lands with a hard thud.

I laugh on the inside.

"I am so sorry. I can come back later…" Alma trails, pointing down the hall to the stairs. I shake my head, and I swear I see her smiling through the haziness brought on by Grey's huge head colliding with mine.

"No, no—we weren't up to anything." I quickly stand and force myself to not hurl on the spot. I stood up too fast, because now my rumbling hangover stomach feels attacked and threatens to spill out of my mouth like a fountain.

"Oh…" she says and glances at her grandson.

Grey is still on the floor, his hands pressed to the hard surface, holding him up. He just shrugs in return and passes me a cocky smile.

I *accidentally* step on his hand—as I planned earlier—and walk over to Alma. "Seriously, he was just being an asshole."

She nods, understanding, and glances at her grandson with a disappointed click of her tongue.

"Once an asshole, always an asshole." She shifts her dark eyes to me and winks at me, and we both wait for what's to come.

"Stop…*calling me that!*" Grey shouts, and Alma and I descend into laughter.

***

"So, Abuela Alma says she caught you and Grey fucking this morning," Sofía, the youngest of Grey's cousins, says casually as she tosses a bag of tomatoes in the red shopping basket I am holding.

I nearly drop the groceries in shock.

I look at her with wide eyes. "W-what?" I stutter like an idiot. Well, I'm sorry I am a little taken aback when one of my ex's cousins thinks he and I had…you know…*the sex* and was caught by his grandmother. I have to live with his family for a few days, so them thinking *that* happened will definitely make things a little awkward.

She nods, her lips pouty as she checks out a pair of peaches. "Yep. Said she was coming to get you to come to the market and walked in on it. He was on top, shirtless, and you were about ready to tear the rest of his clothes off."

"What? That's ridic—"

"I heard the shirt was torn in shreds because you were really desperate for him," another, thickly accented voice rises from behind me. I turn around and find Isabella, who is a few years older than Sofía, nodding matter-of-factly.

My cheeks spark with flames, and I gasp for words. "That is *not* true!" I laugh nervously, and

147

they share glances, then raise a questioning brow at me. I let my jaw drop open and do another anxious chuckle that doesn't exactly paint me as someone telling the truth. "I'm not lying."

"Because you would tell us if you two were banging again?" I whip around to Emilio, Sofía's brother, who is older by one year. He's chewing on a random red straw, his sunglasses perched on his nose. He stares at me intently over the shades and tips his baseball cap down.

Geez, they're all so attractive and dark. I wonder what Grey's offspring would look like. I bet he/she would look just as intimidating, no doubt.

"We are not *banging* because we are not together," I tell them, and they all raise their brows. "I'm telling the truth!"

"So why was his shirt shredded?" Isabella questions.

"Yeah," Sofía adds.

"His shirt was not *shredded*. Your grandmother made that up."

"Why would she do that?" Emilio tips his head to the right, and they follow.

Ugh, this gorgeous cult.

"I don't know," I say honestly and shrug.

"Because you are so good for him." I jump and turn around, finding Alma grinning up at me with an adorable smile. But I've just found out she isn't just adorable, she's also very sneaky. And I mean *very.* I didn't even hear her footsteps or anything.

"I'm...what?" I breathe.

"You're good for him," Sofía says, a little snappy.

148

Easy anger definitely runs through the family bloodline.

"No, I am not," I say with a little huff. Why are we discussing my love life with Grey in the middle of a market, when there is no actual love life with him?

"Yes, you are," Alma speaks up, rubbing my arms. I stiffen. "I can see you are very special to him."

"I assure you, I'm not," I tell her *and* them, strained.

"He hasn't brought any girl around the family," Isabella says, and I am at a loss for words.

"What about Rose?" My throat feels dry.

They all exchange confused expressions.

"Who's Rose?"

Oh...

***

"Mateo...hey," I greet him, shocked, as I am one of the first to enter the house. I kind of forgot he was Grey's cousin, but then I hammer it into my brain. He sets down two suitcases by the stairs. When he turns around and sees me, he grins widely and opens his arms.

"Liv, hey," he says warmly, and we hug, stepping to the side of the stairs as the others bring in bags. I grip the ones in my hands and nervously look around. "What are you doing here?" he asks.

I shrug. "Just here supporting Grey."

He nods. "That's great."

I look around and smile softly. "Mason didn't

tell you I came here with Grey?"

He shakes his head. "He was kind of closed off after I asked him to come here with *me*."

"Oh…" I take in his solemn expression as he nods, expelling a little breath.

"Yeah. He's not ready, I guess…" he trails and begins rubbing the back of his neck.

The silence between us grows incredibly awkward. I want to ask about Mason, but obviously they aren't on speaking terms. And neither are he and I. He didn't make the effort to listen and understand me. I desperately want to make things better between us and fix things, because he must be going through something extreme to turn down coming down here with Mateo at this troubling time. He loves him, he really does. So why not come?

"Well, I should go and say hi to everyone," he says, breaking the silence.

"Sure, I'll see you around," I promise.

He gives me a close-lipped smile before turning on his heels and wandering into the kitchen where everyone else is, taking the bags in my hands.

I bite my lip with a yearning to comfort my best friend, but he wasn't mine when I needed him. So I push the painful thought away with a sigh and bound up the stairs. I briefly admire the many photos running along the wall, wishing my family could do the same. But we haven't taken a collective photo together since that night…

I nearly burst into tears at how many people I have lost, like Mason, Jonah, my parents, possibly Noah…and it's all my fault. Every single one of them. They all nearly connect with one person I love so deeply; he is forever wreaking havoc on my life. But I cannot get him out of my head even if I tried my hardest.

"Hey, are you okay?" a voice booms behind me.

I uncover my hand from my mouth and turn around. Grey stares at me with concern as I nod my head, frantically wiping my tears away.

"Um, yeah, I'm fine," I croak and choke back on a sob.

"You're a bad liar. You should just stop trying," he says. I close my eyes, and he wraps his arms around me. All my worries and despair melt away, and I am able to breathe in his one of a kind smell. I inhale, and he doesn't say anything. I sniffle and let the tears run down my cheek until I can't focus on it anymore.

A cold thing is imprinted on my cheek.

I pull my head back and cry some more.

He's wearing the charm I gave him—*Jonah's charm.*

"You still wear it," I whimper. I had thought he stopped wearing it after we split. But then again, I thought the same about the jacket, yet I found myself wearing it after he had two days ago. Has he really not given up on me?

"Shhh…yes," he admits, tipping my head back. I surrender to his eyes and bite my lip. He watches me do it and smirks. "But I think you need it more, hmmm?"

I don't answer, so he unclasps the necklace and gently turns me around. I close my eyes as he pushes my hair over one shoulder. I suck in a breath and feel his rough fingertips as he clasps it around my neck. My hair falls back down, and I am spun around and met with a smile that does all kinds of things to me, all at the same time, I feel as though I am going to faint from everything hitting me.

"Much better," he whispers, caressing my cheek with his thumb.

I close my eyes and nod as he wipes tears from my cheeks.

Much...

Chapter Sixteen

Two hours later, I'm in the kitchen helping cook dinner. After the really intense and emotional moment between Grey and me triggered by my little breakdown, I couldn't face him. Call me a coward all you want; if I had looked into his eyes for more than a beat as I thanked him, I know I would have lost all my control and done something I would have liked in the moment…but regretted when I returned home. It would wreck what's between Noah and me, and that was already hanging on by a single thread.

In this house, in this *country*, everything is just a dream of sorts. Meeting his family, him being more open to me, flirty, humorous, just like how he was when we started out—it's not going to last. When we get back to Miami, he'll be cold and reserved. I'll go back to feeling like a corpse walking. And I will have two of the most important guys in my life hating me: one who is meant to be my whole future of perfection and check off every bullet on my list, and another who was my first friend at college, a foreign, scary place, but turned into one of my best friends and has always been there for me.

However, when it came time to have their support and full trust…they failed me and acted as if I were some dumb, crazy, obsessive girl. I was no longer their Liv who did her best to feel something when kissed by another. I was no longer their Liv who was by their side with their boyfriend in pajamas watching 80s romance movies or used their shoulder to cry on when complaining about the boy with cold black eyes but the warmest heart. I was Liv, who got up and sought to help a person who she would give all she possessed to make sure he was sane and not taking out his anger via a fucking *gang*. I was Liv, the girl who put all her previous feelings for said boy aside and jetted to another country to be his god damn support system.

But I guess they wanted their Liv who was weepy, depressed, and drowning herself, taking too many pills to stop feeling, and needing their protection and was just so fucking broken! Too bad I can't be that Liv anymore. I need to get closure with Grey. I want to close this door, so I can be the final product of myself—Liv: the girl who goes to college, and attends poetry slams, and smiles at nothing in particular, and is able to breathe, because it's just the easiest thing to do. And even if they hate me because of it, I will strive to be that girl, no matter what. Even if it kills me, anything has to be better than walking around like you've lost a huge part of yourself.

"Liv, can you help me dice the tomatoes?" Alma asks, and I stop draining the rice.

154

I nod and respond, "Of course." I ask Isabella to take over, and when she does, I walk over to Alma. "How many do I dice?" I let my eyes sweep over the large amount. Normally this would be way too much, but considering the massive family grouped in the back, I actually don't think it's enough.

"All of them," she answers.

I pick up the knife beside her and begin dicing the tomatoes. I hum to the beat of the festive song that wafts through the open windows into the kitchen. The atmosphere is laid back and really calming. I love how loud everyone laughs in the back and how well the cousins get along, teasing each other and even throwing a few playful curses at each other. I try my best but fail to contain my amusement when Alma curses at them to stop cursing.

Oh, Grey's family. You gotta love them.

Alma nudges my forearm as I move on to the onions, seeing she could use some help.

"You are good with the knife," she says and raises questioning eyebrows.

I shrug and tell her, "Louise, my caretaker, taught me how to cook at a very young age. I once cooked a meal for her, me, and her daughter when I was *twelve*." I smile proudly at the memory of me standing on my tippy toes to preset the oven.

"That is wonderful—" she praises.

"It smells so fucking good in here," a rather loud, obnoxious voice sounds from behind us.

We turn around and find Grey and Mateo walking in. That was fast. A little while earlier, they left to play basketball down by the playground

155

about ten minutes from here, claiming they were bored out of their minds.

They are matching in basketball shirts and muscle tops. I feel my cheeks fluster with heat. Grey is dripping in sweat, and so is Mateo, but he looks attractive in a whole other way. His golden-specked skin outlines his impressive muscles, and his hair is slicked with sweat. I nearly pass out and die when he brings up the hem of his white shirt and wipes his face.

"Might wanna close your mouth before he sees it as an invitation," a voice whispers haughtily in my ear. I jump in surprise and snap my head to the right. I find Sofía smirking at me.

"Shut up," I hiss-whisper, and she raises her hands defensively. Being annoying sure does run in the family.

"*¿Qué te dije sobre tu maldita maldición?*" Alma curses at Grey...for cursing. (What did I tell you about your god damn cursing?)

He and I both laugh, and his eyes meet mine. I suppress a giggle when he jokingly rolls his eyes to provoke his grandmother, who then threatens to get her belt.

"*Lo siento, abuela, pero estoy tan hambriento,*" he apologizes, but his eyes are glued to me. I blush and glance away, but he's staring at me with a mission written on his face as he comes over to me. "*Y tengo mis ojos puestos en algo en particular.*" (I'm sorry, grandma, but I'm so hungry. /And I have my eyes on one thing in particular.)

I stiffen and tighten my grip on the knife, as if he is about to lunge and gobble me up like the big bad wolf he often represents himself as. My heart is beating faster, and I swallow a lump in my throat when he stops in front of me. He leans forward, eyes drilling through my soul, and I pull the knife back. When he pulls back, he has a mini empanada in his hand, and I feel myself blush and bite my lip. I forgot, there's a huge tray of them on the counter behind me.

And here I thought he meant me…I don't know if I should be disappointed or relieved…

"Oh, hey there, didn't see you there," he grumbles with a satisfied smirk as he chews.

I roll my eyes and use the butt of the knife to push him back. "Lies."

He laughs. "Whoops." He shrugs his shoulders and sucks on the sauce dripping on his thumb.

Shameless, utterly shameless, I tell you.

"Okay, enough flirting. Go back out and play with your little cousins." Alma shoos them out of the kitchen.

"There was no flirting," I groan, putting the knife down, upset but not surprised they're bringing up this topic again. Poor, naïve me prayed our nice little invasive chat would end when we left the market. But no, it has resurrected itself and is proving to me this family are more persistent on giving me heart palpitations than I thought.

Emilio hums as he kicks his feet back and forth, perched on top of the counter, eating an empanada. "There was a little flirting. Right, Izzy?"

"You are very right, Emmy," Isabella agrees, waving a knife at him.

He groans and thrusts his head back, meeting the

counter, causing him to groan again, but in pain this time, causing us to laugh. "How many times have I told you not to call me that?"

"What? It's a pretty name," she defends, pouting.

"Right! Pretty, and it sounds like a fucking *girl's* name!" He flings the rest of his uneaten little treat at his cousin.

She raises her knife and points it at him. "I will shove this up your ass, and you will be shitting butter-knives for a *week!*" she threatens.

"*¿No te advert sobre insultar en mi casa?*" Alma butts in, pointing *her* knife at them. Then she shifts it to Emilio, and he raises his arms defensively. "*Vas a la parte de atrás y juegas con los chicos. No toleraré que un vago se siente en mi mostrador. ¡Muévete!*" (Didn't I warn you about cursing in my house? /You go out to the back and play with the boys. I will not tolerate a lazy bum sitting on my counter. Move!)

I burst into laughter and so does Isabella and Sofía as we watch Emilio gasp, then storm outside, muttering curses, causing Alma to run after him with the knife. We all rush over to the kitchen and watch as she chases him, screaming something about *having no respect for his elders* and how she would *whoop his ass with the knife until he looked like a victim of Krueger Freddy*. Cute. She got his name backward.

The girls are going on about a bet to see if she really does do what she threatens, but I find myself zoning out as I find Grey in the midst of the crowd.

He's playing soccer with his little cousins and Mateo, only now he's shirtless and his sweaty, inked chest and back are on display. He is quick as a bullet on his feet, retrieving and running around with the soccer ball. He chants and mocks and teases the little guys, showing no mercy as he drives the ball into a makeshift net leaning against the wooden fence. I hide a giggle behind my hand as he fist pumps the air and boasts in the little kids' faces. He is so freaking mean…it's kind of cute.

As if sensing my gaze or hearing my barely audible laugh, his eyes find mine through the open window. And he smiles. Widely. Brightly. And perfectly. My chest tingles, and I find myself waving at him, then giving him a thumbs up in reference to him winning the little game.

He sticks out his tongue and winks at me, waving his hand in a surfer dude way.

I laugh some more but stop when I feel two very judging eyes burning through me. I look at both Isabella and Sofía, each not even hiding their grins. I can read their minds. I groan and turn around to head back to the chopping board.

"*Ni siquiera empieces conmigo,*" I warn them, grabbing the knife and pointing it at them, because that's the only way you get this family to listen to you. Or, you know, you could chase them with it. Either or, whichever is more effective. (Don't even start with me.)

***

Dinner was great. Not everyone could fit at the massive table, so some had to eat either outside or in the kitchen despite Alma's protests. They were all so welcoming that I got to meet almost each and every one of them. The food was delicious, thanks to Alma and those who helped, and I almost died at how good her flan was.

Throughout, some reminisce about Nathaniel, Grey's grandfather. Grey held onto my hand the entire time.

Isabella, Sofía, and Emilio, even *Alma*, eyed it the entire time, casting each other knowing looks.

Ugh, Wylers!

But I'm okay with one in particular…as a friend.

I couldn't help but carefully watch Alma listen to each member who told a certain story that included her late husband of *sixty years*.

When I first met Alma, I expected her to be heartbroken and unable to cope with the death of her husband, but apparently, she had enough time to prepare for it since she was told he wouldn't live for much longer shortly before he passed. She has been nothing but sweet and smiles toward me, and I admire her for being so strong during all of this. Although, past all her smiles and joking about Grey being an asshole, which he is, I can see the pain in her eyes. She almost covers it up perfectly. Almost.

Now that it's over and everyone has moved to the back to sit around the campfire and hang out again, I'm on my way to shower. The day felt like it dragged on forever and ever, and I could use some washing up. Tomorrow is the funeral, and I can just feel the emotional torrent everyone will be going through, especially Grey.

I sigh as I send Noah a text, telling him I'll be in the shower in case he decides to text or call.

Though, since our conversation at the airport, he hasn't reached out to me. Not once. I'm confused about where we stand. Does he still hate me and want to end things before they've even started? Or does he want to give me—us—a chance, but is scared of something that will *never* happen between Grey and me, and he wants space? I want to know what's going on in his head, but he's blocking me out, and it's beginning to piss me off more than anything.

I twist on the faucet and turn to the sink while it warms up. I unzip my toiletry bag and begin brushing my teeth thoroughly. Afterward, I pack it away and strip off my clothes. I neatly fold them and place them on the floor, then slip into the shower. Instantly, I am relaxed, moaning as the hot water beats against my aching muscles from cooking all day.

Not even fifteen minutes later, the shower curtain is yanked back.

I shout and attempt to cover my breasts and cross my legs.

Grey beams up at me. "Hey there…" His eyes lower to my right hand, covering between my legs. "Friends."

"What are you doing, Grey?" I hiss. I could have sworn I locked the door.

He rolls his eyes and shakes his head. "It's nothing I haven't seen before." He gestures to my body, and I flush as red as the curtain and shrug my shoulders.

"I don't care. What do you want?" He's over-stepping every boundary to ever *exist* right now.

"What...did...I...want...hmmm?" He hums and taps his chin.

I splash water at him, and he barks at me, but I hold up a finger, cutting him off. "Hurry up and speak before I kick you where the sun doesn't shine."

"Fine, geez." He roughly rubs his face and says, "Me and the gang, my lovely cousins you have acquainted yourself with, are going into town. There's this festival thing going on."

"And? I wanted to get some rest."

"Don't be a granny," he groans.

"I am not a—ugh! Why should I even do what you say? You didn't even ask nicely."

"You're a smart cookie, 'cause I wasn't asking." His hard-ass face is on display now.

I chew on my lip and throw the idea in my head a bit. I was here for him, to be by his side. Plus, a festival sounds nice?

"Fine," I finally say.

"Great." He grins and bites his lip as his eyes wash over me. "And wear something short. It's gonna be hot tonight..." His words sound keenly suggestive, and I just nod. He licks his lips before letting the curtain go and walking out of the room, letting the door shut behind him.

I am thankful for the tiled wall, because it holds me up the rest of my cold shower.

Chapter Seventeen

Grey lied and told Alma we were going to watch a movie at the theater when she saw us leaving the house. He said his grandmother wouldn't allow them to go the festival. According to him, she doesn't trust the lot of them to go by themselves because of the *adult activities* that occur there. Hearing that, I grew very wary of going myself, but the others persuaded me to go, saying I was nineteen and should live a little. Plus, they threatened to tell Grey I was still utterly in love with him and wanted to marry him and have his babies. It's safe to say I claimed my seat in the back as quickly as I could. They are so annoying, but I'm already liking them. That, again, runs deep in the family, straight to Grey.

I end up getting the seat behind Grey, who's driving. We are taking Fernando's truck. When I asked if he knew we were taking it, I was met with silence. They are so sneaky…I kind of like it.

Grey drives out of the space, and I roll down the window. The smell of spices and cigars is extremely thick in the air, but the others don't seem to notice or mind. But of course they'd be used to it, he is their uncle, except maybe Grey, since he's been away for a long time. When I look into the rearview, Grey takes deep breaths, and a smile dances on his lips. I guess he misses the smell. I smile and look into my hands on my lap.

"Okay, before we get there, let me tell you the rules," Emilio announces, turning to me from the passenger seat. "One: do not split from the group. A lot of bad people attend these festivals—"

"Too late there, bud," Isabella interrupts, black eyes glinting with mischief. "She's already with him." She nods in Grey's direction.

Sofía laughs, Emilio cackles, clapping his hands, and Grey merely smirks but keeps quiet as he drives. Me, on the other hand, I feel incredibly hot and swallow a lump in my throat.

"Was, past tense." I string my lips in a tight-lipped smile. "What are your other rules?"

He tells the rest, but I zone out because they become ridiculous. He tells me not to breathe when walking past a man in bones that stands on the corner, whatever that means. And soon enough, he and Sofía get in an argument over something, I don't know exactly. Isabella is snapping pictures with her head out the window to catch the natural moonlight. I'm scared she'll hit her head on something or drop her phone. But apparently, she knows what she's doing. Mind you, she said that while her lips were puckered in a horrendous duck position. I just rolled my eyes and fell into my own little world.

Instead, I lean on the window, let out a breath, and close my eyes. I enjoy the soft breeze as we drive over the tremendously long bridge that connects the country to the city. Despite the odd, sexual way he made it sound, it is hot tonight. Definitely hotter than it gets in the night-time in Miami. I'm very glad I didn't just wave off his words and dressed in a mid-thigh white skirt, flats with cute flower prints, and a loose floral crop top shirt.

"You look very cute, by the way," Isabella says as she gets back in the car.

"Who? Me?" I look around, confused.

"Well, I'm definitely not talking about Sofia," she scoffs, and I stifle a laugh.

"Fuck you," Sofía gasps.

"Sorry, don't believe in incest," Isabella jokes, giving a fake pout.

Sofía responds with a nice little middle finger pointed at her cousin, who slaps it away.

"But she is right. You do look really nice." Sofía suddenly stops bickering with her cousin and gives me an enormous smile.

"Yeah, I wonder why you look all dressed up… hmmm," Emilio butts in, tapping his chin.

Even the girls hum and tap their chins.

"Oh my gosh, shut up." I cover my face in humiliation while they laugh their butts off. I peek through my fingers and make the mistake of looking in the rearview mirror. Grey has this little smile, but he doesn't say anything. His eyes meet mine, and I'm glad my palms are covering my mouth and the smile that mirrors his.

***

Apparently, Emilio's rules do not apply to the others, because the minute Grey parks his car in a lot and enters the festival grounds, they split up...which means I am alone with Grey. However, I don't think there should be a problem. So far tonight, he's been uncharacteristically quiet and calm. I can't help but anticipate for when he snaps, but for now, I am enjoying his tranquil silence.

I try not to feel anything when he points out different things as we walk. The festival is held in the town square. There are a lot of people, maybe hundreds. He says a lot of people come to town just for tonight. Vendors line the cobblestone street. Bright banners of yellow and red hang along the light poles and are draped along balconies of the old-fashioned but beautiful buildings. A salsa song is blasting through the air. Everyone is dancing in vivacious colors and laughing and kissing and singing, and everything is just so perfect.

"This is so beautiful," I breathe in awe, staring up at the people dancing on their balconies. I laugh when I find a woman twirling her daughter to the beat of the upbeat music.

"Yeah, it's pretty something," Grey replies, his voice raspy and velvety. It sparks goose bumps along my arms and makes me beam up at him. I nearly jump in shock when I find he's already staring at me.

"Incoming, love-birds," someone shouts from behind us.

Grey snakes his arms around me and pulls me to

the side in time for Emilio running past us. I laugh as I listen to him hoot and make fist pumps as he dashes to a churro stand.

"Oooh, I want one. Come on!" I grab Grey's hand and feel my stomach bubble at his touch. It's both amazing and insane how, even after all the times we were together in a much more intimate way, simply holding his hand can make my knees weak and stomach uneasy. We wait in line for a few minutes, me bouncing because of my irrevocable love for churros. He just laughs and shakes his head but stays quiet. At this point I'm uneasy. I have never not heard him speak or make some rude or funny comment since the day I met him. I don't like it one bit.

"Which one do you want?" he asks as he begins to take out his wallet.

"El chocolate, por favor," I tell the lady and quickly take out money from my purse. But before I can hand her the money, he grabs my wrist with the money and pulls it back.

"Gracias," he says with a small smile as he hands her the money.

"I can pay for myself, Grey." I brought some money in case of emergencies and if I just wanted to splurge. And this definitely counts as splurging money.

He makes a face as I am handed the chocolate-covered churro, and we walk away from the cart. "I didn't want you to."

"Why not? We're not together."

He winces slightly like my words stung him. "That doesn't matter." He looks around, thumbs resting in his jean pockets. "You're in my hometown, my country. I don't want you spending money when I can take care of it for you."

Wow, that is very gentlemen-like of him. I'm kind of shocked.

"But that doesn't mean you should feel obligated," I point out.

He shrugs. "Who says I do? I wanted to."

I stare at him for a few moments, expecting him to say some sarcastic or sly comment. But when he doesn't, I just hum, and he breaks into a genuine smile. I look away and try to come up with a reason for his random kindness that comes without strings and eat while I do.

We continue strolling along the street, weaving through groups of dancing teens who have lied to their parents to party. I laugh at the thought that I would have never done something like that. Sneak out and go to the library? Yes. But not something as wild and fun like this, not that being at the library isn't fun. It's just not as high-spirited as this.

"Oh, hey, check this out," he says excitedly, grabbing my arm after I throw out the wrapper when I finish my delicious churro. I am shamefully licking my left thumb of remaining chocolate filling when he grabs my right and tugs me from the garbage. My shocked yelp is swallowed in my mouth before I finally let my thumb go and struggle to keep up with Grey's long strides as he runs. *Geez, he can run all the way to Canada in one stride if he wanted.*

He comes to a slow stop behind a large, very loud crowd of mostly men. I blush and apologize like a machine gun as he pushes through to the front. I gasp, but it is drowned out by the sickening crunch of bones and grunts and groans and everything you'd expect from two grown, shirtless men, covered in *blood,* fighting.

I nervously side-glance at Grey, who is beaming at the two men like he's in a candy shop, but instead of candy in gumball machines, there's fighter gloves. He must have been a real hard kid to give gifts to.

"Um, what is this?" I ask, kind of scared of the uneasy glances from some of the men. But they quickly avert their eyes the moment I feel Grey tense up behind me. He must have given them an intimidating look. I blush and look at the ground, not able to look in his eyes.

"*La pelea del año*," he says. "All the fighters and boxers in town come here to compete for a big match."

"In the middle of a festival?" I laugh, and he chuckles a little and brushes his hair back. I watch with fascination as those pesky dimples of his come out to play.

"Yes, they know people come from all over for tonight."

"Ah." I nod, understanding, grimacing as one of the bulkiest men throws his fist across the other's face. I look away and say, "They know they're getting a huge audience and get to show off."

"Yep," he says with sadness thick in his voice. "My, uh, my grandfather was a boxer."

I gasp. "Really?"

He nods and rubs his lower lip, pinches. "Yeah,

it sort of runs in the family blood. But it stopped at my father. He didn't like the idea of it because of the pain the loser had to deal with. Didn't like the violence one bit…that's why he hated me so much." He looks at me, and I want so desperately to hug him. He looks so gutted. "Because I was addicted to the fighting."

"Like you said, it runs through your veins." I tap his forearm with a small smile, and he flashes me one…but the frown wins.

"Yeah, I guess…"

My heart squeezes, and I find myself linking my fingers with his. He looks up and his eyes widen for a second, like he doesn't believe what I'm doing. I don't even know what I'm doing…but what I do know is that I physically can't handle him being so distraught.

"Why don't we go walk around?" I suggest.

He hesitantly nods, glancing at the fighting men. "That'd be nice, actually."

I smile widely and politely ask people to step back, and they do. I give Grey a pointed look, but he just rolls his eyes and I laugh. Once we are free of the crowd, I feel as though I can breathe. The smell of blood seriously makes me sick.

"Why are you being so nice?" I blurt out.

He laughs and looks at me with a confused expression. "Aren't I always nice?"

"Um…not *all* the time." My voice is kind of high-pitched, and he smiles.

He shrugs and kicks a random rock at his feet. "I guess being with a pretty girl at a place like this brings out the pleasant side of me." He nudges my shoulder.

"Don't do that," I whisper.

"Don't do what?" He furrows his brows.

"That—be all nice and stuff. It's freaking me out," I admit, and he laughs. "I'm being serious."

"I think that's the problem, don't you?" He raises his brows in challenge. "It's a festival, Liv. Just go with the flow." He squints his eyes a bit, and my breathing hitches. I have to look away because of all the feelings he's conjuring in the pit of my stomach.

"I'll do that as soon as I do something," I say quickly, and he looks at me weirdly. But I take a step away from him and let go of a breath I wasn't aware I'd taken hostage. I pull out my phone from my white shoulder bag and pull up Noah's contact. My heart squeezes when I see he hasn't responded to the text I sent him before we left the house. I sigh and begin typing a message, letting him know what's happening. In case, you know…

A loud shrill beside me makes me jump and drop my phone. I look to my left, clutching my chest while my heart loses control. A tall man wearing a sharp suit and a black fedora, face painted like he's a skeleton, is screaming at me. What the hell is wrong with him? I feel myself flush bright red when I notice a lot of people are laughing at me, one of them being Grey. I nudge him in the stomach before snatching my phone from the ground and speed-walking away.

"What the hell was that?" I hiss at Grey when he catches up to my side.

"*El cráneo gritando*," he answers calmly. I must look as confused as I feel, because he sighs and explains, "Emilio told you about him in the car. The man in bones?" (The screaming man.)

"What's his problem, though? He can't just go around screaming at people who walk by. That's crazy!" I exclaim, and he laughs. "It's not funny," I whine, and he laughs harder.

"Oh, yes, it is. You should have seen your face!" He laughs his head off, dimples popping into his hair-dusted cheeks.

I roll my eyes and examine my phone that now has a crack in the middle. "Dang it," I curse when I switch it on and see the screen has some weird pixels. "Damn you, skeleton man!"

"What's wrong?" He leans over, his shoulder brushing against mine. I ignore the tingles in my fingertips as I run my hand along the crack.

"There's a crack," I reveal to him.

"Don't sweat it." He shrugs.

I snap my head at him and scoff. "This is my phone I'm talking about here. You know, my means of communication."

He shrugs again. I wish he would just stop doing that. "So?"

"So?" He sounds insane. I can't be laid back about this.

"You're too reserved sometimes," he says. "You need to let go, Liv."

"I can let go," I defend myself.

Oh no…

His eyes sparkle as he works my nerves, like the first time he challenged me to go to that god-awful frat party. "Then come dance with me." He crosses his arms with the smuggest look ever. It makes my blood boil, and I grit my teeth.

"Okay, then—I will!" I stomp past him and faintly hear him snickering behind me as I emerge into the massive group of people dancing. I suddenly realize how good he is at getting me to do things and turn around to tell him to suck it. But I run into his chest, and he smiles like he's won, because, well, he already has. Denying this now would just make me look stupid and like a baby. But I am neither. I just roll my eyes and begin moving around to the beat of an old song, "Maria Maria" by Santana.

He takes my hips in his hands, and I stiffen, beginning to reel back. "No, look." His eyes dash around the vibrant crowd. I look around and feel myself heat up at what I find: couples dancing against each other. But when I look closer, I notice the girls are shaking and moving their hips in a really sexy, intimidating way. They are also dressed in tight-fitting clothes and are showing off their insane wide hips and toned stomachs. I feel myself gulp as I realize I look like I'm dressed for church on Easter Sunday.

And Grey must want them. They're all so beautiful and not afraid to show off their sexy sides. That's why he pointed them out.

"I don't feel good," I lie and begin to pull away again, but his grip on me is like steel—I don't budge.

"Don't lie, just dance. Follow my lead," he instructs. I look down and watch as he moves like the guys, slow and sensual against me. I feel flushed and shake my head. He finally steps back and frowns at me as his eyes roam my face. "What's wrong?"

"I..." I gulp and look around. "I can't...*dance* like *that*."

"Yes, you can. I've witnessed it myself," he argues.

"But I'm not...I'm not like *them*." Ugh! I sound so stupid. I look away from him, ashamed.

He tsks and cups my face, forcing me to look at him. "I don't care about them. I like you for *you*. Now, show me you're different and dance, god damnit." He breaks into a contagious grin, because I mirror it and hesitantly nod my head.

I begin to move again and look around at the girls again, but he forces me to look into his eyes. I smile small, blushing profusely. I close my eyes and actually let myself get lost in the beat of the music. I swing my hips from side to side as best as I can and dance to the music.

"There you go," he praises, voice thick with desire.

I open my eyes and feel my mouth drop open. He looks incredibly sexy: his black button down is open, revealing his tan, tatted chest and chiseled stomach and torso. His black hair looks slicked with sweat or the night mist under the intense light from the bulbs hung all around. And his eyes, oh boy, they're shooting right through me, and they are laced with fire and I feel as though I am out of breath.

He turns me around like he's trying to hold back from doing something, and I find I am grateful he did. I continue to dance and let my head fall onto his back. The laughter and loud music are drowned out...the only thing I can hear is his heavy, hot breathing from behind me. I can no longer feel the vibrations of the music system, but the even more prominent beat of his heart on my back. I lick my lips and bite my lips as his arms drape around my hips, helping me move them from side-to-side. I gasp but it's easily drowned out by his little groan as he slowly slides my skirt up my thigh.

I should get off of him. I should stop him. I should because...oooh, his hand is moving and moving and moving...why should I stop him?

"No..." I begin, then it hits me. "No, Grey—stop." I turn around and place my hands on his hard chest. Oh, such a wrong move.

"Why should I?" he rasps and leans down. I moan when his hands cup my butt, and I fling my head back. His soft lips gently kiss my right mouth corner. "When I know you want this as much as me?"

"Because I am—" I begin breathlessly.

He cuts me off when he smashes his lips onto mine. I am engulfed in flames. My toes curl, and I lean on my toes to help. I find my fingers wrapping in his hair while his squeeze into my butt, making me moan and drop my mouth open. His tongue slides in and teases mine. I smile a little when he finds a certain spot that always makes me laugh because fuck, can he tease.

He pulls away too soon and smirks against my lips as I pant for air.

"You were saying," he breathes.

"Wet..." I mumble.

He laughs a little, and I smile because of it, tracing a tattoo on his right pec.

"Don't be so fucking cocky," I warn, dragging my nails down his chest.

He hisses, but his eyes light with obvious pleasure, and he opens his mouth to say something.

I swallow his immature reply with my mouth meeting his.

Chapter Eighteen

We got home around two in the morning. I have never felt so…energized, so alive. Grey and I danced all night and drank and drank until we couldn't anymore. He said, "Screw being a chauffeur," and forced Isabella to drive, since she was the oldest. I had so many churros and bought a lot of souvenirs for everyone back home. The thought of a certain boy dimmed my mind for a second, but then my lips found a certain pair I hadn't realized I craved so desperately until they devoured me last night. I came back to the house drunk out of my mind and exhausted.

Waking up the next day, I feel a headache the size of Russia swelling inside my brain. I slowly sit up and instantly regret it. It feels like a rubber band is wrapped around my head and pulls me back onto the pillow beneath me. I close my eyes and groan, rubbing my temples in a foolish attempt to ease the throbbing ache. As I thought it would, it does absolutely nothing.

I groan some more and wiggle around as if it will

177

relieve the pain. All it does is set off a low rumble beside me. I stiffen, thinking it's a bear. But then I look down and actually feel the legitimate fear ease off my chest. It's just Grey. I look again and find myself giggling. His mouth is ajar, and his tongue is hanging out of the side of his mouth, like a sleeping puppy.

"An adorable puppy," I mumble to myself, poking his nose. He scratches it and turns onto his stomach. I frown, not able to see his face anymore, and lean up on my elbows. The bed is incredibly small, but he has managed to fit on it with me. He is shoved against the wall, one of his boot-covered feet lapping over mine. One of his huge arms is wrapped around me tightly, like he's a strap meant to hold me down instead of a human being. I fall back onto the bed, extremely confused.

What the heck happened last night? All I can remember is drinking what felt like one hundred shots of tequila and then…nothing. That's it. I rub my forehead and try to find a clear image from the collection of blurry memories in my head like it's a scrapbook. It is a really crappy scrapbook. I can't believe it's mine. If there is one thing that can help clear the fog in my mind, it is a nice, long, hot shower. And if that doesn't work, then I will resort to one of Earth's finest creations: coffee.

I grip Grey's hand and pull it off. I begin to get up when he claims my waist and yanks me into his chest. "Oh, come on," I groan as he snuggles his face in my neck. He raises his leg higher and gets comfortable, exhaling heavily on my neck. He's getting comfortable. And so am I. I close my eyes and begin to drift into a peaceful sleep when there is a loud knock on the door.

"Are you guys still fucking? You were pretty loud night, didn't think you'd fall asleep," I hear Isabella tease as the door creaks open.

I quickly sit up and immediately regret it because of the pins and needles rattling behind my eyes. "Shut up," I manage to groan, falling back down and rubbing my eyes.

"Oooh, they so fucked." I open my eyes and lean over the bed, finding Emilio behind her, snapping his fingers. "Shame, shame, shame—I know your name," he sings.

"Oh my gosh," I mutter, rubbing my nose bridge and watch as Sofía joins the shaming party.

"So? How was the bang?" She holds up her mouth when I prepare to tell her nothing happened. "But please, refrain from *too* many details." She sips the tea in her hand and says, "He's still my cousin, after all."

"Nothing happened!" I hiss, cursing myself for being too loud even though it was a bare whisper.

"Right," they say and nod simultaneously.

I roll my eyes and throw my pillow at them. They all squeal, but the door shuts, and I rush over to it, ignoring all the pain in my body, and lock it. I lean against it and slump to the floor, cradling my pulsating head. I swear, I am *never ever* going to touch another alcoholic drink in my life. The after-pain is just not worth it.

After a couple of minutes of waiting for the beating in my head to stop, I manage to stand. I limp to the small closet and open the door. I gently run a hand down the hung-up lace black dress and feel tears in the bottom of my throat. Today is Grey's grandfather's funeral. I think it's why they wanted to go out so bad. And why Mateo didn't come, because he wanted to be alone to prepare for today. Because they wanted to distract themselves from the hurt that awaited them.

I look back at Grey's sleeping form and feel a sagging wave of sympathy. I walk over to him, ignoring the pain ricocheting in my head, and bend down. I untie and gently take off his boots. I take off his jeans, since it is very hot, and he may be feeling it tenfold. His shirt is next to go. I fold them all and place them in the hamper.

I then leave the room and tiptoe down to the kitchen. I freeze at the doorway. Alma is sitting at the kitchen table in tears and everyone is surrounding her. I feel my heart slow down as I hold back tears. The feeling of a loved one being ripped from your hands is not a great feeling. It makes you think that the world has ended. I rush over, wiggle through people, and hug her, ignoring how I may smell like liquor and blow the lie Grey told her about last night. It doesn't matter. She needs all the love and support she can get.

After a while of her praising me, I kiss her forehead, and she beams up at me like the sun. I smile at her, and she rubs my hand before letting me go. I maneuver around the kitchen, making a cup of herbal tea. When it's ready, I quietly pad back up to the room. Grey is in the same position I left him in. I smile softly at his heavy snores and leave the tea next to him on the table beside the bed. I open the window so some fresh air can come in. I then grab my toiletry bag, makeup bag, my dress and shoes, and run across the hall to the bathroom.

I strip, fold my clothes, and put away my stuff, hanging the dress. I brush my teeth and take my iron pill. I feel guilty finding my morning-after pills. Some part of me knew I'd cave in to Grey, and I had that part of me, but I can't help it. He's like a drug I can't quit. Anyway, we haven't done anything sexual at least, so I don't have to worry about going all the way. I don't take my anti-depressants, though. I stopped taking them after I took too many. They never did anything but make me feel less like myself and I need a clear mind, not a cluttered one.

Since I have a clear mind, I go back to trying to find out what exactly happened last night. The very last thing I remember is a very tall skeleton…and then that's it, weirdly enough. Why would I remember a skeleton? Did we go to a cemetery instead or something? Images of bright yellow and red flash behind my eyes. No, we definitely went to the festival. I think I remember dancing and feeling really hot, but other than that, my mind is a complete blank.

"What happened last night?" I whisper to myself, rubbing my lower lip and biting it.

The curtain is ripped back, yanking me out of my head. I jump and face a naked Grey.

"Morning, beautiful," he drawls, his voice thick with sleep.

"Grey, what the fuck?" I shriek, shrinking and trying to cover my body.

"Oh, don't act so shy." He pouts his lips and does the craziest thing ever: he steps into the shower with me, naked, completely naked, like, really, really, naked…he tips my head back in time before I can voice my naughty, derailing thoughts. "Especially not after last night."

"W-what happened last night?" I reiterate my previous question to myself.

He smirks. "I never kiss and tell."

"You basically just did, you ass—"

He kisses me, hard.

My body takes over and pushes my rational mind behind a locked gate. I thread my fingers into his lengthy black hair that can stand a few snips, then hold his stubbly cheeks. This can stay. I love the way it feels against my fingertips. I find myself lifted by his strong arms, my legs wrapped around his tight torso. I unwittingly moan in need. I want him in me. I need to feel him filling me and claiming me.

"Grey, please—"

"Do you have those morning-after pills?" he asks, tugging my bottom lip with teeth.

"I do…now please—"

He cuts off my plea by doing as asked, plunging into me. I cry out, but he quickly clamps his mouth around my open one. He kisses me to the point where my lungs are drowning in fire. I grip his hair and he groans and wraps one hand around my neck. I moan as he grips my throat a little. I kiss him fiercely and wholly, loving the feeling of him in me. He pounds and grows deeper and faster with each thrust.

"You like that, *princesa*?" he whispers, pulling his mouth off me.

I nod and close my eyes in pleasure when I feel his mouth on my right nipple. "I—ugh…" I bite my lip, swallowing a scream. He tugs the other one, and I tighten my fingers around his hair. He groans against me and shifts his tongue to the other. I roll my eyes back and can't help but yelp.

"You are so fucking perfect," he pants as he removes his mouth and kisses up the valley of my breasts. I open my mouth in anticipation, and he meets it, smashing his lips against mine. I drag my fingers down his neck and smirk when he shivers at my cold, slow touch. However, the smirk dies the minute he picks up speed, thrusting into me so fucking deep and so beautifully fast, hitting a certain spot that causes me to see the stars in heaven. "And all mine, always."

His. Hmmm…it really nice being his to fuck…wait. His? I am not his…but he is—this feels so fucking good. What am I trying to say?

I bite my lip and am drawn out of my muddled mind, humming as he begins to suck on my neck. "Y-you'll leave a mark." I don't want to wear much makeup. It'd be unnecessary since it's hot out. Plus, I don't want to appear disrespectful by wearing so much cover-up to a funeral.

Funeral…why am I going to a funeral?

"Mmmm, Grey. That feels so good." I moan and tug on his hair.

"Fuck, you feel so fucking good," he grumbles, digging one of his hands into my skin.

"G-Grey," I stutter his name and close my eyes,

183

biting my lip. I slowly open my eyes when I feel a familiar pit in my stomach. "I'm, fuck, Grey, I'm—" I try to get out, but the words are stuck in my throat. I feel like I'm being ripped apart but in a strangely good way. I zone out as I feel him clench around me, and I feel myself hitting my high. My eyes widen when they land on my black dress for his grandfather's funeral, which I promised to attend with him despite...

Fuck!

Despite Noah's wishes.

"Fuck!" I voice my thoughts mixed with the feeling of ultimate pleasure as I reach my climax. I writhe against him as he still pounds into me, pulling himself there as well. I grip his neck and arch my back as his lips crash against mine. I kiss him with everything I have and scream into his mouth. I pull back, lightly sucking his lower lip. And that pushes him over the edge.

"Jesus fucking—ugh! Shit," he stutters, releasing inside of me.

I pant, completely out of breath. He pants as well, his forehead pressed against mine. It hits me tenfold when I realize what I've just done and who I've just betrayed and proved right.

"Fuck, Grey," I groan.

"Again?" he jokes with a little laugh.

"I'm being serious." I push his shoulder, and I fall to my feet. I look up at him. "We just had sex."

"Um, and?" He squints his eyes, and I groan, pushing past him to the curtain.

"*And* I am not with you," I remind him as I step out. I grab a towel and quickly dry myself.

184

"So?"

I turn around and gawk at him; he's washing up. I tear my hungry gaze from him and shake my head, saying, "You have no shame."

"Right, but *we* have something you'd never feel with that Ken doll," he says rudely.

I stop as I am putting on my underwear. "Are you serious? I just cheated on him!"

"And how is that my fault?"

I pause as I shimmy into my dress. "You know I am with him."

"Yet you didn't stop me!" he shouts, pissed off now.

I close my eyes and nod. "You're right."

"I'm what now?" He sounds shocked he was right.

I roll my eyes in annoyance and stomp over to my flats. "I said you were right." I hop into them and face him; he is dripping soap suds. Jesus, does he look good...I have no shame. I hate myself! Ugh! "I just can't do this to him. I need to tell him."

"So tell him." He shrugs.

"But what does this make us?" I ask hesitantly, scared of what happened the last time this happened. I mean, the last time we rekindled in this way, he shooed me away like I was dirt on the bottom of boots. So, I am more than a little apprehensive as to the result now.

He shrugs. "Nothing."

My tears come, and they come fast. "Great. No progress has been made and I just broke something that could have meant more with a guy who deserves much more than me, a fucking slut.

Thanks for everything, Grey."

His face falls, and I can see the regret in his eyes. "Liv—" he starts, but I'm too hurt and ashamed to hear the rest.

I rush out of the bathroom and into our bedroom. I am so glad we're leaving tomorrow. It has been amazing being here with his family who are so kind and welcoming. The town and country are gorgeous and a lot of fun, but I can't stay here with *him* any longer.

I grab my laptop out of my suitcase and sit on the bed. I pull up the Skype application and nervously hover my finger above Noah's contact. What if I break his heart too much, and he hates me forever? I won't be able to live with him hating me too. Another tear strolls down my face as I pull my finger back and tug my bottom lip.

The door bursts open. Grey walks in, nearly naked, except a blue towel is draped around his hips.

"I didn't mean it like that," he pants, holding out a hand.

"I know," I huff out.

He looks really confused and taken aback. "Huh?"

"I'm just being really dramatic," I admit, running my hand across my mouth. "It's complicated, I get it. But we'll figure it out later, right?"

He stares at me as if he's trying to solve the Da Vinci code, then slowly nods. "Yes." It sounds more like a question, and I laugh like the anxious, pathetic thing I am.

I flicker my eyes to the screen. "Can you give me

a sec?"

He doesn't respond.

I look up and wipe away a fallen tear. "Please?"

He's biting his lip and looks like he's been kicked in the gut. "I didn't want to ruin this for you. This *thing* you have with Noah."

"It's okay," I say honestly, my voice breaking. "You were right, I didn't feel anything with him. I was still in love with you. I was being unfair. I think I would do this even if we didn't just do that. I would have strung him along, and he doesn't deserve it. He's a good guy."

He takes a step forward, probably to give me a hug.

But I can't. Not right now. I need to do this, and I need him gone.

"Please, don't. Just…just give me a second and…and then I'm yours."

He runs a hand through his hair. "Do you really want to?"

"I have to…"

"Which part?" he questions.

I shrug. "Both. I'm miserable without you, and I can't hurt Noah more than I already have."

His eyes light with an undecipherable emotion, and he nods. "I'll give you some time," he promises, then leaves the room.

I take a deep breath, decide my feelings don't matter right now, and click the button.

His face appears a few seconds later. I gasp. His expression is somber and exhausted. It looks like he already knows and saw this coming.

I don't say anything for a while, and neither does

he.

We just stare at each other, knowing the inevitable has happened—I've fallen in Grey's trap again. And I don't think there is any escaping this time.

Chapter Nineteen

Grey was stiff and cold during the ceremony. I tried a few times to hold his hand, but each time he clutched his hands into fists. When he did it for the umpteenth time, I sighed and cupped my hands in my lap. I gave up on him for the time being. I knew he was just stuck in a bubble of shock and overwhelming pain. I knew he would come around when he felt he was able to. But for that moment, I just sat beside him and was his shoulder to cry on if he needed it.

His gloominess stains him and doesn't budge, even when the service is over. Despite his need to be cold and to himself, I hold his hand the entire way home and whisper sweet inklings of hope in his ear. I even kiss his cheek sometimes, and only then do I see him respond.

He grips my hand harder and closes his eyes. I watch closely and feel my heart slip from beneath me when I notice something very small, you wouldn't have seen it unless you were really, really close: tears dot across his long, thick eyelashes. I quickly grab a tissue from my black purse and try my best to be discreet when wiping them away. But everyone is too distraught to even notice.

I kiss his cheek again. I admire this breathtaking statue and lean on his shoulder. I take a few deep lungfuls, and he follows suit. I have my hand on his leg as an open invitation to take it when he needs it. We park in front of the house and everyone deftly leaves the car that reeks of silent tears and sadness. He finally takes my hand before laying in my lap and bursting into tears.

"Why did this have to happen?" he sobs, and my heart snaps in two like a toothpick.

"I know, it hurts," I coo, brushing back his hair and twirling a piece. I have to try my hardest not to join him in his breakdown. I have to be strong for him or this will just get worse. We stay silent in the car for a few more minutes before I suggest, "Do you want to go inside? Your abuela made a lot of sweets she said you loved as a child." He stiffens, then sits up and stares me in the eyes intensely. I swallow and shake my head. "Or we can go for a walk. Whatever you want."

"What I want is to—" he begins.

A knock on the window next to me cuts him off. I turn around, facing a teary-eyed Isabella.

"Abuela wants to talk to Grey," she informs, dabbing under her eyes.

I nod and offer her a small smile. "He'll be right there."

She glances at Grey, then back at me. "Okay," she croaks. I watch as she heads back into the house. I want to console her too and everyone else

190

grieving, especially Alma, but she wants Grey right now, and I have to give everyone space if it's what they need.

I turn back to Grey. "You were saying something?"

"Nothing," he says firmly, voice cold and face hardened again.

My heart plummets.

"Grey…" I sigh and take his hands in mine. He rips them away and storms out of the car. "Grey!" I open the door closest to me and rush up the stairs. But when I realize he isn't slowing down one bit, I stop and try to catch my breath. Dang it! I was doing so well, getting him to open up. But then we were interrupted and now he's snapped back into off-standish Grey. The most difficult Grey to talk to. However, he probably just needs to let out some steam by himself.

I painfully decide to leave him be until he comes to me like I offered in the church. The church…sitting in the pews while family members and close friends spoke about Grey's grandfather reminded me so much of Jonah's funeral.

The thought makes me dizzy, and I lean against a wall in the living room. I can still remember that somber day perfectly. It had been cloudy that day; a few tear drops broke from the gray sky. There was crying, so much of it. I felt as though I could drown in it indefinitely. I couldn't swim then, and it frightened me. That night is when the nightmares started.

"Liv, are you okay?" I lift my head to Emilio's concerned face. His eyes are bloodshot, and his normally tousled black hair is somewhat tamed by gel. His black tie has come undone and he just doesn't look or sound like his normal self.

"Yeah, I'm fine," I lie and drop my hand from my aching chest. I hate funerals, always have and always will. "What about you?" I am not important now; he and the rest of the family and friends mourning are.

He shrugs and lets out a long sigh as he stares at the floor. "Tired, I guess…I wasn't able to sleep last night. I just kept dreaming of him, you know?" He looks up as if to check if I do understand. I nod frantically. I know about that more than anyone. He goes back to looking at the floor. "We would always go fishing on the weekends, but never catch anything. He was convinced there was this great big fish that was eating all the small ones."

I laugh, and his black eyes meet mine. "He sounded really sweet."

"Yeah…he was." He smiles a knowing smile, shoving his hands in his pockets.

I open my mouth to say something, but I have the feeling like I am being stared at. I raise my eyes over his right shoulder and find Grey staring at me. The look he's giving me sends actual shivers down my spine. He gestures to the stairs beside me, and I raise a brow. He excuses himself from a couple of his uncles, then strides through the packed room like he owns it. I always forget how intimidating he can be. He brushes past my shoulder as he walks by, heading up the stairs.

"I'm sorry, I have to go use the…" I trail, smiling apologetically, and he nods. I give him one last assuring smile and rub his shoulder before walking up the creaky steps. It is quiet and empty up here because everyone is gathered on the lower level.

"Grey?" I softly call his name, opening our bedroom door.

He's looking out the window that faces the front yard. "You wanna know what I was saying in the car?" he asks, foot tapping. He looks much taller with how mysterious he is being, his body not facing me.

"Um, yes?" I croak, not sure what is happening.

He finally turns around and I frown; his top buttons are done, his hair is a complete mess, and his eyes are red and puffy.

"Oh, Grey." I walk over to him, intending to hug him, but he pulls me into his chest and clasps his lips over mine.

My body instantly responds by pressing into him. He walks me backward, and I am pressed against the window. Scared some people may still be out front, I push and turn him around so that he is on the wall. The kiss is hot and leaves me wanting so much more, it's killing me. But then I grip his collar and remember why he is wearing it.

I pull away and swallow, my cheeks flushed. "What are you doing?"

"I need a distraction," he grumbles, pulling me into his lips. I instantly moan and feel myself grow stimulated by his words and what he so desperately wants. But I don't think this is healthy—no, it definitely isn't.

I pull away again and grip his collar. "Not now,"

I whisper, but he just groans impatiently and walks us back to the bed. I fall back on it, and he begins to leave marks on my neck with his mouth and tongue. I moan and nearly forget what I am trying to say. "Grey…we can't."

He forcefully leans up and snaps, "Why not?"

I nearly cower under his intense, heavy eyes. "Because your family is very close by…and you just came from you grandfather's funeral," I whisper the last part.

He rolls his eyes. "So?" He goes back to kissing my neck, but as much as I love it, I can't let this happen when he's like this.

"Grey…no. I said no!" I push him off me and quickly sit up.

He is practically fuming, standing up quickly, hands tugging at his hair. "I said I needed a fucking distraction! If you aren't going to give me that, then why the fuck are you here?"

I grimace, and his face softens instantly. "I know you're just really emotional right now…but you can't talk to me like that."

"I know, I—I'm sorry. I just…" He reaches out to me, then shakes his head and steps back. "I've gotta get out of here. I'm sorry, Liv." I believe his eyes, so I nod and watch him leave, shutting the door after him.

I groan, my head in my hands. I know how he's feeling. He's being bombarded with so many emotions.

"Liv." I look up and find Sofía standing in the doorframe. "Abuela Alma asked if you could help clean up, the party's over."

"Sure, I'll be down in a second," I tell her, and she nods and turns away. But then she stops like she forgot something and looks at me again.

"Is everything okay between you and Grey?" she asks.

"Yes, why do you ask?" I am confused until I figure she saw him storm out of the house. "He's just a little emotional."

"Oh, okay." She nods, eyes darting to the floor. I cautiously watch as her entire demeanor descends into solemnity.

"Are you all right?" I ask her, and she nods quickly.

"I'm fine." She closes the door before I can say anything else.

**

Grey doesn't come back to the house. I stayed up for hours until I'd fallen asleep. I was so worried and tried calling using the house phone the entire day, but he hasn't replied at all. I have to get my phone fixed as soon as I'm back in Miami tomorrow, but until then, I slept on the floor in case Grey came back, possibly drunk, which is understandable, and needs the bed. I don't want him sleeping on the floor, not during this hard time. He needs all the comfort he can get.

The sharp bang against the window above me wakes me.

I jolt upright and peer out the window and find him leaning coolly against the passenger door of his uncle's truck. He really has to pay more attention to his keys. I look around the room briefly and put on a black sweater of his. It's huge on me, but it must be cool outside. I slip into a pair of dark blue flats then leave the room. I'm careful to be quiet as I exit the house.

"Where'd you go?" I ask him as I walk up to him.

"I went for a drink," he explains. "Only one," he adds before I can say anything about him driving while drunk. Thank God. I don't want anything bad to happen to him.

"Are you better now?" I ask, cupping his face, standing on my toes, and bringing his head down so he is practically bent over. He laughs at our height circumstances, and I giggle. I bite my lip when he stares at my lips. I peck his lips just because I've been so very concerned, plus I may miss them even though we just made out feverishly hours before. I can never get enough of him.

"Yes," he says, and I narrow my eyes skeptically.

"Mm-hmmm."

He laughs. "I am not lying. I've calmed down. I swear."

I look into his eyes and the ghost smile on his lips, then nod. "Okay."

"Good." His eyes drop to my lips, and he bites his lip before looking into my eyes again. "Now, have you changed your mind?" I suck in a sharp breath when he brushes hair behind my ear. I blush, knowing I must look insane, my hair wild and dressed in only his sweatshirt and pajama shorts. But he didn't exactly give me a lot of time to get dressed.

"About?" I gulp, feeling the wetness between my legs.

He must have a deep connection to it, because he glances down and licks the corner of my mouth.

Oh God.

"You know what," he groans, and I nod. "Distract me, please? I need you so...*badly,* Liv," he pleads with a whimper that makes me shiver. He presses his excitement against my abdomen, and I barely hold back a moan. I swear, it's like when we had sex in the shower; he ignited this extreme thirst for him, this burning hunger that is ripping its way through me.

"But—" I begin weakly.

He silences my whimper with his mouth. I instantly let my mouth drop and feel his tongue press against mine. I wrap my arms around his neck and stand on my toes to help him reach my mouth a little easier. He cups my face gently and kisses me really slowly, tasting and savoring me. My knees weaken, yet I grow incredibly needy for him...for more. He walks us backward until my back hits the passenger door.

He pulls away too soon and leans his forehead against mine. "Get in the car," he orders, and this time, I don't disobey him.

I nod and press my lips to his again, desperate for his soft lips. I kiss him hard and get a little taste of my own. I moan at how great he tastes and the way my body heats up by his hands gripping me, holding me.

When I pull away, he looks as greedy as me.

"As long as there's more of this," I whisper, and he nods, quickly kissing me.

"This…" He pauses and gently sucks on my bottom lip; a moan slips out of my mouth. "And much more."

Chapter Twenty

He pulls away much too soon. I lean forward to try and re-connect our lips, but he laughs and cups my face. I bite my lip and will my eyes to look into his, not his slightly swollen lips. "Get in the car," he orders, voice gruff, making my knees feel weak. The look in his eyes is intense and makes every nerve in my body stand at attention, much like his erection that pokes dangerously hard, but I love that he's hard for me. "Get in, Liv," he says, and my naughty thoughts fade.

"Why? Where are we going—?"

His lips find mine, shutting me up instantly. "Shut up and get in the car," he whispers haughtily, pulling his lips from mine. I love this dark side of him. I mean, he has always been dark. I've just never admired it so much like I do right now. The glint in his pitch-black eyes, the nefarious crook of his mouth, the look of danger in the way his thumbs are slowly caressing my cheek and lip—it all comes crashing down on me, and I don't mind one bit.

Okay, my subconscious finally swoons.

"S-sure," I stutter like an absolute idiot.

His lips widen, but he doesn't say anything witty, just gives me a chaste kiss on my lips, then rounds the car. His mischievous smile dares me to get in, so I do. He pulls out of the spot as I attach my seatbelt around myself. I quickly undo mine and attach his too. I sit back and blush. What? There's nothing wrong making sure my man is all buckled up and safe. I buckle my seatbelt again before he takes off.

Twenty minutes into the ride, I am quiet, nervous, chewing my lip like it's licorice. Which is pretty impressive considering how much I want to open my mouth and ask him where the heck he's taking us. I want to ask, but I don't want him to tease me. After all we've been through, I am still nervous of being teased. I can't tell if that's a bad thing or good thing.

"You want to know where we're going," he states.

Can he read my mind?

"And you aren't going to tell me," I suggest.

He glances at me with a smirk and raised eyebrow. "Well, aren't we mind readers?" He nudges me in my arm, and I roll my eyes.

We really are, but only when it comes to each other.

I smile and lean against the window, allowing the night breeze to tangle through my unruly curls. I like to think we have a connection, stronger than anyone other than us could possibly understand. Like a bond that ties not only our bodies, but also our minds and souls.

As if sensing my revelation, Grey reaches out and connects my fingers with his. I look at him without holding back how I feel for him. My heart, my soul—everything I could possibly hold in my body, I willingly allow him to take it, conquer it. And as I look into his eyes, I see past all the pain and hurt he has put onto me; I see past the darkness and spot a small spark of light. I want so desperately to reach in there and make a grand light show. I want to show him that he does deserve me, and we do deserve each other, and I do deserve to love him and *be* loved.

Thirty minutes later, we are in the middle of nowhere.

I can't help but be a little confused.

"Where are we—?"

Again, he shuts me up with his lips. The kiss is passionate and makes my heart go wild. He pulls me into his lap, and I tug at the hem of his dress shirt. He kisses me like he's afraid I will disappear. I unbutton his shirt until my fingers hit the cold metal of his belt buckle. I tug at his belt and moan as I grind myself on his impossibly hard member.

"Fuck—don't tease me like that, baby," he grunts, squeezing my bare thigh. "Or you'll regret it."

I nod frantically, believing him.

I gasp in shock when we are flipped, and I am on my back while he is in between my legs. He looks so imperfectly perfect: his dark hair disheveled, inky-black eyes glinting with troublesome intentions, chest, torso, and arms littered with black ink that hold meaning while others are just meant to scare you off. But in all of his blackness, I see light. I want to snuff it out. Who wants a blinding light when you can have this beautiful man with all his flaws and pure love for me in the dark, doing whatever you want, sinful or downright dirty?

"You are so beautiful," I croak, and he bites his lip, furrowing his brows. I watch as he lowers himself onto me, inhaling me from in between my breasts to my neck. I moan and curl my fingers around his neck.

"No, you are the beautiful one," he rasps, making every hair on my body rise. I moan and wiggle beneath him, moving my hips slowly as he drags my shorts down. I impatiently kick my feet, almost kicking him in the face as my flats fly off.

"I am so sorry," I exclaim, sitting up, hands over my mouth.

He laughs but it is soft and not mocking. "It's okay." He glances down, and I do too, blushing even harder. "I'm a little excited too."

I can't help but giggle, and he rolls his eyes and pushes me back. He hovers over me and tips my chin, dragging my head up. Lips touch and a need for him fills me instantly, like I wish he would do to me. Now.

"You know, we can always talk—" I begin, pulling away slightly. But then he grazes his teeth along my teeth and sucks. I moan, wrapping my legs around his waist. "Or not," I breathe, and he laughs, brushing a piece of my hair behind my ear, eyes glued to my lips.

"No talking," he confirms. I gasp and bite my lip when he trails his tough fingertips down my arm…all the way down to my butt. He squeezes it, pulling me toward his chest. "Plus…" he drawls, and I pant with need as he circles his finger around my clitoris. He leans up and sits on his knees. Locking dark, lustful eyes with me, he forcefully pushes my legs apart and smirks. "Abuela always said to never eat with my mouth full." I don't understand what he means until he bends down and cups his mouth around my vagina, tongue running flat down my clitoris.

"Oh my God!" I cry out in surprise and a brutal shock of pleasure.

"Take off the shirt, although you look so fucking sexy in it," he instructs and flicks his tongue, making me cry out again.

I am quick to tug it off and drop it on the floor. I arch my back and weave my fingers through his thick hair, giving it a nice tug. He groans into me, and I make a strangled sound. His tongue flips and circles around me, tasting me on another level. The feeling is almost indescribable. I see stars and push his head harder, greedy for his mouth.

"Please," I moan, gripping my own hair and arching higher. I moan his name and whisper, "Grey mmmm…that feels so good."

"You taste heavenly, *princesa*," he actually moans. I think I am starting to come just hearing it. Then, as if he really wants to make me explode, he grunts in his deepest, yet velvety voice, "*Tan jodidamente bueno. Me haces difícil, lo sabes, ¿Verdad, nena?*" (So fucking good. You make me hard, you know that, don't you, baby?)

I nod, feeling his fingers clutch my thighs. "*Sí,*

Grey. Pero quiero que me enseñes. Por favor, que me jodan. Te necesito tanto que te duela." (Yes, Grey. But I want you to show me. Please, fuck me. I need you so badly it hurts.)

"Fuck, yes," he nearly growls but doesn't budge. His tongue picks up speed, and he even plunges two fingers into me. I scream his name over and over from the shock and pleasure hitting me again and again. He whispers dirty, blush-worthy things while swirling his tongue like the fucking pro he is.

When I finally come, my eyes roll in the back of my head and I yell his name. I am pretty sure the whole of Venezuela has heard. Finally, he puts his weight up on his hands, leaning over me like a dark, fallen angel, lips moist with my release. "Give me a kiss." His voice is rough, but I don't care. I kiss his lips covered with me, and I moan at how good I taste. I lick his lips and suck on his lower one.

"Holy fuck," he drawls, cupping my pussy and playing with my sensitive clitoris. I feel him smile against my lips. "You are just my *Princesa traviesa, ¿No es usted?*" (Naughty little princess/ aren't you?)

I answer him by attacking his lips with mine whilst pulling off his belt. "*¿Qué crees?*" (What do you think?)

"Shit," he says breathlessly, and I giggle, only making him grow in darkness. He kisses me with greed and passion and everything in between. I feel him shift and hear his boots collide with the ground. I unzip his dress pants and tug them and his boxers down forcefully. He leans back until his back is on the wide seat, and I am on top. "Condom," he says just as I am about to get onto his glistening wet dick.

Jesus H. Christ, was I about to get on him without protection? I'm becoming so wild because of him...I think I'm getting addicted to it.

He leans over and digs in his pants pocket. I raise a brow when he pulls out a brand new pack of condoms. "What?" He shrugs, smirking. "I stopped on the way back to the house."

I flush and look away. He had seen this coming. Well, I guess I sort of did too. Like I said, he's started an unbelievable craving for him earlier today.

When the condom is securely placed on him, I smile giddily.

He laughs, but it quickly transforms into a sigh of relief when I slowly sit on him. I do the same and nearly pass out because of how great he feels. "Fuck...*montarme, princesa*," he gripes, holding my waist. (Ride me, princess.)

I nod frantically, slowly rocking my hips against him. "Oh my God!" I exclaim. It feels so deep like this, and I feel like I am going to implode. I continue grinding against him, bouncing a little even, and he cries out my name over and over like a prayer. I splay one hand against his hard stomach while the other is gripped in my curly hair, clutching tightly as if to keep me grounded.

"Fuck, you look...fuck! You look good." His eyes are pinch closed as he struggles to find the right words. "You look so fucking *sexy*," he finally says, drawing the word out.

I suck on my bottom lip before letting both of

my hands fall against his chest. I drag them down and moan while he cries out, lifting his hips to meet mine, "*Y te sientes increíblemente increíble,* Grey. *Tan jodidamente bueno. Oh, mi—*" (And you feel fucking amazing, Grey. So fucking good.) And I'm not lying. Has it ever felt this great? This fucking good to the point that I'm looking down at the planet and the heavens and hell, all combined. I grind my hips harder and feel my sex quake under his cock. "Grey," I groan his name, closing my eyes.

"More," he growls, flipping us over quickly. I don't complain. He grabs one of my legs and throws it over his shoulder and pounds into me, hitting my G-spot too fucking perfectly.

"Grey!" I scream his name on the top of my lungs, my eyes rolling in the back of my head and falling down to my stomach. "Please—" I whimper, not knowing what I mean.

"Please what? Please *fuck you* until you can't remember your fucking name?" he gripes, hitting the spot shaper. I scream his name. "*Fuck you* until your screaming my name so loud, so *hard* you lose your voice?" His hips grow faster, and I grab his torso and drag my fingers down his abdomen, needing something to claw to get my worked-up tension relieved.

"Yes, please. All of the fucking above," I breathe, arching my back while gripping him.

He smirks, and my heart leaps in my chest. He resembles an angel whose intentions are nothing but good. But then he leans down and the light shifts, and his eyes glow through the dark with intentions to rip me apart and suck out my soul. I welcome him all the same and grip his hair as he presses his lips to mine, still thrusting in and out of me haphazardly.

I wrap my arms around his neck and play with the ends of his hair while he works with everything he has in him to slowly drive me to insanity. I migrate my hands down his back, gripping his warm skin between my nails. He cries out in my mouth, and I moan loudly at how it affects me, making me grow tighter around him. He feels it too, and I feel his cock twitch in me. He removes his lips from me and curses my name.

"Come for me, Grey," I moan, my voice guttural. "Please, please, pl—please—ugh, fuck!"

"Fuck, I'm coming, bebé," he announces, leaning back slightly, and I admire the sweat lingering in his hair and across his forehead and muscles, skimming his beautiful array of tattoos. The sight of him makes me come alone.

"Ahhhh!" I scream, gripping his shoulders so tightly, I fear I am causing him to bleed.

He sits up on his knees and fucks me in the deepest, most delicious way possible. "Fuck!" he screams loudly, and I feel his member grow heavy as he comes. I bite my lip and hold in my moans as he continues to pound into me, getting himself off more. As he does, another burst of pleasure hits me and I groan his name, pulling him to me. He sucks my neck, and I stare up at the ceiling of the truck.

Finally, he stills, and I finally breathe for what feels like an eternity. Like I was going to die or implode if I didn't.

He picks me up like a feather and flops down on the seat, pulling most of my body on him.

"I'm—"

He cuts me off by reaching down to the ground and unfurling a plaid blanket, laying it on me completely. I sigh in relief and kiss his chest appreciatively. He really can read my mind.

"Thank you." I blush.

He chuckles, and I stare up at him. "No problem." He brushes my crazy curls past my forehead and pulls me up a little, then lightly brushes his knuckles against my cheek. I close my eyes and lean my head against his warm chest, listening to the soft thump of his heartbeat beneath his chest.

"What are we doing?" I whisper, feeling my eyes grow heavy with exhaustion.

"Shhh…we'll figure it out later." He presses his lips to my forehead for a moment, then pecks my nose. "Just go to sleep now. M'kay?" His soft voice is enough to push me over the edge of sleep.

Chapter Twenty-One

I wake up to the distinct chirping of birds. I groan, shifting slightly, feeling hot yet cold at the same time. I slowly open my eyes and stare through my blurry vision. I sit up and know why I feel cold. I'm sitting on the leather seats of Grey's uncle's truck. Yet I also feel hot because of the Venezuelan morning pouring through the cracked windows. I rub my face and yawn widely, then slump my shoulders. I could really go for some coffee to fully have me up.

I look around to tell Grey we should probably leave now and feel my stomach drop when I don't see him anywhere. He wouldn't ditch me in the middle of nowhere. I know he wouldn't, because I would find him and murder him. I finally settle on putting on clothes so I can get out and look for him. Maybe he went for a morning walk...? Then it hits me, and I snort at myself. Grey barely gets up before one in the afternoon. What makes me think he'd get up when the sun has just risen to *walk*?

When I come up with nothing but his dress shirt

209

from yesterday, I groan in frustration and anger. That asshole took my clothes to wherever he is, including my underwear! I begrudgingly pull on the thankfully big shirt and button it all the way to the top. I am opening the door when I spot a yellow stick-it note on the dashboard on the driver's side. I lean over and snatch it up and read it:

To find me, follow the yellow brick road.

"The hell?" I murmur to myself, flipping to the back in case he wrote something that actually makes sense. I come up with nothing. I crumble it and sigh. "How did I fall for you?"

I jump out of the truck, feeling very exposed and angry. He could have at least left my panties. We are in the middle of nowhere, for God's sake! What if a mad man is driving past, spots me, and steals me away? I would find a way to escape and then kill Grey; that's what I'd do. I look around for a moment before my eyes land on shrubs and the edge of the woods to my right. I look around the barren place, wondering how this is randomly here, then sigh. If he's going to be anywhere, it's in there. In the unknown woods that could be home to how many dangerous species.

"What a gentleman," I grumble, contemplating if I should go find my crazy man in the weird, random woods. I cautiously walk over and look at the ground. There are a group of pretty dandelion flowers. And as I look into the woods, I see there are a rather specific trail of them. There are also more flowers, but they stick out like a beautiful thumb. "Hmmm…" I take a step forward and enter the woods.

I follow the alluring flowers with a little smile. Okay, this is kind of cool and romantic. So, there is a method to his madness. I push branches out of my way as I walk and listen to birds flapping overhead and chatting about their morning, about a weird girl dressed only in a dress shirt with hair that resembles their houses, trampling through their neighborhood.

I stop walking and gasp when I end up in a little hidden stream with a waterfall. The water is incredibly blue, and more of the dandelions surround the edges of it. And in the midst of it is my insane, wild, but romantic man—Grey.

I walk up to the water's edge and cross my arms, watching as he swims under the water, butt-naked. I bite my lip and tilt my head, watching as he approaches me. I sit and place my feet in. The water is kind of cold, but I'm sure it'd be warmer if I were in it.

Grey pops up between my legs with a wide smile. "You made it!"

"Barely clothed and a little pissed off, but yes—I did." I arch an eyebrow, and he smiles sheepishly. "How do you know about this place anyway?" I look around and close my eyes briefly because of the serenity of it all. "It's really beautiful."

"Like someone I know." I open my eyes and look at his smirk.

"Shut up." I scrunch my nose, and he laughs. I admire his dimples. "How'd you find it?"

He shrugs. "Me and a couple of buddies biked

out here one day when I was living here, and we stumbled upon it."

"That's quite a trip to a secluded area, don't you think?" I say in a teasing voice. They probably came all the way out here to do something bad. And I wouldn't be surprised; I know Grey started out as a little baddie and grew into an ever bigger one.

"Okay, so maybe we came out here because Joshua wanted to show off his older brother's BB gun," he says, and I burst into laughter. I knew it! I feel him close to me and open my eyes to find him smiling at me, eyes flickering down at my lips as I laugh. I wrap my arms around his neck. "What? I was curious. Too bad the fucker started testing it out on us."

"Stop," I plead. My stomach is crunching from my laughter. I can imagine a curious little Grey biking out here just to have his ass pelted by a BB gun, running around trying to avoid it, discreetly swearing his vengeance.

"We all jumped in the water and tried to run from it, but he got me in the ass!" he exclaims, and I throw my head back in laughter. "Stop laughing. It isn't nice to laugh at my traumatic past," he whines adorably.

"Oh, I'm sorry." I pinch his cheeks and coo, "How ever did you live after that horrific event?"

"Now you're just mocking me." He smirks, and I shrug.

"You're cute when you're like this."

"Like what?" He chuckles.

I stare into his glistening black eyes and push his soaked hair back. "Open, *funny*—"

He gasps and pinches my waist, and I squeal. "Excuse you, I am always funny."

"Sure." I wink at him, and he narrows his eyes at me. I don't see it coming when he splashes me. "Ahh! Don't do that!" I scramble back on the grass, but he grabs my ankles and pulls me toward him, like he's trying to get me in the water. My eyes widen, and I shake my head. "I can't—I can't swim!"

"I know, I'm going to teach you," he explains, unbuttoning the bottom of the shirt I'm wearing. I clutch it, but then he makes a face like he's saying, "Seriously, being shy? Babe, I've seen every square inch of you." I just flush and let him unbutton the shirt. His eyes stare at my chest, and I bite my lip. He looks into my eyes and grabs my hips. "Hold onto me when you're in, okay? I'm standing over here because it's the shallow end. It gets much deeper over there." He nods over his shoulder, and I follow his gesture, biting into my lip harder.

"Okay…" I say hesitantly. I find it weird how a month or two ago I wasn't afraid of the water. I was diving into ten-foot pools to clear my head when I could have easily drowned. And now, now I'm terrified because I'm more aware of that happening. I guess now I have something I'm afraid to lose…

He gently lifts me, and I stand in the water. I look around, nervous. "I'm not going to let you drown or anything," he says, pulling me further. I give him a small smile and quickly wrap my legs around him when I don't feel the ground anymore, but he's still walking back. I catch him grinning before he spins, and I'm on his back as he swims out to the middle. I close my eyes and lay my head against his back, softly running my fingers along his shoulders. "Having fun back there?" he calls out over the loudness of the waterfall.

"Yup." I kiss just under his ear and laugh when he shudders.

"Wanna see something insane?" he asks, and I hum.

"Will it end with my death?" I ask playfully, and he shifts his eyes to me, shrugging.

"If so, it'd be lovely 'cause I'd be by your side."

"Thanks for making us sound like a pair of toxic teens."

"I'm twenty-one," he argues.

"I know, Grandpa." I stick my tongue at him.

He narrows his eyes, and I giggle. "Do you want to see the cool thing or not?"

I nod and fix myself on his back, biting my lip because of the friction between my legs. He smirks, and I clamp my lips shut and let my head drop against the back of his neck. He laughs at my sudden coyness and continues swimming toward the waterfall. I close my eyes when we pass the pounding water. I gasp when we are in a little cave with a glittering wall that looks like specks of diamonds, but I know it is the light and water making it look that way.

"You can stand," he says, and I hesitantly do.

My feet touch a rock floor, and I look around. "This is amazing." My voice echoes as I crane my head back and touch the wall. It's ragged and sharp. I pull away and look at him. I find him already staring at me with so much emotion, so much

214

passion, I nearly have my knees buckle from the intensity. "What?"

He walks over to me and tilts my head back, the other arm wrapped securely around my waist. "You are just so…perfect."

I blush and glance at the wall. "Thanks?" I say more like a question, and he laughs.

"Do you know how to float?" he asks, tipping me back.

"No, I don't think I can," I tell him honestly, lying flat against the water with his hands supporting my back. I can faintly hear the water rippling around my ears and his instructions. I can't help but writhe in panic even though I can stand up. There is just something about water that frightens me. The finality of it all. That, if you don't know how to swim, you're dead. No amount of fighting against it can help you. You're just gone.

"You need to relax," he says, breaking me from my fearful thoughts.

"I'm trying," I say, fixing my shoulders and breathing deep, but nothing is helping.

He crouches down and lays his hands flat on either side of me, on my stomach and back. "Deep breaths," he says, then adds, "and if that doesn't work, just listen to my voice. Close your eyes." I do as I'm told and listen to him speak, eyes squeezed shut. "Picture yourself on a boat sailing in the Pacific. It's a warm day, and there are not many waves or anything that could possibly harm you. You are safe, and I am right beside you, looking sexy as fuck in a pair of Speedos."

I laugh as I picture what he describes, but he's

rubbing my feet and not showing off his Speedo.

For a few moments, all I can hear is the waterfall and the seagulls overhead. This is oddly really calming.

"Liv?" He sounds like he's been calling my name for some time.

"Hmmmm?" I hum a smile on my lips.

He laughs a kind of laugh that I just have to see. "You've been floating for, like, five minutes."

I panic and stand up. "Really?"

"Yes." He nods, and I throw my arms around him. He spins around and pulls back, accepting my thank you kiss. "But you're not exactly Michael Phelps yet."

"So?" I shrug, staring at his lips.

"Floating gets you frisky, good to know."

I giggle, feeling my cheeks redden with heat. He stares at my lips, then into my eyes with that look he was giving me before. "It's just good to know that I have even a little chance at surviving water."

"What are you talking about?" he asks, and I raise a brow. "You have a *huge* chance with one incredible sexy-ass weapon."

"Oh, yeah? What would that be?" I can't even hold back my smile.

His lips pull up into a smirk. "Me."

"You are so full of yourself." I snort in laughter.

His arms tighten around me. "You were full of *me* last night."

"Grey," I whine, letting my head crane backward.

He chuckles and kisses just under my chin. I wrap my legs around him when I feel him walking toward the opening of the cave. I squeal and close my eyes when we go through the rushing water. He's still kissing me along my jaw. I am very aware of how we're naked and how someone could stumble upon us, but I don't care. This feels so perfect and magical, anyone who dares to mess with this could screw off.

"I thought you were going to teach me how to swim," I whine, gripping his hair and pulling his suctioned lips from my tender skin. I frown at him, and he pouts his lips before kissing me softly. Then again, and again, until I am giggling and trying to avoid him. But he just laughs and marks my neck. "Grey," I whine some more, and he grunts, pulling back, narrowing his eyes at me.

"If you want to swim, you're gonna need a lot more patience," he says, and I roll my eyes.

"Sure."

He splashes me, and I stand since we're in the shallow part.

"Did you just—"

He splashes me again before I can finish what I was saying.

"Oh, you are so getting it!"

"Your pussy? Sorry, got that last night. Not so in the mood again." He shrugs, and I blush.

I answer his snarky remark by splashing him, using a lot of force. I laugh as he sneers at me.

"You got that right. *This*," I gesture to myself, "is closed for business until you apologize."

"I think I'll just find another establishment, then." He looks away from me, crossing his arms.

I gasp, feigning hurt, hand over my chest. "Well,

okay, then." I turn around and begin climbing out of the stream. But he pulls me back in. I go back in the water, and when I come back up, he's hunched over, laughing his butt off. "Come here!" I lunge for him, and he catches me, swimming us back. I push off him and stand, splashing him.

He splashes me back, and we somehow end up in a splash war. Our laughs and declaration of war and shutting down of bodies fill the air and fill my heart. It feels so full, like it's going to burst sometime soon. For a moment, I feel as though we are perfectly imperfect but meant for one another. Our past mistakes are on the back burner, leaving us naked, wild, and splashing each other like insane children. My lips are swollen, and his back is marked when we find ourselves on the blanket from last night laid out on the grass.

We are enveloped in a very comfortable silence, with the exception of the birds, crickets, and his heartbeat beneath my ear. I trace his tattoos, finding solace in being able to find their patterns and hear the stories behind them again. He is telling me about the fiery gray skull on his torso when he says, "Hey."

"Yeah?" I sound as calm as I feel.

There is a pause.

"Where's my charm?" he asks, lifting the hand that is re-visiting his tattoos.

I take a sharp breath and glance at his confused expression, then stare at his chest. "I, uh, I took it off…"

"Well… why?"

"Because I wanted to distance myself from you

and our memories when you didn't respond to my letter," I explain, and he lets out a shaky breath.

"Oh," he says sadly, and I nod.

It grows quiet, but not the comfortable one we were basking in moments before he spotted my wrist.

There goes the blissful ignorance of our problems and our confusing relationship. What are we right now?

"I am sorry," I break the silence.

He cranes his neck to frown at me. "For what?"

I take a deep breath and hold his confused gaze. "For what I did and how I treated you…" I have to get this out there. I have to try and mend us correctly. I don't want us to just get back together, if this is what I think it is, and not really talk about what needs to be talked out.

"Oh." His head falls back.

"I just—I don't know how I could ever make you really see how much I regret doing what I did," I continue. His silence is killing me. "Do you think you'll ever be able to forgive me? Do you—do you ever think you could maybe…*love* me again…?" My heart braces for impact.

He lets out a winded sigh, and I follow the slow rhythm of his chest. "I never stopped loving you, Olivia."

So why does it feel different when he just called me Olivia? He never does unless he's extremely pissed at me.

"You sure?" I sound insecure, and he makes it known.

"What the fuck did we do last night, Liv?" His

voice booms, and I cower. He rubs my shoulder but doesn't change his tone. "Did you not feel me in you, getting as close as I can because I fucking needed you to know that I wasn't imagining it and losing my mind? Did you not see me look at you as if you were a fucking goddess? Someone I could never ever deserve but am glad to have and hold and to make love to or fuck so hard because I need to claim you? Olivia, do you not know that I am desperately in love with you?" His voice breaks, and I can only stare at the emotions pouring into me via his dark eyes. "I'm saying your full name because I want you to understand how serious I am," he says, again reading my mind.

"I just...I don't know what we are and—and I need to know that you forgive me—"

He rolls over, pinning me to the ground, arms above my head. "What you did was fucked up," he says harshly. I look away. He forces me to look into his eyes by moving my head. "I trusted you, and you broke that. You will have to earn that back. And it will take a very long time. As to what we are..." He shrugs like he doesn't really know. "We will figure that out as time goes on." His hands tighten around my wrists. I bite back a moan when he moves my legs apart and glares at me. "But as for my love, never doubt it. Because after all the bullshit we've been through...it will be there for you and you only, always. Understand?"

I nod quickly, cheeks and chest painted red. "Y-yes." I love how open he is being with me. How he's speaking directly from the heart, not holding back like he usually does. He's being upfront, and I want to show him *my* love. "And my love will always be there for you too…" I bring my foot up and brush the inside of his thigh. His eyes widen, and he bites his lip. "Always…"

Chapter Twenty-Two

Grey

We leave the hidden stream after another session of mind-blowing sex. Speaking on the blowing part, that alone was fucking fantastic. I never truly knew how much I missed her soft, responsive body and lips, full and perfectly made for me. I filled her in ways no other man ever would. And although we have not yet titled whatever the hell we are, it still felt amazing knowing how open she was to me. To touch her, caress her, kiss her, *claim* her.

I have half a mind to just have us continue like this without any title, but I know she wants one. She still has to win back my trust first. To be honest, that's just what my pride is telling me. What I really want to do is have her back in my life again. I have been so fucking dead on the inside ever since that day in December. And now that I have her slowly falling in my palm like putty, I want so fucking desperately to just sweep her off her feet and live blissfully in ignorance to the many, *many* reasons why we shouldn't be together.

You have to protect your heart, Grey, my rather reasonable but pretty fucking prideful subconscious reminds me. *She's hurt you before and you didn't see it coming. The same thing can happen.*

I grip the leather wheel and tap my fingers anxiously. "You won't hurt me again, right?" I need to hear her say it. I need the reassurance, or I will go internally crazy and it will spill over and—fuck, I already feel my skin itching. Without my meds, I feel like I am slowly driving myself insane. I have to admit, when I was on them, I felt calmer and more rational. But I am who I truly am without them. And I am determined to show everyone that I can be sane without any fucking pill.

I feel her eyes on me, so I glance over at her. She's staring at me with an unreadable expression, and that's not good because I can usually read her mind with one look. Her huge brilliant blue eyes are squinted, and her lips are bunched to one side.

"What?" I say, feeling a little analyzed. I don't like the feeling. I didn't feel it the first time around, and now I feel paranoid that's what's happening now. "Stop that."

"Stop what?" she asks.

"*That*," I snap, and she flinches. I let out a breath, grip my hair, and stare at the deserted roads. "I don't like it when you look at me like that."

"Like what?" she asks. I see her shrug in my peripheral vision.

"Like you're studying me," I say, and my knuckles turn white. I peek a glance at her and see she's frowning at her hands, like she's about to burst into tears. "Just…promise me that you won't hurt me again."

"You know I won't," she says, her voice hoarse with tears.

Fuck—I shouldn't have let my crazy-ass mind speak. Now she's all hurt and shit.

"I'm—" I begin, briefly rubbing my face, fighting a battle in my head.

"I already lost you," she croaks, cutting me off. "I have apologized a million times. I burned the book. I pled for you—I did everything I could. But I can't go back in the past and erase what I did."

"I know you can't, Olivia," I gripe through clenched teeth. She's getting all emotional again. I wish she knew how much I just want to burn the past and resume what we had. How much I want to get rid of my horrendous pride and slap my heart on my sleeve, all for her.

"Stop calling me that!" she screams, and I pull over.

"What do you want me to call you, then?" I face her, letting my random burst of anger get the best of me.

She just stares up at me with eyes like the sky. I watch as a raindrop falls down her cheek. "I don't know," she says, closing her eyes briefly, then settling her deep baby blues on me. I surrender to them in an instant. "I just want you to look at me the same. I want us to be *the same*. And most of all, I want you to trust me without having to ask if I will *hurt you*."

"After what you did, you want me to treat you the same, like nothing happened?" I look at her as if

224

she's the crazy one. And I very well can, because what she wants is greedy and nearly impossible. "When you did what you did, my heart broke in two, and you took one half of it. I am only now getting it back. And I'm still healing. So I'm sorry if I am a little cruel or rough with you, I just want to make sure I'm not making a mistake."

She looks down, and it is quiet for a moment. "I know, I'm just selfish enough to want us to resume what we had," she admits sullenly. She looks up and reaches out to me. I don't move when she holds my face, and she looks relieved. "But I will do everything in my power to get us back where we once were."

I look into her eyes and see past the normality of them. I swim in her deep oceans, and I search for the truth. It takes me a while, maybe seconds, minutes, maybe even hours or years, but I finally find what I am searching for—her sincerity. Her desperation for us to be *us* again. And I latch onto that too, because I need every last bit of help to hold onto the idea of us being okay. Not in pain or miserable or losing our fucking minds. I just need her…

I nod, feeling tears in my eyes as well.

"Okay."

She looks a little taken aback, and I smile. "Okay?" she questions for assurance.

I lean forward and take her lips in mine. "Okay," I whisper when we pull back for a brief second.

***

"Do you have the food I cooked for the flight?" Abuela asks, dark eyes wide as she gestures wildly with her hands, as she always does when it comes to how well fed I am. I swear, sometimes I worry she wants to fatten me up to the point where she *must* intervene and take care of me for the rest of my life.

"Yes, Abuela," I assure her with a little sigh. I can't be harsh with her. She just lost Grandpa and is going through a lot. She tries her best to show she's strong and dealing with it fine, but I know she isn't. I can see past everything she puts up. I wrap my arms around her, and she stiffens; my cousins raise eyebrows at me. I barely show affection toward any family, but she deserves this. And to be honest…I kind of need it too. "I'll call you when we land." I kiss her forehead, and she makes a strange sound between a cough, a laugh, and a coo. I just roll my eyes, smile, and hug a little harder.

"Oh, my bebé has grown up so much," she whines and pulls back. The heavy emotion of love in her eyes as she holds and squishes my cheeks together makes my heart hurt. "You take care of yourself, you hear me?"

"Yes, Abuela."

"Oh!" she exclaims suddenly. "Before I forget, I have something for you, left by your abuelo." She scurries off, and I walk back inside our room.

Liv is finishing up packing her clothes in her luggage. I'm surprised she didn't do this after the funeral. But then again, she didn't have time since we were out and kind of busy. I smirk at the images flashing through my pervy mind.

"Hey." She touches my arm, and I look into her

226

eyes expectantly. "You okay?" Her lips dance with a little amusement.

"Yeah, I'm fine," I say, cupping her face and rubbing my thumbs over her soft skin. I watch with satisfaction as she sucks in a deep breath. I love how much of an effect I have on her with just one touch. "Just thinking about last night and how amazing you felt as I was fucking you..." I run my thumbs over her lips, and her tongue peeks out to bite or suck like the naughty little princess she is.

"And here it is!" Abuela calls out behind me, ruining the moment.

"To be continued," I whisper to Liv, watching her reel back to planet Earth. I chuckle a little as I drop my hands and turn to Abuela.

She walks up to me, holding a wooden box. "What's this?" I ask her. It has some type of carving around it and a ruby embedded in the middle of the lid.

"This is...*was* your grandfather's," she says, gulping. I catch her slip up, and I want to hug her to soothe her, but she continues, "He loved this thing because his father gave it to him. It was handed down generation to generation. And since your father is gone..." She pushes it out to me, and I gingerly take it, feeling the pressure in such a little box.

"It's mine," I finish for her and look into her solemn eyes.

She hums as a reply. "Now, he said you will find something important in here."

Curious, I flip the lid open and am met with a bunch of crap. I look at her with skepticism.

"Random papers and paper clips are important?"

She shrugs, expelling a sigh. "He said you'd know what it was when the time came." I look up and hold her gaze. "You know how weird your abuelo was," she says.

"Yeah, I know..." I trail, feeling the memories clog up my mind again. I close the lid and press a finger to one of my temples, rubbing gently.

She cups my face again and sniffles. "You behave, okay?"

"Okay, Abuela," I sigh, and she rubs my cheeks.

"You need a shave," she says, and I laugh. I wrap my arms around her and breathe in her scent of cinnamon and dish-soap. "*Te extrañaré, bebé.*" (I'll miss you, baby.)

"*Yo también te voy a extrañar,*" I tell her honestly, and she makes that weird sound again.

When she leaves, something she said is stuck in my brain. (I'm going to miss you too.)

I walk into the bathroom across the hall. "Did you take the pill yet?" I am referring to the morning after pill. I almost forgot about our little "connection" in the very shower behind her yesterday morning. But when Abuela said the word "bebé," a fire was lit under my ass to remind Liv.

Liv stands up straight from the sink and wipes her mouth. "Just did," she says with a sort of sad smile.

"You okay?" I ask, and she nods. I stand back as she passes me and enters our room. I follow her and watch her carefully as she zips up her luggage and stands it up. "Well, you don't look it."

"I am, Grey," she says with a sigh.

"I'm just asking to be nice," I snap, and she looks confused. "Tell me what's wrong."

She shrugs and rubs her palms together, avoiding my gaze. "I just...I was just thinking about our future. I mean, I know we aren't really *anything* right now, but I'd still like to know if we can ever take a large step past being a couple."

"Seriously?" I tilt my head.

She nods. "I would still like to have a family in the future."

I scoff and bend down to my luggage, zipping it shut after throwing a few shirts in it. "Well, I don't."

"I get that—" she says, closing her eyes again, like she's fucking tired of me. I don't like it.

"Then you may as well go back to Noah because I won't give you children—don't want 'em," I tell her, standing up and catching the brief flicker of hurt cross her face. Her lips tremble, and she looks away, biting them. Fuck. "Sorry, but I'm just telling you the truth."

"Is there a reason?" she asks, daring a glance at me.

I nod. "There's no point to them."

"Not even...marriage?" she suggests lightly, and I grimace.

"Fucking Christ, Liv." I hold up my hands. "Do you understand that we aren't a couple, yet you're talking about marriage and children?" It's fucking scaring the crap out of me thinking of mini-mes or mini-hers running around. I actually shudder. Like, Jesus fuck. We aren't even together and she's thinking of kids. I've already told her I don't want

229

them. There's nothing about a slobbering, snot-nosed child that appeals to me.

Again, she looks hurt and turns her gaze to the ground.

I don't like it when she looks like that.

I walk over to her and cup her face.

"Let's take this one step at a time, yeah?" I lamely suggest, and she frowns. I kiss her forehead and rush out of the door, luggage in hand.

Chapter Twenty-Three

Liv

I am nervous the entire plane ride back. I haven't spoken to the girls or any of my friends since I spontaneously went to Venezuela with Grey. I know I shouldn't have alienated them, but I was afraid of what they would have said. I expect them to be angry at me for not telling them or answering their calls or responding to their texts. I was and still am not prepared to know how they really feel about me. I lost nearly two major people in the span of ten minutes.

Just before I left, both Noah and Mason chewed me out for my decision to be there for Grey. I knew Mason would be confused but thought he would still be there for me. I mean, he's my best friend. At least that's what I thought. He of all people knew how much Grey meant to me and how I wasn't one hundred percent over him. I expected him to be a little pissy but supportive of me doing what I thought was best. And I had expected Noah to be upset; I was leaving with my ex-boyfriend. The very man I was so in love with.

I understand how I lost Noah. I can't lie and say I was hurt that he didn't trust me, because look at what happened. I fell right back in step with being so caught up in all things Grey. We reconnected like he thought we would. I betrayed him and broke his heart by ending things between us. So I get that he hates me right now. I saw the resentment coming the moment Grey and I were in that shower together. Because I knew, and even he did, that I wouldn't be able to resist the temptation of both the physical and soulful need of Grey, my first and, I believe, my forever love.

However, when I left, I hadn't expected Grey and me to sort of make up with the high possibility of us getting back together. And although I am ecstatic, I know there will be consequences, some big and some small, because of it. My friends may think I'm stupid for going with him in the first place. Or weak-willed for sleeping with him *twice* before even identifying what we are. And I know on some plane they could be right, because I didn't *think* before bending to his will and giving in to this desperate need to have him and be with him again.

There was no way I could have detested him enough to step out of that shower or ignore his breakdown on the roof. I could not have pushed his head off of my shoulder on the way to Venezuela. I could not have found the strength within me to hold back the smile or laughter that always came so easily when around him. I just couldn't have. He brings out the wildly compassionate side of me. The side that doesn't question his shoulder on me, or step back from his touch, or keep from joining him in a stream. He brings out the absolute best and worst of me, and I freaking love it because he makes me feel so…so *alive*.

I don't know I am smiling at him until he glances over at me from the driver seat, laughing that laugh that makes his eyes crinkle and his dimpled cheeks redden.

"Why are you smiling at me, creep?" he asks in a playful tone.

I bite my lip and shrug. "I'm just happy."

He hums and leans over the center console to rub my thigh unconsciously, at least I think it is… "Why are you happy?"

"Because of you," I say before I can stop myself. But it's true.

His slight smile falters, and he looks at me again, forehead creased. "What'd I do?"

"Nothing." I slink my fingers through his cautiously and watch for a negative reaction. When he doesn't pull away or make a face, I quietly sigh in relief. "I just like the way you make me feel."

His face does twist up a little with a smile as he looks at me. "Really?"

"You asked why I was smiling. That's the reason." I laugh with a little shrug.

"Yeah, but I thought you would answer with: my massive co—"

"Do not finish that," I warn, my hand over his mouth.

He bites my hand, and I let go. "It's just a word."

He bursts out into laughter, making me redden and regret even saying anything in the first place.

"One that I really dislike."

"Why?"

"Because I hate the way it sounds and just *bleh*."

He's snorting up a storm now. "You are such a little wuss."

"I am not!" I cross my arms.

"Oh, you so are!" He bops my nose, and I swat his hand away. More laughter.

Bastard.

"Am not," I mumble.

"So, you wouldn't mind me screaming the word 'cock!'" he screams, and I jump. He is basically cracking himself up now, hitting the wheel, face redder than a firetruck.

"No," I say through gritted teeth, chin up as I face him head on.

He holds my gaze before looking back at the road. "Co—" I raise a brow, and he grins as he finishes, "—*ck*."

"Ugh!" I hold my ears, but I can clearly hear him roaring in laughter. "You are such an asshole!"

"Your asshole," he croons with a cocky smirk. I open my mouth to respond, but he cuts me off with a sharp, "And the owner of your *beloved cock*."

"Jesus—Grey!" I can't be any redder from embarrassment. And he can't be any more of an asshole as he laughs and teases me with a word that is so displeasing in my ears.

He does this the entire way home, and I fall a little bit more in love with this annoying bastard who has my eternal love and doesn't even know.

***

I arrive home about fifteen minutes later. I stand at the front door for maybe five minutes with sweaty palms. I know what everyone's reactions will be when I walk in. It is what I'm scared of. I'm just not ready to go in yet. I prep myself and drill it into my head that they just care for me and want what's best for me. But I will have to drill it into their heads that Grey is what's best for me. I know he is. And they will have to put their feelings toward him to the side and focus on how he makes me feel.

With a few deep breaths, I finally unlock the door and open it.

"Hello?" I call out, closing the door behind me and staring up at the marble staircase. "Char? Jaim'? Julia? Anyone here?" I anxiously stuff my hands in the back pockets of my jeans. I crane my neck back and slide my tongue through my lips, humming. They aren't here. I don't know if I should be even more on edge that they will jump out and pummel some sense into me now or relieved that I don't have to deal with them right now.

"Olivia, is that you?" I hear Louise say, and I freeze.

Oh, I did not prepare for her yelling. Welp, I am in for it now.

"Hey," I say nervously when she rounds the corner from the kitchen.

She gasps as her hands fly to her mouth. "Olivia! You are not dead!" she exclaims, rushing over to me. I'm crushed by a constricting hug that literally takes my breath away. But soon enough, I wrap my arms around her and hug her back.

"Of course I'm not dead," I say and pull back, staring into her teary hazel eyes. "You thought I was dead?"

She shrugs, wiping away a tear. "Kidnapped, actually."

I gasp and put a hand to my heart. "Kidnapped?" I choke out, then pause. "Did you have the police look for me?" I am seriously regretting not leaving a note.

"I prayed."

Well, yeah.

I grin and rub her shoulders. "I have missed you, Louise."

She pulls me into another bone-crushing hug. And I do not pull away this time. I deserve to have her feel my warm flesh and not cold bones. God, I could never imagine putting her through this again. She rambles on and on about how worried she was and how she couldn't sleep at night knowing I was missing, probably dead in her mind. I hug her back even harder, promising to tell her when I am abruptly leaving the country. After all she has done for me, she deserves that much.

"Olivia, is that you?" I hear my mother's shrill voice and freeze, as does Louise.

"Oh no…" Louise and I both whisper as we hear her heels click against the stairs.

"It is you! Do not move, little girl!" she demands.

Louise pulls back and caresses my cheeks. "Good luck," she teases, and I laugh nervously. She kisses my cheek and stalks off to the kitchen.

"Olivia Renee Westerfield!" my mother shouts as she storms over to me. She looks just as terrifying as I last saw her. Dark brown hair pinned up in a beehive hairstyle, pearls glimmering under the crystal chandelier. Her loose, sheer red dress flows behind her and, with her matching Louise Vuittons, she looks like a really glamorous but horrifying she-devil.

"Mother." I grin at her. "It's great to see you a—"

"Where did you go without my permission?" she barks.

I wait a few seconds to make sure she is serous. But then again, when is she never *not* serious?

"I went to Venezuela with a friend to support them. Their grandfather had just passed a—"

"Venezuela?" she exclaims, blue eyes sparking with anger. "Who is this *friend* you'd leave the country for, so abruptly without my say?"

"First, I do *not* need your say so or *permission*— I am nineteen, an adult," I state firmly. "And, not that it is any of your business…Grey."

She freezes like a glitch, then breaks into a frightening smile. "Grey?" she asks through gritted white teeth. "You are back with…*him*?" she spits out like he is pure poison.

"Not officially, but we've realized we are much better together than apart," I tell her, and she scoffs, shaking her head at me like I am the ultimate disappointment.

"You're just a little girl obsessed with the thought of love, but that is not *this*." She gestures me up and down with a disgusted snarl. "*This* is a crazy obsession. A fad. This is a phase of bad boys you will get over in a month's time."

"That is not what this is," I argue. "I truly do love him, Mother. Why can't you see that?"

"Love does not make someone lose their minds and try to kill themselves!" she screams at me, and I flinch.

"I did not try to kill myself!" I snap, feeling my cool steadily melting away.

She laughs a haunting laugh whilst nodding at me. "Oh, yes, you did, dear. Because he has twisted your once intelligent mind into believing whatever he's feeding you is love. Trust me, it is nothing of the sort. It's just a trick. He's using you to get off on whatever goes on in that insane mind of his."

"He has not twisted anything, Mother. What I feel for him is real!" I scream, and she laughs coldly.

"He is a mere distraction for the time being. But he will stop being one when I get you the right help—"

"I do not need help, Mother!" Why doesn't she understand this?

"You are not well, Olivia!" she snaps, stepping closer, glaring down at me from the tower of her high heels. "You are obsessed with that toxic boy, and I will not allow it anymore..." She pauses and looks me up and down like she truly resents the sight of me. "And here I thought you were more than a stupid slut for any boy who lays a hand on her and tells her she's pretty."

I gasp loudly and literally reel back, feeling as

though she's stabbed me straight in the heart. Hot tears blur my eyes. I can't believe she just said that.

"What kind of mother says something like that?" I can't help but whimper, holding my chest.

"The kind of mother who wants the best for her child and won't let her screw up her life over some *boy*," she spits out.

"He is not just some *boy*, Mother. He is the love of my life!" I croak, frustrated.

"You do not get to raise your voice at me!" She points a finger at me.

"But you get to call me stupid and a slut?" That hardly seems fair!

"Yes, because you're acting like both of those things!"

"I can't change how I feel about him."

"Yes, you can, with the right treatment."

"You cannot treat love, Mother! Even though you don't feel it anymore because Dad stopped loving you the minute you turned into this—this insensitive monster doesn't mean you can decide who I can and cannot love!" I scream, instantly regretting it, knowing their rocky marriage is an extremely sensitive subject.

Before I can take my words back, her hand collides with my cheek.

I reel back and trip over my feet in shock. I cannot believe she just *slapped* me! Her daughter, her only child! And she doesn't even look sorry. I hold my cheek and listen to the ring in my right ear, staring up at her with wide eyes and a breaking heart. She clenches her fists but says nothing as she glares down at me.

"How dare you speak to your mother that way?" she hisses, and I grimace.

Tears run down my face unapologetically as I scramble to my feet. "You aren't my *mother*," I whisper, and she looks slightly taken aback. I turn around and run to the front door. I grab my luggage and run down the driveway without looking back.

***

A little under an hour later, I am dragging my luggage up the first place I thought to come to. My feet are on fire and my knuckles are white from lugging the heavy weight for so long, but they don't outweigh the war going on in my mind and the breaking of my heart with each step. I'm still reeling back from the fact that my own mother slapped me for loving someone. It isn't even the slap, but more so the fact that she hated me so much she did it.

I press the doorbell and wait numbly.

The door swings open.

Grey tilts his head, confused. "Liv…what are you doing here?" He eyes my luggage.

I gasp as an overwhelming sob ripples through my mouth. I drop the suitcase and barely hear the metal handle collide with the ground. I drop to the cement steps and let the emotions pour. He falls after me and pulls me into his chest. I wrap my arms around him and cry harder than I have ever cried before. Because I have just lost another family member. I have just lost my mother.

Chapter Twenty-Four

"I am going to kill her!" Grey roars as he shoots to his feet. I grimace and clutch the hem of his black shirt, pulling him back in his seat. I have just told him about the argument with my mother and then the slap. I was more hesitant about the latter because he's sorry there's a rift between her and me. But to be honest, it isn't all his fault. It's hers for thinking she can mold me into whatever her insane mind desires and my realization that maybe it isn't what I want.

"You are not going to *kill* her," I mumble, pressing the ice pack he gave me to my cheek. It stings, and I grimace, but I know it will stop the swelling. He watches with crazy eyes, teeth grinding like a madman. *Oh God.*

"Oh, yes I will." He nods frantically. "She can't get away with hitting her child! My fucking girl!" My heart squeezes at his words "my girl," but it isn't the best time to point it out.

"There's nothing we can do, Grey," I tell him. I'm nineteen years old, an adult. It's not like she can get arrested for slapping me with no witnesses or have Child Services called on her. I'm not a child anymore. But this doesn't register in him, because he widens his eyes before jumping to his feet again.

"There's something *I* can do," he says, gripping his hair. "I have connections, we can—"

"Don't you dare finish that sentence!" I point a finger at him, and he groans before plopping back onto the couch beside me. I am not cool with the idea of him being in the gang. I definitely am not okay with the idea of him using said gang connections to *kill* my mother.

He rubs his eyes. "I can't let anyone get away with hurting my girl."

"It's okay…" I shake my head, closing my eyes to barricade the incoming tears.

I had seen this coming, but I couldn't *not* tell him. Especially after haven broken down into tears the moment he opened the front door. I tried to tell him that I was okay, because I knew he would want to take vengeance. But I can't let that happen, not when it is my mother. Though, at the moment, and for a long while, she hasn't felt like one. I wish I could change her and insert a compassionate mother chip in her coding because then I wouldn't have to deal with this, her slapping me for loving a boy who could very well be *the one*, as cheesy as it sounds. I just wish she could understand.

He grabs me and pulls me into his arms, pressing his lips to my forehead. "No one gets away with hurting you, *princesa. No one.*"

"Please do not send a hitman on my mother," I say with a pathetic little sigh that sounds like a laugh. I swallow the dry lump in my throat. My voice breaks like a hiccup, and I clutch his shoulders for stability.

"Shhh…" he coos, rubbing my back soothingly. I close my eyes and wrap my arms around him. I let out a sigh and listen to him whisper sweet nothings in his native tongue. This is him. This is the man I fell in love with. The sweet guy who can be caring and hold me with so much love it nearly drives me insane but glues all my broken pieces back together. He is my superglue and the only man who makes me feel like…*me.*

"Don't let go," I plead in the most broken voice.

"Never, *princesa.*" He kisses my hair for a moment, and I sigh in contentment, feeling my entire body relax around him, around my *home.* "Never…"

***

"I am going to kill her!" Charlotte threatens with the same vigor as Grey. "I am going to whack her across the face with this—"

"You need to calm—oh my God, you really do have a hammer in your purse!" I gasp at the heavy metal *weapon* she wields out of her shoulder bag like it's a *sword.* I can't believe—I thought she was kidding this entire time!

"I'll swing on the bitch. You know I will." She points it at me with crazy eyes.

"There's no need for that—put that away before someone calls the cops," I hiss, nervously looking around.

"I'll swing at the snitch too, and then the cop for coming to the snitch's rescue," she says, and I groan, pulling and rubbing my lower lip in frustration. I love how she so quickly comes to my rescue and defends me, even if she is threatening to smack people with her purse-hammer. But I do not love the idea of her being behind bars because of me.

"I say we order an assassin, like John Wick, Jason Bourne, something like that," Jaimie suggests with the same wide eyes as she comes up to the food court table.

"I think we should plant a bomb in the house," Julia says, plopping down and shoving curly fries inside her mouth. I glare at her, and she holds her hands up defensively, chewing loudly. "We'd evacuate the house of your dad and her mom, of course." She gestures to Charlotte, who nods and picks up a few fries from Julia's plate, stuffing her face with them.

"Um, why does she have a hammer and where can I get one?" Jaimie says, pointing a finger at Charlotte, fascination in her brown eyes.

"Right, this is the SX *plus* model," Charlotte begins to describe the large hammer, running her hand along it like it's a brand-new car model. "Super sturdy and a nice weight, easy to hold—"

"Stop!" I shout, making them all stare at me. "Please, can you all just stop?"

"No, we cannot *stop*," Jaimie says. "We care about you, and what your mother did is not acceptable—"

"But you can't plan to *murder* her." It's the most

insane thing I have ever heard.

"We're not actually serious, Liv," she tries to defend them.

"Oh, really?" I point to Charlotte, who is breathing on the top, then rubbing it with her palm like it's her most prized possession. We all shift our attention to her as she hums with a sadistic smile as she cleans her choice of weapon. I finally clear my throat to get her attention, and she looks around sheepishly.

"What? Oh, yeah. Totally not going to murder her. Psssh." She laughs nervously then clamps her lips in a thin line.

"Has she kicked you guys out?" I ask, nervously biting my lip.

"No, but I am not staying there if you aren't going to be there," Charlotte says, finally putting her hammer away. "We're staying at a friend's place for the rest of the summer." Ugh, I feel horrible. They came here for a good time and for us to have fun. But now they're being forced to stay somewhere else because of my insane mother. This was not the plan, and it makes me sick.

My hands fly to my face, and I rub to try and relieve some tension. "I am so sorry, guys. I didn't even think about where you guys would go after, and I…" I begin to shake as tears bubble in my eyes. "I should have just backed down and let her send me to my room or something. I didn't mean to inconvenience you guys—"

"Hey," Julia says, bringing my hands down, and Jaimie wipes a tear away. "This is not your fault. Neither you nor anyone else ever thought she'd *slap* you. If we did, we would have been there and dared her to try and go through us to get to you."

I cry even harder at her surprisingly sweet words. Her icy walls she once held up have completely melted away, showing her true compassionate side.

"Oh God, I just made it worse." She nervously laughs and pulls away, looking to her girlfriend for help. "How do you make it stop?"

"We can change the subject," Jaimie answers and narrows her eyes sharply. "To the fact that you jetted off to a different *country* without letting us know."

"Oh, geez," I groan. I also saw this coming. "I couldn't stick around for you guys to…*judge* me the way Mason did. I understand where Noah was coming from, but I was still hurt. And when Mason came in…" I shake my head and try my best to hold back the tears. "I was scared of your reactions. But I really am sorry. I could have answered your calls or something. But I was also trying to be there for Grey and—"

Jaimie envelops me in a hug out of nowhere, rubbing my back. "It's okay, if you're happy. Are you happy?" She pulls back as a tear runs down my flushed cheek that has a little redness from the assault. I nod, feeling my shoulders shake. She pulls me back in and gently rocks me side to side. "Then we're all good with it."

I hug her even tighter as I realize how much I love her and the girls.

"Thank you, Jaimie." I pull back, and she waves a dismissive hand.

"Now let's change the subject again: what went

down with you and Grey and how did it happen?"

"And don't you dare hold back the juicy details," Charlotte warns, peeking the hammer above her purse.

"I'll get us some more fries," Julia announces with a smile.

***

"Can I join you?" Grey asks as I am stepping in the shower. He's already shirtless and is taking off his basketball shorts. "Let me rephrase: scoot the fuck over." His smile is mischievous. I blush and look ahead.

"Sure." I laugh but do as I'm told, stepping forward so he has some room behind me. I grab my loofah and squirt some vanilla-scented body wash on it. I can feel him settle in behind me. I close my eyes and tilt my head to the side when he places a kiss on my neck. A sigh tumbles out of my lips as I rub my chest and he holds my waist.

"Let me do the honors," he mumbles into my wet skin, and I nod in anticipation. I hand him the pink loofah, and he takes over. He glides the fluffy thing over my stomach and rubs against my hip bones. He proceeds to go lower and lower and lower…I bite my lip and he laughs. I heat up and open my eyes and look to the side. He's bouncing his eyebrows at me. "Turn," he whispers darkly, making me shiver and moan lightly. His erection presses into my stomach, and I move around just to tease him. His eyes darken, and his lips turn up. "Don't test me when I have the power."

"Fine," I groan as I face him and lay my face in his broad chest. He laughs, and I smile against his warm, inky skin. I bite my lip as he rubs my butt with his hands. My eyes flutter closed on their own as I am wrapped in his warmth and the tingles he never fails to make me feel when he presses against me like this. "This feels good," I admit, wrapping my arms around his torso.

"Does it?" he teases, and I pinch his butt. He jumps, and I laugh loudly. He pinches mine, and I do the same thing. I pull my head back and stick my tongue out at him. He leans down and lays his over mine, kissing me gently. My stomach feels like it's on cloud nine as I kiss him slowly, cupping his ever-growing stubble. Contrary to our last experiences in a situation like this, it doesn't evolve into sex. It's just a slow, sweet, passionate kiss that makes us both smile and laugh at the end of it.

We get out twenty minutes later. He's in the living room waiting for our pizza to come, watching some UFC show while he waits. I get ready in a pair of workout shorts and a gray tank top. But then I decide to wear one of his shirts without a bra since it's more comfortable that way. I am brushing out my stubborn curly hair when I give up and decide to put it up. Only problem is, I don't have anything to put it up with. I think I left my hair supplies back in Venezuela.

"Grey?" I call out from the doorway. "Do you have a rubber band?"

"Yeah, in the left table next to the bed," he calls back.

"Thanks!"

His response is inaudible as he shouts at the TV. I giggle as I rush over to the bed and jump on it. I crawl over to the left table and throw it open. There are a bunch of junk things in here. I quickly glance around the messy room and promise myself to clean it up later. I turn back to the little table and push some things around.

"Wait!" he shouts, and the rest is drowned out by the loud TV.

"It's fine, I'll find it my—" I stop talking when my eyes land on a scary object. I gasp and reel back on the bed, scared to touch it.

He skids to a stop and rubs his hand over his mouth. "Uh, did you find it?" His voice is shaky as he rubs the back of his neck.

"You mean the huge gun?" I hiss in a low voice, afraid someone like the FBI is listening in.

"Calm down, we're not bugged," he says with a little eye roll, reading my mind.

"We may as well be." I point at the silver gun and whisper, "You have a ginormous gun next to your bed."

"It's not the best neighborhood," he says ridiculously.

"There's a flamingo in the front yard," I exclaim, throwing my hands around. "Where did you get it and why do you have one?"

"I have a permit for it, so—" he tries to say.

"Where...and why?" My tone is firmer now.

He stares at me like he's debating whether or not to tell me. Finally, he breaks and huffs out, "Dean gave a lot to members, and it's to keep myself safe."

My heart drops.

"Safe? There is no *safe* with that thing!" I shout.

"I am in a fucking gang. Of course there is no safe! It's why I need it to protect myself in case—"

I burst into tears and fall on my butt on the bed.

"Why are you crying?" He sounds agitated, but I feel the bed shift as he crawls over to me. He wraps his long arms around me and gently rubs my side. "Hmmm? Why are you crying?"

"Because there's a chance you can get hurt, or arrested, or—or *worse*," I sob and clutch his shirt. I don't want him to be in this freaking gang because it will only end in a horrible way. And I just want the best for him. "I want you to get out," I plead, sniffling and cupping his face. "P-please get out. I don't want you in it."

His brows furrow and his tongue peeks to the side. "I'm already in too deep." I cry even harder because the probability of this ending badly is very high, and I just can't lose him when I am so close to him being mine. "But I promise to be safe. I won't be killed or anything."

"You can't promise me that." I pull away from him. He's so stupid being in it.

"Yes, I can." He pulls me back and presses his lips to my hairline. "I will not screw up for you, *princesa*. Just…just please don't leave me. I promise you won't even notice I'm in it. I won't get caught or anything." I groan some more and clutch his forearms, and he sighs. "Just…just let me hold you now and we'll figure the rest out later, yeah?"

We are already figuring out what we are, but this is so much more important because it deals with his *life.*

250

I nod and let him kiss my tear-stained cheek. "Fine. But I swear to God, if anything happens to you—" I turn to him and look in his eyes seriously. "I will kill Dean."

"Okay, *mi pequeña princesa mala,* okay…" he says quietly with a crooked smile. (My little bad-ass princess.)

Chapter Twenty-Five

Grey

The week has gone by painfully slow, but sickly sweet. Painfully slow because I have been pushing myself to train harder, without the help within the gym. I haven't been there since David dropped the nuke-bomb that he's moving here to Miami. I'm not even angry that he's staying—I'm lying, I am fucking *furious*. It's the fact that he didn't tell me beforehand. I would surely tell him if I was moving to a whole new state with my fiancée, which I will never have, but you get the point. He just treated me as if I was some kind of kid he couldn't talk to. Not like I was his fucking brother. And it pissed me off. I am *still* pissed off.

I push harder as I run, my thoughts nearly drowned out by the rock music blasting through my earbuds. I weave through people and am gunning for the outskirts of town. It begins to drizzle, but it doesn't stop me for one second. If anything, it makes me run even faster, causing my calves to scream at me to stop. But I do not ease up. My phone keeps buzzing the entire time I run, but I don't answer because I know exactly who it is. And he can fuck off. An hour later, I arrive at a crowded park that's damn near on the other side of town.

I hunch over and take long, deep breaths. I can barely hear the loud music over my heartbeat and panting. "Fuck," I curse as I stretch my aching back and stand. I thread my fingers through my sweaty hair and plop onto a bench. There's a beach nearby, and the air is warm. This place is so freaking peaceful. Sometimes I wonder how something can look so beautiful yet be filled with so many betraying assholes, David being one of them. Dean being another. The city may look alluring and sweet, but up close it holds dangerous feuding gangs, monopolies, strippers, and everything your mama would warn you about.

My pocket buzzes with an incoming text. I groan and rub my face. I have ignored him all week long; he won't let this go on any further. I hastily pull out my phone and swipe it open. As I expected, it is Dean. He wants me down at The Spot at ten. That's all. I know he has something shifty up his shady-ass sleeve. Knowing him, dodging his advances, and him saying he wants you for a simple run-down and not cussing you out means you're going to regret avoiding him. But I can handle him. He's put me through shit I can never repeat, not even in my head.

I am yanked out of my thoughts of the menacing gang leader by a particular ringtone I have set for Liv. It's some stupid color song by a girl named

Hashley? I don't know. She stole my phone and set it along with a photo, saying a plain ringtone and a default background was both disrespectful and just plain mean. Apparently, this song is so me...? The girl can be weird when she wants to be.

"Finally wake up?" I tease. "Gosh, we did so much *not*-fucking, I must have tired you out."

"Do not *tease* me, mister, or there will be a *much* longer time of no-effing," she shoots back, and I can just see that little cute smile of hers and narrowed eyes that always appear when she wants to appear threatening. In reality, she's as intimidating as a bunny wielding a carrot around like it's a sword. Honestly, I just can't get over the "no-effing." I've heard her curse, so why the censoring?

I laugh then sigh longingly. "What's up, cute-butt?"

She growls her little growl, and I laugh a little more. "I'm hungry. Do you mind getting something on your way back?"

"Sure," I say and begin to head back in the direction of the house. I didn't notice it before, but I'm pretty starved myself. "What do you want?" I'm going to treat myself to some greasy burgers because I fucking deserve it."

"I could use some salad from Panera, and maybe some ice cream from my favorite parlor downtown?" she says sheepishly. "Remember to get extra—"

"Sprinkles. Yes, I got it," I cut her normal order off with a laugh. "Anything else? Maybe some plugs?"

"Plugs…?" she questions.

"Yeah, to plug up the bloody captain sailing the bitchy ship down south." I quirk a teasing smile even if she can't see me. She's been having her lady-time for a few days now and has been quite a bitch on and off, but I get it completely. It's her time to be bipolar, I get the rest of the month, it's just nice that way. Equal, you know?

She makes a really unattractive sound that could only sound cute on her. "Stop being so insensitive and get me my damn stuff, okay?"

I am ready with a comeback when I hear a very distinct male voice in the background on her side. I stop walking at the bottom of the hill and grind my teeth.

"Who the *fuck* is that?" I boom, giving her no time to defend herself. I listen to her speak as I begin to run back to my car that's about thirty minutes away. But hearing a *guy* is with her, I am so fucking pissed I will reach it in *twenty*. "Liv!"

"It's no one!" she squeaks, and I growl impatiently. "Seriously," she mutters, and I perfectly imagine her biting her lip.

"That didn't sound like no one." I sound as pissed as I feel, maybe even more.

"Well, it was…just the TV," she lies. "You left it on that fighting channel."

"Do not lie to me, Liv." I just want her to tell the damn truth. I don't think she'd ever bring a fucking *guy* to my—our—kind of—house. Not unless she wanted to see more blood than she has for the past few days on my hands.

"Don't forget the sprinkles. 'Kay, bye, drive

255

safe." She makes a kissy sound in the phone before hanging up.

I grunt angrily as I shove my phone on my basketball shorts and begin running. All kinds of thoughts of bashing a fucker's face into the ground and demanding why she brought him to the house in the first place play through my mind like a horror film. I'm pretty sure I knock down a few people here and there as I run harder and faster than I had running, but I couldn't give less of a massive shit. They are simply in my way.

When I finally get to the house half an hour later, I storm in, nearly throwing the front door off its hinges. I have not cooled down one fucking bit as I drove like an absolute madman on the road. A cop tried to pull me over a while back, but I lost that fucker easily. Partly because he's a shitty newbie, and I am a pro when it comes to ditching cops. Don't ask.

"Olivia Renee Westerfield!" I belt out her name as I throw open the bedroom door.

She jumps up a little. She is on the bed in the same clothes I left her in, one of my black shirts and boxers. Her hair is thrown up in a ragged, curly ponytail, and her laptop rests on her thighs.

"Aw, where's the food?" she whines when she looks at my empty hands, about to throw a period-bitch fit.

"Don't start that period-bitchy shit with me," I warn her, pointing a finger. I look around for any signs of a boy, and she watches, chewing her lip, basically making it known she is a guilty little adorable shit. "Where is he?"

"Who?" she tries to play dumb.

"You know who!" I snap, walking over to her.

"No, I don't!" she hisses, shoving her laptop down a little.

"Yeah, right." I turn to search the house when I hear the voice again.

"Olivia, are you there?" The voice is close, really close...

I look to her laptop, and she does too.

"Shoot." She bites her lip.

I rush over and snatch the laptop out of her small hands before she can close it. I walk over to the door and throw it open fully. I am taken aback, lifting an eyebrow. It's the dude she spoke to once back in December. You know, the sweater-vest, khaki-wearing motherfucker she clicked with so well? Yeah, that preppy fucker. But he was only talking to her about the program I didn't really know about then, so why he is talking to her again now? Maybe their friendship runs past the program...?

"Why the fuck are you talking to this prick?" I make a face, and he laughs like the good guy he is. Asshole.

She runs over and grabs the laptop from my hands. "Matthew, can I please call you back later?" she asks sickly sweet with a smile and a bat of her eyelashes.

The fuck!

"Of course, good—" he begins, but I am tired of his polite voice.

I slam the screen shut, and she screams, but I cut her off. "Are you cheating on me with him?"

257

Her eyes blow open and she mouths for words, but finally squeaks out, "There is nothing to cheat on. We haven't discussed what we are officially."

"So?" I shrug my shoulders violently. "You're saying it's okay for me to go out and fuck a random girl?"

She looks so hurt, she bites her lip and shakes her head. "Of course it isn't, but he and I aren't doing anything wrong."

"Then what the fuck are you doing?" I scream.

"Can you please not scream at me?" she pleads in a small voice, hands drawn up. "All it does is give me headaches and scares me a little. So, please, inside voices."

I rub my palm over my lip roughly in agitation and sit on the edge of the bed. "Talk," I demand, and she sighs.

She sits next to me, fiddling with her thumbs. "You have to promise not to get mad at me."

I scoff and tug at my hair. "Can't promise that."

"Fine, but just…don't walk out. Do not *assume* and let me speak. Please, I will only tell you if you promise me that."

Whatever it is must be worse than I thought. Fuck.

"Talk," I demand again, and she nods.

A few tense seconds pass before she finally says, "I got accepted into the…into the Psych Program…again."

I snap my head toward her, but she is staring at the floor. "That's good…right?" I rub my neck, and she finally looks at me, tears bundled up in her eyes.

Oh no, here comes the tears.

I grab the tissue box on her side of the bed and hand it to her. She's been crying non-stop ever since her lady-time began. She mumbles "thank you" and begins to sniffle as she wipes her face religiously. It hurts my heart to see her this upset over something so amazing. I help her dry her tears and cup her red, puffy face.

"You're not mad?" she mumbles, bottom lip trembling.

I smile but shake my head no. "Of course not, silly."

"But...w-why not?" she stutters, sucking her bottom lip.

"Because you've wanted that spot for a long time."

"But it's what ruined us the first time," she points out, voice scratchy. I make a mental note to make her some tea for her throat. "Aren't you even a little upset?"

I take a deep breath and look away. "I...I think I should be...but no. It doesn't make me upset," I say honestly, ignoring my pride and grudge that's fighting to break through.

The thing did tear us apart, but it wasn't just that. It was also her, and I am already working on building my trust for her. But she was willing to go so far for the thing; it means that it means a lot to her. And I love her so much it physically hurts, so who am I to step in the way a second time? I know for a fact that I will not let it rip me away from her again. I almost didn't survive the last time. And I'm not going through the misery again.

"Really?" she croaks.

"Yes," I laugh.

"Yay," she says softly, cheeks glistening with warmth. I crack up in laughter, and she gets hotter and hotter. But then she pouts and whimpers, "But the food…?"

"I'll get it for you." I wink at her, and she launches her arms around me, sniffling back tears.

"You're the best in the world." She kisses my neck, and I grow slack in her arms and *accidentally* fall into the bed. She giggles, and I laugh so hard my stomach is in pain, but it doesn't matter. Because she is to me the very air I breathe and the flicker of warmth I've craved so desperately for months. But now that I know I can't live without her, I will never let go of this little light. Never.

***

After getting her food, which she practically inhaled, blaming her lady-time, she had me take her to this store called Nerdstrom, or some geeky shit like that. The place looked like Micah's nerdy ass and Liv threw up all over it. Khaki-everything dripped down the walls and plaid socks littered the rows and ugh, the sweater vests. I am surprised I didn't die of boredom and disgust. But I barely bit back my tongue as she shopped for clothes for the program.

I am seriously surprised I'm not super upset about it. I mean, it is kind of the reason we split the first time around. But then I just had to admire her drive, however fucked up it was. Plus, she really has to be really fucking destined for it or extremely talented if they are taking her again. By the way she was gushing to me about it, I could tell she's very excited, so I will keep quiet about the wrong it has done to us and focus on how genuinely happy she is, because her happiness overrules everything. And I mean *everything*.

My smile when thinking about my brilliant, foodie girl drops when I pull up at The Spot around the time Dean said I should be here. I just want to get whatever this is over with so I can go back home to my girl and tuck her in. Fuck! I am becoming so fucking whipped again! I told myself I'd stay tough this time, but how can I when she's all pouty faces and cute smiles? I catch myself falling into a daydream about her and clear my throat.

I stare into the rearview mirror and point at myself. "You are a tough motherfucker. You're about to walk into a gang meeting. Act like it."

I get out of the car, popping the collar of my leather jacket just to prove my douche-thoughts. I head inside and ignore the stares as I walk straight into the back and down the stairs, where I expect I am needed. A lot of bad shit happens down here. Fuck that. If word got out to the PD, I would let my girl and—fuck it—David down too. But Dean has a pretty tight relationship with a few corrupt cops and knows to keep everything low-key. I kind of know what to expect. It's the reason I'm wearing my MMA gloves right now.

I'm not surprised when I find a few members lounging around smoking, Dean in front of a tied-up guy. He looks pretty fucked up as I stand in front of him. Blood gushes from his broken nose, bruises all over his collarbones and cheeks, and eyes so bloodshot, I can't even tell what color his eyes are. And the lovely boss beside me has a baseball bat in his hands. You do the math as to what happened here.

"Ask away," I tell Dean with a sigh as I crack my knuckles, eyeing the prisoner. I bet he'll spill once I get a few punches in. I pop a gum into my mouth and throw the wrapper away as I near the guy, but Dean pulls me back.

"After I ask you…why didn't you answer my calls?" Dean asks, head lolling to the side, toothpick slowly rolling in his mouth.

I hold his intense gaze and shrug. "I was busy with training. You know how the big fight's coming up."

He nods thoughtfully, rolling my answer in his mind. "Get to it," he says, turning his back, bat propped on the floor, almost black-blood shining in the single dim light in the dusty basement. I watch him for a moment before turning to the poor fuck. I don't know what he did or what Dean wants to know, but I know I can't test Dean. He is the most menacing man in Miami, one who could hunt you down and show you hell at its finest.

I throw my fist at the man's face without any hesitation. I do it over and over, taking small breaks for him to beg, then go back at it. My boot collides with his jaw, and he cries out. After a while, I look back at Dean, who has the bat behind his neck, toothpick rolling, rolling…

"When do I stop?" I ask.

He picks his gaze from the man to me, then shrugs his shoulders. "Don't…"

I look to the man, my bloody glove…then continue bashing his face in without any hesitation.

Chapter Twenty-Six

Liv

Something is wrong with Grey. He's been ignoring me for the past few days, and I don't know why. He was okay a couple of days ago. The night he left to spar with some friend, for training purposes. But ever since he got back that night, I've noticed a hostile, cold shift in him. So I've been keeping my distance. I noticed blood on his clothes and face, and when I asked about it, he just told me sparring got out of hand. I didn't buy it, but he promised me not to worry. Obviously, I was right to worry because ever since then, he hasn't talked to me really or been at the house. He's just been out training, but I have a bad feeling it's not all he's doing.

I want to ask what he's up to and if it has to do with the gang, but I know him, and I know he won't just up and tell me. He is an expert at building up walls to keep me out and his dirty little secrets in. I broke them down before, and I could do it again.

Only problem is, I got so hurt with every swing I took.

However, I would do anything to get inside that crooked mind of his. Especially if he's hiding something dangerous. I just wish he would understand how much I love and care for him and how I would do anything to protect him. Though, also knowing him, whatever he's hiding is to protect *me*. We are such a mess for each other. It's both romantic and fucked up.

"So, how's married life going?" Charlotte teases, referring to me and Grey.

I roll my eyes at her smile. "We are *not* married."

"Okay, but when it does happen, I want to be HBIC," Jaimie says, throwing an arm around me.

"Head bitch in charge?" Julia laughs, glancing at her girlfriend.

"You've already earned that title," Charlotte jokes, and Jaimie glares at her.

I laugh and gain a few odd looks from people, but I focus on my best friends. We are currently at the mall because I *needed to get out of Grey central and see the rest of the world*. Their words, of course. But so far, we've been wandering around talking about nonsense and how school is starting in a few weeks. Something these girls are not the least bit happy about. I, on the other hand, am ecstatic. What's not to love about learning?

"I meant head *bridesmaid* in charge," Jaimie clarifies with an annoyed eye roll. I rub her shoulder, and she flashes a kinky little smile at me. *Oh no.* "It is happening, then?"

"No, it is not happening." I drop my hands, and she pouts. "I'm just nineteen, guys. Marriage isn't even remotely on my radar."

"So? Jules and I are twenty, and we're getting married," Jaimie says casually, and I almost have a heart attack.

"When the hell did you propose?" Charlotte screeches before I can. I mean, we are very close. I find it very insulting they wouldn't tell me they're getting *married*! And so young, at that. Not that I didn't see it coming. Their love is extraordinary.

"I second that." I raise a hand, and they laugh.

"Kidding. No one popped any question," Julia wheezes through laughter.

"But we sure did pop something last night, if you get what I mean." Jaimie bounces her eyebrows suggestively.

"Gross, I didn't need to hear that." I twist up my face in disgust, and they just shrug.

"I definitely second that." Charlotte mirrors my facial expression.

A few minutes later, we end up in Victoria's Secret. While the girls browse, I stand off in the corner. I open up a text from Grey, replying to my last concerned text. Apparently, he's at the gym training with some of his friends. I text him asking when he'll be home, but it goes unanswered. I sigh and text him that I'll be waiting patiently and wish him good luck in his training. He very well could have been busy all week with training since the big tournament is coming up soon. But that doesn't cancel out the gut feeling that there's more to it.

"Hey, Liv. How does this look?" one of the girls

calls out.

I laugh, finding a slinky black lingerie piece hung over Charlotte's head, draped against her ripped tee. "I don't think it's your color. Try blue?" I playfully suggest, and her eyes lighten up.

"You know, I think you're right." She winks at me and waltzes over to the lingerie section. I smile and walk into the section, feeling naughty as I gaze over the skimpy outfits. There is lace over everything and barely any actual fabric material. I feel a red one that's lace and holes and just very...sexy. My mind wanders to Christmas time, when I wore something similar for Grey. I let the lingerie go and clear my voice. That was the first time I had ever worn or done something so risqué. But I can't deny how sexy I felt wearing it.

A buzz in my shorts stops me from looking around some more. I pull it out and sigh out loud.

The text from Grey reads,

Thanks.

"Everything okay?" Jaimie asks, rubbing my shoulder.

"No," I say honestly. I can't lie anymore; it's exhausting.

"What's the problem?" she asks.

I just show her Grey and my's texts.

"Oh...cold Grey's making a comeback."

"Yup." I shove my phone back in my pocket and rub my face. "He's been so distant lately, and I don't know why. I want to make things right and get him to let me in, but he's being protective over me again…which I appreciate; it's sweet. But it's tiring and isn't fair to me because he shuts me out."

"Then show him you have control too. *Be* controlling."

I remove my hands and see she is smirking with trouble. "What's that supposed to mean?"

She glances to her right, and I glance around at the lingerie. "What do you think I mean?"

***

"This is so stupid," I mutter to myself, cinching the brown trench coat. I feel like an inexperienced hooker. And it doesn't help that the only thing I have under this ridiculous coat is lingerie. Only I'm not going to sell my body to random men but show Grey that I have control. Stupid, but it wasn't my idea. It was Jaimie's. She says doing this will portray my ultra-sexy side and showcase that I am a strong, independent girl who doesn't need no cold mother-effer. Her words, not mine.

But now that I am outside of the gym, I'm not so sure I should go through with this. I mean, his friends could still be in there and I'd end up embarrassing myself. Or he could just look at me and see through my BS. I much rather the latter, though that would suck. I don't want anyone seeing me exposed like that. Especially not his friends. I could lie and tell Jaimie that he wasn't here when I arrived, so I won't have to be the brunt of this ridiculous stunt going awry.

I feel incredibly exposed when a group of guys walk past and whistle at me. I turn a bright red shade and slink into the gym. There's no going back now. I can't go back out because I've really been spotted. And I do not trust myself being out there dressed in nothing but *this*. Why can't they make lingerie more conservative? I'd love a pair of lace khakis or taller garments. I cross my arms tightly and feel my heart beating rapidly on the tip of my tongue. The lights are off with the exception of one dim light above my head.

I am hoping he's alone now, because I don't think anyone is here. And he hasn't told me if he left or not. He is most likely in the private boxing area in the back. As I walk, I cast nervous glances around. Wearing this thing makes me feel vulnerable, like someone will jump out of the shadows at any moment. What if this doesn't work? Okay, it may not work with the whole control thing. But once he sees me in this, well, the sex thing will most definitely work.

I call Grey as I reach the back. I hear his phone ringing, or *a* phone, and listen to it stop abruptly. Did he just ignore my call? Well, sex is certainly out of the question. I text him, asking where he is, and listen to the ding on his phone. I wait a few seconds for a reply. My phone vibrates, and I read the text, feeling stupid for being here like this when he is blatantly lying to me.

Grey: Went out to dinner w the guys. B home soon.

"Dinner, my ass," I whisper angrily and twist the door knob. Slowly, I push it open, thanking the

Lord it doesn't make a creak revealing my presence. I inch it forward a couple of inches and stick my head in. I gasp, and my eyes widen. There are a group of burly men half-surrounding a man tied in a chair. His face is a mess of blood and bruises. And the man in front of him is the cause of it all.

"Grey," I whisper, then smack my hand over my mouth before backing out. Thankfully their backs are turned to me. Heart in my stomach, I softly shut the door and run to the front, feeling as though I'm going to throw up. I do not know the man in that room. What I just witnessed was a beast torturing prey, and I am questioning *everything*.

***

I am at a loss for words, but my thoughts are running rampant with a few emotions. Anger, confusion, and worry are the highlights. I'm pissed off he'd lie to me. It wasn't just a little white lie; it was a huge one that could have him arrested. And I wouldn't be able to just bail him out so easily this time around. I am beyond confused because, well, why would he beat a man half to death in the gym? Maybe because David is close to the owner and he snagged the keys to the place for after dark? I think it's quite clear why I am deathly worried, because he's getting too close to this dang gang and is doing a violent act for them, for *him*. Dean. Grey was right when he said he was a dangerous man. And such an asshole.

I am not going to let Grey stay in this damned gang. He doesn't need to be in it, nor should he be in the first place. There are no benefits—none that are legal, anyway. He said he's in too deep and that Dean is too unpredictable to cross, but he won't be crossing him. I would. I should be frightened for even thinking of doing that, but Grey's safety outweighs everything.

The guy may be intimidating and scarier than the Boogieman himself, but he's nothing but an obstacle in the way of my future with Grey, whether we are actually a couple or not. I would do anything to protect him. *I* am too deep in love with him, and I will ruin anyone who gets in the way of that. Grey can go on and on about him being his own person and such, but we *are* something, and it is enough for me to try and help him. Getting him out of this damned gang will surely help, trust me.

I wait up for what feels like hours. And maybe it has been. I sit on the bed, still in my crazy outfit and heels, eyes glued to the door, waiting for him to walk through it. I chew so hard on my bottom lip I taste blood. My worry grows with each minute he doesn't enter the room. I texted him that I am worried about him, but he didn't reply. That was half an hour ago. He must think I've fallen asleep after texting that, seeing that it is now one in the morning. If he really thinks that, then he's either lost his mind or doesn't know me at all.

After a while I decide to make some coffee to keep me up. The black coffee zaps me with much-needed energy. I have about two cups and find myself laying on the couch in the living room watching a reality TV show about the Kardashians. I don't keep up with social media that much or know a lot of celebrities, but my gosh, they have gigantic butts. Is that a thing these days? Plastic shoved into your butts so you have extra cushion when you sit down? I sound like a clueless old lady. That is excluding the skimpy lingerie, trench coat, and heels. But throw me a robe and some glasses and I'm your insane cat lady.

The youngest Jenner is talking about one of her skinny dogs when I hear the front door open and the jingle of keys. I stiffen, thinking it's a burglar, and briefly contemplate about going for the gun. But then I think the probability of me getting to the gun and shooting the man is low, while shooting myself is way higher. I have never held a gun in my life, nor do I know how to use one. Plus, I have a tingling sensation in my stomach, AKA my Grey radar is going off.

I get up, finally toeing off the heels. They were killing my feet for so long. I walk over to the foyer and stand at the end of it, arms crossed. I watch as Grey carefully closes the door to keep from waking me. I'm already up and worrying myself out! He lets out a breath of relief once it's shut, then turns around.

"Fuck!" He jumps. "What are you doing up so late? And what the hell are you wearing?" He gives me a weirded-out once over as he unties his boots.

"I think I should be asking the questions, don't you?" I step forward and poke his shoulder when he stands straight.

"Um…sure?" He scrunches his eyebrows together in confusion. Just hold on, buddy, I am about to enlighten you.

272

"Let's start with: Why did you lie to me?" I cock my head to the side and give my best *Don't fuck with me* look. He snorts and bypasses me, clearly not impressed.

"When did I lie?" he asks as he enters the kitchen and throws open the fridge.

"Earlier. You said you went out to dinner with the guys…"

"And?" He shrugs as he kicks the door shut, biting into a sandwich he stored away.

"And you're chowing through that like you haven't eaten all day." He stops, caught. "Weird, right? I would have thought you'd be super full after beating a guy's face in," I spit out, unable to hold it back any longer.

He shifts on his feet, eyes thinning as he looks me square in the eyes. "I'm a fighter, Olivia. It's what I do," he says, voice low and demeanor so icy cold it leaves me shivering. He rolls his eyes at me and tosses the sandwich in the garbage, unable to stomach his lies anymore, probably. Too damn bad, I am force feeding them whether he likes it or not.

"I don't mean your training, and you know it." I chase after him into the hallway but nearly bump into him when he suddenly spins on his feet.

"What do I *know*, Olivia?" he growls, balling his hands into fists.

"You know that you're Dean's bitch," I snap and push against him. I don't like how he's towering over me. I have control; I am still wearing this god damn lingerie! "I know that you were beating up a tied man at Dean's will! I know that you are so fucking stupid for getting caught up in the gang.

And I know that I will not allow it—"

He grabs my accusing finger and presses me into the wall. "You can't boss me around, first of all. And what the fuck were you doing at the gym?"

"I was coming for you, to make sure you were okay. Because you weren't being straight with me," I answer him, and he groans dramatically. "Listen, I understand that you are able to make your own decisions. I do. But what I don't understand is why you aren't fighting to get out of his control. You have a freaking gun for *protection*, for goodness' sake. You shouldn't need it all!"

"Stop that!" He grips his hair and drags his hands down his face, like he's losing his mind.

"Stop what?" I throw up my hands.

"That!" He points at me. "Acting like you know what's best for me."

"Because I do know what's best for you!"

"No, you don't!"

"I care for you, Grey," I cut him off and try to drill it in his head. "Do you expect me to just step back and watch you throw your life away?"

"I'm not throwing anything away!" he argues.

"Then what do you call being in a fucking gang?" I question with a raised voice.

"None of your *fucking business!*" he screams, and I tug at my own hair. He's making me lose my mind. I just care so fucking much it is driving me nuts. But going bonkers for him is tolerable. It is expected, because he is the most complex creature on this planet. However, he wouldn't be him without the complexity or the frustration. God, *so* much frustration.

"Fine! Then fucking go and beat people tied to chairs, sell drugs, be his bitch—I don't care anymore!" I just snap because this is too much. You really can't save someone who doesn't want to be saved. I raise my arms and wave them wildly, going on and on about how much I am done with him. But the entire time, his eyes are on my chest and raking my body.

"What the hell are you wearing?" His voice is thick with lust.

"N-nothing," I stutter and quickly close the trench coat.

"This is not nothing," he says and tugs at the coat.

"Will you pay attention?" I slap his hand away.

He raises his lust-heavy eyes to mine and gapes. "How the fuck can I when you're wearing…*this*?"

"Jesus…" I rub my face some more, screaming on the inside. Why did I fall in love with a man who has such a short attention span at the worst possible times, when we are talking about him ruining his life? I push off the wall and storm into the room, throwing off the trench coat. "I am absolutely done trying to talk some sense into you, Grey. You are on your—what are you doing?" I screech when I am tackled to the bed.

He flips me over, pins my hands above my head, and pushes his legs between mine, leaving me open and exposed to his wandering eyes. "This is…Jesus Christ, Liv." I gasp and move around as I feel his true reaction down south press into my abdomen as he bends down. "You are so fucking sexy, it kills me and makes me feel insanely alive. You make me

275

mad, you know that, don't you?" he whispers haughtily against my ear, licking my earlobe. I shiver and moan his name.

"You're the one who drives me fucking bonkers," I breathe out, my voice raspier than usual. *Whoa.*

"Fuck the bonkers, I'll fuck you." He tugs at the lacy garter then squeezes my thigh. "White, huh? Lady-time must be over." I feel his teasing smirk as he lightly kisses my neck. I instinctually put my head to the side so he has more range. I pull at his black shirt, and he removes his lips enough so the shirt comes off. I throw it away and grip his hair with one hand while dragging my nails up his back with the other.

"Why did you lie to me?" I try to speak through the desire taking over my body.

"Shhh." He grips one of my breasts. I gasp and arch my back. He smirks in approval. "So responsive…I don't know if I want this off or on. You just look so…fuck." His erection digs into my stomach, and I hiss, tugging his hair. I arch my back some more, and his smirk grows inches. "*Princesa* says off." He reaches under me and unclasps the bra. I hold out my arms, and he tugs it off and throws it somewhere.

"Grey!" I moan in sexual relief when his mouth clasps around my right breast, while he toys with the other. I hold his head down and swallow the nervous lump in my throat. The throbbing between my legs is insane. I reach down and hoist his hip up. He holds himself up, and I moan over and over as I unbutton and unzip his pants. I tug them, and his boxers, down his feet until I hear them hit the floor. I push against his shoulder and straddle his hips, pushing him down.

Control. Remember that's what this whole thing is about, I remind myself.

"You are going to get out of that gang," I tell him, and he looks surprised, his eyes finally on mine and not roaming my body with need.

"What? No. I already told you, it's hard cutting ties with him." He doesn't sound like he's here. He is too busy examining my body. Again, I feel sexy even if I am just wearing the bottom part now. "You are too sexy for you own good," he groans animalistically, hands grabbing my thighs and going up to my stomach. He can't even talk to me correctly, he's distracted…but maybe I can use this to my advantage…

"Oh, am I?" I bat my eyelashes, and he hardens under me and grips me tighter.

"Don't fucking do that," he warns, and I pout, tilting my head.

"Do what?" I innocently, *accidentally* rub myself on his erect member.

"Oh, fuck me…" He throws his head back, eyes shut in pleasure.

"No," I say firmly. His eyes snap open, and he looks at me like I've lost my mind.

"Why the fuck not? You can't dress like this, do the whole innocent shit, and say no," he exclaims, and I giggle. His eyes widen as his member brushes against my sex. Shit, this is going to be harder than I thought, the whole seducing and manipulating thing.

"Oh, yes I can…" I trail in a sing-song tune, holding in a moan as I shift down and get on my knees, back arched. His eyes look like they're going to pop out of his head. I kiss the head of his dick and smirk when it twitches slightly, and he curses heavily, voice thick. "But I will fuck you…if you promise you're going to leave the gang."

"I told you—oh, fuck you!" He cries out when I roll my tongue around him. "Oooh, just you fucking wait!" He wags a finger at me, and I genuinely giggle but add in the little bat of my eyelashes.

"You'll get what you want *if* you promise to leave the fucking gang." My voice loses its innocence, and I cock my head to the side, waiting for his response.

His cheeks look sunken as he purses his lips and glares at me, in deep thought. He is weighing his options: stay in the gang and don't have sex with me or promise to leave and get what he—and I—obviously wants.

"Fine," he grumbles, rolling his eyes.

"Sorry? What was that?" I tease, cupping a hand behind my ear.

"Fuck you," he hisses.

"As you wish, babe." I wink at him, and he grows pale for a second. It's empowering how I can make him this distressed.

My lips twitch into a smirk as I take him into my mouth as much as possible. I lick and bob my head up and down, feeling him twitch and hearing him curse above me. I pull my mouth off. He doesn't deserve much more of that. He's been an ass to me for a very long time. He is lucky he's getting me at all tonight.

He watches me with desperation before I turn around and pull open the nightstand. I bypass the gun and pull out a condom from the boxed set he has. I turn back around, tear it open, and roll it onto him. I unclip my garter and watch him from under my eyelashes as he eyes me taking off the lacy material. I nudge my hips from side to side as I slide it down my thighs.

"I am going to fuck you so hard." He licks his lips. I barely have the thing kicked off when he grabs my hips and pins me to the bed. He maneuvers me around so I am facing the pillows and am on my stomach. I'm confused because we have never done it *this* way—if it is a way—before. "New position, babe. This is for fucking teasing me so god damn much." He grabs a fistful of my hair and pushes my back down before slamming into my sex from behind.

"Oh my God!" I cry out and grip the sheets. I...fucking shit, that felt amazing. This *feels* amazing! I giggle as I roll my hips, and he makes a crying sound. I laugh and bite my lip, letting him grip my hair as he begins to pound into me. Why have we never tried it this way before? It feels a little weird, but I feel like he's hitting the perfect angle in the most delicious way. "This is...wow."

"Yeah? You like the way I fuck your tight little pussy? Fucking minx," he murmurs, and I burn at his words. I nod in response and scream out when he digs his hands into my butt, kneading the tender flesh. "You feel so fucking good, so tight, and so fucking mine." He chuckles, and I imagine the dimples in his scruffy cheeks. I want to poke my fingers in them, but at the moment, I really want to tug at his hair like I usually do. It's hard not to be able to in this position, but I can deal with it with how fantastic it feels.

"All yours, Grey," I promise with a sigh, rocking my hips against him. I feel as though I can feel every inch of him plowing into me. I love the pleasure rolling through me in waves and the pain from his deadly grip on me, but the mixture has me tearing up and screaming his name. "Faster, please. Please—ah!" I grip the sheets until my fingers turn white and I see the back of my head.

Seconds turn into minutes, and minutes turn into hours, then into the eternity of forever as he claims me with passion and need. I clench around him and moan his name, biting into my lip to keep from screaming his name loud enough for the entire universe to hear. He is a black star hellbent on filling me with darkness, leaving me with nothing but the memory of this indescribable pleasure.

"Promise me you'll be safe," I breathe, rolling my head to relieve the tension building up in my bones.

"I'm wearing a condom, babe," he replies.

"I mean with Dean, the gang—"

"Let's not talk about this right now, please," he pleads and thrusts deeply.

"P-please, Grey. Promise me."

"Yes, yes—I promise. Fuck. Now shut up and let me fuck you," he demands, and I nod quickly, unable to speak anymore.

"I love you, *princesa*," he grunts as his hips go

crazy, thrusting at a much faster pace. I'm not going to last long. My hair sticks to my sweaty face, and I can hear my heartbeat lose its control, pounding almost as fast as he's pounding into me. I lick my lips and plead for more, please, so much. "*More…*"

"I love you too, Grey," I reply, breathless as I feel my stomach tightening. I make a strangled yelp and grip the sheets so hard, I think I hear it tear a little. But I couldn't give less of a fuck. He's fucking me too good. My God, I think I'm going to explode from pleasure. "I'm going to—" I begin but stop when a shriek leaves my lips.

He laughs, but it soon turns into a little scream of his own. "Shit! Come for me, bebé." I scream his name and jerk forward when he reaches under and plays with my clit. "I want to feel you tighten around me. Release for me so I can eat you up," he drawls, pushing me over the edge.

I come to my high and moan his name. "Grey…" My hair is tugged, and I feel him slam into me, releasing himself as his dick grows heavy in me.

"Oh my…fuck. Too fucking good," he groans while he rides his climax out.

I lean back and tip his chin down, bringing his lips to mine. The kiss is slow and passionate, and he grips my throat. I moan as he pumps into me, slowly caressing me inside. I pinch my eyes closed and fall onto the pillows. I tense and mewl in bliss as he brings my butt up again and does as promised. He licks between my folds until I literally can't take it anymore and fall onto the bed.

He chuckles and stands up to discard the nasty condom. I scrunch up my nose before he falls beside me, pulling me onto his chest. "And *that* is what I call fucking," he sighs. I close my eyes as he pulls the thin sheet up and over my body on top of his.

"We should do it more," I joke and yawn, lazily caressing his tattooed chest.

He exhales deeply and kisses my hair for a moment, rubbing my back. "Sure, minus you fucking *teasing* me like a damn vixen," he hisses, and I blush, peeking from under my curls.

"Oops?" I wink, and he rolls his eyes but holds a pretty cute smile. "Goodnight kiss?" I lift my head and purse my lips, closing both of my eyes expectantly.

His lips gently press against mine, smile and dimples and all. "*Buenas noches mi pequeña princesa vixen.*" (Good night, my little vixen princess.)

I poke his dimples and listen to him laugh in confusion before kissing his neck and wrapping my arms around him. "*Buenas noches mi pequeño luchador…*" (Good night, my little fighter.)

"Little? Shall we go for a round two?" He tickles my sides, appalled.

"No!" I shriek and writhe like crazy as he kisses my cheeks and moves his fingers all around my stomach and up and down my sides.

Chapter Twenty-Seven

The next morning, I wake up thinking the house is on fire. I quickly sit up, dazed and confused and sweetly sore from last night. I smile and breathe out when thinking back to last night. The way he held me and filled me and talked dirty, it made me feel perfectly sinned. I distinctly feel the caress of his fingers scoping for laughter as he tickled me, and the smoothness of his lips, like velvet, and sugary-sweet like cotton candy. I blush and bite my lip when remembering what those lips did to me afterward.

The house could be on fire and you're daydreaming about last night?

I push the sheet off me and stand up. I stretch with a yawn and scoop up his shirt he wore last night. I pull it on and discreetly sniff his homey scent. I leave the room, blushing at my subconscious; that seems to be the only part of me left unaffected by Grey. I am honestly so thankful for it, because without it, I would be helpless against the man. And Lord knows how he can be—

283

all-consuming. It's good that I have a little sensibility left in me to keep a part of myself grounded while the rest of me is in the clouds.

As I am nearly exiting the hallway, I look into the kitchen and smile broadly, semi-blinded by the sexy sight. I lean against the wall and bite my lip, tilting my head. Grey is shirtless and standing in front of the stove, struggling to flip a burning piece of pancake. That's why the house smells like burnt char. He's cooking. I am too slow to hold back a laugh when he finally flips the pancake, but it goes splat on the ground. He looks up like a deer caught in headlights, a nervous smile crooked on his lips. His eyes look me up and down, lust forming in those black eyes of his.

"Morning, sexy." His voice is thick with remnants of sleep.

My heart skips a step. "Morning," I mumble shyly, tugging at the ends of the shirt that sits at my mid-thighs. I walk over to the kitchen island and hop onto one of the leather stools. He laughs as I struggle to get up for a brief moment. I glare at him, and he raises his hands defensively. "Need a little help with that?" I stare at the empty pan as he throws away the burned pancake on the ground.

"Absolutely not, I am a grown man. I don't need little elves to help me." He waves the spatula at me, and I stick my tongue out at him. He does the same, and I grin.

"First, I am not an elf." I hop down from the chair, and he gives me a knowing smirk. I grunt at him and round the counter, bumping his hip and making him stumble to the side. "And second, I would like breakfast that isn't as black as your eyes."

"For your information." He bounces into my hip, and I scowl at him. "My eyes are a unique dark *brown*."

"Whatever helps you sleep at night," I mumble, and he hits me with his hips again. "Stop doing that."

He bends down to my height and coos, "Aw, is the little elf mad at me? Whatever shall I—hey, give that back!" I grab the spatula and run out of the kitchen just to spite him. I dodge him as he lunges for me in the living room and laugh like a maniac as I rush down the hallway into the bedroom.

"Not until you stop being an asshole!" I say and laugh harder when he almost slips and falls when entering the room. I hop onto the bed, then jump down and rush back into the kitchen when he jumps after me.

"I'm going to catch you eventually!" he shouts after me, but I just laugh.

I love this. Us playing around like nothing bad has ever happened. We are growing closer, slowly repairing what was broken. And I couldn't be any more elated. I want us to stay this way without ever running into some obstacle. I know wishing for nothing bad to happen is childish and unlikely to come true, but in moments like this, I want the world to stop. I just want to pause the world, eliminate the gang and my mother, then press play and live in innocent bliss with the love of my life. Is that so wrong?

He finally catches me by my waist when I try to

dash into the living room. "Caught you!" he announces, and I squeal as he sets me on the counter and grabs the spatula from me. "You are insane." He shakes his head, smiling.

I lean forward and peck his lips. "Insane for you."

"That you are." He tips my chin up and pulls me in for a toe-curling, slow kiss. I revisit every single inch of his mouth and cup my hands around his neck, splaying my body against his. He wraps an arm around my waist and slowly slides a hand up, revealing my tender skin from last night. I gasp into his mouth when he grabs my butt, and memories from last night make me moan.

A vibration pulls him away too fast, too soon.

"Sorry, sorry…" He pulls his phone out as I try to catch my breath. He scowls at the phone and then at the ground as he puts it back in his basketball shorts.

"What's wrong?" I pull him back in between my legs and cup his face, trying to meet his eyes.

He smiles as he looks up. "Nothing. Hey, I'm gonna have a few fights today in over the next town, but I'll be back in the morning, maybe a little later. Okay?"

"Okay…" I say unsurely. I know there's more to what he's telling me. I know by the way his cheeks paled when he looked at his phone. He smiles wider and kisses me softly, almost like he's hungry. I kiss him back and almost get lost in his lips. He pulls back.

"Shit! I almost forgot something." He grips my thighs before jogging out of the kitchen and into the bedroom. I jump down and think he means his shirt, maybe his duffel bag, but then I freeze. He looked like he saw an angry ghost when he looked at his phone. Code word for a very pissed off Dean, who has gotten under his skin. And then I think of what's in the room that he could have forgotten.

He comes back out wearing a dark grey Nike tank top and holding his black duffel bag.

"Got it. I'll call you when I get the chance," he promises, and I mumble a reply after he gives me a chaste kiss on the forehead.

I watch him leave, then wait a few seconds before going to the bedroom. I open the bedside table and sink into the bed, feeling tears coming rapidly. My worst nightmare has come true. The gun is gone. He took the damn gun.

***

I am frozen in front my parents' beach house door. I am too afraid of what, or rather *who*, lies behind this door. I told myself I would never forgive my mother for acting un-mother-like toward me and physically assaulting me. I am not here for her. I am here for Grey's charm.

I feel like I am slowly imploding. I have tried contacting Grey until my fingers have gone completely numb from all the typing. I need the charm; I know it will calm me down a tad because of what it represents: love, hope, and him. I need even the littlest of assurance or I won't last until he arrives home. *If* he does.

I whimper at the sullen thought and wipe away a

tear. I shouldn't think like that. I have to be positive, so I wait by the door expectantly. He will come back to me in one piece, and I will throw the damned weapon in the ocean. I'm not allowing him to be taken away from me in a violent way like that. There is just no way.

I press the doorbell since I forgot my key. My mind is in a complete fog by this point. I wipe away any extra tears. I don't want her to see me so weak. I inhale and hold it, preparing myself. When she opens the door, I am just going to barge past her and into my room. I will take what is mine and leave without even opening my mouth. Yes, that is the plan. Not the best or nicest plan, but it will let me leave unscathed by my mother.

I am completely thrown off when the door opens. "Mason?" I question, feeling tears prick my eyes.

His brown eyes blow wide open, and he makes a little strangled sound. "Hey…" He didn't expect this either. It has been so long since I last saw him. We left things so shattered, so terrible…it hurts to look at his overgrown hair and little stubble on his kind of chubby cheeks.

"What…what are you doing here?" I croak and blush when I hear how rude that sounds. "It's just, after what happened, everyone else left."

His brows concave. "What happened? I knew the girls left, but no one told me why."

I lose my breath for a little while. "You don't know?"

His eyes rake over my face, and he shakes his head. "No, tell me."

I inhale deeply, but I end up in tears. "My mother and I got in a heated argument that ended with her slapping me."

"Oh my God. I am so…" His eyes widen, and he takes a step forward to comfort me but stops, confused, and rubs the back of his neck. "I'm sorry. I didn't know. I would have left too—"

"And gone where?" I question.

He shrugs. "To my parents'? It's where Rose is staying."

"I didn't know they were down here too." Gosh, is everyone staying in Miami for the summer? That's very strange, but Mason did mention his parents liked to visit here a couple of times per year.

"Yeah, they are." He rubs his neck a little harder and sighs. "Now I feel like an asshole for staying after that. Are you okay?" He notices my continual tears, and I nod, then shake my head when he cocks an eyebrow.

"No," I admit. "I know you're probably still mad at me and I don't know where we stand, but I have to say: I am losing my mind a little. Grey is back in the gang, and the leader or whatever isn't letting him leave. And this morning he left, but with his gun. A fucking gun. He lied to me saying he was going to fight, but I don't know if he's going to really get in trouble or—or even worse."

"Shhh…" He pulls me into his chest and rubs my back. I'm racked with tears, and he moves me side to side in a soothing motion. "Fuck our fight. I'm over it, and you need a shoulder to cry on. I'm sorry for what I said and not being there when you needed it." He pulls back and offers a small smile. "Are we okay? Can we *be* okay? Please?"

I crack a smile and nod furiously, rushing back into his warm chest. "Yes, please. I missed you, Mase."

"I missed you too, Liv." He kisses my hair, and I smile against his chest. "Come in and we can talk." I let him pull me into the house and nervously look around as he closes the door. "Don't worry, your mother isn't here. And Louise is out grocery shopping."

I nod, feeling a little better knowing my mother isn't here. But I'd like to see Louise. She's probably heard what my mother did to me and is worried. I want to assure her that I am fine. I'll just have to stay around and wait for her to come back, but I'm concerned my mother will come back and start something again. I am not ready to face her again.

"Oh, and Rose is here. I'll just—"

"Rose," I breathe, finding her sitting in the living room.

She looks up when I say her name and looks shocked but offers me a warm smile. "Hello, Liv. Long time no see...are you feeling all right? You look a little woozy."

I try to speak, but I'm stuck. I haven't seen her since the night before Grey and I jetted off to Venezuela the next morning. I feel incredibly guilty because I wasn't thinking about how she felt when he let me accompany him instead of her, his obvious girlfriend. She said they weren't a couple, but I saw the way she looked at him. She still loved him; maybe she still does even after he's made it clear that we are working on being together again.

She is so sweet and doesn't deserve the heartbreak.

"I—" I look to Mason, who mirrors his sister's concerned expression. I plaster on a wide smile that hurts and take a step back. "I just came to get something…so…I'm—I'm sorry," I squeak and run toward the stairs.

"Wait!" both of them call out.

I hear someone chasing after me, but I plead to be left alone and rush up the stairs. I nearly slip and fall over a few, but I manage to make it to the grand second floor. I dash down one of the many hallways and charge into my old bedroom. I lock the door behind me, tears falling down my cheeks, and jump onto my bed.

"Come on, I need you. Please be here," I whisper like a mess and throw the pillows away. I remember tucking it under my head the night of my first date with Noah. My heart stings at the mention of him. I still have yet to talk to him. I'm just hurting everyone in my path. I am so selfish.

"Please be here, please, please, please…" I am basically begging now as I push the comforter off and stand beside my bed. It isn't here. Where is it? Did one of the workers wash the sheets or throw it away or something?

I toss the bed, using all of my strength until I fall to the floor and burst into tears, from worry over Grey, guilt from seeing Rose, and anger at myself for being so god damn selfish.

Chapter Twenty-Eight

Grey

It is two in the morning when I finally get back home. I don't expect to find Liv waiting up for me. I already told her I would be coming around this time. Though she is naturally paranoid enough to stay up, I'm just hoping she's asleep. There is no need to be up. I did what I had to and now I'm coming back to rest beside my girl. I'll feel guilty if she sat up in bed nervous to see me come home. My phone died a few hours in, and I didn't have my charger on me. Damn, knowing Liv, she is most likely up right now, burning her eyes out with the lack of sleep. I have half a mind to head straight into the kitchen and make her some coffee to soothe her.

I exit the car and wipe my semi-bloody hands on my basketball shorts and heave my duffel bag out of the backseat. My shoulder is a little sore from the punches I threw all day, but I suck it up. I've been through much worse. I haul my ass up the stairs, ignoring the pain, my girl fresh on my mind. I want nothing more than a hot shower and to snuggle up with my *princesa*. Just a few more steps and I will get all of that.

I close the door after me and kick off my shoes. I walk into the kitchen and rustle around in the fridge for water and some lasagna made a few days ago. While the food is warming up in the microwave, I plug my phone into the charger attached to the kitchen counter. I didn't have any time to get the most nutritious meal between taking fuckers down and gaining rank numbers. My fists are practically itching to go against the toughest of the toughest fighters out there in the big tournament, the very event that will seal my fate as an official MMA fighter. Fuck, I am getting hyped up just thinking about it. To be legally right when bashing guys' faces in. Ah, I smell the blood and gore right around the corner. And I am chasing after that fucker.

I tear through the delicious lasagna Liv made in five minutes and chug down some orange juice to wash it down. I am putting the dishes in the sink when my phone rings. Without thinking about it, I grab it off the charger and swipe my finger across the screen. A little blood gets on it. I grumble a curse while I rub it on my black shorts. I let out a sigh and hop onto the counter, finally looking at the kind of reddish screen.

It's a text from Dean, an address.

I clam up, instantly knowing what he means. I type a response and am so lost in the tapping of my thumbs that I almost don't notice.

Liv is watching me from the hallway.

"What are you doing up, Liv?" I sigh and hop down from the counter. "I told you I would be coming home very late." I tilt my head as I walk up to her and she takes a little step back. Hurt, I stop. "What'd I do?"

She stops from biting her lip and croaks, "I tried calling and texting. W-why didn't you answer?" Her voice is thick with emotion, and it sounds like she's been crying. But why would she be crying? Did someone hurt her? I will literally *kill* any fucker who hurt her. Shit! Do I need to start chaining her to the bed when I'm gone? 'Cause I will if it keeps her safe. I hang with some very bad people, people who have no morals, who aren't afraid to hurt the girl I love.

"Did something happen to you?" I take another step, but this time she isn't fast enough to move away. I caress her cheek with my hand but stop when I realize there's a bit of blood on the glove I am still wearing.

She notices and whimpers, taking a step back. "You didn't...y-you wouldn't—"

"What are you going on about?" I shrug, truly not understanding what's going on.

"You promised you would be safe! Y-you promised!" she screams and begins crying.

"What are you talking about?" I raise my hands defensively, shaking my head. She shakes her head, and I step forward to comfort her, whatever she's going through, but she takes another step back and lands with her back against the wall. "Liv—"

"The gun is gone, Grey!" she shouts, and I widen my eyes.

She thinks I took it to hurt someone…

"It isn't like that—" I begin to defend myself, but she pushes me away with her hands on my chest.

"You promised me, Grey! Do your promises not mean anything?" She is crying tenfold now, eyes bloodshot and voice shaking. I push through her tiny hands and pull her into my chest. She fights and screams and cries. I just shush her and stroke her hair and gently rock back and forth. I bend down and press my lips to her forehead. Finally, she grows limp in my arms and lets me talk.

"I didn't use it or anything," I tell her, and she stays silent, except for her sniffles and soft cries. "I gave it back to Dean because I knew how uncomfortable it made you. I really was fighting like I said I would be."

"B-but, the blood…" Her voice is rocky, and my heart breaks at the sound. I kiss her hair and sigh.

"I showed none of my opponents mercy. I do that a lot." I pause and pull back, cupping her face and brushing away tears, falling into her sparkling oceans of eyes. "But if it scares you too much…if *I* scare you too much…" I reluctantly pull my hands away, and she whines and pushes her face into my chest, wrapping her arms around me.

"Don't go anywhere," she whispers.

I smile and feel my body come alive under her touch. I kiss her head again and mumble as I squeeze her a little and rock us side to side. "Never…*me tienes princesa*." (You have me, princess.)

***

Some hours later I awake to the most obnoxious sound of an alarm. I instantly know it's Liv's because I don't fuck with alarms, nor have I ever set one in my life. I mean, what's the point of it when it cuts your sleep off and just gets you pissed before the day even starts? Speaking of which, why the fuck does she have an alarm anyway? Is she going somewhere she didn't tell me about?

"Sorry." She comes rushing through the door a few seconds after I begrudgingly sit up in bed.

"What the fuck was that for?" I grumble, rubbing my tired eyes and letting out an exhausted yawn. I side-glare at her as I scratch my stomach lazily. She laughs at me before crawling onto the bed after she shuts the thing off, looking sexier than ever. Dressed only in one of my black shirts, maybe the one I took off last night before falling into bed next to her, hair messy and lips puffy from the number of assuring kisses I gave her before falling asleep.

"I had a therapy session today," she sighs and falls onto my lap, straddling me, hands playing with the ends of my hair. "But after what went down between my mother and her mind-state...I just don't see the point anymore. She was forcing me to go in the first place. And now..." She smiles and tugs a little at my hair; I crook a smile at her. She tilts her head and breathes, "Now I don't have to listen to her anymore."

I frown because I have ruined her relationship with her mother. And it isn't the first time. Mine with my mother is tarnished forever. I don't think

I'll ever be able to forgive her. But Liv's is salvageable. Not now, of course. In a few months, maybe even years, just until it hits her mother that her daughter is a woman and not a child who can make her own life decisions.

"What's wrong?" Liv asks, her voice small.

I shrug and rub her waist. "I'm sorry."

"For what?" She laughs a little and sucks on her bottom lip.

I meet her searching eyes and shrug again, feeling a little guilty. "For causing all of that between your mother and you."

"You didn't cause that, Grey," she says, and I shake my head adamantly.

"I did, and I'm sorry I can't be what you need." My voice wavers, so I clear my throat and avoid her eyes. "I don't mean to worry you about whether or not I've *shot* someone. I just want to love you, but I can't do that correctly. How do you even care about me without fearing me?"

She wraps her arms around me and kisses the crook of my neck. "Don't you ever think like that. I love you more than you will ever know." She pulls back, tears streaming down her cheeks. I wipe them away, and she shakes her head. "I only worry about you *because* I love and care about you. Why don't you get that? I would never fear you…I could only fear how much I love you. Because sometimes it drives me to the point of insanity." She smiles so brightly I have to squint my eyes, and she laughs that cute smile of hers where her cheeks grow red and that tiny little dimple rests on her cheeks. "But it is definitely worth it in the end. Grey, loving you is worth *everything*…"

I suck with words, so I respond with my lips. I pull her forward and tell her with a passion-filled kiss how much I love her and will always love her. I whisper irrevocable and undying love in my native tongue. I caress her cheeks with promises to be there for her for whatever she needs and to protect her with my life. I pin her to the bed and spread her legs open with a string of curses just to show her what she does to me.

She moans when I pull back and lick her bottom lip.

"I love you, Olivia Westerfield," I tell her, resting on my elbows and admiring her flushed cheeks and blown-out blue eyes. "There aren't enough words in the world for me to explain. So just remember that."

She smiles widely and nods. "There's no way I can forget it."

I laugh, and it hits me square in the heart: I want this girl, officially. I want her to be mine, and I don't want anyone else to ever have the chance of taking her from me. I let that happen once before because I was such a blind, prideful fool. But I'd be damned to let it happen again.

"What would you and that therapist talk about?" I ask her, and her smile drops.

She shrugs and writhes a bit under me. "How I am still, or was, hung up over you. How my love for you was weighing me down…" She bites her lip, guilty. But I get it. I was still hung up over her too. And my love for her could bring down the world if I let it.

"How would she respond?" I rub her hips, and she bites back a blush, but I still see the redness and the baby dimple.

"Something along the lines of 'You should learn to move on and look toward a brighter future...'"

"Well, I say fuck that." I grip her hips, and she gasps but grins. "Go for what you want. I am...do...you?" I shrug, and she tilts her head.

"I don't know what you're getting at..." Her eyebrows stitch together in confusion.

Fuck! I told you, I am horrible with words.

I would tug at my lip contemplatively if my hands could stop holding her—never.

"Like that Ryan Goose guy said, we should know what we want and take it." Does that sound any fucking better?

Her puzzled features give me my answer. "You mean Ryan Gosling?"

"Sure, yeah, him." Sorry, I don't know the actors of modern-day life. The only TV I watch is the UFC channel.

"Wait, when did he say that?" She tilts her head, lips pursed.

"When the Allie chick didn't know what she wanted," I refer to that one stupid rom-com movie I know that Jaimie forced me to watch when she was going through her romance movie-watching obsession.

She clamps her lips tight.

"Well, I definitely want you," I say sheepishly and clear my throat looking away. This is fucking stupid. I sound and feel fucking stupid.

She leans up and presses her lips to mine. "I

299

understood what you meant at *Ryan Goose*," she admits, and I gasp and narrow my eyes at her.

"That was mean of you. I was struggling there!" I whine but can't help to laugh as she cracks up in laughter, mocking me.

"Sorry." She laughs even harder.

All I can do is stare down at her in awe and place a simple kiss on her lips. She stops laughing and looks up at me with those oceans for eyes and baby dimple and a comically goofy, wide smile.

"Mine, okay?" I whisper, hovering over her lips.

She nods and whispers back, "Yours."

Finally, our lips meet, and our hearts also meet in a beautiful, disastrous collision.

Chapter Twenty-Nine

I can feel my heart pumping fast enough to make me wonder if it's going to jump out of my chest as I run. Everything in me is begging to stop, but I have to push myself to the limit and far beyond that. The tournament is in two weeks. There is no way I can hold back now. If I don't win, let's just say my life will have no meaning. Not to sound dramatic or anything, it's just the only way I can legally fight, which is my passion, and get some really good money out of it. I can't just keep looking for underground or back-door fights. I want my girl to see me beat people's asses on national television.

My run comes to a stop twenty minutes later. I catch my breath and chug the rest of my bottled water as I enter the gym. A few guys greet me with a nod as I walk past them. Others don't pay me any attention. I've been coming to this new gym ever since David decided to be a traitorous, lying bastard. The fucker still calls me to this day, wanting to apologize and *explain*. But what is there to explain? He held back an important thing…him moving multiple fucking states away. I mean, what kind of friend just happens to *not* mention something as fucking massive as that? Especially when said friend has been there to save your ass more times than you can count.

I rotate throughout every machine in the gym. I push past my limits, nearly breaking the fucking boundary until my body is sore and aching. But I push through that even because, like I said, there is no time to be a pussy. I have to be better, stronger, faster if I want to win this thing. My dream lays beyond my win at the tournament. I will face many skilled, talented guys who want the same thing. But none of them have trained as hard as I have. None of them have dreamed of being an MMA fighter for their entire lives. They haven't had their ass beaten night after night when they first started out, only to push as hard as they could and could finally hold their own. No one, and I mean *no one*, wants this as badly as I do.

"Yo, Grey," a familiar voice booms behind me.

I set down a two hundred-pound weight and turn around. "Jake—took you long enough." I smile as he walks up to me and we exchange a little bro-hug. "Did you get lost or something?" I tease, and he rolls his eyes and sets down his duffel bag.

"Sorry that I didn't know exactly where this unknown gym was." He rolls his eyes, and I shrug. He looks at me for a moment and exhales, tilting his head. "Why don't you two make up already? Everyone misses you down at the gym."

I exhale too and walk over to the weights. "The minute he admits he acted like the scum of the

Earth, maybe. But until then, I'm training for the biggest fights of my life." I glance over at his contemplative expression and grunt as I lift the heavy weight. "Are you going to stand there acting like a pussy mediator, or are you going to spot me and train with me?"

He quirks that smile that makes the ladies swoon and walks over to me, all confident-like. "You already know the answer."

"I know, now get the fuck over here, Martin," I call him by his last name, teasing him.

"Just for that, add another hundred-pound weight." He smiles sarcastically at me.

"Fuck you," I spit, setting the weight down and adding another.

"Nah, not really into meat-heads."

"Shut the fuck up." I laugh, glad I had him come here. To be honest, I kind of missed his cocky-ass. I have been coming here for a while, and after a while I missed the usual faces at the old gym. I would still go there happily, if fucking David wasn't there. But that fucker is there nearly every single fucking day. And there is no doubt in my mind that he would try and corner me to speak his peace or some shit like that. I'm just not ready to look at him right now, nor am I prepared to *talk* to him.

He spots me through the heavy lifting that lasts about half an hour, then spars with me in one of the rings that aren't already occupied. I work on my quick dodges and uppercuts that I need some work on. I have to be in tiptop shape in every way if I want to win. This lasts for about another half an hour until I feel like I'm going to cough up a liver or intestines. Could be both, who knows?

"Oh, I almost forgot," he says as I'm texting Liv, asking if she wants something before I get back to the house. There is a string of short and late replies from her from the past few days above, and I pull at my bottom lip. She has been a bit distant lately. I fucking hate it. She's usually always…*there.*

I turn around and shrug. "What?"

A smile slowly breaks out on his face. "Happy early motherfucking birthday."

"Ah, fuck. How'd you know?" I run an agitated hand through my sweaty hair, gripping it just to instill how much I am fucking pissed he found out.

He shrugs and puts his gloved hands on his hips. "I have my ways."

"Well, I fucking hate your ways," I spit, and he just laughs at me. I grumble curses under my breath as I turn around and begin walking.

"Have a great day, Grandpa!" he calls after me as I am exiting the gym and storming to my car.

"Fucking August 18th," I mumble as I slip into my car.

***

"Honey, I'm home!" I announce as I enter the house. Liv didn't respond earlier, so I just got her some kale salad and a milkshake. She eats like a freaking rabbit. Adorable, but so freaking nasty. I'm treating myself to a nice greasy burger. I can already see her disgusted reaction and hear her lecture about being healthy and blah, blah, blah. I

304

only pay attention when she does that because she looks like an adorable angry chipmunk bitching about hibernation or whatever.

I drop my duffel bag and kick off my boots. As if sensing the mess, she steps out of the hallway and glares at them, then at me.

"How many times have I told you to put them to the side?" she chastises.

"About a million." I kick them to the side, and she begins to whine before going into a lecture about keeping the place neat since it technically isn't ours. Her cheeks puff out and her big eyes shimmer. Aw, upset chipmunk time.

"You can't keep doing tha—" she begins.

I cut her speech off with my lips. Her hands slide up my sweaty chest and cup my neck. I lift her up and firmly place her against one of the walls. I will never get tired of her mouth. Or these curvy hips. Or her soft, soft skin. My hands are roaming all around her. She moans, and I smirk. I bite down on her bottom lip, and her mouth falls open. I sneak my tongue in and listen to her moans as I knead my fingers in her ass under her thin dress.

She pulls back so I begin to kiss her velvety skin. "You're so sweaty," she whines, and I laugh.

"What did you expect? I just came from the gym, babe," I explain and nip at her skin—it will surely leave a mark. Good.

She moans my name and begins to say something when a ring punches through the air.

"Shit. That's me. I have to go." She pushes against my chest and lands on her feet. "Don't worry, we'll continue this later," she promises with

305

a smile and seals it with a kiss. Falling back onto the balls of her feet, she leaves me wondering what the fuck that was.

I will interrogate her on her weird behavior later; I'm fucking starving. I set her food on the counter island and tear through my food. I'm throwing the trash away when I hear hushed whispers. I narrow my eyes skeptically and tip-toe over to the bedroom. The door is cracked. I softly push it open a crack and find her looking out the window, talking on the phone. Who is she talking to? She ends the call and tosses her phone on the bed. Sighing as she rubs her eyes, she turns around. Why the hell does she look so stressed?

I fully open the door, and she snaps to attention. "Who was that?" I ask slowly.

"No one," she lies. I know because she's playing with the charms on her wrist. A typical identifier for when she's dishonest.

"Mm-hmmm, sure." I nod my head, and she smiles. "Actually, I have another question...where have you been lately?"

"What do you mean?" she asks.

I sit on the edge of the bed, and she stands in front of me, arms crossed.

"It's just that, well, you're barely around. And if you are, you're off on the phone doing God knows what...so what have you been up to?" I speak easily, carefully watching for any signs of dishonesty.

"I've just been a little busy with the formalities with the program," she says with a small smile. I hum and look her up and down for any sign, but I find none. I guess it does make sense. She's the type of person to gather all the information on something she's soon to dedicate her time to. "I'm sorry if I've been a little distant. I promise, it wasn't my intention at all."

I shrug. "All good." I may seem cool about it on the outside, but I'm a freaking mess on the inside. I've missed her a lot. I didn't know how much I loved her company until she started pulling away.

She chews on her lip. "No, it obviously isn't…" She suddenly drops to her knees and looks up at me through her curtains of eyelashes. "Let me make it up to you."

Fuck.

"Don't let me stop you." I grin from ear to ear.

I am breathless by the way she giggles like she's the purest feather yet yanks my basketball shorts and boxers down like a fucking vixen. This girl is a fucking *gem*. I suck in my bottom lip when she stares at my lengthy cock before leaning forward and rolling her tongue around the head, swiping up the pre-cum. I hiss a curse, and she smiles and winks at me. I almost bust just by that.

"Don't tease me, *princesa*," I say through clenched teeth. She murmurs before finally, fucking *finally*, wrapping her beautiful lips around me. "Oh, fuck," I grunt and wrap my hands in her thick hair. Her mouth glides up before taking me again. Then again and again until she's found a rhythm that is just way too fucking good. Her lips, her fucking tongue—they both feel incredibly amazing as she takes me until I feel the back of her throat and I nearly lose my fucking mind.

She should be distant more often. I swear she was made just for me, with the way she's going. But it's not just that. It's the natural passion between us. The drive to be as close to one another and even closer. The lust that simmers in those big blue eyes of hers. It's the sheer fact that with her, I feel like I am complete. But without, I am miserable and cold, and I fucking hate the feeling.

But back to this fan*tastic* blowjob.

"Fucking—if you keep looking at me like that, I will not last another second," I tell her as she locks eyes with me through her lashes, batting them even. "Fuck—you really hate me, don't you?"

She smiles around me.

I grip her hair, and she moans. I do it again, and she grips my thighs. I smirk and guide her head up and down. She closes her eyes and moans. I feel myself tighten and bob her head faster.

"Oh, fuck, that feels so good, bebé," I say in a jittery tone. "I'm so fucking close… just like that."

She continues to move against me, taking me past her limit, licking and swirling and fucking driving me insane. I grunt and curse and grip onto her head, reveling in her moans and mewls. I fucking love the sound. Makes me want to fuck her right now, but first she has to finish this.

"Fuck, I'm coming," I grunt out and lift my hips.

She stays on me and hollows out her cheeks. I bite my lip and feel my heart increase as I release into her warm mouth. I curse loudly like a bark and watch with greedy eyes as she licks it all up. Her throat bobs and I pant out. She just…

"I fucking love you, princess." I pull her up after

she pulls my shorts and boxers up.

She giggles. "Happy?"

"Fucking ecstatic."

"Good." She smiles even wider and kisses the corner of my mouth. "Now I have to go and chat with Matthew about a few details with the program."

"Fuck that." I grab her hand and pull her onto the bed. She laughs, cheeks puffed, eyes bright and all. I take off my shirt and tug at her dress. "And let me *fuck* you."

She pushes her hands underneath her head and shrugs with a wicked smirk. "Don't let me stop you."

Chapter Thirty

Liv

Grey and I spent the rest of yesterday watching his fighting channel. Well, he watched that barbarian channel while I was making some...plans. I thought I'd been discreet the entire week but turns out he's really observant. More than I actually thought he was. Not that I'm saying it's bad, it's just kind of terrible timing because of how important what I am doing now. The good news is he hasn't figured out what I'm planning. If he did, everything would be ruined. So the next day when I wake up, I make sure to show him some affection and pay extra attention to him.

"What was that for?" he asks after I've given him a long kiss.

I shrug and straddle his hips, splaying my hands against his chest. I stare at his unique tattoos and almost find myself falling into their backstory and complexity when he lifts his hips, jarring me out of it.

"Can't I show my *lovely* man some love without

there being an underlying motive?" I question with a playful tilt of my head.

He just hums and looks me up and down.

"I'm serious, Grey," I say, trying to convince him I'm not lying.

I am not lying, well, not *fully*, anyway. Sometimes I really do have to touch him, kiss him even to make sure this is real. That we're really together. He isn't yelling at me to go away or pushing me away. I am not diving into bottomless pools or having mental breakdowns. Nor am I accidentally downing anti-depressants to relieve the heartache inside of my chest.

I gently drag my nails down his hard stomach, and he hisses while I smile bashfully. He is one hundred percent real. And my love for him is unfathomable and irrevocable. It is like the air: I can feel it nourishing me, yet instead of not being able to sense it physically, I can taste it when I kiss him. I can feel it when he does the little things like kiss my cheek or randomly hold my hand. And I can see it the way he looks at me, the way his black eyes shine just for me and a crooked smile breaks out on his face.

"Is this real?" He reads my stunned thoughts, interlocking my fingers with his.

"Does this feel real?" I lean down and press my lips against his. I glide my hands up to his pecs and squeeze. I receive a low growl that causes me to reverberate. I smile against his soft lips and rock my hips gently against him.

I never imagined we would be doing this—*here*. When he left me all those months ago, I felt my heart crumble to pieces around the horrible person I had become. I didn't think my lips or body would ever find their home again, against his. I finally feel like I am whole again.

I hate that I say that because I shouldn't let anyone, not even Grey, define my well-being. But let's be honest, I was horribly miserable without him. To the point that I needed multiple therapy sessions each week and anti-depressant medication. And now that I have him, I don't ever want to let him go. Sounds obsessive and a little crazy, but love does things to you. I never expected it when I saw him, but it made itself known by smacking me square in the chest. Now it's bigger than ever and is itching for me to be closer to Grey.

A familiar pinging noise coming from my laptop across the room sounds, causing Grey to groan as he shoves his head into the pillow and writhes like an upset child.

"Turn it off," he pleads.

"I'm sorry, I'll get it—" I begin to get off him.

"Good." He rubs his eyes.

"I think it's just Matthew."

His hand wraps around mine, and his scowl stops me. "Hell no." He tugs me back into his chest; he's sitting up now. "He's interrupting something. The fucker can wait a couple of hours." I smile when he presses a longing kiss against my chin, looking up at me expectantly. Like one…oh, two…okay, that's three, and—fuck—it feels good…kisses can, um, can change my mind. Wow, his lips are doing quite the works, huh?

"No, I'm sorry. It's about the—"

"I swear to God, if you say the word *program*, I will flip my shit," he grits through his clenched teeth, eyebrows screwed together. He looks like a pissed off pit-bull. He instantly softens when I peck his lips. His eyes glaze over, and I laugh and do it again, moaning against his lips. I pull back before his hands can hold me.

"We won't take long, I promise." One more kiss and I'm walking over to my laptop. The ringing has stopped, but I shoot him a text to give me twenty minutes to get ready. I've just woken up and I look like a mess. "Take a shower with me?" I take off Grey's shirt and look over my bare shoulder. I'm topless, and he looks like a cartoon character with his tongue out and eyes wide. Just hang the word "Wowza" over his head, and you can toss him in a *Looney Toons* show. He scrambles off the bed, and I squeal in laughter as I leave a trail of my underwear behind me, entering the bathroom.

The shower doesn't take long, much to Grey's dismay. He constantly tried to start something, but I kept reminding him that I have Matthew waiting for me in the next room. That only fueled his jealousy. I can't say that I don't find it attractive. The way he grabs my hips possessively and tries to show me I am his. It's all very alluring in a strange way. Unfortunately, I don't have time for jealousy. So I appease him with a very rushed quickie and am still glowing afterward.

Grey glares at me with those dark eyes of his as I curl my hair and style it so most is over my right shoulder. His eyes go up and down, scrutinizing my white shorts and my strapless blue shirt.

"Do you not like how I look?" I turn in the desk chair, and he shrugs on the bed. I frown and consciously tug at the shirt I thought was kind of cute. "I look bad…?"

"What? No, of course not. You look beautiful as always," he says. "Just a little too much for Mark."

"His name is Matthew. Why can't you remember a name so simple?" I shake my head. The laptop rings again, and I face it.

"Because he's a fuck-head," he says, and I hear him walking up behind me.

"He is not. He's a kind man." I peer up at him; he's scowling at Matthew's icon, him dressed in a button up, dark blond hair gelled. "Please leave. We'll only be chatting for a little while." I push at his legs, but he doesn't even budge.

"Chatting about what?" he huffs out, crossing his arms, eyes unmoving.

"You know what, now please, at least get out of the shot," I plead, and he grumbles and reluctantly shifts a few feet away. *Finally*…I plaster on a smile and finally press the accept call button. It takes a second, but his face appears on the screen, and I am blasted by his radiant smile and warm blue eyes.

"Hello, Liv! Good morning," he greets me politely, and I look around at the gorgeous scenery around him. He looks like he's at a park or maybe a golf course.

"Hello, Matthew, and good morning to you too," I greet back and hear a mumble next to me. Grey. But I keep my eyes on the screen. "I'm sorry, but I have to ask: where are you? It looks amazing."

He chuckles a cute little laugh that makes me

smile just by how happy he looks. Grey growls beside me, and I shoot him a look to shut his trap. He rolls his eyes and mumbles to himself. I look back to Matthew with a smile.

"I'm in California. The CEOs of the program have decided to expand across the country," he explains, and I gape in awe. He laughs at me, and I chuckle, reddening how foolish I must have looked. "I've been touring with the manager of the branch in Pennsylvania, checking out the HQ buildings and such. Pretty soon they'll be in every state for many college students."

"That's amazing, Matthew," I tell him honestly.

"I'm going to the beach soon," he says and slants his lips in an uncharacteristically playful smile. "Maybe you should come out here and catch some waves."

"Maybe I will." I mirror the smile he is ridiculously making, and we both burst into laughter.

"No, nope—not—fuck no. I think that's enough for today." Grey tries to snatch the laptop from me. I gasp and grab it from him, kicking his thigh and making him stumble back.

"You promised!" I'm red as I set the laptop back, him very much known to Matthew now.

"I ain't promised shit. You two were nerd flirting, and I do not tolerate it," he accuses, and I gasp.

"We were not!" I snap through gritted teeth. "I don't even know what that is."

"Flirting: it's when two people tease and joke around with the intentions of fucking—" he says

315

crudely, but I stop him, unfortunately not soon enough.

"Jesus…" I pinch my nose bridge and hear Matthew clear his throat. "Matthew!" I straighten up in the chair and nervously smile, feeling hotter than the sun as he laughs lightly, looking between me and Grey, who is standing behind me, head on my shoulder.

"Should I call back later?" he asks and catches Grey's very intense gaze.

I shift the laptop a little, but he just nudges over too. I sigh and shake my head. "No, please, just don't mind him." I point to Grey peeking over my shoulder like an eager puppy. A mean one that doesn't understand staying out of the *way*. I should have known the jealousy thing would bite me in the butt.

He laughs easily, and I bite back a smile, because Grey surely would rip the laptop from my hands and hold Matthew hostage, thus losing his mind. He and I talk about the program branching out and what I should expect when I begin. I admit that I'm a bit nervous to be a part of something so elite, but he laughs it off and tells me that I will do great. I can't even help but blush at his kind words. Grey almost went crazy at that point, but I whispered in his ear what we could do later if he left me alone with Matthew. He reluctantly left, but he left all the same.

"All done?" he asks when I come into the living room twenty-five minutes later.

I plop onto the couch next to him and kiss his cheek. "Yep. Now I'm all yours."

"Good, and I'm not letting you go." He smiles and lifts my leg, pushing me down on the couch. I smile against his lips, but before it can get any deeper, my shorts buzz. "Oh. My. *Fucking.* God," he grunts each word harder with each one as I sheepishly smile and pull my phone out. "Who is it now?" he complains, letting my leg fall.

I sit up and read the text message, hiding a smile. "The girls. I totally forgot, they promised to take me out to celebrate me getting into the program." I smile widely and pinch his cheek to cheer him up, but he has crossed his arms and is staring at the blank TV. "Raincheck?" I give him a chaste kiss and feel horrible when he mumbles something and shakes his head.

"Sure. Have fun."

"I—"

He clicks on the TV, cutting me off.

I bite my lip and hesitantly rush out of the house.

***

"You know, when you said *raincheck*, I thought you really fucking meant it," Grey complains as I help him tie his tie. His head is tilted back and his Adam's apple bobs furiously. With the way he keeps fidgeting, you'd think he was an impatient child.

"Will you please stop moving around? I'm almost done," I ask and bend a little. I'm on the bed, so I am slightly his height and am able to do this easier. "And I did mean it. Just after this dinner party, then I am all yours."

317

"Heard that before," he mumbles, and I frown but keep my mouth shut.

We are currently getting ready to attend a dinner party. I am having them come to my parents' beach house since Mason says my parents are still gone. The place is huge, empty, and all the hard work my mother put in it will definitely wow them. It is with some very important people from the program. They have agreed to meet with me, so I can familiarize myself with them and help them see me in a good light. They're here because of the expansion, so I am grateful they are taking the time to have dinner with me.

"There. All done and pretty." I cup his chin and pull him in for a sweet but short kiss.

He rolls his eyes and turns away from me. I hop down, and he assists, wrapping an arm around my waist.

"Tell me why I have to go too." He nudges the tie, irritated.

"Because I want to show you off. Now, let's go." I grab my phone and glance in the mirror, giving myself a once-over. I'm wearing a pretty white lace dress, white heels, and a pair of silver drop earrings. I glossed my lips and put on a little eyeliner, mascara, and blush. Simple, but I'm not the best at makeup. And I didn't want to go over the top and end up looking like a clown.

"Wait," he says when I open the door.

"Yeah?" I turn around and find him rubbing his lower lip before throwing his hands in his dress pockets, which I fought hard with him to put on. He doesn't like dressing up, but he was quick to put everything on when I offered him a little something for tonight. He's such a horn-ball. It's a bargaining chip I will shamelessly use. Well, a little shame will be accompanied with its usage.

"Do you...are you forgetting something?" His voice sounds a little weary.

I look around and feel my heart drop when it hits me. "Yes!"

He grins. "Finally. I thought you forgo—"

I rush over to the dresser and snatch my white clutch. "Thank you, you're a life-saver." I walk back over to the door and stuff my phone and wallet in it. I clasp it shut and frown when I find him pouting at me like I just stomped all over his heart. "What's wrong?"

"Um..." He's fiddling with his fingers now, biting his lip. "Do you...know what day it is?"

I raise a brow and shrug. "Friday?"

His face free-falls. "Oh..."

"Now that we have that clear, can we please go?" I walk over to him, grab his hand, and drag him out of the room.

***

"Okay, something is definitely wrong," I say for the millionth time, and Grey sighs, avoiding my worried eyes.

"Nothing is wrong. Get out of the car," he grumbles, stepping out and tugging on his blazer he swears he will burn the minute this "stupid thing" is over.

I sigh and quickly leave the car, catching up to

him on the stairs. "Wait up!" I grab his hand, and I catch him rolling his eyes away from me. I stop him before he can ring the bell, holding up my keys. "Are you sure you're all right? Because you know I will make it up to you later."

"Yeah, you're a pro at that." He smiles sarcastically, and I sigh.

"You know I love you," I remind him, gripping his hand.

He mumbles incoherently, and I sigh again, then finally unlock the door. I push it open and close it behind us. The darkness swallows us whole, and he curses to himself.

"Why is it so fucking dark in here?" he questions.

"I don't know. Turn on the light beside you," I suggest.

The light flips on and reveals the room full of people, all holding confetti poppers.

"Surprise!" they all scream as the poppers go off.

Music blasts through the air, and I laugh as I look up at Grey. He is stunned as he gawks at the shiny banner that reads "Happy Birthday, Grey!" in big bold gold letters. The air is littered with colorful confetti, and the sound of laughter and cameras going off fill my ears until I am smiling so hard, my cheeks are on fire. I spot my group of friends among the people I don't know and wave at them. They wave me over, but I hold up a pointer finger to signal I need a minute. They nod in understanding and laugh at Grey, who is still like a deer caught in headlights.

I tap his shoulder, and he slowly faces me.

"Today is August eighteenth, the day the love of my life, Grey Nathaniel Wyler, was born." I cup his neck and stand on my toes, pressing my lips against his. Confetti falls all around us as he holds my waist and tastes the secrets I've been keeping so I can plan all of this. I pull back and laugh a little as he kisses all around my face. "I will never forget this day, ever," I say through the laughter as he kisses me all over.

Chapter Thirty-One

Grey

"You sneaky fuck." I've just been staring around in amazement and confusion. My first thought when I flipped the light on was: *what the fuck*? I questioned when the hell and *how* she got all of this done. I didn't even think she knew when my birthday was. But then it hit me: my grandmother loves to talk about me and share embarrassing stories. So, of course, she would reveal that, my middle name, and much more. I'll chew her out for that later, but not too much; it shows how much she cares for me.

She giggles and looks around at her handy work. "It's nice, right? You see the waiters?" She points out a tall girl with a short pixie cut wearing a button up and a horrid black vest and carrying a tray. She waves her over. "Your abuela revealed to me that you were obsessed with gummy worms when you were a kid. I wanted to see if that obsession is still there."

"I am going to kill that woman," I sigh and shake my head in slight embarrassment.

"Hush. She's a sweet woman who just loves to gush about her grandson." She taps my cheek and laughs when I turn to bite her hand. She's flushed red as she realizes the girl is near us. "Now, here—thank you," she says to the girl as she picks up two colorful sugary worms, then hands me one. I reluctantly take it, rubbing the back of my neck with my free hand. "Apparently you wouldn't leave the dinner table until you got your dessert worms." She raises a cheeky eyebrow as the girl walks away with a plastered smile.

"I guess you can say I was kind of a chubby kid," I tell her, unable to hide a little smile as I hold up the worm, reveling in arguments with my abuela to give me my *damn worms*. Ah the amount of ass-whoopings were worth the pity worms. "Got teased a lot."

"But you beat them all up?" she questions. I almost don't notice because I am so in my head, but our hands are clasped together and we're walking through the crowd.

"Hell no!" I say, and she gasps. "I had to get beat down a lot before my grandpa stepped in and taught me how to *really* fight. See this scar?" I point to the one above my right eyebrow, and she nods, staring at it. "From a fucker named *Chuck* that would throw *rocks* at me."

"Aw." Her hand lightly touches the scar. I take her wrist and pull it to my lips. I close my eyes and can practically feel her heavy blue eyes watching me. I pull away and brush my knuckles against her soft, fair skin.

"Don't feel bad. It got me to where I am today," I tell her, finally opening my eyes. "Here, with you." She smiles before standing on her toes and bringing my head down to meet her sweet lips. I grasp her hands and pull her into my chest, then wrap my arms around her waist. The kiss is slow and gentle but filled with my love. I deepen the kiss, tracing her tongue and finding that tender spot that makes her giggle. I smile as she does it and cup her face.

I am so in love with this girl it physically hurts me. I did not expect this magnitude of a grand, meaningful party. But then again, I should have seen it coming. Liv is the most compassionate human I have ever had the pleasure of knowing. She is the best thing that I have ever had in my life. I don't deserve her. She and I, and the whole damn world, know that. But I am the most selfish person and I will not give this amazing, cheesy girl up. Not for a damn thing.

"*Te amo*, Grey Wyler," she whispers as she pulls from my lips.

I press my forehead to hers and kiss her nose. "*Y te amo*, Olivia Westerfield."

I will never get tired of saying that. Ever.

Suddenly, the lights are shut off, sheltering us in the dark again. Only a few feet away from us there is a huge cake with sparklers in the top rolling over to us slowly. I feel myself flush, which is really fucking rare, as people I don't even know start singing the horrible tune of "Happy Birthday." I stand awkwardly as Liv wraps an arm around me and joins in, staring up at me. I furrow my brows and grimace at the cake that is now in front of me. It is delicately designed in blue frosting.

I quickly blow out the candles to end the terrible, off-key singing. Everyone claps, and I stare at Liv to ease the awkwardness that comes with birthday cakes. I mean, what are you supposed to do when people are singing at you? It's weird and one of the main reasons why I don't broadcast my birthday around. That and how fucking conceited is it to be rewarded for being born into this fucked-up world...by chance at that?

"Cake?" Liv holds up a slice toward me.

"No thanks. I already got my sweets." I smirk and pull her into my chest.

"Ugh, don't be gross." She backs away, but I kiss her lips.

"If this is gross, then I am disgustingly toxic," I murmur against her lips.

"Guess it isn't that bad." She shrugs, and I raise a brow and nod, pulling her in and deepening the kiss a tad. I wish I could erase the people surrounding us. It's too loud and polluted. I just want for it to be her and me, alone.

"Hey, break it up!" someone screams behind us. "There are people eating, you know."

I reluctantly pull away and force on a smile as Jaimie winks at me.

"Hello, Jaimie," I say when Liv lightly grips my arm.

"Happy birthday!" She launches her arms around me, and I hug her back, slightly. She pulls back and holds out a blue-themed card. "It's from all of us," she informs, gesturing to Liv's group of friends. I read the card and chuckle. On the front, it says: *Happy Birthday, Asshole.* That's it. On the inside it says: *Happy 50th*, obviously written by them with sharpie.

"Thank you, guys." I give her a quick hug, which surprises her and everyone, especially Liv. I cough awkwardly and rub my lip.

"I picked the card!" Charlotte, I believe, announces proudly, pointing at herself with an award-winning grin.

Mateo rolls his eyes and steps forward, giving me a bro-hug. "You already got my gift. But happy birthday, man."

"Thanks." I give him a nod and unintentionally glance at Mason.

He catches my gaze and nods at me. "Happy birthday." His voice is tight, and I shift on my feet.

I just nod and clear my throat. I always fucking despised this kid. Always sneaky and bright-eyed and smiles. It freaks me the fuck out. That and I'm pretty sure the fucker persuaded Rose to cheat on me because I wasn't *good enough* for her. He was right, but still, that asshole started a world of trouble without even knowing it.

"Okay, I have to give you your present," Liv pipes up, clearly trying to diffuse the tension.

"You got me something?" I shouldn't be so surprised.

She nods and tugs at my hand. "It's in the car—come on. I'll see you guys soon." She waves to her friends, then proceeds to pull me through the crowd. There's a parted opening as I glare at anyone in our way. They shift, and Liv leads me to the door like an angel in her all-white get up. I have to stop and admire how beautiful the color causes her hair to glow and makes her seem all the more innocent. But if everyone knew how I had my hand wrapped in her hair, tugging her head back or how fucking great her pouty lips around me felt, well, she wouldn't be painted so innocently anymore. But to me she will always be my pure angel I can't help but taint with my darkness.

I take off the stupid fucking blazer she forced me to put on and shove it into the backseat. I lean against the tail of the car as she pops the trunk open and searches through it. I loosen my tie and pop open a few buttons. May as well take off the abominations that are these fucking loafers and change into a pair of shoes I keep along with a few clothes in case in the trunk. I run my fingers through my hair and groan in satisfaction as the fuckers pop off my feet.

"I am never going to another dinner party with you again." I wave an accusing finger at her.

"I had to get you to come with me. I knew how much of a loving, supportive boyfriend you are." She tries to kiss me, but I duck, grab the shiny shits, and toss them in the back. She makes a huffing sound, and I laugh loudly as I grab a black pair of Converse. Not my favorites, but I don't exactly have my boots with me.

"Now, where is my present you promised?" I perch onto the open trunk and raise a brow at her.

"Um." Her hands are behind her back, and she shrugs. "It's me."

"Well, okay." I make a move to grab her, but she squeals and jumps back.

"I was kidding, you horn-ball!" she exclaims and gives me a look that makes me laugh.

"Excuse me, but you said it was you! Not my fault you wanted to be *funny*." I throw quotes around the word, and she gasps, hitting my chest.

"I can be funny when I want to be," she defends.

"Oh, yes, you're the most comedic person I have ever known," I say sarcastically, rolling my eyes in the air.

"If you keep making fun of me, you won't find out what your present is," she threatens.

"Okay, just hope you've kept the receipt." I shrug, and she gapes at me. I laugh and bring her between my legs, cupping her face and smiling at her sullen expression. "Kidding, babe. You know I'll love whatever it is you've gotten me."

"Seriously?" She lifts an eyebrow.

I sigh and latch my pinky with one of hers and bring it up and kiss it. "Pinky-promise serious."

"Okay, that was cute." She kisses our interlocked pinkies, a smile on her luscious pink lips. "You deserve your present now." She holds out a long, blue-wrapped box with a white bow on top. I wonder what it is. Maybe some cheesy shit like a wand if my abuela also revealed on top of many other things that I was obsessed with *Harry Potter* for a *very* short while. If so, I will *obliviate* her and my memory of a grandma.

"Oh, thank you for the honor." I take the box from her, not missing the look of excitement written on her crooked lips and shining eyes. I feel a sort of weight on my chest in anticipation as I slowly unravel the bow, watching for her reaction. She has the crook of her index finger clenched between her pearly white teeth.

She taps my knee impatiently and mutters, "Hurry up and open it, Grandpa."

"Hey, I'm turning twenty-two, not *eighty-two*." I chuckle and toss the long piece of ribbon behind me. She just shrugs. "How'd you get this in there without me noticing?" It is my car after all, and I throw in and take out my duffel bag basically every day. So how did I not see a wrapped box with a fucking bow on it?

"I put it under a pile of blankets," she explains and holds up a finger. "Why do you have so many anyway?"

I pause in opening the lid. "I like to have a lot of blankets around in case."

"In case of what?" she shrugs.

I shrug myself. "You never know…"

"If?" Her lips are curving now. She sees my answer coming.

I blush and cough into my hand. "In case of avalanches and shit."

She falls into a fit of laughter that makes me red.

"That's it, I'm not opening it." I begin to put the gift away, and she finally stops laughing. "That's what I thought."

Finally, I pop the lid off and tilt my head. It's a…belt. But it's not an *ordinary* belt. Facing me is a long buckle that is the word *Champion* in bold letters. On the right side at the end is an engraved *G*. I don't know what to say, so I just look up and find Liv fumbling with her hands against her chest, bottom lip being chewed out like it's taffy.

"Do you get it?" She pushes hair behind her ear. "Because of the huge tournament coming up. You probably won't win a belt like this or a belt *at all*. But you get it? With the fighting show you watch? How they win those champion belts…do you not get it?" I watch her ramble and feel my smile getting bigger and bigger. "I can throw it out. Not really carry it to the store because I kind of got it custom because of the G. Do you see it?" She taps the *G,* but I can't speak. All I can do is stare at this marvelous woman standing in front of me. "Can you please say something?" She's covering her face now.

I stand up, remove her hands, and tip her chin up. "I love it…and I love you." I take a deep breath and briefly close my eyes to keep from blurting out every thought that is tied to this petite girl who has the heart of a thousand full moons. "My love for you is too profound to be explained in words."

"So explain it using something else…" she suggests, her eyes lingering on my lips before suffocating me with her cerulean eyes.

I nod and lean down, smashing my lips against her. Her hands grip my elbow as I hold onto her face but then migrates to my neck. She leans up, and I lift her up, close the trunk, and place her on it. She is finally at my height, so it is easier to show her how much she has my heart. I gently pull away and press her small hand over my exposed chest. I suck in a deep breath and find the courage to say the next words to leave my lips.

"This…this is what you do to me," I say in a shaky voice, licking my lips as she gasps when feeling my heart race, more than any lap around the *city* could cause. So fast that it is burning bright and practically glowing against her hands. But that could be my mind that loses all sense when I am around her. "You have my whole heart, *princesa*." I flick my eyes up the same time hers look up, and I smile shyly. "The entire thing…"

Chapter Thirty-Two

Liv

I am glowing like the moon above our heads. The words that just came out of his mouth leaves me stunned; I can't even speak. All I can do is press my hand harder against his chest, like I want to reach in and grab his erratic, tattooed heart. Mine. His heart is mine. I can't be any hotter or blush any harder even if I tried. His affection toward me makes me giddy, and I want to get up and dance even if I look like a fool. He loves me whole-heartedly. I can see it in his eyes as he takes in my shocked, blushing state with that little crooked smile of his.

What he doesn't know is that he has my heart. I've told him countless of times how I love him, but I don't think he understands how he truly and one hundred percent has me. There is no turning back from this, from him. He has a hold on me that I know will never loosen. It's a good thing I don't want him to. I have never felt such heartache from the amount of love pouring into my veins, and I somehow just know that I won't feel this love again, not for anyone else. Only for him.

"Say something," he begs softly, nudging his nose with mine.

I hum and circle a finger around his inked skin. "You have mine too, Grey. You stole it the minute we met."

"I was quite the catch, huh?" he jokes with that cockiness I love dearly.

I laugh and lift my eyes to meet his, admiring his dimples. "And you still are." I offer him a genuine smile, and his lips lose his arrogant smirk just a tad. They soften into a smile that reflects the light beat of his heart as I slip my fingers through his unbuttoned shirt and bounce my fingertips over his tattooed skin that protects his matching heart. I lean up and he bends down, our lips meeting in the middle. A single hair of electricity wraps around my heart and squeezes tightly until I find relief in his mouth.

We should probably go back inside; my friends must be wondering what's taking so long. The thought of their assumptions makes my stomach tighten and my face to heat up in embarrassment. But I can't seem to pull away. His lips draw me in and pull me away, tugging at a desire for more. So much more. Especially when his hands slither up my dress and grip my thighs. A moan slips out, and I grip the back of his hair, earning a throaty groan from him.

"Sick, dude!" a person behind Grey shouts.

I pull away and hide in his neck as one of

Charlotte's friends passes us.

"Fuck off!" Grey snaps, and the boy quickly nods before scrambling into the house. "Fucking ruined the moment," he mumbles, turning back to me with a pout.

I laugh. "It's okay; I think we should head back inside anyway."

"Because of that ass-wipe? Hell no." He pulls me closer to him, and I laugh harder.

"We can continue this later when we're home and not in front of my parents' beach house." I take my hand out of his shirt and push him back. He begrudgingly steps back and helps me down. I open the trunk, grab the belt, and hand it to him.

"What's this for?" he asks as I close the trunk again.

"For you to wear," I explain, and he scoffs.

"I am not wearing this," he says and moves to open the trunk.

I step in his way. "Why not?" I ask, and he opens his mouth. "Do you really not like it? Do you h-hate it?" I pull out the big guns: widened eyes and pouty lips. The puppy dog look. He falls for it every time. I even tug at my dress and twirl it a bit. It's one of the reasons I decided to wear it tonight—he's a sucker for the whole innocent look. Can't ever say no to it or me. A flaw I will definitely use in the future. With a lot of guilt, of course…

"I really hate you," he grits out through his teeth.

"Funny, I thought you loved me two seconds ago." I bat my eyelashes, and he glares at me but slinks the belt through his dress pants loops and clasps it on. I tap the buckle and then his nose. He bites my finger and I gasp, poking his chest. "Don't bite or I may have to reciprocate later." I wink at him, and he slaps a hand to his chest.

"You wouldn't dare," he says.

"Wouldn't I?" I back away, and he chases after me. "Grey!" I scream as he scoops me up and tosses me over his shoulder like a lousy sack of potatoes.

"You bite, I bite back," he threatens, and I consciously rub my thighs together. "That's what I thought." He bites my thigh, and I laugh, then moan in pain. He puts me down in front of the door and pecks my lips, holding my chin. "Don't tease me if you know what's good for you, *princesa*." I frown, and he kisses me, but I keep my eyes open to glare at him. He laughs like a dictator before pulling me from the door and opening it.

We walk back into the party, and it hits us full force. The lights are slightly dimmed. Red cups are beginning to litter the floors along with colorful confetti. Everyone is dancing to some hip-hop song I don't know the name of. This is going to be a bitch to clean tomorrow. But for right now, we should focus on having fun and enjoying the night.

I pull Grey into the kitchen where the drinks are. He wraps his arms around me. I first think it's because he wants to be closer to me, but then I notice how every boy I pass looks like they're about to poop their pants. I roll my eyes but keep walking.

I stop in my tracks when Rose's eyes lock with mine. She looks a little uncomfortable but is dressed prettier than ever in a red wrap dress and perfect makeup. Grey stiffens behind me as she smiles at us and waves us over.

Oh God.

I haven't officially spoken to her without running away. I mean, I practically ripped Grey from her hands. They weren't really a thing, but still, they were something. And I just swooped in and jetted off to another country with him and started something up again. She's a really sweet girl, and I hurt her. I didn't ever want to put her through any more pain after what Grey did to her. But I just dropped a truckful of betrayal, and I hate myself for it. What if they were meant to be and I just destroyed everything?

"She doesn't hate you, bebé," Grey whispers in my ear. "I told her what happened, and she said she saw it coming. It's okay." He kisses my cheek, and I close my eyes and take a deep breath.

I needed that.

With his helpful words, I finally plaster on a smile and walk over to Rose.

"Hi, guys," she says, genuinely spirited. Her eyes flicker to Grey, and she nods to him. "Happy birthday, Grey."

He nods at her and tightens his arms around me. "Thanks."

A little more awkward silence, then I clear my throat.

"Do you know where the others are?" I ask her, referring to her brother and everyone else.

"Out back," she says, and I smile, beginning to leave. But her arm grabs mine, making me stop and look into her sad eyes but bright smile. "It's really good to see you guys together…" She pauses and glances at Grey, then smiles a little bigger. "Happy.

You two are really meant for each other." She sounds like she really means it, and I feel even worse on the inside.

"Anyway." She clears her throat and turns to the counter. "I was going to bring some out to the others, but I want us to clear up any tension or anything between the three of us." She holds two shot glasses out to us, looking me in the eyes. "To start over, you know?" I stare at her, then at the shot glass in fascination. How can she be so kind after everything? She's a truly compassionate human being, that's why.

"I'd love that." I take the glass, mirroring her blissful grin. I look over my shoulder at Grey, who is staring at Rose with slightly narrowed eyes. "Grey," I whisper, and he makes an incoherent sound before taking the glass.

"Sure," he mumbles, knocking the glass back then sets it on the counter.

She and I giggle at his brutishness.

"To new beginnings," she promises, clinking my glass with hers.

"New beginnings," I repeat and down the vodka. My tongue tickles, and I grimace as the hot liquor slides down my throat. *Well, here's to new beginnings…*

***

I awake with a raging headache and aching limbs. I slowly lick my dry lips and sit up, wherever I am. I am in a hell of a lot of pain as I move every inch until I am fully sitting up. I open my eyes one at a time and look around. I am in my room, in my bed, and a few of my friends like Mason and Charlotte and Mateo are passed out on the ground, each snoring like hungover bears. I look to my side, hearing a familiar deep snoring closer to me. It's Grey. He's shirtless and pantless, but he still has his socks on.

What the heck happened last night? I question myself, rubbing my eyes.

I'm hit with a strong urge to pee. I coach myself to take deep, soothing breaths as I slowly stand. My legs protest like the jelly sticks they are, and I fall to my stomach. My bladder is pressed, and I whine as I try to stand, but my body feels like iron. Strong and sturdy. I drag myself using the very little strength in my upper body and pull myself up.

I walk along the wall to the bathroom, stepping over loose limbs and messy hair from my friends until I'm finally in the bathroom. I pee like I have Niagara Falls in my bladder, then wash my hands. I make the mistake of looking into the mirror. Gross. I grimace at my ragged appearance. Hair that stands up every which way like I was struck by lightning, dry drool on my chin, makeup that is a complete mess, and my dress is fully unzipped.

Seriously, what the heck happened last night?

I don't remember anything after the few shots taken with Rose and Grey. I know I'm not one to handle my liquor, but geez. You'd think after a while I'd get used to it.

"Ugh," I groan as I rub my head to conjure something, anything from last night. All I get are buttons bouncing on the floor and gold—that's it. "I am never drinking again," I promise myself.

I shower, taking a long time to loosen my aching muscles, rinse out my hair, and brush my teeth until I can't taste any of the puke I did conjure up while showering. Which was the grossest thing ever, but at least I washed up quickly after. I had to lean against the tiled wall for a good portion of the shower.

Now I feel a tad better, but hell still resides in my head. I'm dressed in a pair of khaki shorts and a simple white tank top and Converse. I brush my unruly curls into a ponytail and put on a headband. I take the opportunity to pack all of my clothes into more suitcases. It hurts that I'm not staying here anymore and my mother and I haven't talked in such a long time since the incident, but she hasn't reached out to me. So why should I?

After working my exhausted body out, I decide I should reward myself with some breakfast.

I descend the stairs while yawning, when I see him.

"Noah?" I croak and almost slip down the stairs from shock.

He is quietly opening the door but stops at my voice and freezes. "Liv?" He turns around, and I feel my heart skip a beat. His green eyes meet mine, and I feel myself flush as I finish coming down the stairs. What is he doing here, leaving? I didn't see him at the party last night. But why would he come anyway? It was Grey's birthday party. And considering what went down between us...well, I thought he hated us—me specifically.

"What are you...I didn't see you last night," I

breathe, tilting my head.

"I wanted to drop by and talk…" he says, jaw tightening.

"I…d-did we?" I clear my weary voice. "Did we talk?"

He shrugs, looking away. "I don't remember anything."

"Me either," I admit.

He looks at me and stiffly nods. I bite my lip and look away. I hate this awkward, angry tension between us. We were great friends before anything happened romantically between us. I want that friendship back, and I will not stop until we have it.

"I'm sorry," I whisper. I finally look up into his eyes, and he merely shrugs.

"I honestly saw it coming," he says and smiles sardonically. "You never truly loved me. I saw it in your eyes, when we *kissed*…" His voice breaks, and he closes his eyes.

My heart breaks looking at him, this sweet boy I've ruined because I was so damn selfish and didn't think about his feelings.

I take a step forward. "Noah, I am so sorry—"

"I gotta go. I'll see you around, Olivia."

Olivia?

The door slams behind him, and I am left here, shocked, angry, and heartbroken. And it's all my damned fault. Why couldn't I pull my head out of the grey cloud and actually pay attention to *him* and how this would affect him?

I scream at myself and shake my head. "I fucking hate myself," I murmur. My skin crawls, and I feel like I'm being watched. I look up but see no one. I shrug and conclude it's my jittery body. I still feel like I am going to implode. I should get something to eat and hydrate myself before I actually do implode.

I shuffle into the kitchen and make myself some cereal and pour out orange juice. I shovel the Lucky Charms into my mouth, silently wishing I could be a better person. I wish I could go back in time and just be *better*.

"Hey," a strained voice says behind me.

"Morning," I reply when Mason sits on the stool beside me.

Silence.

"Do you remember anything from last night?" I ask him, curious.

He juts out his lip and shrugs. "A little, but not much. We partied pretty hard last night."

I hum in reply, shoveling more cereal.

"You?" he asks.

I shake my head, my mind stuck on Noah's defeated face and words.

"Nothing."

Chapter Thirty-Three

Grey and I left the minute he woke up and found his clothes. Oddly enough, they were hanging off the chandelier in front of the stairs. He had to use two brooms taped together to get them down. I wondered how they got up there, but my brain, once again, betrayed me and offered absolutely no memory. I just don't understand how my mind draws up a complete blank sheet whenever I try to find memories of last night. It's like someone dragged an eraser over the foggy details.

I spent that day dealing with the worst hangover I have ever experienced. I felt a little disconnected overall, but especially with Grey. I didn't mean to, but after my little interaction with Noah, I was left stunned and unsure of myself. The guilt that hit me in the gut was overwhelming; it still has me reeling back for balance. I was so focused on Grey, even when Noah and I were sort of a thing, I didn't take into considerations how he would feel. I truly never meant to put him in any pain or make it seem like I didn't care about him; I did and I still do. I just wasn't done with Grey and forced him into my life. I was selfish.

I want to make things all right between us. I won't be able to move on without repairing our friendship. It wouldn't be right if I just went on about my life with him feeling so angry and hurt by me. I am not the type of girl who fools around with boys and leaves them in the dust after I grow tired of them. I develop feelings and care for people.

Plus, Noah deserves to know why and how hard it was having Grey re-enter my life after I thought he and I were done. I had no idea we'd reconnect the way we did in Venezuela. If I could go back in time and warn him, I would. And I would also warn myself of the feelings bursting to life once again that nearly rendered me incomprehensible.

It is now the morning after my horrid hangover, though there are still some remnants, like the slight headache and dryness of my mouth. But I guess I deserve to suffer for hurting someone so close to me who didn't deserve any of the heartache I caused him. I just rub my temples and take yet another pain medication.

I lean on the kitchen counter, staring at my phone, pondering over the text I have typed to Noah.

Liv: Can we please talk? At the very least, I would like to fix our friendship. Xxxx.

The question is: Is it good enough? Would he even reply? Judging how he left before I could utter a word of explanation, I would say no. But I also know him well enough to assume that he did feel something for me. And it didn't even have to be romantically. We were friends, and I know somewhere deep inside of him, he wants an explanation, even if he thinks it's BS. I just need one chance to speak to him, to explain.

"Hey, you okay?" Grey's raspy voice breaks my thoughts. I look up. He struts into the kitchen, yawning, and I quickly hit send. Now, all that's left to do is pray he lets me talk to him properly.

"Yeah, I'm fine." I smile, but he doesn't seem to buy it.

"Sure you are. Really, what's up?" He leans on his elbows and exhales roughly, dark eyes watching me, examining my features.

I play with my charms and shrug noncommittally. "There is nothing up," I answer him, and he hums, tilting his head. "Nothing but the, uh, s-sky," I accidentally stammer. I'm sorry, but I crack under pressure when he is staring at me like this.

"Very funny," he says, and I spare a glance at him. He's chewing on his cheek but sits down on the stool and lets out a deep breath. "What's for breakfast?" he asks, gratefully changing the subject.

I knew there was a reason I loved him.

"You're looking at it." I point at the ceramic bowl of Frosted Flakes in front of his folded, tatted arms.

He looks down at it and pushes it away with a look of disgust. "Yuck. I was expecting more of a glamorous meal for your glamorous, hard-working boyfriend." He raises his arms and looks at me pointedly, like he's disappointed.

I narrow my eyes at his expectation of me cooking at his whim. I am not a housewife, but his girlfriend. There is a major difference between the two. "Too bad. There is barely anything in the fridge, so your *glamorous* breakfast will have to wait until the fridge is stocked with food I can actually work with, because ketchup, an onion, and a box of popsicles aren't going to cut it."

"Fine." He draws the word out and digs in his jeans pocket. "Have fun shopping." He places his car keys on the counter next to my hand.

I lean over and flick him in the head, causing him to groan. "You're coming with me, jerk." To think he thinks I'm his maid. I glare at the audacity and round the counter.

"Prude!" he calls after me.

I hold up my middle finger. I speed up to the bedroom when I hear him running after me. I squeal and move to close the door after me, but he has fast reflexes and grabs me by my waist, tossing me over his broad shoulder.

"What was that, princess?" he questions, pinching my butt.

"Ow! Let me down, you barbarian!" I demand, biting back the laughter.

"Okay." He drops me onto the bed.

"Rude!" I shout at his back as he strides out of the room.

"Nerd!" he sing-songs back.

I stick my tongue out at him and roll it rapidly like a temperamental child. I can practically hear the skid marks as there is a pause.

"What was that?" He comes back in the room with a crazed look, but I don't miss the smile ghosting his lips.

"Nothing! No! Grey, we have to get ready!" I scream, but it goes unheard as he picks me up, and all of my worries and hangover vanish the second he makes me come alive with his silliness.

**

"Grey, we do not need a pack of gummy worms," I say for the millionth time as he brings them over to shove in my face. I kind of wish I had never learned he loved them as a child. Now that obsession has exploded up again, right in my face. That's what I get trying to be a good girlfriend.

"You may not need it, but I certainly do," he says, tossing the huge bag in the grocery cart. He ignores my glare as he leans against the cart, watching as I pick up a large bottle of milk. "Are you cold or am I so good you're just turned on by my presence?" he asks with a cocky smirk and an even cockier waggle of his eyebrows.

I look down at my thin white t-shirt and gasp, covering my chest. "Shut up. We're in the frozen area."

"Sure, keep telling yourself that." He winks at me.

I blush and thrust the long list into his hand. "Go get the items that are in the next aisle while I get the others, please."

"Fine," he groans like I'm sending him off on a mission to trek the Sahara Desert. He walks over to me and kisses my cheek. "You're lying about the nips, and we both know it," he whispers in my ear, and I gasp.

"Leave, Grey!" I push him away, and he bursts into laughter. He winks at me one more time before disappearing round the aisle. I can still hear his obnoxious laughter. With flushed cheeks, I grab whatever is left I need from this horrid section and wheel out of the aisle.

I hum a random song as I guide the cart down to the meat section. I tap my chin as I check out every meat I want and decide on a whole chicken, ground beef, steak, and a few more things. After that, I venture out to the junk food aisle with much distaste. I would much rather munch on lettuce or bite into a fresh apple than eat these processed…*things*. But Grey loves chips and these types of foods, so who am I to turn down getting them for the house? I pick up a few of his favorite chips, candies, and other assortments I have never heard of. He is quite the junkie; you would have never expected it by taking a single glance at his ripped muscles.

I enter the aisle that has pasta when I accidentally bump into another cart.

"Oh, I'm sorry," I am quick to say. "I didn't see you—Noah?"

Am I hallucinating, or is he really standing in front of me?

Noah's eyes widen when they meet mine. "Liv…what are you doing here?" I squint my eyes and glance at my filled shopping cart. He looks at it too, then laughs. "Right." I glance at his half-filled cart then look back into his assessing eyes. "You're living with him now, right...?" It kind of sounds like an accusation.

I feel myself blush. "Something like that, yeah." I nervously play with my charms, and he smiles with a nod.

Silence lingers between us while I try to figure out what to say. Obviously, there is a lot, but none makes sense. Finally, I find two words that should get the ball rolling.

"I'm sorry," I say, but he blurts it out at the same time.

We laugh, and I gesture for him to go first. It's the least I can do.

"I am really sorry for yesterday," he says with a little disappointed sigh.

"What? You have nothing to be sorry for." I am the one in the wrong.

"Yes, I do, for being rude by walking out while you were talking," he explains and takes a really deep breath, rolling his shoulders before shoving his thumbs in his jean shorts' front pockets. "I was just really upset. I just...I really liked you, Liv." I look away, guilty. "But that doesn't mean I don't want us to be friends."

I look at him and gape for a few seconds, shocked. "I'd love that! There's nothing more I want than fixing what I stupidly broke." I pull on my lip, a habit I unintentionally inherited from Grey. I drop my hand and find my voice. "I—I was really selfish for what I did. I betrayed you and didn't consider your feelings...and for that I am eternally apologetic. I didn't mean to hurt you, I really didn't…will you ever be able to forgive me?"

His green eyes turn a tad dark as he licks his lips, contemplating. Then he breaks out into a grin and laughs. "Yes, I will need some time to heal. You hurt me, but please, don't feel bad."

"Of course. I understand." I nod and fight the urge to hug him. I feel tears form in my eyes, but I just tug at my bracelet and look at his cart. "So, what are *you* doing at the supermarket?"

He follows my gaze and blushes. "Oh, just doing some shopping with someone."

"Who's that someone?" I ask playfully, but I hope I'm not pushing our barely forming friendship.

"Her name is Kelly; I met her a week after we, you know, broke it off." He nervously scratches the back of his neck, and I smile forcibly.

"That's amazing…so is it serious?" I glance at the cart, and he shakes his head.

"We're not living together or anything like that, just helping out," he explains and nods. "She's a really sweet girl. She's actually a lifeguard. We met on the beach while I was eating my broken feelings in an ice cream cone."

I rub my arm. "Whoops."

He chuckles. "I will heal, I promise. I'm a tough nut to crack."

"Well, I would love to meet her one day—she sounds nice."

That sounds awkward.

"Maybe one day." He laughs, and I blush even harder.

"What do we have here?" a familiar voice drawls as a hand snakes around my hips.

"Grey, so nice to see you," Noah says with utter sarcasm, a forced smile curving his hips.

"I wish I could say the same, but my very polite girlfriend says it's bad to lie," he quips back, gripping my hip possessively and kissing my hair while shooting Noah a mocking grin. I drown in his cologne and cigarette smell, but I don't smile at the bittersweet scent. I glare at his chest then soften my expression toward Noah.

"Right, well, I'll see you around, Liv." Noah nods at me.

"Goodbye, Noah." I smile widely at him and nod back at him.

He casts a single uneasy glance at Grey, then turns and wheels out of the aisle.

The minute I'm sure he's gone, I turn and smack Grey in the chest.

"Are you serious?" I hiss-whisper at him, since there are a few customers around us.

"What?" He sounds and looks annoyed with me.

"You know what." I jab a finger at his chest, and he rolls his eyes like I'm a pestering fly.

"I seriously have no idea what you're talking about," he booms down at me through gritted teeth.

"Then how about you figure out what I'm talking about while you check the food out. I'll be waiting in the car," I snap, fed up with his childish behavior. I quickly dig his car keys out of his jacket pocket and storm away before he can stop me. He can be such an asshole sometimes!

Chapter Thirty-Four

I do not utter a word to Grey the entire way back home, because I have nothing to say to him. I know how he can be a cruel asshole, but he didn't have to be one back at the grocery store. He knows I chose him, everyone knows that. I am with him now; he has me. He doesn't need to show me off or rub anything in Noah's face. He's already hurt enough as it is. But of course, asshole Grey just had to come out and emphasize why everyone is so hesitant with me being with him. Because, when he wants, he can flip a switch and turn into a vile man who does the most hurtful things.

I'd rather he did so with me and not toward Noah. As horrible as it sounds, I'm used to it. And I don't want my friend, who is on the fence with me already, to be the brunt of Grey's less attractive side. As much as I love him as a person, that side will always be ready to strike, and I will always despise it. Unfortunately, it makes up about eighty-percent of him. Like I said, I'm used to it. I send Noah a text apologizing, and he replies saying it's

351

okay. I wish it was, but it most definitely is not.

When the car pulls up in front of the house, I grab the house keys on the dash and climb out of the car.

"Wait, Liv! Aren't you going to help?" he asks.

I continue toward the house, ignoring him. He wants to be an asshole, he can bring the things inside.

"Olivia!" he calls after me, but I don't answer him.

I unlock the door and am entering when my arm is gripped, and I am spun around.

"Why are you being like this?" he asks, more like *barks,* through grinding teeth. His anger is coming alive; I can see the sparks in his deadly eyes. But I don't give a damn. I have adapted to the burns.

I rip my arm from his hand and push him away from me.

"Do not touch me."

"Since when are you resistant to my touch?" he scoffs as a nefarious smirk slices into his dimpled cheeks. I gasp at the underlying sharpness beyond his words. Is he really implying that I am so easy when it comes to him?

"Since you've started acting like a barbaric ass, that's when!" I shout, not caring if anyone hears me. His face falters a little like I chipped his ego. Good. He freaking deserves it. I spin around on my heels and enter the house.

"Why the fuck are you being like this?" The barrier that shields his anger finally shatters as he chases after me into the kitchen.

"Why do you think, Grey?" I don't face him as I open the fridge. He is very smart; I know he can figure it out without much trouble.

"I don't fucking know. That's why I am asking!" he exclaims in a *duh* tone.

I shift my glare at him. "Get the groceries and *think*." I slam the fridge door closed and ignore his eyes following me as I round the island and sit on a stool. He looks at me with wide eyes and a gaping mouth. "Get the damn groceries, Grey!"

He opens his mouth to scream something at me, but I give him a pointed look that says *try me, I dare you*. He backs down instead and grunts before storming out of the house, muttering Spanish curses I full well understand, but I don't say anything. Not to him directly. I spew my own curses in other languages he wouldn't even begin to comprehend. I rub my face and wonder how I fell in love with someone like him, but then I remember how charming and sweet he can be and—ugh.

A few minutes later, all the groceries are on the kitchen counters. It's quiet as I put away everything while he just sits on the island, staring at me with narrowed eyes. I think I just need to cool down and maybe I will adapt to yet another one of his asshole tendencies. But all of that is thrown out of the window when he grabs my wrist, stopping me from picking up a loaf of bread next to him.

"Let go of me, Grey!" I snap and try to pull my hand away, but his strength is like a steel—unmoving.

"Not until you tell me what I did wrong," he says, and I groan.

"You showed me off in front of Noah, shoving it in his face that I broke his heart just to be with you—that. That is what you did. And I do not need your help in making him hate me, trust me," I explain, and his grip loosens. I grab the loaf and place it in the pantry, gripping the knob on the door. I take deep breaths as he scoffs and begins talking.

"Seriously? What the hell is wrong with showing off my girl?" he questions.

My stomach flutters at his words, but I ignore them and face him.

"He's already hurt. You didn't need to do that," I say, and he rolls his eyes as he hops off the counter and strides over to me. "I'm serious, Grey. I…I hurt him. And he really liked me. I could have liked him too, but I was—"

"Still in love with me?" he finishes my sentence, but in the wrong way I intended. "I'm sorry you were so hung up over the big bad wolf. I should have backed off and let you *like* the pretty charming boy, right?" His words are seared with malice, and it makes my mouth grow very dry. "I'm not stopping you." He backs away, and I notice how flushed he was against me. "Go ahead and get your prince. Don't let me *stop you*."

"You are such a piece of shit. You know that, right?" I stand up straight against the counter, crossing my arms over my chest. "I love you, Grey. I have proved that to you so many times, it's actually insane. I do not love him—was that not clear enough when I went behind his back and had sex with you? Was it not clear when I left him and went to Venezuela with you to comfort you? If you seriously don't think I love you, or at least *care* for you more than I do myself...then you're stupider than I thought you were."

"I know you love me, Olivia," he says slowly.

"Stop calling me that!" I shout.

"Why the hell not? It's your name, isn't it?" he snaps back, hands thrown up and waving around theatrically. He's trying to piss me off, he really is!

"Because it sounds like you're angry at me for no reason. Because you only call me *Liv* and it makes me feel like *I* am in the wrong when, as usual, it's you!" I point an accusing finger at him, and he twists his face at it.

He bellows, throwing his head back. "Are you fucking kidding me? Do you want to bring up the past?" I shiver at what he's referring to, my one biggest mistake I have ever made in my life. One that still haunts me within, down deep.

I take a step back, feeling my heart drop to my stomach. "I don't know, shall we?" I slither out, referring to *his* more than fucked-up past.

He glares at me, and I do the same right back.

Finally, he rolls his eyes and mutters, "Honestly, I am fucking done with this." I watch him walk to the door, and I rush after him.

"Done with what?" I question him.

He closes the door after he opens it and looks back at me, anger simmering under his skin. "Done with you acting like you love the guy."

"I just told you I don't!" Seriously, has he lost his mind?

"There is nothing wrong with me showing you off, Olivia!" he shouts.

This asshole, I just told him how I felt about him using my full name. It hits me in the gut every single time.

"When you do it to hurt my friend, yes, there is." I cross my arms, and he punches the wall. I gasp and jump back when he stalks over to me and towers over me.

"Your *ex-boyfriend*, you mean," he gripes out.

"He was my friend first," I point out, and he rolls his eyes. "And we were only together because I was trying to get over you."

"Doesn't matter," he says as he shoves his feet in his boots.

"Where are you going?" I sigh.

He swings the open and tells me, "Out," before the door slams behind him.

Chapter Thirty-Five

Grey

I drive to the nearest bar but don't drink anything. Partially because if I do and go home, Liv will just be more pissed, and also because I want to have a clear mind. I want to keep this malignant anger bubbling in my chest and tickling my mouth. I don't understand what is so wrong with showing off what that fucker never deserved and could never have. Okay, that sounds a little like Liv is nothing more than my possession, but in a really, really fucked-up way, she is. I mean, fuck! She is mine. No other guy can touch or have her.

I love her, though. I truly do. More than myself, actually. I just—I hate that some other guy had her. She hasn't told me the specifics of what went down with them, but just thinking of the possibility that they kissed—or worse, *fucked*—it makes me see bloody red, which is what I would love to be coated on my fists. I hate that I took so fucking long to come to my senses. I realized I wanted her back too

357

fucking late, because the asshole probably got as close to her as I have.

And I fucking hate the thought of it. His hands on her hips that I love to see squirm out of her innocent-looking white panties. His mouth swallowing her heavenly moans. Her scratching his chest, his stomach, his back as he fucks her. I can just fucking see her wiping *me* from her memory as she enjoyed the light pouring from that douchebag into her. His member lodged into her tight puss—fuck!

I throw a glass near me against the wall of liquor and grip my hair.

"What the fuck is your problem!" someone screams at me. I can hear people shuffling around and a phone being dialed. The bartender's probably calling the police to complain about me. I hear snippets, like *drunk fuck* and *broke my shit* and *stiff as a god damn board*. He thinks I'm crazy. A drunk. Crazy, maybe. But definitely not drunk.

I rub my temples and mumble that I'm fine, I'm sober, and I did not mean to lose my shit. I try to reason with the man, but my vision is fucked up and I can hear trumpets blasting in my ears. Oh, for fuck's sake! I'm losing it. I need—I can't control my thoughts. They are all scrambling and squeezing my brain. I'm having a fucking meltdown, in a bar, and the cops are on their way. This will all go down perfectly fucking fine.

"Fuck my life," I grumble as I press my palms into my eyes.

Chapter Thirty-Six

Liv

I hadn't been able to sleep since he stormed out of the house. I let him have his space and texted him to be careful and not to drink or take any drugs since he's driving. I don't know what I would do if he got hurt because of me. The stupid fight I brought up. Grey's an asshole. I've known that since the second he opened his mouth. I've just about forgot and gave up on the fight as the hours ticked and stopped at one in the morning.

At that moment, I just wanted him home. Safe and sound.

When my phone finally rang after hours of silence, I felt my heart drop. My mind raced with pessimistic thoughts. I hadn't heard from him all day, and then he was just calling me up out of the blue? But then I began to think the worst possible thing: what if it's the hospital or a cop to inform me the worst has happened...? It didn't help when I flipped my phone over and saw an unknown number. At almost two in the morning. After my hot-headed, angry boyfriend stalked out of the house.

I burst into tears on the spot and thought the worst *had* come. All because I couldn't just think about what *he* was going through. I know about his disorder. And I know how territorial it can make him, plus he hates Noah. I should be used to his crude remarks and asshole ways. I didn't care about any of it if he has hurt himself.

I scrambled to answer the phone and let out a huge breath of relief when the person on the other line revealed themselves to be an automated device for the police department. I was ecstatic because he was behind bars, safe, and *not* injured or dead. I know how he craves alcohol when his anger flares. I would take him being jailed over staying in the morgue any and every day.

My heart unclutched from the little ball it formed into, and I left the house in a messy ponytail, one of his shirts, and a pair of shorts. I looked like a mess, but it didn't matter. I took a cab to the station and prepared for the worst, money-wise and charge-wise. I'm sure he has a lot of strikes against him, considering how just last month I bailed him out of this very station. I was a nervous wreck as I stood in a short line to reach the woman in the front. I mentally prepared myself to be read a list of the charges and his intoxication while driving. Oh, the damage he could have done. Both to himself and others.

Tears stung in my eyes.

"Next," the woman calls.

I walk up to her and lick my lips nervously before saying, "I'm here for Grey Wyler."

She nodded with a lackluster look, typing his name in her computer. "He was picked up for damaging a bar by the name *Lucky Joe's.*"

"Oh no...was he intoxicated or anything?" I ask anxiously, pulling my lip.

She glances at the screen and shakes her head no. "Sober," she answers, and I don't hold back my sigh. She gives me a look. "Bail is two-fifty."

I nod. "Thank you." I give her a tight-lipped smile and walk over to the processing desk. I sit down and wait for a few minutes until it is my turn. I quickly pay and, while I wait for the transaction and paperwork to be handled, I ask to be taken back like last time. But the man tells me Grey doesn't want to see me.

My stomach drops.

"What?"

Chapter Thirty-Seven

"What do you mean?" I ask the man. That doesn't make any sense.

He shrugs. "Don't know what to tell you."

I want to demand him to take me back there, but I know it won't be any use. Grey doesn't want to see me for some strange reason. I slump in my seat and pull my feet into the chair. I wait for who knows how long. I almost doze off a few times as the exhaustion finally catches up and hits me. But I force myself to stay up. I just want this stupid fighting over with. I want to see his uninjured face and kiss it until the thought of his cold skin goes away.

"Let's go," a familiar rough voice grumbles.

I jump to my feet and follow the black blur moving past the glass doors.

"Grey, wait up," I call after him as we walk over to his car they must have brought in too. He ignores me and gets in. I go in after him, and he instantly turns on the radio and revs the engine. I groan and fumble with the seatbelt as he swivels out of the parking lot. "Will you please talk to me?"

Silence.

"I'm over the fight," I tell him, and his fingers tighten around the wheel. "I just…gosh, Grey. You can be such an asshole all the time, but this time you were gunning to hurt one of my friends, whom I am *just* starting to mend my friendship with."

More silence.

I rub my hand over my mouth and shrug. "Why were you arrested?"

He glances at me and then looks back at the road, jaw clenched and sharp. "Misconduct in a public facility," he says stoically. He drives faster.

"What did you do exactly? The lady said you destroyed a bar…?" She also said that he's sober, which is a really good thing. Though *destroying* a bar isn't all right in the least.

He runs a hand through his hair, fingers shaking. "I had an…an emotional breakdown—"

"Oh my, Grey!" I gasp.

"But I'm fine," he finishes through grinding teeth. He is driving a little reckless now. You'd think he'd be a model driver to avoid going back behind bars. Meaning he is not *fine*. There is much more to the story, and I intend to find out more.

"No, you aren't," I say, and he looks out his window, clearly trying to ignore me. "Stop icing me out and tell me what's wrong, Grey!"

Suddenly, the car is pulled to the side of the road.

He turns to me and snaps, "You were with him!"

I search for words. "So? You were with Rose." It is not fair for him to be mad at me for trying to move on when he made it clear over and over that he didn't want me.

"But you…" He grips his hair and turns to the wheel. He takes a deep breath, and I sit up attentively. "I didn't love her. I never did. Even all those years ago. I—I thought I did, but what I felt for her was not love. But what I feel for you…" He turns to me with tears streaming down his cheeks. I unlatch my belt and reach for him, but he sits back and shakes his head. I frown and bite my lip, hurt that he's flinching away from me. "You're still fucking wearing his charm. Where is mine, huh? Are you not mine, for real? Am I still in that fucked-up mindset I was in when I was with Rose?"

"No, no—this was a gift. I swear, for my birthday. It means nothing." I unclasp the necklace with shaky fingers and tuck it in my shorts. He watches with hurtful eyes. I am quick to reach over the center console and explain to him soothingly, "Just a *friendly* gift, before we got together."

He grimaces beneath me, and those eyes pierce through me. "Did you guys…?" He trails, and I can see the breath he is holding as he coyly plays with his lower lip.

"No, God, no!" I shake my head quickly, and he sighs and closes his eyes. "I would never be able to. I didn't ever feel anything with him, nothing compared to you."

"Nothing?" He is looking for assurance, bottom lip jutted out like a hopeful child.

I laugh and shake my head. "Nothing at all. What about…um, y-you and Rose?"

He shakes his head frantically and pulls me onto

his lap. I gasp at the suddenness, but my body instantly clasps around him while my hands play with his slight curls above his forehead. He rolls his eyes, and I giggle, and he smiles against my neck. His lips are divine pressed against my skin, and I sigh in bliss.

"Drier than the Sahara Desert," he says, and I laugh.

I stare into his eyes and breathe, "Truce?" I hold out my pinky.

He looks at it with a blank face but soon turns into gold with his dazzling smile. "Truce." He latches his pinky with mine, kisses it, then silences my laughter with a kiss of my own. Gentle movements turn into harsh ones as he claims me, both with his lips and his hands gripping my bare thighs. I am suddenly glad I ran out of the house dressed in his shorts. It both amazes and scares me how much this man makes me feel and fills me whole in less than point two seconds.

Grey and I fall asleep in each other's arms when we arrive home. The past few tense hours between us fizzle out and leave us content and forgiving. The moment he told me he and Rose never did anything worthwhile, and how he felt nothing when he was with her and not me...I felt the weight of a world I never knew about be lifted off my shoulders. The truth relieved me of the worry. Now I can breathe knowing that he has only felt and been in love with me, and only me. It makes me feel one hundred times better and a thousand more giddy.

Chapter Thirty-Eight

Grey spends the week training, harder than I have ever seen him train. Which is a pretty big thing to say, considering how much he pushes himself regularly. But with the tournament coming up in *days*, he has been pushing himself more and more. I never thought it was possible, but he proves it to me every day when he gets home sweaty, exhausted, and on the verge of breaking down like an over-worked robot. I've been giving him baths every day to ease his cramped, tense muscles. Plus loads more affection, like kisses, sex—hell, after all he is doing to work to meet his goal, he deserves all I give him and more.

To say I'm scared for him and his health would be a disgusting understatement. I want him to win the title and jumpstart his dream career of being an MMA fighter. However, I do *not* want him burning out his body to the point that he can barely function or run himself into the ground. I want him to be healthy and sound of mind. But I can't say his relentless drive doesn't make me proud to call him my man. My hard-working, lovable man, to be correct. I love that he doesn't stop when he has pushed his limit, he goes beyond that with one goal on his mind, and it drives me insane with utter adoration and respect.

I spend today cleaning up the house. It's the least I can do while he works so hard. While I do the dishes and laundry, I am wrapped up in thoughts, and the time flies by in a flash.

In just two weeks, summer will be over, and I will go back to school. And I am a bit afraid. I love college and all it has to offer; I am not scared of school. I am afraid of how our dynamic will alter when we are back in Pennsylvania. He will obviously be done with college and working. And I will be going to school. Since he will be focused on working while I attend school, will we be able to find time for each other? And not only that, but…where will I live? We have just gotten back together and are working out our kinks and trying to solidify trust. But does that mean we are ready to live together after we leave this mini paradise?

It's safe to say that we have a lot to talk about. But when will there be time to discuss them? Along with being tired and stressed out every day when he comes home from the gym, he is very irritable. I know the man well enough to know that if I bring up any touchy subject that can possibly end in an argument, which is sadly not hard to accomplish, he will burst into anger and probably storm out on me. He has a terrible habit of leaving without us talking about it. I hope we can work on that sometime. But for now, we have important things to contemplate and figure out. Hopefully by next week. I want to know if I should apply to stay in the dorms or not.

By the time I'm finished cleaning, I am exhausted. I take a brief nap and wake up rejuvenated. I feel like we should go out so he can take his mind off of the upcoming tournament. He's going to work himself to the bone. Plus, I could use some time with him romantically. Setting the baths and affection to the side, I want to go out. Take a walk on the beach, have dinner at a restaurant— anything out of a cheesy rom-com, like on our first date when he took me out to eat and then to the movie theater afterward. But like I said before, there is no right time to bring anything up. Well, anything that doesn't deal with the tournament or training.

I check the clock on one of the kitchen walls as I eat a turkey sandwich for lunch. It is almost four p.m. I quickly finish my sandwich and walk into the bedroom to get ready. I set up a time for Matthew and me to talk. He has been a great mentor of sorts, guiding me through my millions of questions and just chatting with me as a friend. I hope that we can grow into a full-fledged friendship when I begin the program.

All week, as Grey has been training his butt off, I've been gearing myself for the opportunity of my college lifetime. I have been buying plenty of outfits to wear for the program, which will take up a lot of my time, and other school supplies. Matthew has joked, regarding my purchases as a tad overdone. I blushed at that. But then he quickly reassured me that it's good that I'm getting ready for the new school year. Again, I blushed at that.

I brush out and curl my hair, letting it fall against my shoulders. I am dressed in a pair of jean shorts and a blue tank top. Not the most professional get up, but like I said, Matthew and I have grown a little closer into a sort of friendship. I feel more comfortable around him. Plus, I don't feel like ironing a button up or pinning my hair up in a tight bun. The bobby pins always feel like they're trying to probe inside of my brain.

"Hello, Olivia," Matthew croons in his deep voice as his face appears on the screen. I settle onto the couch, my legs tucked beneath me.

"Hi, Matthew." I wave at him, and he flashes me those pearly white teeth of his. "And please, I have told you time and time again to call me Liv."

He nods, and his eyes smile at me through his round eyeglasses. "I'm sorry, I'll do that from now on…Liv." He winks at me, and I laugh.

"Where are you now?" I question, examining the pebble-stone behind him. He is sitting at a cafe of sorts, and wherever he is looks absolutely beautiful. He has the luckiest job ever, mentoring those entering the program and traveling to check out new location spots.

"Paris, France," he informs me before sipping from a cute, small cup of coffee. I stare at the cup; he's most likely drinking black coffee since it is both of our favorites, he's revealed to me.

"Oh, Paris," I swoon, leaning against the couch, hands against my chest. "I've always wanted to go there. It looks heavenly."

"Then you haven't tried their coffees, or their croissants, or their coffees *with* croissants," he groans and shows me a piece of a buttery croissant roll. My mouth waters as he bites into it, then washes it down with the steaming coffee. "Ahhhh," he sighs in contentment, and I glare at him. He laughs at my expense.

"You are horrible, you know that?" I point an accusing finger at him, but he just smiles.

"Guilty as charged." He chuckles.

"How long have you been working at the program?" I ask curiously. He looks ridiculously young. He looks like he's no older than twenty-six yet is granted the amazing privilege to travel and eat croissants and drink coffee in Paris? He must either be really good at his job or is a naturally lucky man.

"About five years now," he says, readjusting in his seat. "I was doing well in college and was lucky enough to have been spotted by a representative for the program. I was brought in after I graduated. I've worked my way up and smooched a little." He winks, and I laugh. "But it all worked out pretty well, I guess…" He takes a long sip of his coffee.

He is so annoying!

I narrow my eyes at him and sigh. "Hopefully I can be where you are now."

"In Paris or my position?" He quirks an eyebrow.

"Both." I smile, and he slowly matches it.

We chat and talk a little more about the program for about forty minutes. He warns me what and who to watch out for and how challenging it will be, juggling schoolwork and the program's. I tell him that I will be able to deal with both, and he makes an annoying *are you sure?* face that I am half-tempted to raise a middle finger to. Geez, I am becoming Grey in every sense. I don't know if I should blush or be worried. I wish I could talk to him more, but his superiors call him for some job. He promises to call back later tonight, if not tomorrow.

"Goodbye, Matthew." I wave at him, and he smiles at me.

"Have a nice night...Liv." His little wink is the last thing I see.

I glance at the time in the right corner. It is now almost six p.m. I will cook dinner in an hour, Grey usually gets in around eight, and it doesn't take long to make his favorite, lasagna. I grab a novel and a cup of tea before sitting on the rocking chair on the back patio. It is a warm night with a little cool breeze. Perfect weather to sit in and wait for my sweaty, tired man to come in. I read and drink for maybe twenty minutes, and it's relaxing. I can definitely get used to it.

My perfect moment is ruined when my phone rings.

"Ugh," I grunt and set my tea and book down. I pull out my phone and feel my heart skip two beats at the caller I.D. I slowly slide my finger across the screen to answer. "Mother...?"

"Olivia, I need you. Please come. It's an emergency," she says, sounding tearful.

***

I take a cab to the house and rush up the driveway. My heart is in my throat, and my legs are burning as I run. The adrenaline has officially kicked in, carrying me to the front door. I had a feeling something was off when I saw her calling me. Considering we got into a heated argument that resulted in her slapping me, I thought it would be longer before either of us dialed the other up to chat about the other's day over tea. But when she pleaded for my help and said it was an emergency, I bolted into a mode to protect her. After all, she is my family. She is my mother, even if she doesn't act like it most of the time.

I was surprised, hearing her tear up over the line. The last time I witnessed or discreetly heard her cry was when Jonah passed. She was a complete wreck and acted as if both of her children passed away that night. But it was Jonah, but not him alone. She had been pregnant and announced it to us all. That night…she lost everything…but me. And hearing her so emotional and human again, I just had to be there for her to comfort her, like I had when I found her crying in her bed countless times.

I push through the unlocked door and call for her. "Mother? Mother, where are you?"

"In here, darling," her voice tells me, weirdly calm despite how wrecked she sounded over the phone.

I enter one of the living rooms and find her on the pristine white couch. She is dressed in a red-as-a-candy-apple dress, hair pinned up and makeup done perfectly. No tear marks or distressed wrinkles in sight. What's going on?

"How nice to see you, dear." She smiles from ear to ear, and I shiver at the strange sight.

"What…what's the emergency?" My voice feels tight. "I thought there was something wrong with you." I don't like how she's smiling at me.

"There is nothing wrong with *me,* dear. But you, on the other hand." Her head tilts to the side, and there is a pause before she points at me. "Darling, there is something wrong with *you.*"

What?

"Huh?" I voice my confused thoughts.

I hear a grunt behind me and squeal when I am lifted up. I gasp and thrash around, thinking an intruder or a murderer is trying to hurt me. But when I look over my shoulders, I am met with two huge men in all white, mean looks etched into their clean-shaven faces. They kind of look like security guards in the movies. But what they'd be guarding are people…crazy people.

"Mother!" I gasp, facing her creepy grin. "What do you think you're doing?"

"I am doing what any mother would do to help their child," she says with a little frown. "I gave you plenty of time to come to your senses about that nomad of a man you call *the love of your life.*"

"You're insane!" I spit at her, kicking my legs wildly.

She laughs and nods, gesturing to the men to raise me higher. "No, I'm not," she says as I feel my shirt be dragged up and a needle be pressed into my side. I scream and call for help, but no one is home to hear my cries. "You are, my love…"

Chapter Thirty-Nine

Grey

My heart has just about jumped out of my body by the time I have completed my training for the day. I hunch over and try to catch my breath when I exit the gym. I have been tiring myself out, but I can't slow down, not now. The tournament is coming up rapidly in just a few short days. I feel like I'm ready, but that doesn't mean I can ease up on myself. I will finally be able to prove to everyone that I'm serious about this being my life—fighting. I can barely stand still at the idea of using my fists to reach my goal.

I have fought so hard for this opportunity, literally. I can imagine the surging crowd, the thick-like-molasses tension, the mouth guard between my teeth, and me beating up fuckers who have no idea how much I have been yearning for it all. Oh, the anticipation is filling me up like fuel being injected into a machine. I feel like I'm going to explode from the fiery gasoline residing inside of me. And I just can't wait until I am put in a ring and am able to show off my killer skills. All of this training will be worth it in the end, just you wait.

But all I want now more than anything in the world is my girl. She has been in the back of my mind with every weight I lifted and every mile I ran, my little motivation pushing me further and further. I haven't been the closest to her, as I have dedicated the days to training, but she has made it her goal to sprinkle little bouts of affection here and there. Her kindness and compassion are a few qualities I love about her. She is always there: bath prepared and a little more if my body is up for it.

I have never met someone so charitable without wanting something in return. She is rare, but I don't even think she realizes it. I continuously thank fate or whatever made it possible for us to meet, because I have the most beautiful, loving girl on this planet. She's mine, and not in a possessive kind of way. But in the sense that she's my light and savior, my fucking angel-princess.

Gosh, she's turning me into a complete mush of bones—putty in her little hands. But to be honest, I don't mind—because she's turning me into a better man. For my girl, I'd turn into freaking Superman.

It's dark by the time I am leaving the gym, nearing ten p.m. I usually come home an hour or two earlier, but I wanted to push a little harder and get some more workouts in. I've worked myself up so much, I can barely sit up as I drive. However, with my girl on my mind, soaked in the bath, bubbles covering her—I drive faster and feel my body tense, ready to be kissed. I could come undone just sitting here thinking about me on top of her, touching, caressing her while she works her magic and fixes me right up.

I finally arrive home about fifteen minutes later, giddy and practically bouncing to see my girl. My fucking princess. I get out of the car and lock it. I jog up the stairs and unlock and open the door. I kick off my shoes and set my duffel bag down, cracking my neck with a grin plastered onto my face.

"Honey, I'm home!" I holler jokingly. After a few seconds of silence, I frown. "Liv?" I call her name a little louder and take a cautious step forward. Another beat of silence and I begin to worry.

Normally, she runs up to me and quite literally *jumps* into my arms, showering me with kisses, which I happily reciprocate. She'd then drag me to the made bath and I'd have the best night of my life. But she isn't doing anything right now, and I'm worried. And not because she isn't peppering my face with kisses and showing me to a luxury bath. Okay, maybe a little bit because of that, but also because I fucking care if she's hurt or worse.

"Olivia?" I softly call her name as I push the bathroom door open. Nothing. I turn and walk down the hall to the bedroom. "Olivia, are you in here?" My voice becomes a little shaky as I open the door. I feel my heart stutter when I find nothing but a cleaner room than how I left it. It's obvious she's been in here. She's always been such a clean freak.

I pull out my phone and dial her number as my anxiety kicks into high gear. I get her voicemail as I open the glass doors that leads to the back porch. I step out and step down the wooden steps and walk on the sand, screaming her name and walking around. We don't usually come out here, but maybe she wanted to come out and get her feet wet or walk around?

I step on something and look down. One of her books and a mug of tea. She was out here. Maybe she still is…

"Olivia? Are you out here?" I scream, getting looks from an older couple passing by. "Have you guys seen a girl out here? Short, about *this* tall? Dark brown hair, blue eyes?" I gesture just under my pecs, and they shake their heads. I become frantic as I gesture with my hands. "A-are you sure?"

They shake their heads and move on.

"Fuck!" I curse and press the balls of my hands against my eyes, rubbing hard. "Where the fuck are you?" I can't breathe. Where the hell can she be? I remove my hands and storm back into the house. I have to look every-fucking-where. Maybe she went out with her friends? Calm down, Grey. Don't lose your head.

I call every single one of her friends, except for Mason—I don't have that bitch's number—nearly screaming my fucking head off when they say they don't know where she is. They're panicked, though, and promise to begin searching for her in town. I text her a dozen times as I fumble with my boots, shoving them back on. She doesn't reply to a single one of them as I storm out of the house and get in my car, peeling off onto the road, not caring if I hit anyone. I can't fucking focus on anything other than my girl.

I try to track her, but I can't even pinpoint her fucking phone!

Seriously, where the fuck can she be? I call her about twenty more times as I visit all the places she could be, scouring the boardwalk, the ice cream parlor, even the fucking Nordstrom place with all the khakis and shit. She is nowhere, and I'm seriously having a fucking panic attack. My mind is going crazy and my hands are bruised and kind of bleeding from punching the wheel. I rub my face, and I taste the blood. I have been searching for almost a fucking hour. Where the hell is she?

I know she wouldn't just go anywhere without giving me a heads up. Not saying that I have a fucking leash on her or something, but we are together. And if I went fucking rogue and dropped off the planet, she would lose her shit too and go insane searching for me.

"Fuck!" I hit the wheel again as I tug on my lip, trying to think. "Fucking think, Grey. Where could she be?"

It takes a moment for it to slap me in the face: her parents' house.

I furrow my brows but make a U-turn, upsetting drivers; I ignore them and slam on the gas pedal. It doesn't seem like the sanest idea of her to visit her raging bitch of a mother, but it's the only other place I can think of. I just don't understand why she'd ever go there willingly. But this is Liv I'm talking about, and she loves to test her safety. Like how much she loves going to parties even though they literally never end well. Like, at fucking *all*.

When I finally pull up at the ridiculous mansion, I nearly bust my ass as I stumble out of the car. I don't even bother locking it. As if anyone in this neighborhood would steal my hunk of junk compared to their shiny Porsches and Lambos.

"Open the fuck up!" I bang on the door and ring the doorbell repeatedly, not giving a damn if I'm disrupting anyone's beauty sleep. Everybody better get the fuck up. "Olivia, are you in there? Liv—?"

My screams are shut off abruptly when the door swings open, revealing Liv's caregiver's groggy face. She rubs her eyes, and I push past her, screaming Liv's name, jogging up to her room. I burst inside, faintly hearing her call after me and her feet slapping against the marble spiral staircase. She isn't here. I exit the room after quickly checking the ensuite. I check the guest room even though she'd never come here to stay. We've been nothing but great and in-sync the entire week, no fights or anything. She has no reason to come here to escape anything.

"Excuse me. It's too late for all this hollering. Why are you screaming Liv's name?" Lana, or whatever her name is, asks me at the stairs when I walk over to her.

"Because she's fucking missing!" I snap from the building anxiety and anger filling my senses. I feel like I'm drowning from all of the emotions covering me from head to toe.

Her face drops, and she stammers, "What? W- what do you mean, she's *missing*?"

"Are you fucking deaf?" I grip my hair before

rubbing my face, hard. "I got home and she wasn't there. I searched everywhere she could have possibly gone, but I've come up empty." I take a lethal step forward. "If you have any idea where she is, I suggest you tell me right now," I warn her through gritted teeth. Liv is the one thing in this world I would fucking *kill* for.

She shakes her head with wide eyes. "I swear, I don't know either." When I don't let up on her after a beat of silence, she looks offended and pushes me. "I raised her, you know. Don't look at me as if I don't care she's missing. I care about her."

"Sure, you do." I roll my eyes and look away. I catch sight of blue eyes and a trailing white robe before it disappears into one of their immaculate living rooms. "Hold on…" I narrow my eyes skeptically and fly down the stairs.

I stand at the mouth of the living room. Her mother is standing at the lit marble fireplace. The pale orange flicker against her strong jaw and ridiculous bun while she holds a glass of red wine. She looks like that top monster you have to fight to beat some stupid fancy game.

"Where is she?" I growl, balling up my fists.

"You don't deserve her," she says calmly, raising the tall glass to her red lips.

What the fuck?

"I didn't fucking ask you that, now did I?" I stride over to her and glare down at her. "Where the hell is my girlfriend?"

She finally looks up from the raging flames and at me. Her blue eyes gleam with malicious intent as her full red lips curl into a cat-like smile, fucking evil as shit.

"Like hell I'd tell you." She laughs like the insane woman she is.

Okay, I've had it.

"Listen, lady, I am not messing around. Tell me where she is…now!"

"I'm working on getting rid of you, and with her treatment, you will be a blip in her memory just like *that*," she slithers out, snapping her fingers.

"Treatment, huh?" I smirk just to fuck with her, and it works because her face twitches like she's been caught. "Brainwash, really? Do you really have to stoop that low to be the worst fucking mother ever?" Her hand comes to my face, but I grab her wrist before it can touch me. "Where is she?"

I hold her intense gaze. Her lips twisted up ruefully.

"I will never—" she begins.

I squeeze her wrist, and she gasps. "Where…is *she*?" I'm getting my answer now with her wrist intact or in halves.

She groans with her mouth closed before huffing out, "Memorial Hospital…"

"Thank you for that." I push her hand away easily and whisper, "Your daughter loves me and nothing you do will be enough to deter her away from me. Get that through your fucking skull and leave us alone."

I glare at her for a few moments, the only sound in the house her heavy breathing and the crackling fire. I want my calm tone and words to seep into her brain until they are all she sees and hears. She needs to understand that her daughter can very well do whatever she wants and be with me.

I walk away but stop at the mouth of the living room.

"She doesn't love you. You are only a plaything—a phase!" she screams, desperate to hurt me. But nothing this witch can say will hurt me.

"Funny, doesn't seem like it when I fuck her, and she tells me I am everything to her," I say without looking back, smirking as she gasps and throws her glass of wine at the wall beside me. "Don't fuck with my girl ever again, got it?" I say as I walk to the door. I listen to her faint screams of losing as I slam the heavy door behind me.

Chapter Forty

Liv

I was taken to a hospital. I didn't know this since I'd been forcibly given a sedative back at the house. I had dreamed of Grey over and over, picturing him chasing the ambulance and tearing off the back door and flying away with me in his arms like he's Superman. *My* Superman. Only he wouldn't be dressed in diapers and leggings. He's wearing all black and covers my body with his cape like it was a blanket as we bounced from cloud to cloud. I felt like I had been living that dream my entire life but found it to be a cruel, cruel lie when I finally woke up.

I awoke in a hospital room, sedatives dripping from an IV that was attached to one of my arms. I was groggy and could barely open my mouth to lick my chapped lips. I was dazed and confused as to how I ended up in the hospital. My mind went wild as I tried to come up with a solid, reasonable explanation why I would be in the hospital.

I hadn't broken any bones or anything, had I? I tried to move my arms to check for any bruises or a cast, and that's when I noticed it. My freaking arms were strapped down to the bed. I panicked and felt my head burst from the inside out as I thrashed all around. The sharp leather holding me down cut into my skin, and I began screaming my lungs out. Screaming for help and demanding answers. I freaked out and exerted myself until I fell back asleep.

When I finally came to consciousness again, a young female doctor with big green eyes and soft-looking skin was waiting for me. I felt my heart hammer when my muddled brain reminded me that I was tied down and had no idea how I ended up in the hospital.

"Why am I here?" I asked her.

She smiled at me and told me, "You're here for your treatment."

"For what?" I questioned her when two nurses came in, headed toward me. I tried to scoot back, but they grabbed my wrists and pinned me down. "How—why am I here? Please, *please*—tell me!" I pleaded with wide eyes as she peered over me, clutching a clipboard to her chest.

"You're here to forget Grey, sweetie…" she said, then broke out into a grin.

Oh God, I thought. *She sounds like my mother, which means…oh God.*

The sedatives came in waves, knocking me out and pulling me under, pushing me up, and then dragging me back under. I tried to hold my breath and fight against the rough waters, but her soothing words of forgetting the big bad man that has a hold on me kept challenging me. I almost let her overtake me, but the thought of Grey and his soft smile as he watched me run up to him after he'd come home, tired and needy for me, kept me sane. Well, enough for her to stop her "therapist" ways.

After this, I'm not so sure I want to be a psychologist anymore...not if this, trying to convince your patients they should not be with who they love, is what the job entails. And it hurts me deeply to think this way, because I have dreamed of helping others who need it since I was eight years old, since I lost my little brother in a tragic accident that should have never happened. I don't want her or any other cruel people to deter me from my dream, but it's incredibly hard when they continuously tell me my thoughts and beliefs are wrong and should be altered.

Hours later and I am huddled in one of the corners of the hospital room. I am tired beyond comprehension and have a hole inside my heart. I want Grey so badly; my heart is literally yearning for him. I have cold sweats and shaking hands. I want to get up and walk out of this dreadful place, but they probably have it surrounded with armed guards, per my mother's request.

My mother.

I want to say that I can't believe what she has done, but it would be a total lie. This, what she is doing, is sickening and has put the last straw on the camel's back, my freaking back. I thought after the slapping incident maybe, *maybe* we could work out our relationship. I thought maybe she would see me as her daughter and not some clay thing she could mold into the perfect girl with the perfect husband and their perfect kids. I am not, nor will I ever be, that girl! I will be with Grey. We may not have kids or get married, but I will always, and I mean *always,* love him.

But her sending me to the hospital to be brainwashed and treated like I'm not a human being has broken me as a person, as a daughter. She is unbelievable and underhanded. I don't think I can ever recover from this treason. Ever.

A tear falls down my cheek, and I rub my lower lip. I press my face into my drawn-up knees and let it all out, sobbing and shaking until I am dried out as a well. At this point, I just want to go home. I want Grey to come rescue me like the knight in shining coal he is. And I want him to shower me with kisses and tell me it's okay. I need him to come right now, but I can't—I don't even know where my phone is. They must have taken it when they changed me into this hospital gown.

I am praying when there is a loud slam. Thinking it's the nurses to bring me to that room where the doctor tried to scramble my brain, I scream and try to scramble back, only to come up empty, since I'm in the corner, my hands drawn up in fear.

Chapter Forty-One

"Liv!" a voice shouts and, by the way my body and heart responds, I instantly know who it is.

"G-Grey?" I slowly lift my head as if this is another one of the doctor's tests. But it isn't. It's true. Grey is standing at the door, frozen in what I think is shock or anger, maybe a mixture. But I am frozen in pure relief and happiness. "Grey!"

I jump to my feet and run over to him. I almost slip and slide because of how heavy my limbs feel. But seeing his outstretched arms and that wide, relieved smile of his pushes me to suck it up and run harder. I finally collide against his hard chest and jump up, latching my arms around his neck and my legs around his waist. He holds and nearly chokes me in a tight hug while breathing heavily in one whoosh. Like he hasn't been breathing until this very moment.

My heart sags.

It just hit me how he must have felt so wracked with a lot of emotions upon my disappearance. He can be very dependent when he wants as a result of his abandonment issues, first with his mother, then David. He feels as if everyone is leaving him, and I know he's scared of being alone. And to find me gone, he must have lost it. I never want him to feel alone or hopeless. I want him to know that I will never leave him. I will never hurt him, and I will never stop *loving him.*

"Oh my God, I was losing my fucking mind, *princesa*," he admits in a groggy, tight voice, like he's been crying.

I hug him harder and kiss his neck; he shudders in response. "Me too," I admit in a sigh, closing my eyes tightly and breathing in his scent—my home.

"I am going to fucking murder your mother," he growls, his hands tightening around me.

"No, just—please, take me home?" I pull my head back and cup the side of his face, rounding my finger in his dimple, closing my eyes as I let my body re-connect with his, like I'd been detached from my oxygen tank. "Take me home, Grey."

***

Grey

I am fucking livid. What kind of fucking mother does this to their daughter, their *child?* The minute I had my girl back in my arms, all my dread and worry over her safety had flushed away. But anger flared up when she dropped her hands like I was going to hurt her and revealed her paling face and heavy blue eyes that were kind of dull, lifeless. I had never wanted to twist someone's fucking neck so badly in my entire life. But I just held onto my princess and thanked whatever mysterious force that she was breathing and still able to smile, even if it looked as broken as her voice sounded.

I put her in the bath tonight. I whispered sweet nothings and commanded her to not speak and rest her hoarse, practically destroyed voice. I gently washed her body and hair. She looked like a beautiful angel as I touched her soft as silk skin and listened to her soft humming. My body yearned to be close to her, but not through sex. Just to be wrapped around her, protecting her from any threat. And that was what I did.

I was wrapped around her, her little body dressed in my black shirt. I had brushed her hair and fell asleep with her plump lips against my bare chest, hair smelling like strawberries and vanilla. I never wanted to let go.

But, of fucking course, my phone rang like the little bitch it is.

"Fuck me," I groan, craning my neck to look at the buzzing thing on the table beside me. I peer down at my girl, knocked out and content, arms wrapped around me, tongue pressed against me. She looks like a fucking kitten. I smirk, but then the annoying buzzing ruins the fucking moment.

I grab it and lowly bark into the phone. "What the fuck do you want?" I hadn't looked at the caller ID; I just want to tell this fucking person off and get back to dreamland.

"Might want to lose your tone with me," Dean sneered.

I sigh. "It's, like, two in the morning." I pinch

389

my nose bridge, trying my best not to lash out at this very dangerous man.

"I don't give a shit. I want you here; there's a huge fuck-load shipment coming in an hour. I want you by the dock, prepared for…" His words are lost on me. They go in one ear and fly out of the other. Honestly, it just sounds like gibberish at this point. And I can barely decipher it.

My focus is locked on my little princess that needs and deserves me more than this fucking douche-asshole.

"Fuck you and fuck the shipment," I grit through the phone.

A pause.

"Excuse me…" he snarls.

"You heard me. Lose my number—I'm out. Now I gotta get back to my girl." I hang up, turn off my phone, and toss it back on the table. What I just did will definitely backfire on my ass and I will be in major shit, but I don't care anymore. Dean and that stupid fucking gang are not my priority. They never have been, nor will they ever be. I have someone who is more important to me laying on me, clutching me like I am her entire world as she is mine.

I kiss her head for a long moment, savoring her scent and picturing my life with her, content and so fucking perfect. Home. She is and will always be my *home*.

Chapter Forty-Two

Liv

I am strapped to the bed again. I struggle against the restraints, but it is no use. There is no way out. I crane my neck and look around the white room. It seems like the type of place where aliens torture humans for information on their leader. Just the thought of being probed makes me freak out even more, screaming and pleading to be let go.

The door slams open, and I still.

I can't see who it is, but I can clearly hear the tip-tapping on the tiled floor.

I gasp when the person peers over me, lips red and hair delicately draping down her roundish face.

Me.

"Time for your treatment, Olivia," she says, grinning down at me. I kick my legs as I watch her long white fingertips come down to my head.

"No!" I shout as loud as I can as shocks spark my body, making me writhe with nausea.

"Shhh...it'll all be over with," she promises, and

391

I scream for help.

Suddenly, a little boy I know too well appears by her side, holding her hand while sucking his thumb with the other.

"Just forget him and move on," he mumbles around his thumb. "Only pain will come to you by being with the bad man. Run." His face morphs into a sort of demon, and I scream louder, squeezing my eyes shut.

"No!" I scream as I forcibly eject myself from the terribly frightening dream. I scramble up and hit my head against the headboard. My head sways and my hands are shaking so much, I feel like the house is shifting on its foundation and I am perfectly still. I can't stop screaming as hard as I try to stop. I just can't get the fresh, vivid images of my creepy smile and Jonah's face. Oh, my poor Jonah.

I begin crying, and the tears are hot as they flow down my face.

"Liv? Liv!" A banging sound makes me jump. I open my swollen eyes from the crying. Grey is standing at the door looking shocked and heartbroken.

"Grey." I hold my chest as he rushes into the room and jumps onto the bed. He scrambles over to me and sweeps me into his arms for a tight, soothing hug. It takes my breath away and helps calm the raging tears falling down my cheeks. "W-where were you?"

"I was making you breakfast," he explains and kisses my hair.

"Is that why you smell like burnt bacon?" I

mumble into his chest.

He chuckles and kisses my forehead before cupping my cheeks and forcing me to look into his eyes. "I held you all night. I just got up to make you something to eat. You weren't able to keep any of the pizza I ordered down. Are you sick?" he asks, splaying the back of his hand against my forehead.

I smile softly and shake my head, eyes drifting to the floor. "The IVs tend to make people sick." I can practically still feel the sharp needle digging in my skin as I screamed and thrashed around on the hospital bed, begging to be released. Begging for the pain to stop…

"Hey." Grey tugs my chin upward, and I look into his soft black eyes. "Stay with me."

I let out a deep breath and nod. "I'm here. I promise."

"Good." He smirks, and I beam up at him. "Now let me ground you here. I have missed these lips," he whispers. He leans down and gently places his lips on mine. My body instantly melds into his while my hands find their way into his hair. His kisses always rip me off this world's plane and sends me into his without any hesitation.

I stand up on my knees like him and pull him down on me until I'm laying down on my back. His lips rub against mine; he tugs, licks, and bites a little like he is greedy for me. I open my mouth and let my heart collide and explode with his.

"Grey," I moan when his hands slide under my shirt and into my panties. My heart is beating out of control as he rubs his thumb over my clit and sucks on my bottom lip. Oh my God. I can't take this. I grip his shoulder and arch my back, circling my hips for more friction, greedy for his touch. "That feels so good."

"Mmm, you like when I touch you, *princesa*?" he groans next to my ear and nibbles on my earlobe.

"Yes, Grey. I love it," I whisper and kiss him, hard. I rock my hips against his, cursing and hissing as little waves of pleasure hit me. I migrate my lips to his chin, his jaw, all the way down to his neck. I suck and smile as he moans against me, making my body reverberate and feel as though I am on fire. He keeps rubbing and even adds a finger. I scream in surprise then melt into his touch and moan his name.

"I fucking love it when you moan my name like that." His voice is hard and low. I can feel his erection against my inner thigh. I reach down and palm him through his basketball shorts. "Fuck," he hisses through his teeth and rubs himself against me. His finger goes deeper as he inserts another. I scream his name and grip him.

I cup his cheek with my free hand and pull his face down to my chin. I smash my lips against his and rub him faster, feeling him growing and growing.

"I need more, please," I beg, my voice hoarse.

He nods frantically, and I kick his shorts and boxers down using my feet. He stops his finger movements, and I feel cold when his hands leave me and help take my panties off. I take off my shirt, leaving me bare since I'm not wearing a bra underneath it, just how he likes it. I watch as he grabs a condom from the bedside table on the side where he sleeps.

"You need to get back on the pill," he gripes angrily as he tears the foil packet open and slides the rubber on his erect member. I've told him that I stopped months ago when I was sure I would never see him again. But here we are, about to have sex and in a relationship again. Crazy how life works, isn't it?

"I will, promise." I sit up and pull him down by his shoulder, impatient. "Just please…" I part my legs, and his eyes grow dark as he smirks before getting between them. I close my eyes in pleasure and relief as he finally slides into me, filling me until I am moaning in pain that feels way too flipping good. "Oh God…" I mutter, clutching my hair.

"Fuuuuck," he moans, and I open my eyes to find him closing his eyes in bliss too.

I lick my lips as he pulls out a little, then slams into me. "Grey!" I groan his name, gasp as he swirls his hips and plays with my sensitive clit. I reach up and whine as I clutch his shoulder. I need to kiss him. I need something to ground me before I fly away to cloud nine completely. He bends down and rocks his hips against mine, plunging into me and claiming me over and over again.

His lips collide with mine, and I gasp into his warm, open mouth. I sink my nails into his back and drag them down and all around, tracing tattoos and pushing him into me every time he pulls out slightly, only to pound into me mercilessly.

"Fuck, you're so fucking tight. And so responsive," he mumbles as he drags his tongue along my jaw. I moan a strangled moan and lift my hips with his. "I love you, princess. So god damn much, it drives me fucking insane."

"I love you too, Grey. So, s-so much. Mmmm, please." My words slur as my breathing slows, heart beating too incredibly fast for me to catch up. "Mmm, close, Grey." I bite his shoulder as I feel a familiar tinge of pleasure uncoil and tighten in the bottom of my stomach. My head feels light and I'm becoming sensitive. I let my head fall to the pillow and wrap my legs around his waist.

"Hold on for me, bebé." He stands up on his knees and pounds into me, hitting my G-spot perfectly.

"Oh my!" I scream and drive my head into the soft pillow, feeling my heart drum against my chest like it's trying to fly out of me and into the clouds. "Grey, please, d-don't stop," I moan and writhe, latching my hands onto his tatted forearms. I dig into the bed and scream his name; I am almost there. He lifts my hips and I groan, digging my fingernails into his skin.

"Shh, just let go, princess." He bends over and licks my lips, sucking and nibbling all over. I breathe into his mouth and gasp when he lets my bottom lip go, whispering, "Come for me, *now*."

I do as I'm told and come crashing down on him.

"Ahhh, Grey!" I scream his name and hold his neck as I close my eyes, feeling myself release. I feel like I've been hit square in the face with pleasure. I suck my swollen bottom lip and open my eyes. He has his closed as his hips pound into me. He's almost there. "Come on, Grey. Come for me, please." I somewhat moan his name, dragging my nails down his chest to his torso.

My words pull him overboard.

"Oh, fuck! Fucking shit." A slew of curses leaves his reddish lips from our hard, passionate kisses as he slams his hips in me. I moan, feeling how full and heavy his member is as he comes. I lightly drag my fingertips up and down his back, pulling and pushing him away from me, milking him into me.

When he's done, he rests his forehead on mine, and we stay silent as we try to catch our breaths.

"I think the house is burning down," he says after a moment.

I open my eyes and whine, feeling him pull out of me. "You didn't turn off the stove?" I ask, pulling the sheets over my sore but light body.

He's standing now, completely naked since he's thrown away the condom. "Um…maybe?" he shrugs, palms raised in the air.

I pick up a pillow and toss it at him. "Go turn it off and meet me in the shower."

"You got it, dude." He winks at me, shooting me with finger guns.

I roll my eyes and watch him run out of the room, butt naked. I flush and stand up. I nearly buckle under my weak knees but luckily catch myself before I can fall. Lord knows what that would have done to his already massive ego. Tiring me out from amazing sex. Geez. He wouldn't be able to walk around with such a giant head. I smile to myself as I throw the sheet on the bed and steadily walk into the bathroom.

I am warm and content when he finally joins me, arms linked around my waist, neck peppered with his sweet, soft kisses.

"What are you doing today?" I ask him, already knowing the answer. Training. I just miss him. I want to chill with him and have him be by my side.

"Training," he answers, and I can't hide my little sigh. He kisses my chin and peers around to look me in the eyes. "But I want you to come."

I raise a brow, my mind now linked and dirty like his.

He chuckles, cheeks pink as he hides his face in my neck. "I want you by my side."

I smile from ear to ear. "I'll come."

"Is that a promise?" His hands are wandering down below.

"Maybe…" I bite my lip, and he stares at me. I know what's about to go down when his lips twist into that wicked smirk. He is so insatiable. I love it.

Chapter Forty-Three

"Duck," Grey instructs, and I do as I'm told, but a little too late. His gloved hand nearly swipes across my face as I go down.

"This is hard," I groan, stumbling back.

He's teaching me how to *fight*. In reality, he's knocking me around with gloves, but in the gentlest way ever. Like a tiny little baby tap to the cheek or stomach. I'd say it's insulting, but I appreciate it. My body can barely take his soft blows. And I suck, like, really bad at this whole...*thing*. I don't understand how he does this and at a much faster pace with actual hard-hitting punches that leave bruises and cuts.

"Why couldn't you be a baker?" I wheeze as I sit on the ground against one of the rings.

A group of shirtless men with gloves passing by laughs at me, and I stick my tongue out at them. They laugh even harder, and I glare at them, but they just "aww" at me and nod to Grey. I look at Grey, who waves at them. His eyes feel mine, and he looks at me.

"Oh, come on. It isn't that hard," he says, pulling me up. I whine and push against the rope. "All you have to do is pay attention to my hands."

"It's harrrrd," I groan, digging my feet in the mat.

"No, it isn't." He's smiling as he raises his hands. "Now, watch my fists. Even look at my shoulder. If they're rising, *duck*. Simple as baking a pie."

"You'd *burn* the pie." I make a face at him, silently imagining digging a knife into these stupid gloves and throwing an apron on him either way. Anything is much better than getting punched around all day, every day.

"Come on, babe. Hands up," he instructs with a little smirk.

I groan but put them up. The hot-pink gloves mock me. He nods his head, and I nod back. I watch his shoulders and duck as his right hand comes forward. I block the left, duck again, and jab him in his stomach, much harder than he's been hitting me. He grunts and hunches over, winded.

"Oh, come on, babe. It isn't so hard," I mock him in a baby voice. He looks up through his sweaty black hair, and I say, "Whoops."

I take a step back as he stands to his natural looming height, narrowing his eyes at me. "I surrender, I surrender!" I turn around and begin running.

"C'mere." He swoops me up by my waist and spins me around.

"Put me down!" I giggle and kick my legs as I go around and round. "I'm going to barf!"

"Ew, gross." He stops moving, and I smirk, moving my right hand to jab him in his jaw. He easily shakes his huge gloves off, grabs my outstretched hand, and whirls me around so I am pressed into his chest. "Gotta be quicker than that."

I move to the side and punch him in his gut.

He doubles over.

"Gotta be quicker than that," I mock him in a *duh* tone.

He rushes over to me, but I dodge him. "Come here!"

"No!" I stick my tongue out at him and make a childish sound as I roll it at him.

He makes a battle cry and runs after me. I giggle and get calls from guys to *run faster* and *escape the beast*. Their cheering me on makes Grey even *angrier*. I jump onto the rope and escape, when he grabs me by my waist and pulls me back.

"Got you!" he announces with victory in his voice.

Some men boo.

"Fuck off!" Grey curses.

I laugh and wave at them, then spin on my toes and wrap my arms around his neck. "Don't be mean to the men. They were rooting for me, the victim."

"And what the fuck am I?" He twists up his face.

I hum, biting my lip, tilting my head side to side before grinning up at him. "The beast," I drawl, and he smirks.

"Then I'll take pleasure in eating you up." He picks me up, and I scream. He laughs, and I shut him up with my mouth. I grip his hair and clasp my tongue over his, gliding and exploring his warm mouth. I tug on his lips and bite and suck. He moans, and I smile as I drag my nails down his neck. He shivers and whispers, "You are so fucking bad."

"I get it from you." My voice is raspy.

"Fuuuck," he drawls, and I laugh.

I go back to kissing him, hard and thoroughly. I love this man with all of my heart. I truly do not see a world where he is not next to me. Lightly tapping me with a glove. Almost burning down the house. Chasing me around and claiming he wants to devour me.

"Ew, can you guys get a room already?" an annoyed voice says behind Grey. I look over his shoulder and flush. It's a boy with light blue eyes and short brown hair. I notice a scar slashed across his cheek and am intrigued and scared as to how he got it.

Grey pulls me away but slides his arm around my waist, facing the boy. He smiles, weirdly enough. He isn't the best with people, not unless he's already friends with them...

"Don't be jealous I have a girl and you don't," Grey says, and the boy shows off his middle finger.

I laugh, and the boy winks at me. Grey's hand on my hip twitches and grips me tightly. I lean over and softly kiss his shoulder to calm him, and his hand relaxes, but only a bit.

"Liv, this is a *friend* of mine, Jake. Jake, this is my girl, Liv," Grey introduces us.

"'Sup." The boy, Jake, nods at me with a charming smile that makes me blush and shyly rub my cheek against Grey's arm.

"Hi." I nervously wave at him, and he laughs.

"What's up?" Grey nods.

"There's gonna be a party at Mark's tonight. You guys up for it?" Jake says. "It'll be before the tournament."

Oh, the big night! I cannot wait. Tonight would be great to have fun before being thrown in a ring with stress.

"I don't know," Grey begins to say.

"I want to go," I tell him, and he snaps his wide eyes to me, then relaxes them and shakes his head.

"I don't think we should," he says, and I frown.

"Why not?" I shrug.

He shrugs and rubs his lower lip. "It's just…things don't end well when we, I mean, like, *you* go to a party. And I'd rather just chill with you alone, without all the bullshit."

"I doubt anything wrong will happen," I say, but he doesn't look so convinced. I turn to him fully and pull out the big guns—the puppy look, bulging eyes, pouty lips and all.

He groans, knowing how weak he is to the look.

"Please…" I huff out.

A beat of silence.

"Ah, what the hell," he sighs with a smirk. "What *princesa* wants, *princesa* gets."

I lean up on my toes and press my lips to his, ignoring the boy with pale eyes behind us, telling us to get a room and never come out. I laugh into Grey's arms and scream as he picks me up and spins me around. Man, do I love this man.

Chapter Forty-Four

"Are you sure you want to go?" Grey asks for the millionth time.

"Yes, I'm sure." I smile at him through the mirror.

He is being very strange, urging that we stay home tonight. Is it because there will be bad people there, people he doesn't want me to interact with? Like…Rose? No, I don't think so. She is trying to be friendly with us, but partying with us would be going over a clear line of comfort. I wouldn't want to torture the nice girl. Maybe Dean…my stomach tightens at the idea of the monster being anywhere near us. He has been nothing but trouble to Grey.

"Why don't you want us to go?" I ask him as I apply lip gloss. "Will, um, will Dean be there?" I look at him through the mirror, and his face hardens, but then he sighs and shakes his head.

"No, I…I cut myself off from the gang," he says, and I whirl around.

"When?" I gasp. He's always been so adamant about being in it, saying it would be too dangerous if he ever left. So why leave now? Don't get me wrong, I am incredibly happy and relieved that he's left the gang. I'm just curious as to when and why he did so.

"The night we came home from the hospital," he mumbles, looking down at his fumbling fingers.

"That's great," I say and smile.

"I guess. It was just taking my time away from being with someone who makes me happy…you." He clears his throat.

"You're so cute." I walk over to him and kiss his head.

He looks up at me through his lashes. "Thanks," he says as I push his cheeks together.

I smile and kiss his nose. "Now…" I step back. "How do I…look?"

I feel his eyes on me as I struggle but succeed in zipping up this loose pale blue dress that is off the shoulder and stops mid-thigh. I twirl around in it, nearly falling over because of the matching blue wedges, but I catch myself and grin. Grey is laughing, cheeks pink and eyes lighting up.

"You look adorable," he says as he pulls me between his legs.

"You look…" I pause and look down at his outfit: a white shirt that makes for a crisp contrast to his dark, haunting tattoos, his signature leather jacket, washed out Levi's jeans, and boots. *Is drool dripping down my chin?* "Hot," I admit.

"Why, thank you. I try only for you, babe." He cups my face and brings me down to his.

"Only for me, always *only* for me." I grip his jacket and narrow my eyes playfully.

"Fuck, I love it when you get feisty," he snarls, and I laugh as he falls back on the bed, hand sliding under my dress and gripping my butt. I moan against his neck, and he grows hard against me. "Wanna arrive fashionably late?" he whispers against my ear.

"Mm-hmm," is all I can say, well, hum.

His laugh ignites a flutter in my stomach, and I shut him up with my mouth covering his.

Chapter Forty-Five

I begin to feel a little anxious as we leave the house. Maybe Grey is right; something bad will go down at the party. But as long as he's out of the gang and we don't have any enemies, there is nothing to worry about. Plus, Grey's hand on my thigh helps soothe the anxious thoughts until they are all gone.

As we near a line of various off-brand stores and stop in front of a one-level building, I listen to the roars and laughter and loud music, all colliding to make a nervous but excited smile take over my face. There are bamboo trees that line up against the side of the building, and through the little cracks and low height, I can see arms in the air and tall men dancing behind girls in jeans and short shirts. There are strung up lights, and beers clinking together, and cursing.

We enter, passing by a girl getting a tattoo on her lower back. She is biting onto a leather belt while her boyfriend cheers her on. I almost, out of worry, rush over to her and see if she's too intoxicated to get a tattoo, but she raises a glass of dark alcohol and chuckles after taking a large swig. I then look around and notice other people are getting tattoos too.

What a party...

"Which font should it be in?" Grey asks me.

I turn to him and see he is staring at a wall of pinned up sample tattoos. "What are you talking about?" I grimace at a tattoo of a machine-like teddy bear having sex with a big-breasted woman. Gross, why would *anyone* want to get that?

"Your name," he says and looks at me with a crooked grin.

"You're joking," I say with a little nervous laugh. He can't be serious. I love him and everything, but to get my name imprinted on his skin *forever* would be actually insane!

"Oh, I'm doing it. And I'll do it in a nice pretty font you'll love." He taps my nose and sits down on a leather stool, in front of a bald guy covered in tattoos, a metal contraption in his hand.

I widen my eyes and shake my head. "No, don't do that! Are you insane?"

The man chuckles. "You're a lucky lady. This guy's really committed." He winks at me, and I flush. *Committed? Yeah, in the sense of getting a tattoo of my name, but not in the sense of marriage or kids. Just saying...*

"Heh," I laugh nervously, and Grey grabs my hand, pulling me forward.

"Don't worry, babe," he says with a smile, like marring your skin with another person's name is nothing.

"I am going to worry because this is a huge and very *stupid* thing to do," I snap, pulling at my hand, but his grip is too tight. I whine his name.

"Stop worrying, princess." He kisses the back of my hand.

I blush and bite my lip. "If you do this…then I'll get your name on my forehead."

He bursts into laughter and shakes his head. "You're too much of a wimp."

"Wanna bet?" I raise a brow. He knows how much I love to prove him wrong.

"I don't want your delicate skin marred." He presses his soft lips to my skin again, and I burst into a rosy color on my cheeks. "Stay my perfect angel, m'kay?" His voice is rough, but his words are silk, making me gush and nod.

"O-okay." I smile down at him.

He laughs, and the machine in the man's hand starts up. The sound emitting from the metal makes me grimace, and I take a fearful step back. Grey's hand tightens, and he gently pulls me toward him. He lays his forehead against my stomach, and I'm shocked by his tender affection in public around these people. I blush but wrap my arms around him and listen to the clanging sounds of the machine as it presses into his skin.

"Does it hurt?" I ask after a while. He has been still for about ten minutes, unflinching. Given how many he has already, I doubt it even feels like a pinch.

"Nope," he mumbles, then rests his chin on me as he looks up at me with a childishly large grin. "Maybe you *should* get a tattoo."

"Of what?" I thread my fingers through his thick hair.

"My face."

"Shut up." I tug his hair and his lips curl, tongue sliding through his mouth. "Stop that."

"Oh, you want your last name on my ass?" he jokes, and I roll my eyes.

"I wouldn't be the only one embarrassed," I point out, and he shrugs.

"Just don't test me." He reaches around and pinches my butt.

I gasp. "How much longer?" I mumble.

"A few more minutes," the man says, eyes trained on Grey's back.

I stand on my toes to peek at the tattoo that I don't believe for a second is my name, but Grey tugs me down and bites my stomach.

"Hey!" I frown at him, tugging his hair.

"Don't look yet. It isn't finished," he whines.

"Fine." I lean down and kiss his head. I pull back and smile at the grin splashed over his face. I stand around for maybe ten more minutes, lightly gripping his hair, listening to the buzzing of what Grey explained is a tattoo gun.

"Done!" the man whose name I learned is Rick exclaims and rolls back from Grey. "You gotta keep it under wraps and apply the cream I know you already have for a few days," he instructs.

"Got it. Thanks, man." Grey sits up, letting his shirt stay rolled up. He digs into his pocket and hands Rick money. They talk for a quick second before he finally stands up.

"I want to see it," I tell him, nervously chewing

on my lower lip and tugging the top.

He chuckles but nods and turns around. "Like it?"

My eyes gravitate to the fresh tattoo among the others. I gasp when I see it. It definitely isn't my name, but something much better. Something that makes me light-headed and tear up.

You are my middle ground, princesa, the tattoo reads, floating in large, thick gray clouds.

"Oh no, Grey—" I start, throat thick with emotion.

"Don't say it's insane or anything because...princess." He laughs, eyes tearing up. "You're quite literally *it* for me. And I know how you want a family and all that, but I...I just can't do that. But this is my commitment to you." He holds my hands and whispers, "My promise to love you forever and always."

"Sappy," Rick groans behind Grey.

Grey merely raises a middle finger in the air, eyes never leaving mine.

"So...what do you say?" His voice is shaky from nerves. I can see how much he wants to touch his lip out of anxiety, but he won't let go of my hands.

I answer him with my lips pressed against his. I kiss him with every single ounce of love and passion that burns deep within me, all for him. I grip his neck and bring him down while pressing up into his mouth, biting and licking his lips. He wraps his arms around my waist and tugs my hips up. Before this can go any further, I pull away and press my forehead against his.

"I say...forever and always," I whisper, and he

411

grins, kissing me hard once again.

"Fuck, I love you so much." He spins me around, and I squeal, latching my arms tightly around his neck.

"Grey!" I scream his name, and he whispers something dirty in my ear. "You are too bad." I hit his shoulder, and he shrugs, glancing at my lips. I do the same with him.

"Not too bad for you, right?" he asks, licking his lips, my eyes following the action.

"Never…"

Chapter Forty-Six

Grey and I take a few shots and spend most of the night dancing with each other. Jake arrives a few minutes into our dance, and I meet a few more of Grey's fighter friends. They are all blowing off steam and relaxing before going to the tournament that's in forty-five minutes. I want Grey to leave now and get focused for the big fights, but he says he'd rather have my ass grind on him than beat up some guy. I have never felt so giddy in my life. What a compliment from a hardcore fighter.

My phone nearly buzzes the entire time, messages from Mason and missed calls. It became so annoying that I had to text him that I'd talk to him later and shut my phone off. I don't mean to be rude, but my man just did the sweetest thing ever for me and is about to have the biggest fights of his career. I want to be here for him, and that's it. Nothing or anyone matters more in this moment.

"I'm going to go get some water," I scream over the music, pushing from Grey's sweaty chest.

"Hurry back." He smiles as he leans down and

413

kisses me on my open mouth. I grip his shirt and deepen the kiss. I finally step back after I've had my fill and turn around. I gasp when he smacks me on my butt. I hide half of my face behind his leather collar. He gave it to me a while back when I admitted I was cold. Such a gentleman.

"I won't take long," I promise and wink at him. He bites his lip sensually, but I have to turn around and zig-zag through the crowd before I am tempted. I reach the cooler and search for a bottled water. I down about half of it, parched from all the shots I've been taking.

As I turn back, I bump into someone.

"Oh, sorry—" I giggle, sweeping my hair out of my face.

"Liv? Oh, thank God I found you," the person says, and I finally adjust my blurry vision on the person. "Mateo told me about this party and I just had to find you—"

"Mason?" What is he doing here?

He takes a deep breath and stutters, "Liv, i-it's Rose…" His voice is panicked, and I widen my eyes in worry.

I feel my heart drop to my feet, and I blink rapidly as I try to find access to my tongue. I am so drunk, I don't believe I heard him right. "What's wrong with Rose?" My tongue feels incredibly heavy, my words slurred. I'm seeing fuzzy lights around his head. I need to clear my head to pay attention to him. This seems very important. I should really listen…to how amazing this song is. I begin dancing, and he sighs.

He licks his lips. "There's nothing wrong with

her, per se…"

"Then why'd you act like something was wrong?" I mumble before I take a large swig of water. "Drama queen…"

"You're not listening to me." He grabs the bottled water from me.

"Hey, give it back!" I whine, tears bubbling in my eyes. "Why'd you come here if you were just going to ruin all the fun?"

He sighs and grabs my hand, tugging me to his side. "I have to tell you something, and I don't want you to get mad at me," he says, and I raise a questioning eyebrow. "It's too loud back here." He pulls me out of the back, through the tattoo shop, and outside by the huge green trees, away from the party. Sorry, they're called bamboo. I think I've had a little bit too much to drink.

"What do you have to tell me?" I ask him and gasp, pointing a finger at him. "Are you pregnant?" I hunch over on my knees and jab a finger at his tummy. "Hello, little Mason. How you doing in there, hmm? Having fun swimming?" I coo and scratch his stomach.

"Stop that." He pulls me up, face stoic and ultra-serious. "Rose is trying to—"

"Your mouth looks, like, *really* funny." I poke at them, and he groans.

"Liv, I'm trying to tell you something," he groans, squeezing my shoulders.

"Fine, go on and tell your life story. I am all ears." I grin from ear to ear and hold onto his shoulders, giving them a nice squeeze. Hmmm…they are so soft, strong too. Has he been working out? Is this facial hair I see growing on his chin? His lips are moving, but I don't hear a word he's saying because I'm busy playing with his scratchy cheeks.

"Olivia, please, listen to me." He grabs my wrists and holds my hands up. "I am *begging* you now…"

His serious tone finally makes my brain click in the right places, and I nod.

"I am listening, I promise," I manage to say with minimum slurring.

He nods and sucks in such a large breath, I am afraid he's taken all of the air in the world. "Rose is trying to sabotage you and Grey," he blurts out.

Chapter Forty-Seven

"W-what?" I stammer, furrowing my brows.

"She…s-she took pictures of you a-and Noah at Grey's birthday party," he explains, stuttering over nearly every word.

I burst into laughter because I have no idea what he's talking about. He looks at me weirdly, and I pout, stifling laughter.

"Rose? Sabotage Grey and me? What? How?" I shake my head because the thought of sweet Rose doing such a thing is unconceivable.

"You don't remember anything from that night, right?" I slowly shake my head. "She…she drugged a drink she gave you and then after that separated you from Grey and got Noah and you in your room. She…a-and I—I helped…w-we got you both undressed and made it seem you h-had sex…b-but you didn't! I swear!"

"What?" I feel so cold despite the warm air passing by me. "No…no! Y-you wouldn't do that to me. She wouldn't…no! Mason, fuck, no! No, Mason!" I push him, and he stumbles back, tears

417

leaving his eyes as my own pour down my face. "Mason!" I scream, throat tight and heart beating fast.

He nods his head and whimpers, "I am so sorry. I didn't...s-she made me promise her."

"Mason, no." My voice is small as my thoughts race and my stomach churns. This isn't happening. This is not *fucking happening!* Not to me. Not on behalf of one of my *best fucking friends* and a girl I actually trusted. Not like this!

"I am so sorry, Liv," he cries. I hold my hand up when he takes a step toward me.

"What did you promise her?" My voice is thick with heartbreak and dreaded anticipation.

"I—I promised I would help hurt Grey. S-she said that he hurt her so bad, and he did, Liv. So fucking bad. I wanted to hurt him the moment she told me she had the abortion and lost everything. And I mean *everything*," he wheezes, and my heart twists. "She said that if she ever came into contact with him ever again, she'd hurt him a million times worse than he hurt her...no matter what." His eyes take in my flushed face and shaking hands. "S-she, she's in there right now," he whispers, and my eyes widen.

"I can't—I can't believe this. I thought you were my friend!" I don't believe this is the same Mason who saved me from that football my first day at college. The same Mason I gossiped with over cartons of Chinese food. The same fucking Mason I got matching friendship bracelets with.

"I am your friend," he falsely promises, taking another step forward.

"No, you are not!" I scream on the top of my lungs and push him away from me. He lands in the fence behind him and grunts, staring at me wide-eyed like I'm the one who betrayed *him*. "A friend would have warned me about his fucking insane sister! Not help her tear me and my boyfriend, the love of my *life,* apart! After all I have been through, I would have thought you'd be there for me."

"I am so sorry," is all he can murmur.

"You better be." I take off the stupid bracelet and throw it at his chest. He catches it with a fallen expression. "I am fucking through with you! I'm done!"

"Liv," he whines and reaches a hand out to me.

I walk away from him and feel everything crash down on my chest. I feel like I'm going to implode on the spot. I have never felt so much betrayal in my life. I feel like I've been chewed up but never spat out. I just keep tumbling and getting speared by spiky teeth by a monster that goes by the name of *Mason.*

"Grey!" I scream his name as loud as I can. I rush to where I last saw him but come up empty. "Grey, where are you? Please, where are you? Grey—?"

"Looking for someone?" a familiar sweet voice drawls behind me.

I whirl around and find Rose smirking at me, arms crossed. "How could you?" My voice is low, and fresh tears are now falling down my face.

"I didn't mean to hurt you. You were just in the way—a casualty." She shrugs her shoulders and looks me up and down. "I got what I wanted, though. Grey's all wrecked and pissed at you for cheating. Must suck to be you guys." She winks at me. She taps my nose before brushing past me, and something inside of me unleashes. I have only dealt with the force in me with one other person. One other *bitch*.

"Hey, Rose," I say before I slowly turn around.

"What?" She sounds annoyed as she spins on her heels.

"I didn't get what I wanted," I say with a sarcastic smile.

Then I throw my balled-up fist into her nose. She screams and scrambles back. But before she can go down, I drag her by her dress, hear the cheap red fabric rip, and pull her back up. Her mouth meets my fist. I kick her in the chin before throwing my fist across her jaw, hearing a sickening crunch. I let her go and finally hear the yelling and cheering behind me.

She's unconscious, bloody, and bruised.

"Now I got it," I hiss through gritted teeth. I watch as Mason runs to her side and stares up at me, regret and despair sprawled across his face. "You two deserve each other."

"Wait," Mason pleads.

"What!" I snap.

He holds out his hand, and I recoil. "No, look…" He opens his fist and cries, "I took it—as a little kick to hurt you…Rose's idea." My charm. *Grey's charm!*

"You are such a puppet, I can't believe it." I snatch the charm from him, and he cries more.

I walk away and look for Grey but come up

empty once again. My fist is stinging like a bitch, but it doesn't matter. I can handle the pain. But what I *can't* handle is Grey thinking that something actually went down between Noah and me. I may have been extremely drugged and don't remember much from that night, but I do know that I would never do something with Noah. I like him as a friend, but that's it.

I find Jake leaving the party and run up to him.

"Jake!" I scream his name, pulling him from entering a car with two other guys.

"Yeah?" He faces me with a relaxed smile, but he sees my bloody fist and looks shocked. "What the hell—?"

"Are you going to the tournament?" I am out of breath since I've been running around like a chicken without a head.

"Yes..."

"Take me, please." I swallow the lump in my throat.

He nods to the car. "Get in." His normally playful tone is switched out for a more serious one. I nod and slide into the backseat, giving an acknowledged nod to the tall guys next to me.

Hang on, Grey. I'm coming for you.

Chapter Forty-Eight

Grey

I don't believe a fucking word Rose says. Liv would never betray me like that. She told me she never liked the prick, never felt anything when they...*kissed*. Ugh, I rather be bashing his fucking head in...anyway, I don't believe her. But then she shows me the clear photo of her stumbling upon the bodies. They are both naked under a thin sheet. Her hair is messy, and her lips are red. She looks like she does after we have sex...my blood boils as I stare at the way she's latched onto him, afraid to let him go.

Tears pricked my eyes, and I felt my hand begin to clam up as I analyzed the picture. I felt such anger and betrayal, all I could see was fucking red. My eyes scanned over the charm laying between her cleavage, his arm just under her breasts...I had to take a deep breath from smashing Rose's fucking phone. That damn charm. She was wearing his charm yet doesn't have mine anymore. She probably threw it away right after he fucked her for the first time.

I couldn't fucking believe it. My angel, my princess, my fucking *girl* fucked another guy. I thought she was fucking *it* for me. I had just tattooed how much she meant to me on my fucking skin. Talk about fucking karma and timing, huh? If Rose had gotten there earlier, I could have avoided marring a fucking mistake into my skin. She fucking fucked him! That prick, that Barbie doll. That asshole didn't fucking deserve her!

But why? Why do it? Why fuck him then come to me and convince me you love me? My mad mind went crazy with thoughts and possibilities of how she could have been such a fucking master manipulator. I mean, she's betrayed me before. Played me like no one has ever before. Maybe she's writing a sequel. Maybe she's never loved me, ever. And my entire life is just for her fucking pleasure— her gain.

How could I have allowed it to happen again? Her twisting my heart around like it was a fucking toy she could play with freely. I promised myself and my heart that I would not let her or anyone hurt me the way she did the first time. Yet here I am. Hurt, broken-hearted, and pissed the fuck off. I let her in *again*. I let her fool me *again*. I fucking fell for the girl with the brightest smile and devious big blue eyes…*again*!

I roar as I throw my fist into the metal locker, then lay my forehead against the cool surface. I grind my teeth hard against each other as I try to cool myself down, catch my breath. But I can't even hear over the loud thumping inside my chest. I punch the locker again and again and just keep punching until my knuckles are numb. I finally kick it and watch it slam to the ground. I grip my hands and shake my head, letting out another roar as I stomp on it, denting the green metal. I want to fucking tear the door off its hinges and throw it at that prick's fucking face until there is absolutely nothing left.

"Grey, you're up," a voice booms behind me. I didn't even hear the door croak open.

I turn around and face a short guy holding a clipboard. He looks scared as he eyes me and the fallen locker.

"Finally." I crack my neck and knuckles, and he gulps and backs out.

I get to take my anger out the old-fashioned way. Beating fuckers' faces in, literally.

Chapter Forty-Nine

"Come on!" I scream in frustration, pulling at my hair. I stare at the blaring red headlights through the windshield window. We have been stuck in stupid traffic for over fifty minutes. If I'm not quick enough, the tournament will be over, and I'll miss Grey before he goes off the grid again. He did just that after I betrayed him the first time. But this time I really didn't. I was framed, and he has to know that. But he won't know if I am here for the rest of my life.

"Fuck!" I curse and kick the seat in front of me.

"Hey." Jake peers over the passenger seat, and I mutter an apology, crossing my arms. "I'm sorry about this, and what happened…"

"Yeah…" the guys agree in a low mutter.

I sigh and bounce my legs and run a hand through my hair. I bite my lip and peer around his head. We move an inch, then that's it. More red lights. "Thanks for the ride, but I've got it from here," I thank the driver, and he nods at me.

"You sure?" Jake frowns at me.

425

"Yeah, I have to fix this. Now." I unbuckle my seatbelt and am opening the door when a hand touches my knee. I look back and find him unlatching his belt.

"I'll go with you," he says, and I flush.

"You don't have to." I rather do this alone.

"There is no way I'm not coming with you," he says like the gentleman he is.

He and I exit the car and say a brief goodbye to the other guys. We zig-zag through the basically parked cars. We run along the sidelines, and all I can think about is what I am going to say to Grey. He has to believe me when I tell him I never did anything with Noah. God! I still can't believe this. I did not see it coming. And Mason…fuck! I truly thought he was my best friend. I could have never seen him betraying me like this, in the worst way possible. Destroying the relationship between Grey and me. We have only just begun to glue the jagged pieces of our last disaster back together. But then *this* had to happen.

I am too late. We arrive about fifteen minutes later, and the large stadium is being cleared out with hundreds of people. Fuck! I really wanted to see him fight. It's the biggest time of his career, and I had to miss it because of…ugh!

"I'll go see if he's still inside," Jake tells me, rubbing my shoulders.

"Thanks," I mumble and give him a small smile. I watch him nod and rush past the mounds of people into the stadium. I groan and pull out my phone. I wish I had discreetly recorded Mason, but like I said, I did not see it coming.

Even though he has not answered any of my hundred calls and texts, I call Grey. I pray and hope he hasn't turned it off or has already left the venue. Because I know that when I go back to the beach house, he won't be there. He'll be gone…

"Please answer—" I close my eyes.

A loud ringing bursts my bubble of hope with my granted wish.

"Fuck!" I hear a familiar voice curse.

I look up, and my eyes fall on Grey. He's standing tall about ten feet away from me, glaring down at his phone. The call is ended by him, and he looks up. His eyes lock on mine and they roll. He curses again, but I can't hear him this time.

I make my way through the crowd to him, my eyes focused on him. I bump into a few people, but I can't find my voice to apologize. He scowls down at me as I finally reach him.

"Grey, I…" I gulp and shrug, smiling softly. "D-did you win?"

"Yes, not that you should care." He rolls his eyes and looks away from me.

I bite my lip and sigh. I have to fix us, I have to fix *this*. "Grey, I didn't do what you think I did."

He turns away from me and begins walking away. "Fuck off, Olivia."

That stings. He's said that to me many times before we reconnected, and it hurts ten times worse, if possible.

"Please, you have to listen to me." I push through people and grab his hand, pulling him to face me.

He snatches his hand away and balls it into a fist.

427

"I don't have to do anything you say!" he snaps.

"Let me speak!" I snap too, angry he won't even let me speak. He clamps his mouth shut and crooks his head to the side. *Finally.* "I did not have sex with Noah."

He laughs dryly. "The photo says otherwise."

"Rose took it! But it was staged," I tell him, but he doesn't look like he believes me. "I swear! Mason confessed to me and everything. I was drugged, Rose put something in that shot she gave me, but not in yours. Or, yes, in yours. I don't know." I grip my hair, frustrated, as I watch his blank expression. "I swear it, Grey! She said she had this plan to hurt you worse than you hurt her all those years ago. I would never ever sleep with anyone other than you. I l-love you." I begin tearing up and take a cautious step forward, watching for his reaction.

He doesn't move back, which is a good thing.

"Please tell me you believe me. Please, Grey. I didn't know what was going on. If I did, I would have come running to you, never *from* you. Remember when I said that?" I risk it by taking his hand and pressing my lips to his bruised knuckles. I close my eyes and whimper, "Don't you believe me? I love you so much it hurts. You can't believe her. Please, please don't believe her."

"Liv," he breathes. I cry hard as I wait for him to finish what he has to say.

A familiar voice screaming his name cuts us off. I sniffle and we both look behind him. Lots of cars are rolling up, honking people out of the way. Men hang out the window with bandanas around their mouths and glasses covering their eyes.

I feel my heart drop as one of the men scream, "No one leaves the gang, pussy! Have some fireworks to celebrate your victory!" Dean. His voice is indistinguishable, his words haunting.

The world freezes as he raises a huge gun in the air.

Suddenly, the world resumes and goes crashing through space. Shots are fired into the air and all around. People begin screaming, and a stampede ensues. The men in the cars are driving everywhere, mowing people over and shouting crude remarks. My heart is pounding dangerously fast. The men begin viciously shooting people and hitting the glass building just behind us.

I feel my eyes widen as I am frozen, unsure of what to do. I think I'm screaming and gripping Grey. He's pushing me behind him to protect me, but a woman rushing my way pushes me away from his arm wrapped around my waist, pushing me to the ground. The shooting is so loud, it crackles in my ear, and I can feel the air grow tense.

I try to stand, but someone steps on me. I scream in pain as I hear something crack. I push myself up but am kneed in the face. I yell in utter and sheer pain before I finally grab a man's pant leg, and he helps me up. He pushes past me, running in fear. I whirl around and run back over to Grey but stop when I feel a prickle sensation crawl through my skin.

The shooting has finally stopped, and I can clearly hear the ambulance and police sirens. Screaming people everywhere, dead people littering the ground. A massacre.

Grey is a few feet in front of me, clothes messy and eyes bloodshot, tears running down his face.

"Liv," he croaks, voice shattered. He's gawking at me. And his eyes are wide, and he looks like he's seen a ghost. I don't get it—what's wrong? Was he shot? God, I don't know what I'll do if he's hurt. "Liv!" He launches forward and grabs me into his chest. I was fainting, but I don't remember feeling light-headed.

I don't understand until I am saying, "What?" and I feel a thick, gooey substance that tastes like metal on my tongue. I bring my fingers up and gently touch my mouth, then bring my hand out. My eyes widen when I see blood and a lot of it. "What?" My voice is hollow. I look down at a crimson red spreading through my shirt, near my heart.

And then I understand.

I've been shot.

The realization hits me, and I begin to panic. I look up at the beautiful man cradling me. He's calling, screaming, barking—nearly letting out his wrath—for an ambulance, for help. I smile as he faces me, but frown when tears leave his eyes.

"Grey, I—" I mutter. "I…love…G-grey…"

And then, darkness.

Acknowledgements

I can't believe the end is almost here. Just two more books to go. I wish I could write this couple forever and ever. They have such a special place in my heart.

First, I want to thank my family for continuing to believe in me and my writing. And for the unrelenting predictions of these books turning into movies. It may never happen, but we'll see.

Next, I have to thank the readers who have been with me way before I ventured into the publishing world. I still cherish every comment, edit of our #ley, and overall love for our complicated but lovable couple.

Thank you, Toni, my editor, for turning this messy story into something legible to read. If it weren't for you, I'd be blind to many errors and inconsistencies.

Limitless, you already know you have my gratitude for supporting me and getting this story out there.

About the Author

Allison White is a writer spending most of her days creating stories when most people are asleep. She has always been a lover of stories, especially romance. From the very first word she typed, she knew writing was her passion and never stopped. And when she isn't creating stories that tend to break and mend reader's hearts, she's either listening to music or getting way too involved with fictional characters.

Facebook:
https://www.facebook.com/AuthorAWhite

Twitter:
https://twitter.com/AuthorAWhite

Wattpad:
https://wattpad.com/user/authorawhite

Instagram:
https://www.instagram.com/authorawhite

Join our Reader Group on Facebook and don't miss out on meeting our authors and entering epic giveaways!

Limitless Reading

Where reading a book
is your first step to becoming
limitless...

LIMITLESS ◆ PUBLISHING *Reader Group*

Join today! *"Where reading a book is your first step to becoming limitless..."*

https://www.facebook.com/groups/LimitlessReading/

www.ingramcontent.com/pod-product-compliance
Lightning Source LLC
Chambersburg PA
CBHW021122260626
47169CB00005B/1401